THE MAENAD

AGE OF THE FORGOTTEN ONES
BOOK I

BOBBIE ISABEL

Trigger and Content Warnings

This book does not contain many triggers, but there are allusions to childhood trauma of an unknown nature, domestic violence, and neglect.

As this is fantasy, there are descriptions of battle, use of weapons and magic. There are references to multiple deities, religions and religious trauma.

This is a work of fiction. Names, characters, places, and incidents are products of the author's imagination or are used fictitiously and are not to be construed as real. Any resemblance to actual events, locals, organizations, or persons, living or dead, is entirely confidential.

No portion of this book may be reproduced in any form without written permission from the publisher or author, except as permitted by U.S. copyright law.

Cover Artist: Beverly Watkins

Map of Skyemera's World in Book 1

Pronunciation Guide

- Dynami - Die-nah-mee
- Phialyra - Fee-uh-lear-uh / Lyra - Lear-uh
- Eirini - Ee-ree-nee
- Skyemera - Sky-meh-ruh / Mera - Meh-ruh / Meraki - Meh rah-key
- Karielle - Car-ee-ell / Kari - Car-ee
- Eckasia - Eh-kay-see-yuh
- Eustis - You-stiss
- Strimmena - Stree-men-nuh
- Phrixa - Frick-suh
- Sapharnia - Sah-farn-yuh
- Danalise - Day-nah-lease
- Euonsise - You-own-sis
- Canea - Can-ay-yuh
- Nerin - Nair-in
- Nelaira - Nay-lar-uh

- Callisto - Cuh-lis-toe
- Pholus - Foe-luhs
- Rhivy - Rih-vee
- Yevondra - Yay-von-druh
- Mingus - Mean-gus
- Vasilios - Vah-see-lee-ohs
- Sizzsear - Siz-ear
- Rheizaldaru - Ray-zahl-dah-roo
- Purivia - Poor-iv-yuh
- Gericole - Jay-ree-coal / Gery - Jerry
- Gaeleath - Gail-eeth
- Tarkegan - Tar-key-gan
- Krinosera - Krih-no-say-ra
- Palaestra - Pal-ice-tra
- Nereids - Neer-ee-ids
- Alseides - All-see-ids

Chapter One

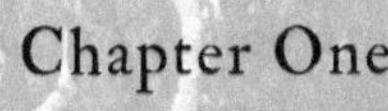

Mera loved frolicking through the forest with her cousins. Rarely did they stick to the visible path, well-worn by supple and cloven feet alike. Instead, they ran zigzagging through the brush, relishing the feel of leaves crunching beneath their weight and twigs snapping at their ankles. Her mother called them careless when she'd make it home, skin afflicted with scrapes and scratches where the bramble had caught her. Mera called it being carefree. Out there in the woods, she had no worries, no expectations, and no responsibilities. She could just run, play, and enjoy the company of others her age who didn't look at her like she had two heads.

No matter where they went outside of the wooded glen they called home, Mera received strange glances and head-to-hoof appraisals that made her want to disappear. If the responses had been ones of mild curiosity, eyes quickly averted when she looked in their direction, Mera would've just let it go by now. It had been happening since she was very young.

Though her family had never said she didn't fit in, Mera felt like an oddity amongst her people. She wasn't unattractive by any means, but she was different. The hair on her head was a beautiful umber that shone with hints of red and gold in the sun. It hung across her shoulder in soft waves, gently framing her face with its wide eyes that shifted from blue to green and their long, dark lashes. The skin of her torso and face was smooth and healthy with a slight tint that said she enjoyed spending as much time beyond the forest's canopied protection as she did running through the underbrush. She didn't even mind the elongated points at the tops of her ears or the small stubby horns sitting atop her head. They both could be covered when she was around strangers or distant relatives, and they gave her hair a little added height and movement, if she was honest with herself. They were really the only parts of her upper body that set her apart from her female relatives.

Everything she hated about her body was below the waist. Where her cousins' bodies were lithe, smooth, and hairless, she had curves and hair in places no other nymph had. This was the part that got all the unwanted attention. She had haunches covered in fur that led down to a pair of hard hooves, and she had a tail. It was like waking up inside of a nightmare everyday. Why in the world did she have to have a tail? And what she wouldn't give for graceful feet better equipped for dancing than the mountain-climber hooves she bore at the ends of her legs. It was just as well that her people preferred nudity to the confinement of clothing because it was nearly impossible to hide the shape of her bottom half where knees, hips, and heels all stood out at unexpected angles. In this way, her people had gotten used to her physical differences and just accepted Mera as one of them.

Whenever they traveled into the city to interact with humans and other creatures, however, Mera had to tie two robes together because she was bigger than all of the other nymphs, and nothing fit. Rather than enduring the stares and not-so-hushed whispers of strangers, she much preferred to stay home and frolic in the woods than make those trips beyond The Great River. In truth, she'd much rather head down to the beach and commune with the ogre oaks, as they were known by her people.

"Mera, there you are! I've been looking all over The Grove for you!"

Mera looked out from her favorite hiding spot amongst the gnarled oak trees along the shore and glared at Kari, her favorite cousin and best friend. Kari's beautiful face was flushed from the trek she'd made from their home in The Thicket. Her ebony hair, usually pulled back into a long braid, was loose. There were random twigs and leaves in her hair, showing that she had taken the long way through the densest underbrush of the forest. Mera nearly laughed at her appearance.

"You looked everywhere?" she asked, eyebrow raised.

Kari's cat-like eyes, a combination of tawny brown and green tinged with gold sparkled in the afternoon sun. "Ok, ok, so I knew where you probably were, but I didn't feel like running all the way out here first. I don't run as fast as you do! Why can't you find somewhere closer to hide?"

Mera climbed out of the safety of the tree copse, looked at Kari squarely and said, "I'm too easily visible everywhere else." She plucked a rather long twig from Kari's tresses. Her cousin feigned nonchalance with a shrug, as her cheeks turned pink. "Besides, we can't catch this sound from The Thicket." Mera gestured toward the waves with a sigh. "Anyway, now that you've broken my solitude, why were you looking for me in the first place?"

"Oh yeah," Kari exclaimed, "The baby is coming soon!"

Mera looked at her sideways. "Is that all? Mother's been pregnant for a while now."

"No, silly. By soon, I mean today!"

"Oh!" Mera exclaimed and started walking away from the shore. She gave one more longing glance to the copse of trees that provided shelter and comfort when she came to listen to the waves.

The sandy beaches were not technically part of The Grove, though Mera liked to claim them. No one else visited this area of the shore, so it was her refuge. Even the sea nymphs stayed away from this side of the beach because they saw the twisted oaks as harbingers of evil, or at least that's what Mera had been told the first time she was caught sneaking out there. Mera, on the other hand, saw them as majestic and beautiful. Their bark was worn white by the wind coming in from the vast ocean rather than covered in the traditional brown garb of all the other oaks in the forest, almost as if Aeolus himself had stripped them bare. They shone in the sun as a beacon for her. The twists and turns of their trunks, gnarled, pulled low to the ground, and protruding in unexpected places were a testament to their strength and resilience. She saw them as kindred spirits, her own body a mirror to their form when compared to her family. Based on the stories told by her nymph cousins, these trees received the same scared, pitying, disgusted stares that Mera did. Thus, Mera felt safe snuggled amongst the trees, hidden within the alcoves of their tangled walls.

The area called The Grove actually didn't start until they walked over the dunes and beyond the short ground coverings growing from the sand there. The Grove was the densest part of the Tribunal Forest flanked on the north and south by mountains and the Great Sea to the east. While it could take one of the short-legged forest nymphs multiple hours to walk from their home in The Thicket near the other end of the forest, Mera could make it in one because her long, muscled legs allowed her to mimic the gait of a deer, with long, powerful strides, rather than a nymph. Still, even with the urgency of her mother's impending labor, Mera maintained a comfortable pace to allow Kari to keep up.

As the sand gave way to packed earth, tall, looming trees stood sentinel overlooking all who sought to enter the forest. Though Mera had never seen it happen, since she was herself a forest dweller, she'd heard tales of the trees closing ranks with their branches to stop outsiders from invading the sanctuary that was The Grove. Mera turned her face up trying to catch a glimpse of the highest branches, imagining how the pine, oak, and maple that hardly touched in the canopy could possibly join forces. She wondered what type of invasion would cause this unimaginable feat to occur and then just as quickly said a silent prayer to Artemis that nothing like that would happen in her lifetime.

"So what do you think Lyra's child will be like?" Kari asked, breaking into Mera's reverie.

"What do you mean?"

"Do you think the child will be a nymph or a satyr…or…" Kari trailed off.

"Or like me," Mera stated matter-of-factly.

"Mera, I didn't mean anything by it. You were so quiet, and I was just making conversation. Are you at least excited for the child?" Kari continued, her features softening.

"I honestly don't know how to answer that question," Mera responded. "I have always wanted a sibling, so I wouldn't feel so alone, but now that I've seen 14 winters, I don't know. It feels awkward."

Kari grabbed Mera's arm. "What do you mean alone? Have you not been blessed with my company?"

Mera laughed. "Oh yes, absolutely blessed. A gift from the gods for sure. But you know what I mean. Some days, I feel like an outsider in the family."

"I know, and I hate that for you."

The cousins continued walking further into The Grove where the canopy was thicker and sunlight was a rarity amongst the shadows.

"The days will be getting shorter soon," Kari stated, breaking the silence again.

"Too soon," Mera retorted.

Kari giggled. "For someone born in the dead of winter, you have a terrible case of apricity," she said, wagging her finger.

"You prefer summer too, so what's your point?"

"Oh, no point at all, just making conversation," Kari said with a grin.

"You do love to hear yourself talk."

"And you love me." Kari linked her arm through Mera's, skipping along the path.

"You're so humble," Mera said playfully and pulled the nymph to a quicker pace as they walked through the hedges surrounding The Thicket. Its name was a misnomer meant to keep outsiders from intruding on the community. While it had at one time been a thick wooded area, The Thicket was a clearing of multiple acres surrounded by thick hedges and tall trees. Lore has it that the village elders combined their earth magic to get the tallest trees to stretch their branches around the outer parts of the village to provide shade.

The living areas of The Thicket resembled a mid-size village with thatch homes of various sizes. Most of the homes closest to the hedgerow were small, generally inhabited by one or two individuals who also served as the first line of defense for the community. In exchange, the community collective took care of the upkeep on those homes. The homes grew, supporting larger families, as they neared the center of the village. Mera's family home, visible from the outskirts, stood near the center since her and Kari's grandmother was the community matriarch.

As Mera and Kari approached the two-story house made of twigs and branches covered in clay-colored mud, they noticed the small crowd gathered in the yard. "Were they all here when you came to find me?" Mera asked, almost afraid of the answer.

Just as Kari was about to respond, they heard a loud scream. Mera recognized her mother's voice immediately and started running, weaving through the groups gathered outside until she reached the door. Helena, the village healer and Kari's other grandmother, was standing in the doorway with an impassive look that immediately quelled Mera's panic. If Helena was calm, then all had to be well.

"Is Mother all right?" Mera asked the elder.

"As well as can be expected," was her response. "The child is larger than normal, nearly as large as you were at birth," Helena stated.

Mera glanced at Kari, remembering the conversation they'd had on their walk back to the village. Was it possible that Mera would finally get the sibling she'd longed for, a child who shared her physical features, someone with whom she could share her insecurities and have them understand, really understand? Suddenly, their age difference didn't seem an issue.

After her mother's next scream and Helena's calming reminder that this was a normal part of the birthing process, Mera sat on the stoop leading into the home and began the other long process of waiting. Kari sat by her side, surprisingly quiet during the long stretches between Lyra's cries of exertion. During one of the more excruciatingly long periods, Mera couldn't take the silence anymore and mused, "What if the child is male? What does one do with a male sibling?"

Helena chuckled quietly, and when the young nymphs turned to her, she said, "The same thing one does with a female sibling."

Karielle laughed aloud while Mera sighed at the poorly-delivered joke.

"I mean..." Mera began when Helena interrupted her.

"I know what you mean, young one. Your experience with male creatures is limited because our village is primarily female. That does not mean we do not birth, and, at times, rear male children. They're not much different, at least not while young. We just believe they are better left to grow with their fathers and learn the ways of the satyr. Though, there have been rare occasions when these children are returned to us for their own safety," she continued.

"Safety?" Mera and Kari asked simultaneously.

A piercing scream of both anguish and release came from inside the house, interrupting their conversation. The eyes of everyone outside fell on Helena who turned and walked through the door. Minutes later, though it felt like forever to Mera, her grandmother, Dynami, came to the door and announced to the crowd, "The child is a nymph," at which Mera's shoulders drooped. The Matriarch then turned to Kari and Mera. "Skyemera, your mother is well and will see you now. Go greet your sister, and wipe that dejected look off your face. Today is a day for celebration, as we add another to our family."

"Yes, Yaya," Mera said quietly and stood to enter the house.

"Karielle, go and spread the news that Phialyra is well and the child has arrived," Dynami told her other granddaughter. "Tonight we feast," she finished.

"Yes, Yaya," Kari answered and left the yard.

Dynami then greeted the people gathered, allowing Mera time to see her mother and sister.

"Meraki, my pride and joy, there you are," Phialyra said, as Mera entered the room, "Come, greet your sister."

Mera smiled with genuine affection at her mother and approached the bed. Her mother was as beautiful as ever. Her naturally pale fawn skin was pink with exertion, making her look younger than her 85 winters. She had pulled her russet brown locks up onto the crown of her head, as stray tendrils stuck to her skin with sweat. Her jade eyes shone in the light from the small window. "I was worried about you," Mera said, looking at the small bundle tucked against her mother's breast.

"I'm sorry we worried you so, but your sister was as large as you were and nearly as stubborn." Lyra ruffled her eldest daughter's hair.

"When I heard of her significant size, I thought, hoped that maybe she would be..."

"Like you," her mother finished. Mera nodded. "My heart, there is no one like you. You are a true gift from the gods." Lyra removed the infant from her breast and shifted, so Mera could get a glance at the child's face, "And now you are a protector."

"Does she have a name?" Mera asked, staring at the small,

perfect features topped by a head of dark, chestnut curls that contrasted her porcelain skin.

"I was hoping you could help me with that," her mother responded with a smile.

"Eirini," Mera said with conviction.

Within minutes, Dynami entered the room. "It is time," she stated. Phialyra nodded.

"Time for what" Mera asked.

"Time to present your sister to her community," Mera's mother answered with a wider smile.

"And as her sister, her protector, it is your responsibility to make the presentation," Dynami said. "This is our way." Mera's grandmother made this last statement with the authority of her position as both family and community Matriarch. Though there were younger children in the village, Mera only had a vague recollection of earlier presentations.

Mera nodded solemnly before she stood and took Eirini from her mother. Babe in arms, Mera followed her grandmother out of the house to where a much larger crowd was now gathered on the lawn. The house had been decorated with woolen garland that seemed to glitter in the twilight, and a huge bonfire was lit in the center of the yard, far from any dry leaves or forest debris that might accidentally catch the flame. Following the matriarch's instructions, Mera removed the infant's swaddle and held her up before the congregation of nymphs. Mera then carried her sister through the yard to circle the fire while everyone gathered wished the child good health and prosperity, beauty and patience, kindness and joy. When Mera returned to her grandmother's side, she once again lifted the babe for all to see and declared, "A sister has been born to us, and her name shall be Eirini, for she shall be a beacon of peace for our community, now and forever." No sooner had Mera finished her speech, and before the crowd could erupt in cheers, a large shadow passed over The Thicket.

"What was that?" Mera asked, pulling the babe close as Kari came to stand by her side.

"Hush," Dynami said, looking toward the sky, attempting to peek through the canopy of leaves.

A loud screech pierced the silence, and a collective gasp went through the crowd when, as if day had returned, the sky lit above the trees. The shadow passed over The Thicket again, the unmistakable sounds of wings following in its wake.

"It can't be," Dynami said as Lyra came staggering outside, clutching tightly to the doorway.

"The dragon is back! He cannot have this one!" Lyra cried, snatching Eirini from Mera's grasp and rushing back into the house.

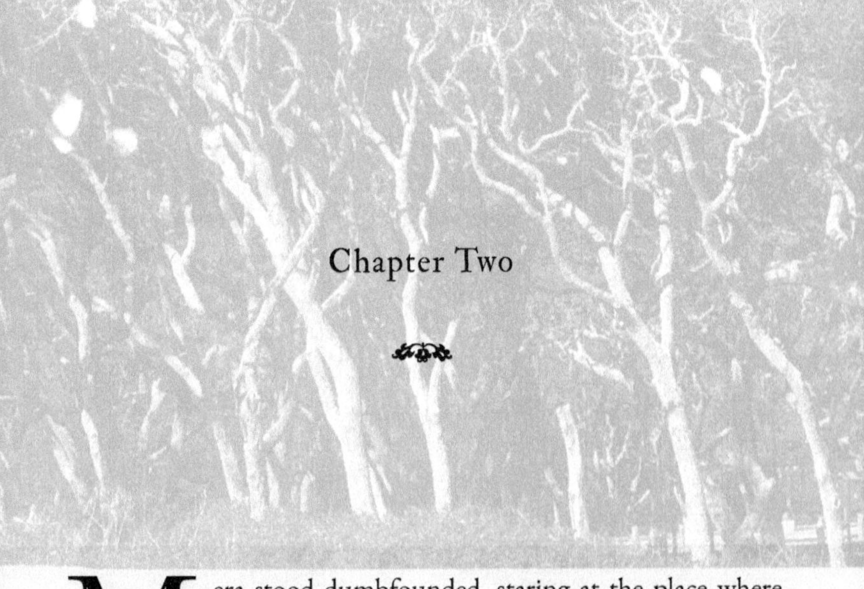

Chapter Two

Mera stood dumbfounded, staring at the place where her mother, her normally quiet and controlled mother just left in a crazed state. "What just happened," Mera asked, looking back and forth between Kari and Dynami.

Kari shook her head and shrugged. Their grandmother, on the other hand, looked worried. Although nymphs maintained their beauty for most of their long lives, Dynami's furrowed face appeared as if her age had doubled in mere moments. "I can't believe the dragon has returned after all this time," Dynami said aloud to no one.

"Returned? That's the same thing Mother said. What do you mean returned? I've never heard tales of a dragon here in The Grove." Mera's mind raced. "Have you heard of such a thing," she then asked her cousin.

"No. I mean, I've heard the ancient stories of dragons from faraway lands and stolen, hoarded treasures, but nothing about anyone having seen one in the flesh," Kari responded.

Both of them looked up at the approaching footsteps of Helena. "I think we should all go inside. Rumors will be spreading soon, and silenced stories will once again resurface," she said, putting a hand on Dynami's shoulder. "I know you and Lyra had hoped to never tell the story to anyone, but if the dragon has returned on the night Lyra has once again given birth, it is time for Mera to know, to remember what this means." Helena look into Dynami's tired and weary eyes.

"Will someone tell me what is happening here," Mera demanded.

"Let us go inside," Dynami said and turned to enter the house.

Helena headed toward one of the back rooms. "I will check on Lyra and the babe first, and then we will try and recount the story of the last time the dragon came to our forest."

"Let's sit in the parlor," Dynami said as she moved into the large room and began lighting candles.

Each flicker of light created an eerie dance of shadows along the ceiling. Though she normally only lit one or two candles in each room with a flick of her wrist, Mera and Kari watched their grandmother use one long taper to light the tall candelabra that stood in front of the hearth, each sconce in the four corners of the room, and every candle sitting on the tables and mantel inside the room. When all 30 candles were lit, Dynami put the taper back in its holder, and Mera caught a glimpse of her hand shaking before she quickly put it into the pocket of the ceremonial cloak she had been wearing for Eirini's Amphidromia. It was a ceremony meant to be a cheerful presentation with eating and dancing. Now, she wore the cloak like a shroud. By the time Dynami sat on the cushioned armchair and gestured for the cousins to sit on the larger settee, the shadows had hidden behind the carefully carved furniture and artwork the matriarch had received as tributes from the community over the years. Because of its ornate decoration and exhibition, the parlor was a place for visitors and important emissary meetings where Dynami could show off her people's creativity.

Mera ran her hand across the back of the settee and its carefully woven branches and vines before taking a seat. While they awaited Helena's return, the cousins looked about the room, taking in the paintings and sculptures. They had never before spent time in this room, only seeing the furnishings in shadows from the hall. Helena's footsteps echoed in the quiet, when Kari nudged Mera with her elbow and pointed at a portrait tucked into an alcove alongside the mantel. It was framed in gilded wood, but the opulence of the frame wasn't what caught Mera's attention. It was the large blue and red dragon prominently featured in the center of the painting. The dragon stood with its wings fully extended and gold-flecked green eyes directed forward as if it were staring right at whoever painted the portrait. In front of the dragon stood a man. He wore dark blue pants with black boots and a billowy red shirt crossed with a black and gold sash. His hair was wavy with medium brown curls. His eyes also stared forward with the same golden green hue as the dragon's. Those eyes looked vaguely familiar to Mera. "What is that painting?" Mera asked, as Helena entered the room.

"They're both asleep," Helena said, walking to where the matriarch was seated. Dynami sighed, and Helena put a comforting hand on her shoulder.

"When your mother was much younger," Dynami began, her eyes locked on a spot above the mantle. "She had an absolute lust for life. She loved to dance and found her way to many parties throughout the forest and beyond. She also had a lust for men, as many of us do, but hers was different. It was like she was searching for something, and that was when she met your father, Mera. He was not from the forest, nor was he a human from neighboring villages across The Great River. He was a faun from a far away land." Mera sat in stunned silence, as her grandmother continued the story of her birth, a story she had never before heard. "Because he and your mother served different pantheons, the gods decided that rather than you simply presenting as faun or nymph, as what happens when we mate with satyrs, they would give you features of both parents. You, my child, are a true maenad in service to both Bacchus and Dionysus."

"What does that even mean," Mera asked, wide-eyed. "I knew I was different, but you're telling me I'm some weird abomination of the gods?"

"You're not an abomination, Skyemera. You are a gift, and you have been given gifts that you've not yet explored."

Mera stood and began pacing, shaking her head in disbelief.

"Yaya, if I remember the old stories correctly, maenads were human women compelled to follow and fight for the gods. How can Mera be one of them?" Kari asked.

Helena answered while Dynami watched her eldest granddaughter walk back and forth through the large room. "It had been many ages since a daughter of mixed pantheons was born...and the gods are egotistical." She added the last part under her breath. "They enjoyed the element of surprise that came from having female warriors to unexpectedly spring on their enemies. But consider why the stories tell of these women adorning themselves with garb made from the flora and fauna of the forest."

Kari's eyes grew wide. "To mimic the true maenads," she stated enthusiastically before snapping her mouth shut and looking at the her cousin in awe.

Mera stopped pacing and turned a resentful stare on her grandmother and Helena. "Why are you telling me this now?" Mera fumed. "We gathered to speak about the dragon. If no one thought it important to explain to me why I don't fit in anywhere before, why tell me now?" Her voice caught and she sat down on the settee, hand covering her mouth, eyes clamped shut.

"Because there was a time when you did know. You knew, and the dragon knew," her grandmother said, "and it was that knowing that brought the dragon here in the first place."

"What?" Mera and Kari shrieked at the same time, both jumping to their feet.

"Please sit down, and I will try to explain the unexplainable,"

Dynami said. She gestured for Mera to retake her seat next to Kari who had already followed the command. Mera did as she was bid, though she perched on the edge of the seat as if she might jump up and bolt out of the room at any moment. "As I said, you were the first maenad born in centuries, at least since before I was born, and your birth caused a ripple of power throughout the connected earth. The trees in The Grove shook in excitement, and the ensuing explosion of leaves and birds to the heavens gained the attention of the dragon. When he came to us, though, he did not show his true form."

"Is that him in the painting," Mera asked. Her grandmother nodded, giving a quick glance to the portrait before turning her eyes back to Mera. Mera's eyebrows rose quizzically. "Who painted it," she asked, "and why would you keep it if he is as dangerous as you're making it sound?"

"I painted it," came a voice from the hall.

All eyes turned to the doorway where Lyra stood, pale and disheveled.

"What? Why? How? He just let you?" Mera interrogated her mother in rapid succession, unable to believe this above everything else she'd just been told.

Lyra walked to the painting and ran her hand down the frame before she turned to her daughter and said, "He was my mate."

Mera stared at her mother, mouth agape. As far as she had known, her mother had never had a mate, well, not a true mate. Of course she'd birthed Mera and just now delivered Eirini, so she'd obviously have mated in the physical sense, but to call someone her mate, and a dragon. On top of all Mera had just heard about her own parentage, this was almost too much. If Mera looked dumbfounded, Kari was the exact opposite, energy radiating from her as she bounced in her seat.

"How is it we haven't heard of this? You were mated? And to a dragon? I didn't even know that was possible? Ok, until tonight, I didn't even know dragons existed, but still. Gods," Kari exclaimed at the end of her litany of questions.

"Breathe, both of you," Lyra said, "and I will continue the story." She looked to her mother and then back at both young nymphs. After a brief pause, she squared her shoulders and began. "When you were born, Skyemera, there was, as your grandmother stated, a tremendous outflowing of energy, as if the land had known something great had arrived. And you were that great thing. Based on what I heard your grandmother saying when I came down the hall, I believe she has already told you that your father was a faun from a distant land." She sighed and then looked directly into Mera's eyes as if no one else was in the room. "I was young and foolish, and I fell for his charm. His dancing took me away from The Grove and our forest, and all I wanted to do was to see the world through his eyes. Your eyes are so similar to his with the intense blue they become before shifting to the green of our people. His long, dark lashes, just like yours, were entrancing. Needless to say, I was under his spell."

She turned away and walked toward the large candelabra, waving her hand over the dancing flames where the wax had already begun to run. "And then I got pregnant. He had no intention of staying in the area and left for other lands almost immediately." She turned and walked back to kneel in front of her daughter. "While I was sad he left, I had you," she said taking Mera's hands in hers, "and though I did not yet know what that would mean, I knew my life would forever be the adventure I had been seeking."

Tears welled in Mera's eyes eyes, and she stood, abruptly dropping her mother's hands to start pacing again. What she wanted to do was run from the house and keep running until she sat amongst the gnarled oaks along the shore. This was all too much! Her sister's birth. Her responsibility as protector. The arrival of the dragon. And now the fact that she was a maenad, born from a nymph who mated with some random faun from a far off land. She shook her head. None of this seemed real, and yet no one had answered the pressing question that started this whole conversation, and that was bothering her most. "What does this have to do with the dragon whose shadow we saw this afternoon," she asked emphasizing each word in hopes that someone would get to the point.

"She is getting there," Helena responded. "We know this is a lot, especially for you, young one, but it is important that you get all of the details in order, so you can put the puzzle together. There will be things we cannot tell you, not because we don't want to, but because we do not know. So, let your mother continue."

Mera stopped pacing and looked at the grandmothers who seemed to have gained years in these couple hours, much like the candles that had already shrunken halfway from the intensity of their flames. She softened her scowl and sat back down next to her cousin who was still bursting with intensity. Mera put her hand on Kari's knee to settle it for a few seconds before looking up. "Please continue, Mother."

Lyra continued the story, and when Mera thought she could no longer take the exposition of how wonderful her pregnancy had been, her mother finally got to the dragon's arrival. "Much like what happened today, once you were presented to the community, we heard a loud screech through the forest canopy. We could not see what had made the screech, but we knew it was something large. Our warriors and guards prepared for some sort of aerial attack, thinking that whatever flying creature had made that sound would come from the air. We were all caught off guard when the forest creatures warned of a lone man wandering through the forest from the direction of the northern mountains. Thinking he was a lost traveler, and worried the creature we were preparing against might cause him harm, we sent scouts to find him and bring him to The Thicket."

"The law says we're not to bring anyone into The Thicket, especially not a man," Kari exclaimed, unable to contain herself.

"We know. That rule was created because of this incident," Dynami stated, staring at her hands, twisting the ring she always wore.

Both of the young nymphs went wide eyed at the unexpected statement. As far as they had known this was a long-standing rule. To think it was something created during their lifetime was unbelievable. "We're made to study our people's history, and yet there's so much we're not told," Kari muttered with a wrinkle of her nose.

"Karielle, that is enough," Dynami said in a way to show she was no longer entertaining the young nymph's outbursts. "We brought you into this conversation to support your cousin because she will need your support. If you are unable to contain yourself, I will send you home and allow Skyemera to decide how much to divulge later. Since I know how thirsty for all the world's knowledge you are, I am sure that you will be able to stay for the remainder of the conversation." She locked eyes with Kari until the young nymph acquiesced.

"I understand your shock, Kari. Now imagine my embarrassment at being the person for whom this rule was created," Lyra said to calm the tension. "Please understand that there are many things unknown to the full community, but most of them were put in place to protect Skyemera."

Mera always knew when a conversation was serious because her mother rarely used her full name. "To protect me?" she asked. "I have never felt unsafe in The Grove, or really anywhere between the river and the sea. What could I need protection from here in my home?"

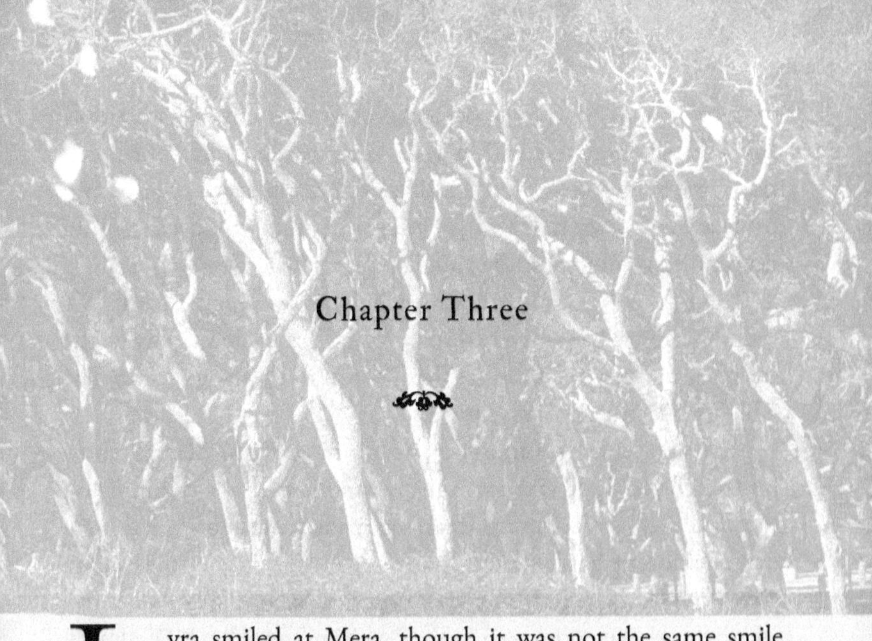

Chapter Three

Lyra smiled at Mera, though it was not the same smile she'd given her daughter when introducing her to Eirini. Her heart had been at peace in that moment; she was overflowing with joy and pride for both of her children. Now her heart was being squeezed from the inside out, as she tried to hold herself together for Mera's sake. It was hard to keep her smile from turning to a grimace. "I'm glad to hear you say that. It means our work to maintain your safety was successful, but I'm afraid that in our efforts at overprotection, we've left you unprepared for today's event and what it might mean for the near future." She took a deep breath and was relieved when the matriarchs took over for a minute, so she could get her thoughts straight.

"I know the elders have taught you the human tale of the sheep in wolf's clothing, right?" Helena asked the young nymphs. The cousins nodded. "Well, the dragon entered The Grove disguised as a man." Lyra looked up at her pause to see Mera and Kari with their mouths agape. She would have laughed had this been any other conversation. "You see," Helena continued when the young ones settled down again, "dragons are natural shapeshifters. They are able to take the shape of a man and even live as a man for long periods of time. They are powerful creatures, not just physically but also mentally, and with magic. Their magic, unlike ours, does not come from the earth. It is innate. The fact that we had not seen or heard of dragons for ages relegated them to myth and an unimportant topic of study and discussion."

"Until Vasilios came to our forest," Dynami interrupted. "We did not know what we were dealing with. It is my job to ensure the safety of our people, and I let that demon not only walk into The Thicket but into my house as well."

"Mother, do not blame yourself. He did not immediately show his true form," Lyra said, stopping her mother from continuing on the trail of self-loathing that happened whenever the rare conversation of Vasilios came up. If anyone should be guilt-ridden about the effect he had on the community, it should be her. After all, she's the one who tied herself to him eternally. "We already mentioned that I was young and naive," she reminded them. "I was also a new mother and concerned about whether or not I could rear you into the goddess you were meant to be by myself. While I knew I would never be fully alone here within my community, none of us had any idea what the development and maturation of a maenad would entail. You, too," she said, turning to her daughter again, "were a myth. So when Vasilios arrived looking uncertain, as if he had lost his way and needed our help, I grasped onto him because I knew how to do that. I knew how to help lost travelers. I knew how to take care of others. He was what I needed to feel secure in myself. So just like with your father, I fell head over heels."

"With a dragon," Mera said with a sneer that Lyra did not miss.

"You've seen the painting, my daughter. When he's in his human form, there's nothing, aside from his eyes, that would distinguish him from a human male. And since none of us had ever encountered a dragon or even believed they were real, it was easy for him to pass himself off as human." But he had a magnetism, she remembered with a shudder. "His powerful appeal should have warned me, but it didn't. I wanted him and his strength. He made me feel good and beautiful, intelligent and valued. He got into my mind." Lyra watched Mera's face contort, and she once again wished she could save her daughter from the rest of this story, her history.

"The next thing we knew, your mother was leaving you with us for days at a time, returning a bit more distant, that longing for adventure stronger than ever," Dynami cut in. "Within a year, she announced that she was mated to the rogue and taking you to live with him in the northern mountains. There was nothing I could say to sway her from that decision, and I tried."

Lyra tensed at the memory of the argument she and her mother had that day. Dynami insisted that Mera be left in The Grove, within the safety of the community, and she had refused, arguing that the best and only place for Mera was with her because no one could care for her or maintain her safety like her mother. Lyra had regretted that day for so many years now that it was like a constant cloud following her around.

"So we threw them a wedding," Dynami said with a sneer, "right outside on the lawn, and wished you all well." She turned to Mera then, "and we made your mother promise that she would bring you to visit regularly."

"And I did," said Lyra quietly before continuing. "I did bring you back to The Grove for you to spend time with your grandmother and amongst our people. By the time you were five, it was obvious that you preferred being here to being at home. I had no idea why, but I could feel it before you even said it." Lyra pulled up a footstool and sat in front of her daughter with her head in her hands. "You wanted us to come back and live here. You said you wanted him to come visit, but you didn't want to live in his mountain home anymore," she said, looking at the floor between them.

She looked up into Mera's eyes, and for a second, she considered lying, placing all the blame for her poor decisions on

Vasilios. "It hurt me to think you were unhappy, but it hurt my pride to consider leaving my mate." She took a deep breath. "Yes, he had me enthralled, but I was prideful. I saw changes in you, but I thought they were just loneliness for not having any other young nymphs around. So we would invite some of your cousins to come visit and stay with us, until suddenly you stopped wanting them to come. I was at a loss." She felt the sting of tears, but her daughter needed her strong for this. Both of her daughters needed her strong. Still, it was so hard to control herself.

"When did you know he was a dragon, Mother," Mera asked when Lyra paused.

"Somewhere around when you were three. We had gotten into an argument one day, and I saw his eyes flash crimson. In the blink of an eye, he had me by the throat hanging over one of the cliffs outside. He showed me his form that day as a warning that we were under his control." Lyra began to shake as she remembered the fear she felt. Mera had been in her room napping when Lyra told Vasilios that she wanted to return to The Grove, that she was lonely and missed her people. The anger in his eyes was terrifying, but the fear of leaving her child alone with him if she couldn't get out of his grasp and on solid ground was what broke her. He'd said 'Stay or leave, the maenad is mine, and then he'd leapt from the cliff with her still grasped by the throat, until she wasn't anymore, until she realized she was cradled in humongous talons. She shook her head to clear the vision and steadied her breath before finishing, "It wasn't long after that when you began to pull away and behave differently."

"Why don't I remember any of this," Mera asked. "I realize I might not have remembered those early years, but I don't remember any of this. I don't remember a dragon, or even anyone named Vasilios. You said I began asking to come home at five, but I don't remember ever leaving home. None of this seems real. Kari, do you remember coming to visit us, or us being away for any periods of time," she asked her cousin. Kari shook her head, but no words came from the usually chatty nymph.

Lyra could hear the panic rising up in Mera's chest, and she knew there was nothing she could do to lessen this pain. What a mistake they had made by keeping the past from her. "We came back to The Grove when you had seen nine winters, yet a babe to our kind. Karielle had but three winters at the time." She struggled to keep her own breath steady. "Even if she were able, she would not have remembered any of this."

The cousins looked at each other. "That's impossible," they said together, "we're the same age."

"That is false," Dynami interjected. "Have you never wondered why Skyemera seemed so much taller, more developed, and more mature than you, Karielle?"

"We just assumed she was bigger because she was different. I mean, her hooves have to add some height, right?"

Lyra saw Mera scowl at her cousin. References to her hooves always made her daughter uncomfortable, and it was obvious that the new knowledge of her father did not make that reality any easier to talk about. Lyra locked eyes with her daughter. Could Mera feel all of the emotions swirling inside her? Would it make Mera feel better if Lyra were to share those feelings? She'd had years to process all of this, and yet they were throwing it at her daughter of fourteen...no...twenty winters, like a river cuts through the glade. Would Mera ever forgive her? Was it fair to ask for forgiveness? Mera shook her head, breaking their eye contact.

"I still don't understand how we don't remember any of this. If I was nine and Kari three, I, at least, should have some kind of memory. We celebrate together each year, together, Mother," Mera exclaimed, her voice raised in a crescendo.

"I know. We did that to help you forget," Lyra responded quietly, guilt settling in like being pressed with Sisyphus' rock.

"Forget what," Mera retorted, jumping to her feet. "What did I need to forget?"

"I don't know," Lyra responded with a sob as tears ran down her cheeks. She could feel her daughter's emotions shift, as anger set in. She knew that anger, deserved that anger.

"That doesn't make any sense, Mother," Mera responded, voice harried with emotion. "You said you did that to help me forget, and you don't even know what I needed to forget? What did you do? Do you know that? Do you remember?" Her breathing had sped to a pace where the last word came out as a whispered sob. Mera held her gaze, looking for an answer Lyra didn't have. The tension between them grew, like a palpable charge in the air, until Eirini's muffled cry from the other room broke the silence.

"I'll be right back," Lyra said and walked toward the door, looking back at Mera before exiting into the hallway. She nearly ran to her room in the back of the house. Every thought of fleeing the anger in her daughter's eyes swirling around her brain with the fear of her mate's return and concern for her newborn.

She lifted the babe from her cradle, tears streaming down her face and falling onto the swaddled form at her breast. "How can I protect you, little one, if I could not protect your sister?" she asked aloud, hoping the gods would hear her. "What am I to do?"

A presence caused Lyra to turn. She jumped at the sight of a figure near the window. Lyra instinctively pulled the babe closer to her bosom and began walking backward. The figure shifted into view, and she saw an attractive man, at least he looked like a man, but his presence felt—like a god.

"You know me, Lyra, daughter of Dionysus. We met many years ago."

In that moment, Lyra knew a panic she never had before. "What are you doing here? And what is this illusion, or was the faun the illusion?"

"I am here to protect my daughter, Lyra, something you should be grateful for, no?"

Protect her, she screamed internally. "You left the moment I quickened."

"That does not mean that I would never return, and now it seems I am needed. Now that she knows who she is, she's in danger."

"What do you mean?"

"Her powers will be cresting soon. They will be uncontrollable at first. Your people will not know how to help her manage it. She will need guidance to protect you all and herself. She must learn what it means to be a goddess of protection because even protective measures can backfire when not properly channeled."

"How? What do we have to do? Bacchus, tell me what to do."

"Ah, you do know me. Call for the Ancient One, Callisto. She will know where to take her for proper training."

"Take her?"

"You really don't think it would be safe to let the daughter of a god come into her full power within the close quarters of your little hamlet here, do you?"

"Oh gods, I must send her away? Will she be safe?"

"She will be safe until she learns to wield her powers effectively. Then the trials begin."

"Why? Can you not just train her yourself? Can you not just tell us what to do for her?"

"I have, and now I must go. You are as beautiful as ever, Phialyra."

"And you are as treacherous as ever, Bacchus," she spat out as he faded back into the shadows with a smile and a bow before he disappeared completely. Lyra fell to her knees and wept, Eirini held tightly in her arms as protection from the cold that slowly began to creep into her skin.

Chapter Four

"Please don't be too hard on your mother, Skyemera," Dynami said, breaking the prolonged silence. "You were having nightmares. You would wake up screaming multiple times a night. You wouldn't talk about them, almost as if you would forget they happened once you awoke, but they were terrifying. We didn't know what to do to help you, Meraki."

"By the time they called me to try and help, the nightmares had gotten so intense that you would wake up with a bloody nose from the power of your screams," Helena chimed in. "There was no healing spell I could devise that would prevent the bleeding."

"I don't remember any of this," Mera cried. Nothing they'd told her made any sense when she had no recollection of anything.

"We know," Helena continued. "We tried appealing to Morpheus to protect your dreams and he refused."

"Refused, why?" Kari asked in surprise.

Though her lip curled like an irritated cat ready to show its fangs, Helena's voice remained level. "The gods are fickle, and their reasons are often unknown to us. Even when they are known, dwelling on them is not helpful. It is enough to know that the God of Dreams refused. So the three of us, Dynami, Phialyra, and myself, pooled our collective energies and called on Lethe, the Goddess of Forgetfulness. She agreed to help us, but under one condition..." Helena trailed off, face softening into one of sadness, or maybe it was remorse.

"What was that?" Mera asked, more curious than concerned.

Lyra entered the room, babe in hand, and responded. "She told us that the entire community must be made to forget everything related to you from the age of three to nine." Mera noticed that her mother looked much more resigned than the panic-stricken face she had left the room with mere minutes before. "It was not an easy decision to make," Lyra said, gazing at her mother who looked exhausted. Mera had never seen her grandmother so forlorn and uncertain. Her pale blond hair, normally perfectly coifed atop her head was falling, mirroring her disheveled gaze. She'd always been steadfast and self-assured that Mera had to fight tears of sympathy. "You were suffering terribly, Meraki, and the community as a whole was beginning to feel the toll of your night terrors. So we agreed to the terms, and the three of us," Lyra said, gesturing at the two elders, "with the goddess' help, erased the memory of you from everyone in The Thicket. As far as they knew, we went to the mountains when you were still an infant and returned when you were three, the same age as Kari, and thus, you grew up...again."

Everyone looked at Mera, but she turned to look at her cousin, her best friend. The elder nymphs were talking about Mera's life, but everything they said was also affecting Kari. Her cousin's unusual calm showed how much she was also struggling to make sense of this story. "So I have seen twenty winters," Mera asked, hoping she misunderstood.

"Yes, though you have no recollection of six of them," her mother confirmed.

"I don't know how to feel about this," Mera admitted. "I don't know what to think." The sun peeked through the windows, catching her attention. "May I be excused to take a run through the forest. I need some time, some space to process all of this."

Her grandmother sighed. "You will need someone with you. We are not sure you are safe with the dragon's unexpected return."

For the first time in nearly an hour, Kari spoke. "I can go with her, Yaya. I, too, need some time to process, as this was all so much. Since I already know where we'll be heading, I can give Mera space should she need it and, yet, ensure she is not alone."

The matriarch nodded. "If that is ok with you, Phialyra."

"Yes, Mother, that will be fine." Turning to Mera, she said, "I can understand the need to process all of this. We will be here when you are ready to continue the conversation as we try to work out what Vasilios' return means."

Before another word was uttered, the young nymphs were out of the room, down the hall, and onto the empty path. They left The Thicket in silence. Mera did not feel like talking, and Kari seemed to be in her own head as well. Their elders had dropped much on their young heads this past evening, and it was taking a toll. Mera had so many emotions coursing through her body that she didn't know whether to take off running, climb the tallest tree and jump, or fall to her knees and scream. In fewer than 24 hours, she had welcomed a new sister, became that child's protector, learned she, herself, was destined to be a goddess due to her unusual parentage, and that her mother was somehow mated to a dragon who triggered nightmares so bad the memories of the entire village had to be erased. It was all too much, and if she had not seen the shadow of the dragon or its fire herself last night, she probably would not have believed any of it. As it was, she was having a hard time accepting it all. She could only imagine what Kari was thinking about everything, and she was surprisingly pleased when her best friend started talking.

"So little of what they said makes sense," she said, waving her hands to the trees. "If it was just the idea of a faun seducing your seemingly level-headed mother, we could probably overlook it as a fanciful excuse she gave her own mother for running around. But then, it actually makes sense considering your hair, coloring, and physical features. I mean, your eyes change colors, for Artemis' sake." This last part probably would have made Mera chuckle if everything didn't feel so dire, but Kari continued her musings as if Mera wasn't there. "Then you take the fact that a dragon just happened to show up following your birth because the trees exploded into the air? If that doesn't sound like a myth the gods told to make their births seem more supernatural than the rest of us, I don't know what would." This time, Mera did chuckle, which caught Kari's attention, and she too started laughing. "It is all so ridiculous!"

"Tell me about it," Mera said between giggles, "I'm the one who is supposedly this rare cross-pantheon goddess and yet, I can't remember six years of my life because my family did what, obliterated all memory of me from the community's collective history? Is that even possible? And, if it is, what does that truly mean? We sat there listening to them for hours, and I still have more questions than understanding."

"And let us not forget the fire-breathing dragon," Kari exclaimed, as if announcing the arrival of one of the carnival caravans that sometimes passed through parts of The Grove on their way to the human towns on the other side of the river.

"How could we possibly forget a dragon? Big thing. Flies. Shoots fire. Oh, and not only are they real, but they are shapeshifters that can pretend to be human. If the humans think we are dangerous and a little out of place, I can't imagine how they'd respond to finding a dragon in their midst, no matter how well-dressed for a portrait."

"I still can't believe your mom painted that portrait. I mean, he was quite handsome, if that's what he truly looked like in his human form, but also quite terrifying."

"I wonder if she painted the portrait out of the love she felt for him early on, or did he compel her to paint it? She said that he didn't show his form until he was angry with her, so the portrait would have had to come afterwards. I have so many questions, but I had to get out of the house for a while. It was getting hard to breath, Kari."

"I understand. It was definitely a lot to take in. I had so many questions, but I was afraid YaYa really was going to send me home. I am far too nosy to have waited for you to tell me."

"I'm not even sure I'd have known what to tell you, so I probably wouldn't have said anything."

"Really, you'd have left me out in the cold with this? My feelings are hurt." Mera looked up at that last statement, feeling guilty until she saw the gleam in Kari's eye as she stifled a laugh.

"I should have left you home," Mera said, picking up the pace just to make her cousin suffer a little as she tried to keep up.

"Mera, I know you are running on purpose, and that is completely unfair," Kari yelled from 20 yards back. "I am simply trying to make sense of all of this the same as you. I'm torn about asking my mother what she remembers about your birth. What if she says 'nothing'?"

"Well, they said they did not delete my birth from anyone's memory, just those years after the dragon became violent." Mera stopped walking and turned to let Kari catch up. "What do you think could have possibly happened to cause nightmares so great our elders would feel it necessary to mess with others' memories?"

"I'm stuck wondering what would have caused Morpheus to deny their request to protect a child from nightmares so great she was bleeding from the nose?" Kari wrinkled her nose in obvious disappointment.

"Like Helena said, the gods are fickle and egotistical. Maybe they couldn't offer him anything worthwhile for his service."

"Maybe, but I'm not sure his denial is any more disturbing than the fact that Lethe required everyone's memory be erased just to settle the mind of one child." Mera nodded in agreement at that, and the young cousins continued their walk toward the shore. As they crossed the dune, they could smell the sea air and see the gnarled trees ahead in the distance. Mera felt the tension in her shoulders relax.

"You go ahead and commune with your tree friends. I promised to give you space, and I think I just want to walk along the water's edge anyway," Kari offered as she changed direction to the south.

"Thank you for coming with me and for being my friend. Seriously, you're the best."

"I knew you'd come around," Kari said with a giggle and took off at a run before Mera could respond.

"Mother, we need to talk," Phialyra said almost as soon as the young nymphs had left the room. Helena started to rise from Dynami's side. "This is important to all of us, and you are like a second grandmother to my Mera. Please stay and provide comfort to my mother." Her mother looked exhausted, and she could see the events of the last two days, and eleven years ago, etched into her beautiful face. It broke her heart to know how much damage her hasty, youthful decisions had caused, and would likely continue to cause. No, she wouldn't think of that now. Right now, she had to focus on Mera's safety. She felt her mother's penetrating gaze and knew she couldn't prolong the inevitable. With a deep breath, she told them about Bacchus' visit.

"There was a god...in my house?"

"Yes."

"Are you saying Mera's father isn't some random faun from a distant land. He's actually Bacchus," Helena asked, a dumbfounded look on her face. "I mean, that would explain some things."

"Explain what?" Lyra asked, sitting on the settee across from the elder nymphs.

"The gods do not often interfere in the affairs of other pantheons. Her father being a god and not the servant of one trumps your request as a servant of Dionysus. I cannot say for certain if that was Morpheus' motivation for turning down our request, but it is possible."

"The gods have forsaken my child. They left her to be terrorized by nightmares. They have left her unprotected. I care not one whit about the gods' motivations."

"Take care with your words, Lyra," Dynami said firmly. "They do not always provide what we wish, but they will mete punishment as they wish. Also, it appears that we have a goddess in this household now, so we would do best not to make her feel any more isolated."

Lyra deflated and slumped down into the settee. "He said we would need to send Mera away. I don't know that I have it in me to do so."

"What did he say exactly?" Helena asked.

"Oh, not like that," Lyra responded picking up on the elder's tone of concern. "He warned that Mera's powers would soon... crest...yes, I believe that's the word he used. Unlike our powers that build as we become more connected to the earth, Mera's powers come as a wave."

"A wave she will not be able to control," Dynami speculated.

"That is the way he made it sound. He was clear that we would not know how to help her harness those powers and made it sound like she could be a danger to herself and others when the time comes. Mother, I'm scared for her."

"Did he say anything else, give any suggestions?" Helena asked, focusing the conversation.

"He said that we should search out the Ancient One, Callisto. He said she could help my Mera."

"Callisto!" Dynami and Helena shrieked.

"She's not been seen in ages," Dynami said. "How in the world are we supposed to..."

Helena held up a hand. "I have an idea for how to contact her. There are tales of her seclusion in the southern lands beyond The Tribunal Forest. We could try to send word to her, or I could go in search of her."

"He made it sound like reaching her would not be so difficult. Could we not just beg Artemis for help?"

"We could try, but I'm not sure that will result in any better outcome than our pleas to Morpheus, but we can try," Helena said. "I will go now and attempt to contact Callisto. Do we know exactly what we are asking from her?"

Lyra shook her head. "He only said that she would know how to help Mera learn to harness her powers. He didn't explain what that meant."

"Very well, then. I will simply plead that she come and advise us on how to proceed."

"Thank you, my friend, for everything," Dynami said reverently. Helena nodded, squeezed Dynami's shoulder, and left the house.

"I wonder if it will take long for her to get the message and to arrive should she agree? I'm afraid time is not on our side," Lyra mused.

"I trust Helena to convey the urgency," Dynami responded. Lyra nodded and stood.

"I am tired and would like to rest while Eirini is resting."

"Yes, daughter, get some rest, as we all may be sleep-deprived soon."

"Mother..."

"Hmm.."

"I am sorry for all of this."

"We all have our regrets, but none of that will help the present. Let us focus on what we can do differently this time around. Go, before the babe wakes."

Lyra felt the sting in her eyes and left the room. As she made her way down the hall to her sleeping infant, she prayed that Mera was finding some solace in her favorite place along the shore.

Chapter Five

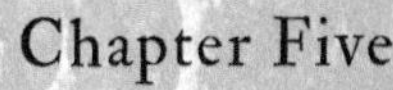

Mera found her place amongst the oaks where she could see the waves wash over the shore from a semi-hidden vantage point. It was her favorite place because no one expected anything of her there, and no one was there to scrutinize every aspect of her person. The trees didn't judge her. From her alcove, she could see Kari's head bobbing along the water's edge. Occasionally, her cousin would dip out of sight, and Mera imagined she was picking up tide-tossed shells.

Kari was truly beautiful, even by nymph standards. She had the typical petite frame, but she was fierce. She had strong cheekbones that gave her a noble look, much like Mera imagined their grandmother looking at their age. No, Kari's age, Mera reminded herself. Mera had seen twenty winters, her mother confessed, though six of those years were missing from her memory. Does that mean she cannot actually claim the full twenty or...she had no idea what that might mean.

Instinctively, Mera looked across the beach for her younger cousin. When she could no longer see Kari's bobbing head, Mera crept from the copse of entangled tree trunks to look for her. She was nowhere to be seen, and Mera nervously began making her way down the beach, listening carefully for Kari's voice on the wind. The young nymph loved to sing while she was walking alone. That thought made Mera smile. It was true that Kari loved the sound of her own voice and was almost never silent, or at least her silence never lasted for long. As Mera got closer to the curve around the bluff, her concern grew. She could not hear Kari, not even her footsteps. All Mera could hear was the sound of the surf. For the first time, she found herself wishing it wasn't so loud.

Picking up the pace, Mera quickly maneuvered around the cliff wall, the lump in her throat threatening to take her breath until she finally spotted her cousin. There, not 100 yards in front of her, Mera found Kari talking to another nymph. Mera didn't recognize the nymph, so she must not be from The Grove. Was it possible her outgoing cousin was making friends with one of the nereids? All the time that Mera had spent on this beach, she had never had an encounter with a sea nymph. She'd never thought about it before, but as she slowed her pace and quieted her breaths, she wondered why they'd never approached her.

Mera's thoughts quickly refocused on the scene in front of her, where it became obvious, as she closed the distance, that her cousin was quite animated in whatever story she was telling. Mera was surprised that neither nymph acknowledged her approach, especially once she'd gotten close enough to overhear their conversation. Just as Kari said, "So we had to get away for a little while," the unknown nymph turned in Mera's direction. Her head snapped back immediately, though, when Kari finished with "and my cousin's favorite place is with the ogre oaks up the beach a bit."

"Ogre oaks," the other nymph repeated, a questions clearly written on her face.

"The large, twisted trees at the north end of the beach," Mera said. "I like to spend time among them and listen to the ocean."

"Oh, The Strimmena," the nymph responded, her face relaxing. "They are the Watchers of Wind here on our shores. And you are the maenad. My name is Nelaira, and I am one of the guardians of this shore." Though the nereid appeared to be of a similar age to the cousins, her bearing said she was much older. Her black hair was tightly twisted away from the copper skin of her face and adorned with small shells from the sea. She held a spear in her hand, the base of the shaft sitting in the sand. She was fierce, and Mera was both comforted by her reverence of the oaks Mera loved so dearly and unnerved by her intimate knowledge of Mera when they'd never met.

"What have you been telling her, Karielle?" It was rare that either of them called each other by their given name, but this nymph's nonchalant acknowledgement of news that she was still trying to process put her on edge.

"Nothing, just that we came to the beach to get out of the house," her cousin answered, looking at the ground.

"This young nymph told me nothing I did not already know. My people know who you are. We watch over you while you're here. The burst of energy from your birth caused a tidal wave that shook our shores. We remember every time you've come to this place in your short twenty winters."

"Wait, you know my age? How do you know my true age when my village does not?"

"I don't know what you mean when you say your village does not know your age, but you have been coming here since your birth, though much more often in recent years. You have always played and hidden amongst The Strimmena, even when you were quite small."

Though she could not see them for the obscuring cliff face, Mera looked toward the oaks at the mention of them. "Did I always come here alone?"

Nelaira laughed. "No, of course not. You came here for the first time as an infant and then at least twice each season as you grew. We do not track time quite like you forest folk do, since our tides change daily, and our oaks are always bare. According to the sun's position, I would say it was at least five or six times per year."

"Oh, so my mother would bring me then? I wish I could remember."

"Yes, your mother brought you when you were very young, and then there were times where others would bring you."

"Others?" Kari asked before Mera could process the words.

"Yes, there were two different males at different times. One appeared human, though he had a powerful aura around him. He came most often and watched the young maenad play in the surf." She turned to look where the water touched the sandy beach. "Later, there was a satyr who would bring her, but they would stay in the shadows of the cliff, so we could not see much."

Mera stared at Nelaira, unsure how to process this new information. Kari had no such difficulty and trudged headlong into her analysis of the situation. "Presumably, the human-like creature was your mother's mate."

"Your mother was mated to a human?" Nelaira asked, and Mera wasn't sure if her tone was one of confusion or disgust. "We were sure that one was not actually human."

"Oh, he wasn't," Kari chimed in whimsically, " but for the sake of keeping the two separated, it was just easier to call him human. Anyway, who was the satyr, do you think?" All Mera could do was shrug. "Was it possibly Eirini's father," she offered. "Had he been around that long without anyone knowing?"

"There's so much no one knows," Mera stated, sitting down in the sand. She found a small stick and began drawing swirls in the sand. Without looking up, she asked, "If it was Eirini's father, why was he bringing me to the beach while my mother was presumably still living with her mate?" Kari plopped onto the sand near her, and the cousins sat in quiet contemplation for a few minutes before Mera shook her head free of the confused thoughts. The sea nymph stood vigil, her bronze skin glowing in the afternoon sun. "None of this is making any more sense than what we were told last night. Nelaira, is there anything else you can tell us about that time?" Mera asked, trying to stave off the hopelessness threatening to overpower her.

"As I said, when you were born, there was a disturbance felt all around, even in the sea. We heard rumors from the creatures who live along the forest's edge that a dragon had come to The Tribunal Forest and was often seen circling above the northern mountains. It wasn't long after its arrival, maybe a couple months before your mother started bringing you to the water's edge. It was a couple years later when that human, as young Karielle has decided to call him, began accompanying you and your mother. We noticed then that you were spending more time among The Strimmena than out on the open beach."

"What was Mera's mother doing?" Kari asked.

"We're unsure. We know she stayed near the human. We kept our attention on you in case you should stray too far into the surf or upon the dunes. We do not usually meddle in the business of other nymphai, but as The Maenad, you fall under our protection while on our shores," Nelaira said with a respectful head bow. Mera didn't know what to say, but she returned the gesture instinctively.

"Was it always you who stood looking over me across the years, or were there others who may have overheard the adult conversations? I am most curious about what my mother and the dra...human discussed while I played in the sand or beneath the trees."

"I was your primary guardian here, though, as I said, my job was to watch from afar to ensure you did not leave the safety of the sand. I did not get close enough to overhear any conversations, even those that happened when you were brought here without your mother. I will ask the others if anyone saw or heard anything when I was not able to attend you."

"Thank you," Mera said, looking at her cousin and then up at the sky that was already showing past midday. "I suppose we should begin our return to The Thicket, else it will be dark before we arrive, and there will be no food left from the evening meal." They both stood and began wiping sand from their lower halves, Mera giving up quickly as she realized it was all in her fur.

"I wish you safe travels, Maenad," Nelaira said with a bow.

"My name is Skyemera. I don't know what all this maenad talk means yet, so please just call me Mera."

"Very well."

All thoughts of food fled when Mera entered the house through the rear kitchen door and heard her mother and grandmother talking in the receiving room. As much as she wanted to interrogate them about what she had learned from the nereid, she was too tired to process anything they could have told her. Kari had decided to go home with a promise to return in the morning, so Mera snuck up the stairs and fell into her bed exhausted. Rather than her normal peaceful sleep, though, Mera dreamt of the dragon.

She was a young maenad with the upper body of a nymph and the lower body of a faun standing on a cliff overlooking The Tribunal Forest. She really did love her homes, both the one below surrounded by beautiful trees and the one above that gave her views like this. She could see The Grove, The Great River, and the Great Sea from her vantage point. Such a beautiful mixture of colors, much like the paintings on her grandmother's walls. Mera hoped that they'd go back and visit Yaya soon. She couldn't understand why her mother hadn't taken her off the mountain yet while her poppa was out of town. They almost always went down to The Grove while he was gone.

Mera hated being up here among the crags by herself. She hated even more that her mother always told her to stay inside. She didn't want to stay inside all day. She wanted to run and play with her cousins. She was a forest nymph after all. She wondered where her mother went when she left her alone at home. At least in The Grove, there were other creatures and the nymphs of The Thicket. Here in the mountains, there was no one. She had no one to play with and no one to talk to when her mother wasn't home. Her poppa didn't really like a lot of people around, so it was rare that they had visitors. Mera found herself wishing she was off the mountain. Maybe she'd ask her mother if they could go to the beach tomorrow.

A loud screech broke the silence. She had never heard an animal make that sound, so she ducked behind some rocks and tried to figure out where the sound was coming from. Suddenly, a huge shadow passed over the cliffside, bringing with it a bone-chilling cold. She looked up into a huge underbelly and caught sight of taloned claws. A dragon. She froze. Dragons weren't real, or if they had been, they didn't exist anymore. The cold remained until the beast had passed around the other side of the mountain. Afraid it would circle back, Mera ran to their stony home. She nearly screamed in fear that it would swoop down and grab her in those terrible claws, when she heard its wings high overhead, but she managed to duck into the doorway and slam the door, hoping it hadn't seen her.

There, behind the door, breath ragged, Mera listened intently for another screech or something that would tell her if the dragon was still around. In those few endless moments, Mera wished her mother and poppa were home. She wished for anyone bigger and stronger than her. She thought she heard flapping wings closer to the house and looked around the kitchen for anything that could protect her. The pots and pans hanging along the wall wouldn't do much against a dragon, nor would anything in the larder. She thought about grabbing a knife, but that would required her to let the dragon get close enough to use the knife, and she wondered if a knife would even work against its scales. With no other options, she hid under the kitchen table, pulling all the chairs in around her. Something scraped on the stone walkway outside, and she held her breath. It can't hear you if you're not breathing, right? Tears rolled down her cheeks, as the scraping got closer. When the door flew open, she screamed.

L yra ran into the room, followed closely by Dynami, and grabbed her daughter who was still screaming. She called Mera's name, rubbing the maenad's hair, pleading with her to wake up. Dynami stood inside the doorway, eyes wide with concern. Lyra caught her gaze and held it, pleading with her mother to somehow help. Still asleep, Mera thrashed against her mother who held her tight until the screams turned to sobs. Then she continued holding her, rocking back and forth, cooing to her elder child, trying to console her.

"This has to be related to Vasilios' return. What are we to do?" Lyra asked her mother.

"This is no mere coincidence," Dynami conceded. "I am not sure why, though. She did not know who the dragon was until we told her."

"Maybe we shouldn't have told her, mother," Phialyra exclaimed, voice cracking. "Maybe breaking the silence also broke the spell. What if everyone's memories have returned?"

"I hope that is not the case, but I am not as worried about them as I am this child," Dynami responded. "I do not know anything we said that would have caused the return of her nightmares. To know that dragons exist should not have been a catalyst for this," she continued, gesturing toward the still sobbing maenad.

"No, but something attacked her in her sleep," Lyra whispered, as Mera's sobs quieted. Moments later, Mera's eyes fluttered open, and she gave a disoriented look around the room until she landed on her grandmother in the doorway.

"What's going on?" Mera asked, trying to extricate herself from her mother's arms and sit up. "Mother, are you alright?"

"The question is, are you alright?" Dynami responded as Lyra lifted Mera's chin and wiped a tear from her child's eye. Mera reached up to her own cheeks, concern contorting her face as she found them damp with fresh tears.

"Mother," Mera said with a hint of trepidation.

"You had a nightmare," her mother answered the unasked question. "You were screaming. I couldn't wake you, and you were fighting as if a demon was trying to grab for you. I held you until you relaxed into sobs and then kept holding you until you woke up. It was like you were a child all over again."

"Do you remember anything about your dream?" Dynami asked, having moved close enough to place a hand on her granddaughter's head.

"I remember being in some kind of cage with bars on all sides, and something was reaching for me through the bars. I couldn't get away from it." Mera shuddered and moved closer into her mother's arms again.

"Do you remember what it was?" her grandmother pressed.

"I tried keeping my eyes closed, but it had claws. No, wait, it had hands. Actually, I think both were reaching through the bars," Mera answered, pulse and voice rising simultaneously. Lyra tightened her grip.

"At the same time?" Lyra asked.

"Yes, they were coming from different sides."

"What could that mean?" This time, Lyra directed the question at her mother.

"I do not know, but Helena and I will contact Lethe today to see if we can get some answers regarding why the forgetting spell has worn off." She lay a hand on her daughter's shoulder, and smoothed her granddaughter's hair once more before turning to leave the room. "There must be some kind of explanation for this," Dynami muttered, barely audible as she exited the room.

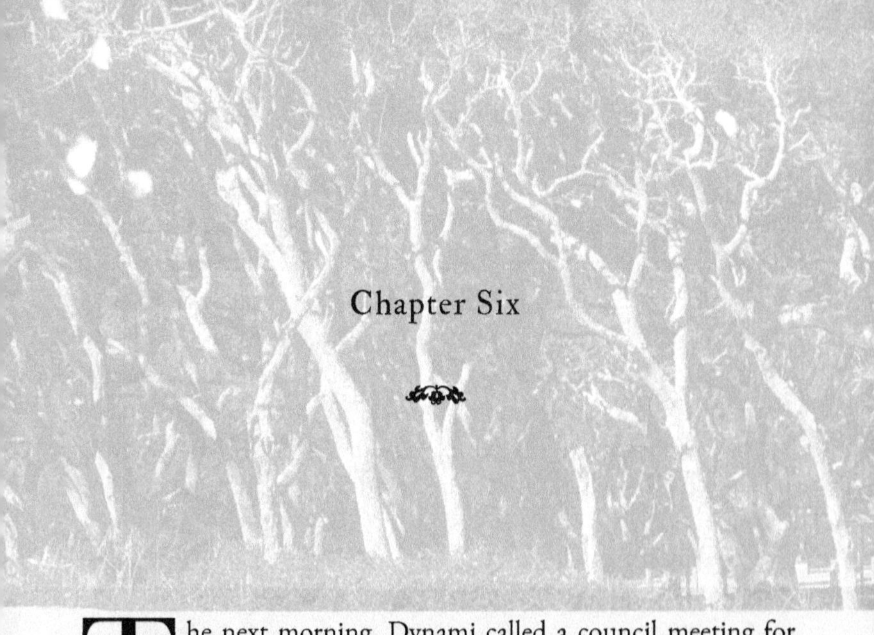

Chapter Six

The next morning, Dynami called a council meeting for the leaders of their community to talk about what happened the previous evening and what may be coming now that the dragon had returned.

"Are you sure we want to tell everyone about the spell?" Helena asked Dynami on their way to the meeting hall.

"I think we have gone far too long holding everyone's memories hostage without their knowledge."

"Yes, but will it make things better for them to know the memories were taken intentionally and could suddenly return?" Helena continued.

Dynami stopped and looked at her best friend. "I do not know." She opened her mouth to say more, but instead turned to continue their walk. As the elder nymphs passed through The Thicket, Dynami said, "I hope they will understand, but more than that, I hope they will be prepared. I want them better prepared than Skyemera was. Than we were."

Helena looked down with a sigh, and they both turned onto the path that led to the meeting house. The revelation that

Skyemera's nightmares had returned was frightening in so many ways.

The matriarchs silenced their conversation as they neared the long, single-room hut set off from the homes near the northwestern edge of The Thicket. It sat in the middle of an open field and only the council and special guests were allowed to enter its doors. The council was made up of family matriarchs. Each of these leaders had seen well over 100 winters and were held in high esteem within the community. In total, there were eight council members, though there were many more individual families living in The Thicket. These eight represented the founding families and their descendants.

Dynami had been the community Matriarch, her title as well as descriptor, for nearly 80 winters now, not long after she had birthed Phialyra, and she was proud to serve as their leader. She could only hope that the secret she told the council today would not make them regret the years of her service.

"Good morning, Matriarch...Mother," Phrixa said in greeting as Dynami and Helena arrived at the hall's entry. The tall, redheaded nymph gave a quick bow as she moved to open the door, her pale skin reflecting the morning sun like ice.

"Good morning, Phrixa," Dynami responded with a nod. Phrixa's family had been in The Thicket as long as Dynami's, and Phrixa had long coveted the Matriarch position.

"Early, as always," Helena responded.

"When your Matriarch calls an emergency meeting, you do not dally," Phrixa said with a smile Dynami knew was as insincere as the statement that preceded it. "I only arrived moments before you did, Helena."

"Let us make our way inside to await the rest of the council," Dynami said, breaking the repartee between the two nymphs.

The inside of the meeting hall was sparse. A fire pit had been dug into the middle of the room to allow for warmth and sacred ritual. There were flaps over the window-like openings that could be rolled up to allow smoke to escape and air to circulate. Around the fire pit, there were trenches dug to create earthen seating. The council did not behave as a hierarchy, though they did have an elected leader, so they all sat in a circle where they could see each other and speak freely. There were mats placed around the outside of the circle along the walls for the rare visitors to the council.

"I will open the window flaps to allow more light to enter. I do not believe we yet need a fire," Helena offered.

"Thank you," Dynami said, sitting herself within the circle, facing the doorway, so she could see everyone as they entered. She was hoping to gauge their moods prior to the meeting's start. She was fairly sure how Phrixa would respond to the revelations, but many of the other elders could be swayed if their mood allowed.

The next members to arrive were Sapharnia, another redheaded nymph of medium height with emerald eyes, and Danalise, a petite, olive-skinned nymph with Jade eyes similar to Lyra. Danalise' brother was Lyra's father. Though green eyes were the dominant color of their kind, it was not unheard of for nymphs to develop varying eye colors depending on their parentage. Helena, for example, had gray blue eyes, the color of the sky before a storm. The two nymphs entered the hall arm in arm, whispering and laughing. Dynami was glad to see them in a cheerful mood. She greeted them with a smile and a nod. "Your invitation was a surprise, Matriarch," Danalise said to her as they sat next to each other at Dynami's right.

"Yes, I am sure it was," Dynami responded, "and I apologize for any inconvenience it may have caused."

"No inconvenience, Matriarch," Sapharnia said, "more curiosity. We hope all is well with Phialyra's new babe."

Dynami smiled at the mention of Eirini before her smile faded as she thought of her eldest granddaughter and their reason for meeting today. "The babe is fine. I will make it all clear once everyone has arrived," she said with what she hoped was a calm tone. She felt anything but calm. Helena sat to Dynami's left and placed a supportive hand on her friend's knee, as it was starting to bob up and down like driftwood on the ocean. Dynami looked down at her knee and then smiled back up at her friend. "Thank you," she mouthed silently.

A loud, "I hope I'm not late," came from the doorway, as a large, muscled nymph with terra cotta skin entered the hall. If not for her green eyes, flowing, sun-streaked hair, and unbelievable earth magic, one would never think Euonsise a nymph. She was unimaginably strong and yet unceasingly kind and gentle.

"You are right on time, Mother," Dynami said, loud enough to be heard across the hall. "How comes the harvest? Will we be set for the winter?"

"The harvest is coming along great. All of the crops were fruitful this year, and we should have food to spare," Euonsise responded with a smile. Her farm at the southwestern end of The Thicket was the primary source of food for the entire community. The strong harvest and her good nature led Dynami to believe that Euonsise would be an ally in today's meeting. That only left two members to arrive.

Canea had served as Matriarch before Dynami, and while she was at all times cordial, Dynami couldn't help but think Canea was still upset about losing that status. Dynami wasn't sure she'd be able to count on Canea during this difficult conversation. Nerin had held a grudge against Dynami since they were children, over 300 years now. Dynami had no idea what the elder nymph was angry about after all this time, but Nerin was nothing if not consistent. She would be late to the meeting because Dynami called it, and she would naysay every argument the Matriarch made. In truth, Dynami would be better off if the two nymphs did not come to the meeting, but she had no delusions. They would be there.

As she finished the thought, the door opened, and Canea walked in leaning a little heavier on her walking stick than at their last meeting. "Are you all right, Mother," Dynami asked respectfully. Canea glowered, though Dynami was unsure if it was for being addressed at the same level as the others or on being called to the council unexpectedly. She knew the elder disliked giving up the Matriarch title.

"I've been better, but I am here," Canea responded. "I will say I'm grateful that the seat here closest to the door was not yet taken."

"We are yet missing Nerin," Dynami stated to the room. "We will begin as soon as she arrives."

"You know she's going to be late," Sapharnia said, shaking her head.

"Yes, she has no respect for the Council's time, so why must we wait for her," Danalise stated in agreement.

"She is a member of this council," Canea reminded everyone, "and thus must be in attendance for us to begin. Unless," she continued, "anyone has heard from her and knows she will not be coming."

"She was never late when you were our Matriarch, Canea," Phrixa said, glancing at Dynami from the corner of her eye.

"I don't believe that to be true," Canea responded. "That nymph was late to her own birth."

Helena laughed aloud while the other members chuckled, Euonsise covering her mouth to hold in her laugh. Just then, the door opened, and the final council member arrived. The nymph entered with a flurry of movement, going left and then pivoting right, as if she were dodging the wind. Nerin had the impulsiveness of a young nymph, and her clear, supple skin belied her 350 winters. She was loyal to a fault and held grudges the same way. In many ways, Karielle reminded Dynami of Nerin, though she hoped her granddaughter would be much more levelheaded rather than running on both ends of the spectrum at all times.

"Now that we are all here, Nerin, if you will take your seat, we can begin," Dynami announced.

"Tell us what's on your mind, Dynami," Canea said directly.

"Thank you, Mother," Dynami responded, ignoring the lack of proper address before speaking to the council as a whole. "Mothers, I have invited you all here to discuss the events from the past few days and to share a painful secret we have held for the past 11 years."

"A secret? Held from the council?" Phrixa asked, malicious curiosity written in the tilt of her brow and purse of her lips.

"Yes. I will try to make it all clear in time, and Helena will fill in any gaps should I inadvertently omit some detail," Dynami said quickly to ward off any further comments. "As you are all aware, a dragon flew over The Grove on the night my youngest granddaughter Eirini was born and presented to the community, as is our way. We have reason to believe that dragon was Phialyra's mate," she said, pausing at the gasps from around the room.

"What do you mean her mate?" Sapharnia asked.

Dynami lifted a hand to regain control of the murmurs before they derailed the entire conversation. "If you will think back to the year Skyemera was born, you should remember two things that happened. A dragon, much like the one from the other night, flew over The Grove, and a human male was found wandering The Tribunal Forest at the edges of The Grove," Dynami began.

"Oh yes, I do remember that," Euonsise responded. "I remember Phialyra taking such a liking to that human and moving away with him."

"Yes, my daughter did develop affection for the man. They insisted on getting married within the year, and she moved away to his home in the mountains with my granddaughter."

"Whatever happened with that relationship? I don't remember

much except that they moved back to The Thicket after a couple years," Canea mused.

Dynami looked at Helena, took a deep breath, and said," That is precisely what we are here to discuss."

"You're not saying that man was the dragon we've now seen twice, are you? That's absurd," Nerin chimed in before Dynami could continue. That nymph was astute, if exasperating.

"If everyone would let Dynami speak freely, she would tell us. I can't imagine that airing family secrets is going to be easy without distractions, let alone with repetitive snide comments," Helena said in support of the Matriarch, drawing pointed stares from the more vocal council members.

Dynami stood, as the tension in the room grew, "Thank you, Helena. You are right that this is not easy for me; however, ridiculing each other will not make this any easier either."

"Please continue, Matriarch. There was a purpose for which you called this meeting, and you deserve the respect of being heard," Canea said, looking around the room at the others. Nerin and Phrixa both slumped back in their seats, deflated.

"Thank you, Mother. I will try to make everything as clear as possible, and then I will address all questions and concerns as best I can. As I was saying, my daughter married this unknown human and moved away when Skyemera had seen but one winter. You likely do not remember, but they used to come back to The Grove and visit us regularly for the first few years, and then the visits began to come less frequently."

"First few?" Sapharnia began, caught up in the story, before Danalise placed a hand on her knee stopping her words. She looked around sheepishly and gestured for Dynami to continue.

Dynami nodded in her direction. "Yes, as I said, you likely do not remember these details, but that will make sense shortly. During those early years of Skyemera's life, I did not see them except for when Vasilios, Phialyra's mate, was away. He would leave for weeks at a time, though no one knows where or why, but those times were when my daughter would bring her child home to commune with our people. Over time, the visits became shorter, and both of them began to change. It is hard to explain, but there was something different in their personalities and behaviors. They were more subdued and distant. Then the visits stopped altogether, until shortly after Skyemera's ninth birthday." Dynami paused, taking a deep breath and letting it out slowly. "I don't have all the details of what happened in those years, but I can only imagine it was something horrid," she said before pausing again, tightness growing in her chest.

Dynami thought back to when Phialyra and Skyemera returned to her home. Neither spoke much that first day, other than to say that they were home for good. The look on Lyra's face was burnt into Dynami's mind. Her once beautiful, lively, and adventurous daughter looked wan, lost, and broken. It took every ounce of strength not to grab her daughter by the shoulders and shake answers from her. Dynami had wanted to call on the guards and the community at large to chase down that human who had broken Lyra's spirit and did who knows what to Mera. She wanted to break down his door and unleash all of her power on him, but propriety and responsibility to her people stayed her hand. She could not let her lust for vengeance wreak further havoc on her family.

"When Lyra returned home, she was but a shell of her former self. Now, I understand that some of our people may think that a good thing, as my daughter was always too carefree and prone to wandering, but there is nothing as painful as seeing your child broken and unable to fix it." The council stared at her, rapt by the raw emotion in Dynami's voice and surprised by her use of Phialyra's nickname, which no one, save Helena, had ever heard the Matriarch use before. "It was on this return home that I learned Vasilios was the dragon. He apparently has the ability to shape shift between human and dragon form, and he had used our nature of helping lost travelers against us to get his claws into Skyemera."

"Skyemera?" Eunosise exclaimed. "What would a dragon have wanted with that poor girl? She was but a babe."

"I struggled with this as well, until I had chance to contact the gods. Skyemera is a maenad, a true maenad, blessed by the gods of both of her parents with the strength of both." Dynami omitted the newly learned fact that her granddaughter's father was actually a god because none of them knew what trouble that widespread knowledge might cause, and it wouldn't change this conversation. "Skyemera does not yet know or understand what that means, but the dragon felt the rush of power at her birth and came to The Grove to find its origin. Unfortunately, he found her mother easily pliable. According to Phialyra, Skyemera was three before he showed his true form."

"His abuse escalated after that, from what we were able to gather from Lyra when she came home," Helena added. "No one, not even Lyra knows exactly what happened to Mera while they were on the mountain, but we could tell from her behaviors that something significant had happened to the young nymph... maenad." She corrected herself with a shake of her head.

"She came home with uncontrollable nightmares," Dynami continued, having caught her breath while Helena filled in the gaps. "It was terrifying when Skyemera suddenly began screaming in the dead of night. Her screams were inconsolable. She would fight us, as if the Onerois themselves were holding her hostage. We'd start the next day scratched and bruised. Subsequent nights only got worse. She began hurting herself in the throes of those nightmares. She fell from her bed, hid in closets, and ran through the house, banging into furniture, all while asleep. One night, we had to chase her through The Thicket and out into The Grove. Her powerful legs had nearly propelled her to the edge of The Great Sea by the time we caught her."

"That night, her screams as she ran through the streets woke many who helped in the chase. I, myself, had taken to staying at the Matriarch's house to try and help contain Mera, but it was just too much. We were all sleep-deprived and scared for the young nymph," Helena continued.

"How is it that I don't remember any of this? My house is closest to yours. I would remember nightly screaming," Danalise said, looking at Dynami. "It is not that I don't believe you, Matriarch, but it is difficult to comprehend this missing time."

"We're getting..." Helena started but was cut off by Dynami with a hand on her arm.

"That night, after we brought Skyemera back home, Helena and I both went to speak with Morpheus. We begged him to help my granddaughter. It was from him that we found out Skyemera was a maenad. He refused to help her and did not give a reason. We believed it was due to the fickleness of the gods, but now I'm not so sure."

"He refused to help a child? A child who was being tortured in her dreams," Euonsise gasped, tears in her eyes.

"Yes, he refused our request outright," Dynami responded. "Not knowing what else to do, we turned to Lethe and asked her to take away the memories that were plaguing Skyemera. She agreed to help us, but there was a cost."

"What sort of cost," Canea asked with a raised eyebrow. Dynami knew the rest of this conversation was going to be extremely difficult, and the weight held her tongue. She looked to Helena for support, and her friend began the tale.

"Lethe was adamant that removing Mera's memories would only last if everything related to her during those years was removed from the entire community. In other words, we had to agree to remove everyone's memories of Skyemera from the age of three to the age of nine when she returned to us," Helena said, looking around the room as she spoke.

"What!" Nerin and Phrixa exclaimed at the same time. "You

stole our memories?" Phrixa cried. "How dare you?" Nerin followed.

Canea stood at her seat, silencing the outbursts around the room. "Let me make sure I understand the implications of your story. The Goddess of Forgetfulness agreed to help you protect your granddaughter from nightmares the God of Dreams refused to address, and her agreement required that all memory of young Skyemera be removed."

"Yes, that is correct," Dynami responded quietly.

"I can't imagine how difficult that decision must have been and how heartbreaking it must have been to listen to that young one scream in her sleep every night. I am not sure I could have handled it," Euonsise said before anyone else could respond. Dynami felt the tears burn the backs of her eyes, but she held her head high and looked at each of the council members in turn.

"Did we lose any other memories," Danalise asked, holding Sapharnia's hand for support.

"No," Helena and Dynami responded together. "We verified with Lethe that the spell would only remove memories related to Skyemera," Dynami explained. "She promised that all other memories of those years would remain intact.

"I can hope I would have made different choices had I been in your place," Canea said once Dynami's declarations were finished, "but I cannot honestly say I would never have considered the decision you made. I must know, though, why you decided to tell us now. It has been eleven years if my calculations are correct."

At this, Dynami stood to her full height and addressed the council, "As everyone knows, Phialyra birthed another child mere days ago, and the dragon has returned. We do not know what it means, if anything, as this child is a nymph. So far as we can tell, she holds no additional power or status different from our own. What everyone does not know is that Skyemera's nightmares have returned unprovoked. Something is happening, and I want everyone prepared."

"Prepared for what," Phrixa asked.

"We do not know exactly, but something is coming. The dragon's return at the birth of another child to my bloodline and Skyemera's nightmares after eleven years of oblivion does not portend well for the coming days," Dynami said in response.

"Maybe it's an omen for your family alone and will not affect the rest of us," Nerin said.

"Perhaps," Dynami agreed, "but I did not want to take that chance by leaving the council in the dark, in case whatever is coming comes for us all. Additionally, Skyemera is much older now, older than she even imagined, and she is still unaware of her powers. We are unaware of her powers as the only true maenad in ages. I am concerned how these nightmares will trigger her before she is able to control those powers."

All eyes widened at that revelation, and Dynami remained poised at the back of the hall waiting for the shouting to begin anew. Instead, Sapharnia and Danalise stood and nodded in her direction, followed by Euonsise and Helena. Danalise spoke for all of them when she said, "You are our Matriarch, rightfully chosen, but beyond that, your family is alseides, one of us. We take care of and protect our own." At that each of the nymphs raised her open left hand to the sky, as the trees of their grove, and saluted Dynami.

Phrixa and Nerin turned toward Canea. "Mother, can you believe the danger she's putting us in," Phrixa cried. Nerin opened her mouth to speak her agreement when Canea once again stood. The nymphs at her sides smirked in triumph until Canea raised her open palm to the sky in salute. "But..." they began in protest.

"Dynami has protected her family with the help of but one other in order to safeguard our community," Canea began, addressing the unspoken protests. "She shared a painful secret and acknowledged the negative effects of that secret, which shows great courage. At the return of the threat, she recognized that there are forces at work beyond their capabilities, and she called on the community for support. We would be remiss if we ignored her pleas and warnings," she finished before turning to address Dynami directly. "I support your leadership, Matriarch, and your cause. You must simply give word on what preparations we must take, and my family will be ready."

"Thank you," Dynami said, voice shaking, in the direction of those who'd stood by her. After a deep breath, she addressed the other two council members. "Phrixa and Nerin, I know that we have not always gotten on personally, but whenever I make decisions for The Thicket, I keep your families in mind as part of this community. I do not expect us to be friends. That may be a bridge far too charred, but I believe that when the time comes to protect The Grove, you will do so alongside every other nymph in this room and family in The Thicket." Finally, she sat down, the gesture followed by the other nymphs in the hall. "As of now, there are far more questions than answers, so let us return home to break our fasts, for I know we have all missed the morning meal for this meeting. We shall reconvene this afternoon to begin making preliminary plans.

Chapter Seven

Dynami walked back to her home for lunch, having dropped Helena off at her house down the street. She weighed the outcomes of this morning's council meeting in her mind and tried to think ahead to what she would need to do this afternoon and in the coming days. She cursed her lack of foresight. She never considered the dragon returning or what might happen if it did. All these years, and she thought her granddaughter safe from the nightmares. What had happened to her all those years ago? What did her nightmare mean? Two sets of hands grabbing at her through a cage, one clawed, one not. She could assume the clawed hand was that of the dragon, but was the human-like hand also that of the dragon? Could it have been someone or something else? It was all so hard to work through.

She waved as she passed by small groups of young nymphs running through the streets. She envied their carefree nature. Responsibility was weighing heavily on her heart as she entered the door to her home. She hoped that there was some happy medium between responsibility for her people and that for her family. She hoped she wouldn't have to make the distinction again, but when she saw Skyemera with her head on Phialyra's lap while Eirini nursed, she knew which side would win.

"Welcome home, Mother," Lyra said with a smile. "I hope the council meeting was not too difficult."

"You had a council meeting this morning, Yaya?" Mera asked.

"Yes, there was a meeting, and it went much smoother than expected. I confessed to the council that we enlisted the goddess Lethe's help with taking everyone's memories, and while there was some anger and derision, most seemed to understand. I believe we will have allies should we need it, but we must create a plan for preparation after lunch."

"Preparation for what?" Mera asked, sitting up with furrowed brows.

"Come help me make lunch, and we can talk about it. I am hungry after having spent so much time at the meeting house."

"Mother, are you sure this is something to be discussed with Mera?" Lyra asked, raising worried eyes to her mother.

"We have kept enough from her, and if she is to suffer through this nightly, she can at least have some agency during the day." Lyra lowered her eyes and instinctively curled her arms tighter around Eirini. The movement was not lost on her mother. "Though she is still young, Mera is no longer a child, Lyra. That was taken from her long ago."

Mera looked back and forth between her grandmother and her mother. Dynami knew this was a lot for her mind to take in all at once, but it would be unfair to keep anything more from her. They could not protect her from what was coming when they did not know what that would be. Mera's words strengthened Dynami's resolve.

"I'm stronger than you think, Mother. I don't know what is happening, but I would rather do something than sit around scared and wondering."

"Yes, Meraki, you are stronger than I have ever been. Go with your grandmother and prepare lunch. I will join you when Eirini has eaten her fill."

Mera followed her grandmother into the kitchen area. Not all homes had kitchens inside the living space or even covered cooking areas outside. Most homes, especially those on the outer circle of The Thicket, had small fire pits outside the door. Some families agreed to share larger fire pits between their homes. The Matriarch's house, however, had all three. There was a larger pit out front that was used for community events, such as the presentation of Eirini mere days ago. Then there was the outdoor grill area. Family history said that Dynami's mate had built the cooking area for her when their first child, a satyr, was born. It was built out of blocks of dried clay with a large internal area for burning twigs and wood underneath where a large spit or flat surface could be placed for cooking. This is where Dynami usually cooked the evening meals. For smaller meals, such as lunch, though, there was a hearth built into the kitchen wall where she could reheat small bits of food in a clay pot. Dynami loved cooking and was always glad when Mera would join her for the preparations.

"Get out the basil, Mera, a tomato, and grab some of the graviera. We shall make some quick sandwiches with this warmed pheasant." Mera disappeared into the small larder they kept inside the kitchen proper to gather the items. When Mera exited the larder a few moments later, her eyes were as full of tears as her arms were of food. Dynami cried, "What is wrong, child?" Mera dropped the food and fell weeping into her grandmother's arms.

"I had a vision," she said between sobs, "or maybe a memory. It was so real." Just then Lyra walked into the kitchen with a sleeping Eirini and locked eyes with her mother, both of them holding back tears.

"Tell us what happened, Mera," Dynami said, rubbing Mera's hair with her calloused hand. When Mera didn't immediately respond, Lyra silently left the room to put the baby down. She returned and began picking up the food that had scattered across the kitchen floor before laying a hand on her daughter's head.

"Please tell us what happened, Meraki," she said with a sob, unable to maintain her composure.

"Why is this happening," Mera asked, pulling away from her mother's hand. "What happened to me? What is happening to me?" She pulled from her grandmother's arms and stood to her full height, her faun legs causing her to tower over both nymphs. "I walked into the larder, knelt down for the basil, and suddenly felt myself cowering in a space not much larger than the larder. I felt my fear, felt myself shake. I heard echos of screams or cries or something else terrible. I could not make out the voices, but each raised cry made my heart jump."

"Oh, Meraki," Lyra whispered, reaching for her daughter and sighing when Mera pulled out of reach. "There were times when I would find you hiding in your wardrobe as a little girl. Sometimes, by the time I found you there, you would be asleep. I would pick you up and put you in your bed. You would never talk about why you closed yourself in that small space."

"I'm not crazy, Mother. I felt my fear just now. Something happened or was happening while I was hidden." Lyra's eyes trailed from Mera to Dynami, a silent plea for reprieve. When it didn't come, Lyra looked around the room. Dynami watched her daughter look at the back exit and both hallways as if searching for an escape.

"Phialyra," Dynami asserted with enough authority to get her daughter's attention and break the flight impulse. "It is time you stopped hiding what happened up there in the mountains. You spoke of Mera never telling you why she hid in the closet, but you have never talked about what you have been hiding all these years. We need to make sense of this."

"I can't go back there," Lyra said, panic in her eyes. It was the same look she'd had when she came outside and grabbed the baby after the dragon's arrival. Mera grabbed her mother's hand and led her to a stool at the table.

"Help me, Mother, please," Mera pleaded.

"If I speak of these things, he will come for me."

"We will not let that happen," Dynami declared. "He took you away once. He would not dare come into The Grove for you again."

"He would not have to come here physically to come for me," Lyra said with a sad shake of her head.

"You don't understand," Lyra said with a whispered sob, "but I will do what I need to try and help my Meraki." She reached for her daughter, and put her arms around Mera's waist. After a few minutes, Lyra pulled away and sighed. "As I've told you, Vasilios was a dragon, much older than The Grove, and much more powerful than I had imagined. I met him in his human form, and though I felt a power within him, I was unable to even comprehend what I was feeling. It was like I was in a trance most of the time. He controlled me and my thoughts. I knew what he let me know and nothing more. I am sorry I could not protect you, Mera. I could not protect myself."

"You seemed fine when you would visit The Grove," Dynami said.

"I was fine, I suspect, when he was gone. Distance reduced his control, or maybe he was focused on other things, so his focus on me slipped. At any rate, after the initial fright when he revealed his true form, I didn't know what to do. I had hoped that coming home would maintain enough distance between us that even when he came back to the mountains, I could be free, but he'd call to me.

I was afraid if I didn't return, he would come destroy all of us here, so I went back."

"That explains why you would run off and leave half of your belongings home," Dynami reminisced.

"Yes, I always hoped I could one day return home for good, and I knew I couldn't carry everything for both of us. So, I brought things little by little as often as I could get away." She trailed off, looking toward the windows. "On one of the trips through The Grove, I met a satyr. He walked me to the edge of The Thicket, but I dared not invite him in. He was waiting when I was compelled to leave and walked me back to the edge of the forest below the mountain cliffs. I believe Mera had seen five winters at the time. He was sweet, and we talked the whole way," she said wistfully, lost in the pleasant memory.

"Lyra, you didn't," Dynami cut in, breaking the reverie.

"What?" Lyra asked, still stuck in the memory, "Oh, no, at least not right away." She shook her head. "I had just met him, and my mate was calling me. I could feel him in my head, patiently at first. As time went on, though, his calls became more urgent, more forceful, but that really wasn't until a year or so later. This time, we just walked and talked until we were about to leave the cover of The Tribunal Forest, and then I begged him to stay beneath the canopy. Vasilios' sight is astounding, and I didn't want him to read anything into the encounter."

"Oh, Lyra," her mother sighed.

"No, it wasn't like that. He was just nice enough to accompany us to and from the village is all. As time went on, and things got more difficult at home, I looked forward to him being there, waiting for us at the edge of the forest. Finally, he asked me if I would be able to meet him, just once, without Mera. I didn't see a way that would be possible. I couldn't leave the mountains when Vasilios was there, and I wouldn't leave The Grove without her, so I told him no. He still waited and continued being there, steadfast. I don't know that I had any true feelings for this satyr, but I knew it felt good to talk and be listened to. I appreciated his attention for sure, but it was the freedom to talk that made the difference."

"What did you do, Lyra?" her mother asked pointedly.

"One day, while Vasilios was gone, instead of coming to The Thicket, I left Mera at home and met the satyr at the lake on the northern end of The Grove. He was sweet and gentle, nothing like my mate had become," she said with a smile while looking out the window. She sat like that for a long time before she felt Mera touch her shoulder. Suddenly, a rush of fear assaulted her as memories flooded. She stared hard at her daughter. "I felt his presence. I was at the lake, and you were home alone, and I felt Vasilios' presence. He had returned, much more quickly than normal. I panicked and took off running. I had to get back to you!"

"It was not unusual for you to not be home when he arrived, right?" Dynami asked.

"No, but I always had Mera with me. I didn't know what he would do, so I ran. I knew I wouldn't get there in time, that I wouldn't beat him home, but I ran. In running, I forgot about the satyr. He followed me up the mountain to our home."

"Who was this satyr," Dynami asked, and Mera nodded as if she had the same question.

"His name doesn't matter. I didn't see much more of him after that day."

"Much more?" Mera asked. "Was he around during most of the time I can't remember?"

"Well, yes, but let me finish explaining what happened that day," she said with a gesture for patience. It was hard to lay herself bare like this when what she really wanted to do was forget. All this time, she had envied her friends in The Thicket who had no memories of those years. "I ran all the way home not knowing the satyr was climbing the mountain pass behind me. I don't know what I would have done had I known. Maybe warned him. Maybe been more emboldened to stand up to Vasilios. I'm not sure, but I honestly didn't know he was coming. All I could think about was

Mera being there by herself when Vasilios landed and what he would do."

"Had he ever done anything to harm her before," Dynami asked.

"Not that I knew of, Mother," Lyra answered, "but I'd have never intentionally taken any chances. He loved Mera and treated her like his daughter, even when he was unhappy with me."

"Was he hurting you, Mother," Mera asked putting her arms around Lyra's waist.

"As I said, things were not easy with my mate after the first couple of years. I just want you to know that I would have never let anything happen to you intentionally." Mera smiled at her and gestured for her to continue.

"I got near the top of our mountain when I heard the flapping of his wings," Lyra said with a shudder. "I didn't see him, but I knew I was too late. He had beat me home. By the time I could see the house, I heard his voice calling my name, not just the call he sends to my mind. I continued to run. I don't know what I was going to tell him, but maybe if I was close enough, he'd think I had just gone for a walk. He didn't," she said, eyes brimming with tears. "I got to the door and saw him hunched down near the table, reaching between the chair legs. It took a minute for me to register that Mera was under the table. I called his name. I said, 'Vasilios, what are you doing? You're scaring her.' The look he gave me over the top of the table as he stood froze me in place. I had never seen him shoot fire, but I felt the heat of his anger the same as if he had opened his mouth and breathed flames across the room. 'Where have you been?' he asked me. I couldn't answer. I didn't know what to say. He repeated it louder, snarling." Lyra paused, hugging herself and shaking slightly.

The memory was still terrifying. The fact he was close nearly sent her into a panic. Her chest rose and fell quickly with each erratic breath. Why couldn't these memories have just stayed hidden?

"What happened next?" Dynami asked from a stool next to Mera. Lyra saw the tears and understanding in her mother's eyes and felt even more guilt. That day was Mera's nightmare. She was responsible for so many things, and she didn't know how to make it right. So she plowed through the rest of the story.

"He accused me of all manner of things, not the least of which neglecting Mera by leaving her home alone. I had no response, no retort," she said, looking at her daughter, hoping she might one day forgive her. "I felt the guilt of each accusation, but as he stalked toward me, I also wanted to run. For a moment, I forgot she was there beneath the table, and I just wanted to run.' She saw Dynami sit up a little straighter at that. Her mother had always chided Lyra about running from responsibility. She didn't say anything, though, so Lyra continued.

"He must've seen the fear in my eyes because he grabbed my arm and dragged me outside toward the cliff again. 'Do you think you could run fast enough?' he growled, 'Or maybe you think you could hide.' He laughed then, actually laughed, and I knew I'd never get away. But then the satyr came out from around the rocks and grabbed Vasilios. They stood there on the cliff's edge, wrestling, and he told me to run. So I ran into the house, reaching for Mera, trying to get her to come out from under the table, so we could escape. She wouldn't. She just screamed and screamed. I tried pulling the chairs away from her, but she grabbed onto the legs and held them tight. She was so little but so strong." She looked at her daughter, guilt and pride mixing. Mera was far stronger than she would ever be in every way possible, and she was going to need that strength for what was coming. Lyra dropped her gaze and lowered her voice.

"I heard them fighting outside, and then I heard what sounded like a yelp. I turned and peeked out the door around the house. The satyr was on the ground, but I couldn't see my mate. I took a step forward, and he grabbed me. He pulled me toward the cliff, and before I knew it, I was falling. We were falling. His talons were wrapped around my body, holding me tightly, and he flew us away."

"What?" Dynami and Mera exclaimed at the same time. Lyra kept her eyes averted, looking at the loose garlic skin that was left from where Mera had dropped the vegetables earlier.

"What do you mean, Mother?" Mera asked, eyes wide, obviously reeling by the story.

"You just flew off?" Dynami asked much quieter, and Lyra felt the accusation in those words. "He just took off and Mera was left there at the house?"

"Yes," Lyra said with a sob.

"How long were you gone? How long did you leave me alone in that house?"

"I'm not entirely sure," she answered honestly, the guilt tightening her chest until she thought she might pass out from lack of air. She watched her daughter turn away, tears streaming from her beautiful green eyes. "I," she hesitated. "He took me to a large cave. I don't know how far away we flew, but it felt like we had flown for hours before he landed us inside the cave. There was no way to mark night or day, and he locked me inside of a cage when he left to find food and water. I nearly went mad with worry and from his constant voice in my head. He made sure to remind me that he controlled my mind by calling my name repeatedly while he was away from the cave."

"How is it that you have not heard nor been compelled all these years?" her mother asked, a hint of suspicion in her voice.

"While he has not compelled me to return to the mountain, and I've been able to live a normal life here in The Grove, including having my beautiful Eirini wrapped in the arms of my community, his voice has ever been in the recesses of my mind."

She watched the Matriarch sit up straighter and set her jaw. Even Mera turned back around to look at her. She looked directly at them both and said, "He calls me still." She could feel the air being sucked out of the room at her words. She could sense their fear, and she hated that she could no longer keep them from the chilling reality she had been living with for eleven years. She knew the danger for them all would grow now that she had acknowledged his presence in her head. She hadn't wanted to tell them anything. She didn't want to relive her own waking nightmares. Now that she had opened the gates, though, she was ready to unburden herself of all her secrets, and just as she was about to tell the rest, Eirini began crying from the other room.

As she made to retrieve the babe, Dynami stood and left for the afternoon council session, leaving her and Mera together in the kitchen. Lyra was torn between her crying daughters, an additional weight on her heart telling her to decide who she would console first. Minutes passed as Eirini's cries became stronger, and Lyra stood in the doorway. Then Mera looked up at her with a combination of hurt and anger that shattered Lyra's tenuous resolve. When her daughter rose and left the house behind Dynami, Lyra broke, collapsing to the floor in sobs that rivaled the babe's wail.

Chapter Eight

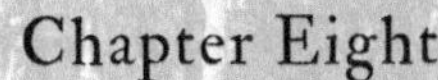

Dynami felt just as uncertain walking back to the meeting house as she had on her way home. Lyra's confession hung heavy on her heart and was muddying the plans she needed to formulate with the council. Finding out that Lyra not only left her young daughter alone to spend time with an unknown satyr but that she was then stolen away by her mate for days, possibly even weeks, leaving Mera alone again both infuriated and frightened her. What could have happened to the child? What more did they not know? The kicker, though, was Lyra's final words before Dynami left the house, "He still calls to me."

Dynami was halfway to the meeting house when Mera caught up with her, barely out of breath. "Yaya, can I accompany you to the council meeting?"

"You know, child, that we do not allow visitors to the meetings. What would be your business there?"

"Everything that is happening now and that happened years ago seems to revolve around me. I can't just sit at home with mother right now. I'm angry and hurt. I also don't know that running to the ocean would help either, as I feel hopeless. Please let me be of use, even if it is to lend support to your recounting of all we learned today."

"You are far too mature, Meraki. I am surprised this had not previously given away your truths. You are no fourteen year old child, and I am sorry for your lost childhood."

"Then let me try to fight back, please." Her grandmother acquiesced, and they continued walking in silence to the field where the meeting house stood.

The other council members were already inside when Dynami and Mera entered the hall. The conversations they'd heard through the door were silenced as all eyes turned on the pair. There were looks of confusion, compassion, disbelief, and resentment. Dynami's back stiffened as she continued her path to the circle, but Mera held back under the torrent of emotions. "Come Skyemera," the Matriarch said, using her full name as a show of authority. Her grandmother only used her given name around others outside of their home, and Mera was drawn forward by that tone.

"What is this about, Dynami?" Canea asked. "Council rules state that visitors from within The Thicket are not allowed to our meetings." The use of her name rather than her title for this admonishment was not lost on anyone in the room, including Mera.

"I must agree with the elder on this, Matriarch," Euonsise said with a slight smile and shrug in Mera's direction.

"I am aware of the rules. I helped create them. In fact, most of the rules of our community we now adhere to are related to what happened after Skyemera's birth." Phrixa rolled her eyes, and Nerin sneered, obviously still put out from this morning's session. "I invited Skyemera here because our discussion is relevant to her especially, and there have been additional revelations since we were last together."

"Something else happened during lunch?" Helena asked, eyes

widening in concern. Dynami nodded slightly in her direction, hoping the look conveyed the need to not share too much now.

"Please sit, and we will try to impart all that has happened and begin to make plans," Dynami directed. With little fanfare, the council members took their seats. Mera sat on one of the mats behind her grandmother against the wall, trying to be as inconspicuous as possible, though even seated, she towered over the elder nymph. "While we were making lunch, Skyemera had a vision...or a memory. I'm not sure how to categorize it, as it seemed a bit of both." There were gasps and whispers around the circle at this. Their people were not known to have visions. Only those who were known as oracles had visions, and those began at such a young age that the nymphs with the sight were separated from the community to serve the gods. When everyone was calm again, Dynami called on her granddaughter. "Skyemera, please come forward and tell the council what you saw."

Mera rose from her seated position and stepped down into the lower pit, so that she was not hovering over any of the council members. She stood in front of her grandmother as instructed, and Dynami hoped her presence would offer quiet strength to bolster the recounting of the afternoon's occurrence. "I had gone into the small larder on the side of the kitchen and was stooped down gathering the ingredients Ya...," she paused, "The Matriarch needed for our lunch. It was in that position, I was whisked away to a small wardrobe, where I was kneeling on the ground, covering my ears and cowering. I felt tremendous fear and thought I could hear booming, arguing voices from outside my hiding space, though they sounded to be at quite a distance. I was shaking and my heart was racing when I was finally able to stand and exit the larder." She bowed her head at the council and returned to her seat.

"Skyemera was ghostly pale and shaking. She dropped all of the food on the floor and was barely able to stand on her feet," Dynami said, adding veracity to her granddaughter's words.

"Why is this memory important to the council?" Danalise asked. "It simply sounds like she remembered a fight between her parents. It happens, even amongst our people."

"Yes," Canea began, "domestic disputes, particularly ones that are very old do not seem like an appropriate topic of conversation for the council, though I empathize with your family over the impact they may be having on your granddaughter."

"That is not all," Dynami said, standing to address the council as their leader. "You are correct. Though I am hurting for the pain my granddaughter is feeling again, I would not have brought these secrets to bare had they not had import for the greater community, and The Grove as a whole. This is but one occurrence. Two nights ago, Skyemera had a terrible nightmare, as was alluded to this morning. In that nightmare, she hid under the table of the kitchen after having seen a dragon fly overhead. Understand that she did not previously know her mother's mate was a dragon. She dreamed of both a clawed hand and a human hand reaching for her through what appeared to be a cage. We learned today that the cage was, in fact, the table surrounded by chairs. This, again, was a memory, though a broken one until Phialyra filled in details of the dragon's return home earlier than expected. The details of what happened between Phialyra and Vasilios, and even the fact that Skyemera is having these nightmares again, are not as important as Phialyra sharing that he held her in thrall all those years and still calls to her."

"What?" Phrixa exclaimed over the collective gasp. "Can he take control of her? Could she hurt the community? Would he do that? What does this mean? Are we safe with them here?"

"They are Alseides," Canea asserted, "and are part of our community. We will not again question whether they belong, but we must discuss what this means for us and how to keep all of us, including Phialyra and Skyemera, safe."

"Thank you, Mother," Dynami said, bringing her hands together at her forehead in a formal gesture of gratitude.

Euonsise stood, "If this dragon had mental control over Lyra all those years, and she is now hearing him again, shouldn't someone be with her at all times to ensure she doesn't go back to him." Everyone turned to look at her, including Dynami whose eyes went wide. "Be calm, Matriarch. I will send someone." She opened the hall door and whistled. Soon, a young, brawny nymph Mera recognized as Eckasia, Euonsise's daughter, came to the door. Within seconds, the girl ran off toward the center of the village.

"I hadn't even considered the need to have someone monitor her when we cannot be there at the house. Thank you for your compassion and practical thinking," Dynami said to her after the girl had gone and Euonsise had once again joined the circle. "Now, to discuss a course of action if everyone will take their seats," she said, addressing the full council.

"What is the actual threat we need to be preparing for?" Danalise asked. "I understand the concern, and I, too, am concerned, but I'm not sure I fully understand what we are up against." Around the circle, the other council members nodded. Mera nodded right along with them. Though the young maenad knew that her own nightmares were affecting her family, Dynami doubted she'd considered what the dragon's control over her mother meant for the Alseides as a whole.

Helena stood then, and with a nod from Dynami, she began. "The implications of Eirini's birth, the dragon's return, and the control it has over Phialyra are significant beyond just The Grove because of Skyemera's lineage. If her birth was powerful enough to call the dragon to The Grove and keep him around without causing significant harm to Lyra and Mera, there is a reason. I can only imagine it is to gain control of her powers once she comes into them, particularly if she has yet to learn what they are and how to control them. Whatever we decide to do to protect The Grove, we must also consider how to help Mera learn about her abilities." She gestured at Mera. "This young maenad holds power we cannot fathom but can be felt across realms. We cannot allow it, or her, to be influenced by a dragon. Normally, we would expect a nymph's mother to introduce her to her powers, but not only does Lyra not know what powers Mera possesses, the dragon's control makes her incapable of managing Mera's lessons."

Murmurs of agreement rose around the hall. Dynami took a moment to look at Skyemera, and found her seated against the wall with her shoulder's drooped. The poor child had had little time to process any of the revelations from the past couple of days, and here they were discussing powers she didn't even think about having yet. Most nymphs didn't begin to feel their powers surging until they had reached fifteen winters, which meant that Karielle should get hers in the coming months, but now that Mera knew she had seen twenty winters without gaining any of her powers, it had to be weighing on her mind.

"Excellent point, Phrixa," Dynami heard Canea say and realized she had stopped attending to the meeting. She was about to ask for suggestions when the doors to the hall flew open and Eckasia came running in.

"She's gone," the young nymph squeaked out between heavy breaths. She was holding onto the door handle trying to steady herself. Dynami realized the girl must have run all the way from the house, and she closed the distance to her before anyone else even got to their feet.

"What do you mean gone?" Dynami asked, grabbing her shoulders.

"She's not there, Matriarch," the girl said after a second. "I went to the house as quickly as I could. I knocked on the door, and no one answered. I thought maybe she was sleeping or in the back feeding the baby, so I opened the door. No one was in the house, and when I entered the kitchen, I saw that the back door was left open. Neither your daughter nor the babe are there." Dynami stared at her until the sound of running caught her attention. She looked up to see Mera dash out the door, her long, powerful legs carrying her faster than any of them could move.

"Gather the guardians," Dynami ordered. "We must find her and the babe. Someone find Karielle," she said as her knees buckled. Helena's arms grabbed her around the waist, so she could sit on the earthen seat. "I have failed her again," Dynami cried in her friend's arms. "I have failed them all."

Chapter Nine

Mera's heartbeat rang in her ears, but she kept running. She had to see for herself, had to know for sure that she had again been left behind. That thought made her eyes sting, but she kept running, hooves tracking divots in her wake. She'd never run so fast in her life. When she arrived, the front door of the house was wide open as if Eckasia had just taken off running back to the council meeting when she found Lyra and Eirini gone. Eirini, Mera thought with a sob, as she slowed her pace at entering the house.

Mera went straight to the room her mother and sister shared. No one was there. All of her mother's clothes remained in the closet, though that didn't mean much. The nymphs rarely wore clothes unless receiving formal visitors or traveling to the human city. They preferred communing with nature in their natural states. Mera looked around the room and her eyes stopped on her sister's cradle. The blanket Kari's mother had handmade for the babe was gone. She walked to the empty cradle and ran her hand along its smooth wooden side before dropping to her knees. She screamed then, a terrifying guttural scream of anguish that drew nymphs in the immediate area from their homes.

Dynami heard her granddaughter's pain from the meeting house where she and Helena had begun making their way back to the village center. As she increased their pace, as much as two 350-year-old nymphs could, tears streamed from her eyes. Helena took her hand and followed the trail Mera had left in their direct path minutes before.

Kari had already been walking toward The Matriarch's home when she heard Mera's scream. Not sure what was happening, she took off running, dodging between the other nymphs who had gathered in the road outside of her grandmother's house. "Stop gawking and move out of the way," Kari cried with an authority and urgency she'd never used before. They all parted, as she sprinted into the house full tilt. She followed her cousin's sobs to the back bedroom and found Mera on the floor beside the cradle rocking back and forth. She entered the room and kneeled beside Mera, smoothing the maenad's hair back from her face.

For several seconds, Mera looked at her until recognition set in and she fell into Kari's arms. "She's gone, Kari," Mera gasped out between sobs.

"I'm sure she'll be back," Kari said, trying to console her friend.

Mera snapped at that, grief turning to anger in a millisecond. "She left me, Kari," she said through gritted teeth, as she got up and began pacing the room. Kari stood and walked to sit on the edge of the bed, watching Mera closely as she walked to and fro in the small space. When Mera's anger had dissipated, her shoulder's slumped, and she said, "My mother left me alone—again." The last part came out as barely a whisper, but Kari caught it and brought up her hand to remove a wayward tear from her own cheek.

Kari still had little idea what had happened in Mera's childhood, since she had been but a toddler when everyone's memories of Mera had been removed. It was only days ago that she learned her cousin and friend had actually seen six additional winters, though they celebrated every birthday together as if they had been twins. She hadn't seen Mera since they came back from speaking with the sea nymph, so she was completely at a loss as to what Mera meant by "again," but it didn't change how obviously distraught Lyra's disappearance had left her cousin. "Do you have any idea where she might've gone?"

"Back to the dragon, is my guess," Dynami said from the doorway. Kari's eyes snapped open nearly as wide as her mouth.

"Back to the dragon? But why," Kari asked, looking back and forth between Mera and their grandmother.

"Likely because his call to her was too strong for her to ignore any longer," The Matriarch responded. "I am sorry, Mera," she said with a quivering voice that made Mera look up from the hands in her lap. "I hadn't even considered the possibility, even after she sat here and told us he still called to her. I was so wrapped up in worry about the council's response to our having taken their memories and protecting you from whatever might come that I once again failed to protect my daughter from the imminent threat. Tears were running freely down Dynami's face now, and Helena entered the room to steady her friend.

"Why don't we come into the study where we can all sit comfortably and discuss what is to happen now," Helena suggested. "Come, Mother, you should sit now. Today's exertion and emotions are taking a toll on you, and you must rest your bones to allow your mind to work as it needs." She gently nudged Dynami to leave the room, and the two elders walked down the hall to the same room they all sat in when the young nymphs first learned about the dragon and Mera's lost childhood.

Mera was the last to enter the room, and she walked past the sitting area to stand in front of the dragon's portrait. She stood there for a moment making a silent vow. *I will find a way to punish you for all that you have taken from me. I promise you that!* Dynami sat with Helena's consoling arm around her shoulders. Kari was the only one who noticed as Mera's back stiffened and her hands balled into fists. It wasn't until a wind came sweeping through the room, lighting all of the candles that Dynami and Helena looked up and saw Mera's defiant pose in front of the painting.

"Mera," her grandmother said without any real force. "Child, come sit down next to your cousin," she stated clearly and precisely when the wind continued to swirl with the flickering candles, but Mera did not move. Dynami heard people yelling outside the house, but she maintained eye contact on her granddaughter while she gestured something to Helena. Helena then directed Kari to go see what was happening. The girl returned moments later, her face a mask of terror.

"There...There's..."

"Spit it out, child," Helena said, waving her hands at Kari.

"There's a cyclone swirling around the house," Kari said, making spinning gestures with her hands. Helena jumped from her seat and went to try and look out the window, but it wouldn't open. Kari continued, "The wind and dirt are spinning around the house. I couldn't even see where they were going." Helena left the room heading for the front door.

"Mera," Dynami said again. "Meraki, I know you are upset. I am angry too. We cannot let our anger overtake us."

"We must stop the wind, Dynami, or it's going to pull the house apart," Helena said, raising her voice above the roar of the wind outside. "I cannot even see through the dirt and debris to tell how the rest of the village is affected."

"Skyemera," the Matriarch tried again, more forcefully, getting up and approaching her granddaughter cautiously. Kari and Helena watched them from the doorway, holding onto each other as much from fear as from the winds that still circled through the room blowing the candle flames to and fro. Helena reached out with her own powers to try and calm the squall inside before the flames danced off the candles and onto either the furniture or walls.

While her energy reached out to the kinetic energy floating

around them, Dynami's hand reached out to her granddaughter's fist, trying to release the tension holding the maenad in the throes of fury by uncurling her fingers. She first tried pulling at those fingers, but they were frozen in place. Then she began slowing running her hands down her granddaughter's hair, humming quietly. She ran her wizened hands down Mera's arms and onto her legs, smoothing the reddish-brown fur that distinguished her from her nymph cousins, all while continuing to hum. She noticed the change in Mera when the wind inside the house slowed slightly, the candles settling their frantic dance into slight gyrations. Dynami again tried to uncurl Mera's fist, this time successfully. One and then the other, which she took in both of her hands and stared into her granddaughter's unblinking eyes, steadily humming the same tune.

Kari raised her voice above the diminished winds to sing along with her grandmother's humming—
Mother Earth's blessed hands
They come forth to mold you
Seedling's sprout and saplings grow
Here our forest anoints you
Respect the land from river to sea
And it will rise to protect you
Mother Earth's blessed hands
Have placed their power upon you
As Kari got to the last line, Mera joined her, and the two sang like they had as children. Mera looked at her grandmother fully then and squeezed the hands that were still holding hers. "I don't know what happened to me yet, but I will not let the same happen to Eirini. Mother did not, perhaps could not, protect me, but I will not let my sister suffer the same fate. I am going to make sure she is safe. That is my promise." Dynami nodded at her granddaughter deferentially and squeeze her hands back before letting them go.

"Before we go making plans for how you will accomplish that goal, let us go make sure there is still a village for you both to return home to," the matriarch said as she swept out of the room and down the hall. Helena looked at Mera one last time and quickly followed her leader out of the house. Mera grabbed the back of the nearest chair and half leaned, half sat on it. Kari sat on the bench in front of her and let out a big sigh. Mera snorted at her friend's dramatics and smiled.

"I'm not well, Kari, but I will be. I don't know why all of this is happening, but I know I have to do something to stop it, else I'll go mad." She pulsed her hands out in front of her as if she were emphasizing the need to both go after her sister and steady herself from the weight of it all.

"I want to help. I have no idea what is happening or what just happened right now, but you are my cousin and my best friend. Besides, you'll need me to spark up conversations with random people along the way." She nudged Mera's knee with a laugh. "You will either stare them into submission or cause the wind to blow them all the way to Aeolus' realm."

"What do you mean?" Mera asked, head tilted to the side.

"You don't remember what just happened? You don't remember bringing a squall into the house, lighting all the candles, and then trying to set the house on fire?"

Mera balked. "What are you talking about?"

"You don't remember the cyclone that surrounded the house?"

"Cyclone? Are you mad?" Her words belied the nervousness that made her look around the room at all of the lit candles and the odd way the wax was lifted around the edges of each one.

"No, but you were, and I'm sure Yaya will be once she makes sure everyone, including you, are alright," she said with raised eyebrows. "Let's head outside and survey the damage. Maybe that'll help you remember," she said in a sing-song voice before she jumped up, nearly pulling Mera's arm out of its socket as she tried to lift the maenad's weight from the chair before she was ready to stand.

"Ow, alright already, I'm coming," Mera said with a wince and a shake of her head. Let me go see what kind of mess I've made now, she thought to herself.

Chapter Ten

Mera sat on the stoop awaiting her grandmother's return. It appeared the Matriarch intended to check in with every family in The Thicket to ensure they were safe and calm after the impromptu weather pattern of the day. Kari had since gone home to let her mother know she was safe and returned. The young nymph was surprisingly quiet for most of the time they sat waiting for the elders to arrive. Mera sat tapping her hooves and brushing her fingers through the fur on her legs. She was itching to run. Though Mera had no recollection of the wind inside or outside of the house, the knots in her fur and the hair on her head said something definitely occurred. This recognition gave her pause and was the only thing keeping her in place at the family home when all she wanted to do was go after her sister and mother.

It was way past time for the evening meal when the elders returned to the house. Mera and Kari had gone inside and prepared a simple combination of roasted meats and root vegetables. Dynami was the cook of the family, so the young nymphs were unable to prepare anything elaborate. "Smells delicious," came their grandmother's voice from the entry. "We are starving," she called out, and the girls hurried from the back rooms to prepare plates. When they brought the food out to the sitting room, they found the elders were not alone.

"I didn't realize we had a visitor," Mera said, her cheeks reddening, as she handed her grandmother a plate and then passed her own plate to the stranger. The being, as that was the only word that came to Mera's mind, who had joined them for dinner was unlike anything Mera remembered meeting before. She appeared a nymph, lithe and strikingly beautiful. Her hair was the color of wheat laced with reds and orange. It framed a perfectly rendered face untouched by the sun that appeared far younger than the wisdom Mera caught in her emerald eyes, as the stranger took her in as well. There was something more to her, though, some underlying, almost animalistic, strength. Mera had never noticed the smell of others before, unless they hadn't bathed regularly, but this creature carried the scent of fur, though she had none visible. Mera's curiosity nearly got the best of her when Kari entered the room.

Kari gave a plate of food to Helena. She then realized the additional person, saw Mera had no food, and passed the last plate to Mera who tried to wave it away. "I'll make myself another," Kari told her and headed back to the kitchen once Mera finally accepted the food with a smile.

"I will make introductions once my other granddaughter returns from the kitchen," Dynami stated between bites of her meal. Kari returned shortly, and Dynami put down her plate. "This is Callisto," she began, only to be interrupted by Kari, nearly choking on her mouthful of food.

"Like the legend of the constellation," she spit out around the half-chewed wad of meat in her mouth.

"One in the same," her grandmother responded. "Now, child, if you will let me continue." Kari looked sheepishly at the ground and nodded before returning to stare wide-eyed at the visitor. "Callisto is one of the oldest nymphs on our planet. As the village matriarch, I am able to call on her wisdom, and she has graciously come to aid us."

"You're the bear," Kari said more than asked before she squealed with delight. Mera had never seen her cousin so excited, though she knew how much Kari loved to learn and talk about legends surrounding the ancient ones.

"The bear," Mera repeated in a whisper. She remembered the legend now. Zeus had taken advantage of Callisto, and she was banished from Mt. Olympus because of it. Mera didn't see how that was fair, but rarely were stories of the ancients fair, particularly for female creatures. Even the goddesses were often overshadowed or beholden to the male gods. Mera wasn't a fan of those stories, but this one made sense. Callisto had been banished, and Zeus' wife decided to further punish the nymph by turning her into a bear. According to legend, though, Callisto's son nearly killed her on a hunt, and Zeus turned them both into constellations.

"If you are Callisto, The Ancient One, The Great Bear, prior handmaiden to Artemis, weren't you sent to the heavens with your son?" Mera asked. From the corner of her eye, Mera saw the stern look that passed over her grandmother face, but she held her ground looking directly at the visitor.

"I am all that you said and more," the visitor responded without a hint of consternation. "Zeus felt guilty," she said with a slight snort of laughter, "and he created the constellation in my name so that Hera would leave me be to live out my life. I have kept a low profile, only making my presence known when my people have need of me. Dynami implored my help, and here I am."

"Please forgive my granddaughters, Ancient One," Dynami said with reverence. "This is Karielle." She gestured toward the younger nymph. "She is a lover of legends and will talk your ear off if you but give her a chance." Callisto smiled and inclined her head in greeting, and Kari, who had since put her plate down to focus completely on the nymph in front of them, smiled widely, showing all of her teeth. She was holding tight to the edge of her chair to keep herself from bouncing out of it.

"And this is," Dynami continued with another gesture toward Mera. She was unable to get the words out before the ancient nymph completed her sentence.

"The Maenad." Callisto spoke with reverence, and there was a flicker of awe in her eyes. "I have not seen one of your kind for over a millennia and dared not hope to see another in my lifetime. You are perfect," she said to Mera, and the young maenad blushed at such a compliment. She had always found herself lacking. She wasn't quite nymph, at least not from the waist down, and she wasn't even faun from the waist up. She did not know what it meant, but she knew that she always felt out of place. Now, here was an elder calling her perfect.

"What would you need of me, Matriarch," the ancient nymph asked, using Dynami's honorific rather than her name.

Dynami's face showed her surprise in light of such unexpected address, and it took a moment for Dynami to respond. "First and foremost, Ancient One, we need your guidance. My granddaughter is a maenad, as you have stated."

"Not a maenad," Callisto countered with a dismissive wave of her hand, "The Maenad. The only one in over a millennium."

"Yes, my apologies. Skyemera is The Maenad, but none of us really know what that means. Prior to today, she had shown no powers, not even the powers of our or her father's lineage. Then today..." She trailed off with the memory of this afternoon's demonstration.

Helena chimed in, as she so often did when Dynami was struggling to find her words, or when she got lost in thought. "Your eminence, this afternoon, Skyemera created a controlled cyclone both inside and outside of this house. The winds inside lit candles and spun around the single room we were all occupying. The winds outside picked up dirt and debris from the yard, creating an impenetrable cone from the ground to beyond the canopy above The Thicket. We were unable to see out through it, and no one from the village could see within."

"Interesting," Callisto responded. "And you have never used your powers before, Maenad?" It took Mera a minute to answer, as she tried to understand the nymph's use of the word almost as a title rather than a species descriptor like nymph, satyr, faun, or even dragon.

Mera stood and walked to the window. She turned around and looked at Kari before turning her gaze back to Callisto. "Honestly, I don't remember any of that. If I was the cause, I didn't know it."

"Will you show me the room, Maenad?" Callisto asked while rising from the chair. Everyone else stood to accompany them when Mera began toward the hall. "Please stay and finish your meal," Callisto said to them. "I would like to have a moment alone with The Maenad to see if I can ascertain what occurred here this afternoon." Dynami looked solemn, and Kari was pouting, but they sat back down at Callisto's insistence. Helena also sat, but she was the only one more curious than dejected.

"This is my grandmother's receiving room," Mera shared as they arrived at the doorway. "It's hard to believe I had never been in this room before this week. So much has happened these past few days."

"I would like to hear all about it, but first, let us try and recreate the situation from this afternoon. Where was everyone?" Callisto asked, walking fully into the room and looking around at the shadows from the three lone candles lit at different corners. Mera entered the room behind her, and with a rush of wind, all the candles lit. "Interesting," Callisto said, and the repetitive response from earlier made Mera turn to look at her.

"What's interesting?" Mera asked, brows knitted, head tilted to the side.

"How did the candles light themselves?" Callisto asked, staring at Mera with patient eyes that said she was waiting for an answer.

Mera looked around. She did not remember all of the candles being lit when they were in the hallway.

"Didn't you do it?"

"Me? No. It would be a bit impertinent of me to walk into your home and begin lighting all of your candles, don't you think?" Mera looked at her, confused at the situation and the question. "Let us get back to this afternoon. We can talk about candles later," the nymph offered. "Where was everyone earlier this afternoon?"

"I'm not sure. I ran home to find my mother and sister missing. I was hurt, angry, and scared. The grandmothers arrived and suggested we come in this room and talk about how we might find and save my sister." Callisto sat on one of the benches at the center of the room while continuing to give Mera her undivided attention. She gestured for the young one to continue. "I came in and was drawn to the portrait of the dragon. He's my mother's mate, you know. I promised him that I would make him pay for all he'd taken from me," she said with more vehemence than she'd planned. She walked over to the portrait. "This thing, this demon, stole my childhood, and now he has taken my mother and newborn sister. I want to watch the wind tear at his wings, watch him writhe in the air until he can no longer stay aloft, and then I want to watch him crash to the ground." As she made this last statement, the wind entered the room and began circling it, the flames dancing a frenetic pace, casting excited shadows along the walls.

"That's enough," Callisto bellowed right before the other nymphs came crashing through the door. The wind responded, reducing its intensity until it was but a draft that slowly seeped out of the window. The candle flames returned to their gentle sway. Everything and everyone in the room relaxed, except Mera. The Maenad maintained her gaze on the portrait. Her lip was curled in a sneer, and her brows were pulled tightly together in a scowl. Her back was stiff as the mighty pines of the forest, and her fists were once again balled tightly.

Callisto turned back toward the doorway. "I see what you mean. The power is controlling her by latching onto her hurt and anger. That is a dangerous combination. If she were to take that response before the dragon, as I'm assuming is the plan, she is more likely to hurt herself and those on her side than she is that ancient beast." She left the room, allowing Dynami and Kari to attend to breaking Mera's trance, and she returned to the sitting room with Helena following close behind. Soon, humming and singing came from the inner room.

Just as they were settling onto their seats, the front door flew open. Helena and Callisto both jumped to their feet, Callisto's hands already lifted in a protective stance. Helena stepped in front of the ancient one when she realized who had barged into the house. Lyra stood there, breathing heavily, eyes wild. The babe, Eirini, was tied tightly to her chest. Mera's mother looked around the room, eyes passing over Callisto and landing on Helena. "Where is my Mera?"

Chapter Eleven

T he sudden exit of her mother and daughter left Lyra in a vulnerable state. She didn't know what kind of reaction they would have to her painful revelations, but she never expected them to just walk out on her. The disappointment on Dynami's face would have been enough to break her spirit if the pain on Mera's face hadn't already shattered her. Life with Vasilios was an absolute rollercoaster of the ultimate heights early on and the lowest of lows near the end. She didn't know who she was for most of the time they lived with him in that isolated mountain cottage. The only thing she knew was that Mera depended on her, and she had failed somehow at that one task.

The thought of Mera, scared and alone, in the cottage for however long the dragon had taken her away reminded Lyra of Eirini and allowed the babe's cries to penetrate her misery. *Eirini needs me now*, she thought as she got up from the kitchen floor and headed toward her bedroom. The babe was so small and so vulnerable. Lyra stared at her for a moment, afraid to lift her while carrying the weight of the past on her shoulders. "I need to clear my head. I have to be strong for you, my sweet. Your sister will soon be called to protect us all, but for now, I am here for you."

Lyra picked up Eirini, cleaned her bottom, and swaddled the babe to her own chest to feed while she readied a small pack of dried meat, nuts and berries. Babe at her breast and pack on her shoulder, Lyra walked out the back kitchen door and through the north side of The Thicket toward the mountains.

As she made her way through the concentric circle of homes toward the outer hedgerow, Lyra changed direction. The babe she carried was not Mera, and she was not heading to the mountain home to heed her mate's call. He was not there, at any rate. She could feel the distance in his mental connection. She shuddered at the thought of what he was up to, having shown up mere days ago and then flown off again. There was no way he simply came to say hello with his show of flames. She headed east toward the most serene place she knew, the sea that Mera so often loved to visit. Walking would take her hours, but Lyra had a special ability few knew about. Since the time she had spent with Bacchus, Lyra was able to commune with the deer of the forest. Their help is what allowed her and Mera to reach the mountains in time to meet Vasilios upon his return each time they visited The Thicket. She called on the deer and was soon making swift time toward the distant shore.

Holding the swaddled babe close, she dismounted at the edge of the Tribunal Forest and walked over the dunes toward Mera's gnarled oaks. Laying her hand upon the blanched bark of one of the trees, Lyra said a prayer of thanks to the copse for sheltering and providing peace for her daughter. She prayed that they would likewise protect the babe in her arms should she need their strength. The wind whistled like pipes through their bent forms as if in response.

"We haven't seen you here in many years, Mother of the Maenad," a raspy feminine voice came from behind Lyra making her jump. Though her heart was beating erratically, Lyra steeled herself and turned slowly to try and hide her fear. She wasn't sure who out there could possibly have known who she was. She did not recognize the voice. The nereid who stood in front of her was beautiful, with copper skin and tight, gold-tipped curly black hair decorated with small shells and bits of sea grass.

"How do you know me?" Lyra stammered.

"I'm responsible for watching this shore and protecting The Maenad each time she is here. I watched you and others bring her here for many years until she started coming alone, or with that cousin of hers, the talkative one."

"Karielle."

"Yes, it was entertaining to talk with that one when they were here the other day."

"You spoke with my Mera as well?"

"I spoke with The Maenad, yes."

"How do you know what and who she is?"

"We felt the aftershocks of her birth, though we didn't know what it meant right away. Once you and the others began bringing her here as a small one, the Strimmena told us what she was. We have been watching over her ever since, at least when she comes to our shore."

"Others? Strimmena? What are you saying?"

"The Strimmena are the sacred trees you were just communing with before I spoke to you."

"Oh, I didn't realize they had a name. But what did you mean when you said others brought Mera here when she was small?"

"Mother of the Maenad, were you not aware that the goddess regularly visited these shores with the human who came with you a time or two and a satyr later on as she grew?"

"Human," Lyra said, closing her eyes with a deep sigh.

"Yes, the Maenad told us that he was not likely human at all."

"He was a dragon and...wait, you said she came here with him as she got older? When I wasn't with her? And a satyr as well?" She began visibly shaking as she considered how long the dragon had kept her from Mera. "For how long? Over what period of time?"

The nymph paused before responding, and Lyra barely held

her patience in check. "Over a period of two years, Mother of the Maenad."

Lyra tightened her hold on the babe still swaddled to her chest. "Two years? Gods, what have I done?" Nelaira quickly wrapped her arms around Lyra whose knees buckled. She slunk to the ground, wracked with sobs.

"I don't know what you mean, but I can tell you that nothing untoward happened while The Maenad was on our shores. We still kept watch over her, though from a distance. She spent most of her time hiding amongst the Strimmena. Neither the human nor the satyr could fit in amongst the gnarled trunks and branches, so they mostly watched from the dunes."

"Thank you," Lyra finally responded after her breathing returned to normal and the tears slowed. She felt Eirini fussing within the wrappings and loosened them slightly to allow her room to move.

"Is that The Maenad's sibling?"

"Yes, her name is Eirini. Mera named her in the Amphidromia, according to our tradition of presenting newborns to the community."

"She is a nymph then?"

"Yes, she is Alseides."

Nelaira eyed that babe for longer than seemed necessary before nodding at her and sitting back on the sand. "How did you not know that The Maenad was coming here to our shores all that time?" Lyra felt no judgment in the nymph's question, just a genuine concern.

"My mate, the human, had caught me unaware one day." Her guilt made it hard to tell the full story again. "He was so angry with me that he pulled me off the cliff near our mountainside home. I thought I was going to die there on the side of that mountain," she said with a shudder, "until he shifted at the last minute to his dragon form and flew us far away. It felt like we had flown for hours, but now I'm not so sure, as I don't remember time having passed, especially not two years worth of time. He took me to a large cave somewhere in a mountain range, high in the peaks. And he would leave me there to hunt and bring back food."

"He just left your child alone there?"

"That was my thought, but now that you've said he was here with her while I was stuck in that cave, I am left wondering. Did he leave me to go back for her? If so, why? What did he get or want from her? And why was she with Rhivy other times? I thought for sure he was dead."

"Is Rhivy the satyr who brought her?"

"He would've been the only one she knew. I can't imagine she'd have comfortably traveled this far with another. She was so little then, as little as she could've been. What did they want? Why even bring her to The Grove?"

"These are all important questions, though I am not sure they could be answered by anyone besides the human or the satyr. The Maenad had no recollection of these visits either when I spoke with her."

"Oh, that is worrisome."

"Why? Should she remember?"

"No, she shouldn't, but I'm afraid she may soon, and..." They both turned toward the forest as birds rose in a cacophony of squawks and wings from the forest's canopy far off in the direction of The Thicket. "Mera!" Lyra jumped to her feet, wrapping her arms tightly around the once again sleeping babe.

"What is happening? I've never seen the birds behave like that aside from the Maenad's birth." Lyra didn't hear Nelaira's question, as she was already running toward the dunes and the forest. "This cannot be a good sign," the nereid said aloud to no one before diving into the surf.

Lyra registered the shocked and confused looks at the same time she heard her mother's voice singing in the other room. "What is happening?" she asked, making her way toward the hall.

"Lyra, thank the gods you're alright," Helena said, reaching for her.

Lyra turned toward the elders, head cocked to the side. "What do you mean? Of course, I'm fine. Why wouldn't I be?" She watched the unfamiliar nymph look to Helena with uncertainty and Helena look at the floor before meeting Lyra's gaze. "What is happening here, Mother, and where is my Mera?"

"You disappeared so shortly after the council meeting began this afternoon, after Dynami told us of the dragon's call. We thought..."

Understanding dawned and hit Lyra in the chest. "Let me guess. You assumed I had returned to the dragon." There was venom in her statement that she hadn't expected to release. "Everyone assumed I would just answer his call after all these years because he decided to show up out of nowhere. Everyone believed me that weak to abandon my child again." She knew Dynami and Helena thought her impulsive, knew they were waiting for her to disappear again, but she didn't think they believed she'd intentionally hurt Mera.

"Where is my daughter, Helena?" She had never before used the elder nymph's given name, but her concern for Mera outweighed her concern for propriety. She called out, "Skyemera! Meraki!"

"She is in the receiving room with Karielle and your mother," the stranger said quietly with her hand on Helena's shoulder.

Lyra made her way into the hall and stopped short at the doorway to the receiving room. She saw her mother kneeling before Mera, holding both of her hands while singing the same lullaby she'd sung to all of her children and now her grandchildren. Kari was singing along while stroking Mera's hair. It was such an intimately beautiful scene that Lyra's anger dissipated. They were soothing her Mera. No matter what Dynami might think of her, Lyra knew her mother would move the heavens for Skyemera, and she was grateful.

Lyra joined her voice to the lullaby and slowly entered the room. Eirini had begun fussing with the earlier outbursts, but even she was settled by the calming song. Kari noticed her aunt first and jumped into her arms, careful not to crush the infant.

"You're here. Oh, Lyra, you're here!"

Lyra held her niece for a moment before she let Kari go and directed her out of the room, all the while singing along. She was not sure if her mother had registered her presence yet or not, as the elder maintained intense eye contact on Skyemera's face. Lyra made her way to kneel in front of her daughter as well and took both sets of hands in her own. Dynami's fingers trembled as she came out of the trance that connected her to Skyemera through the song. She wrapped her arms around Lyra and wept. There were no words and no need for them. Lyra heard the door close behind them and looked up into her daughter's face still stiff with anger.

She raised a hand to smooth back Mera's hair and caressed her cheek. Mera's skin was warm and soft. Lyra rubbed her thumbs over Mera's brow, smoothing away the tightness. Her daughter was beautiful whether she believed it or not. She rubbed down Mera's arms from shoulder to elbow, stroking away the tension. "Meraki, come back to us. There is no need for so much anger now. We are here with you. Your sister needs you. Your grandmother needs you. I need you."

Mera blinked, and Lyra felt her body relax. "There you are, my Meraki." The look Mera gave was one of confusion. It quickly shifted to recognition and then surrender as she melted into Lyra's arms. "I'm here. I did not leave you, would not leave you." She held her child, rubbing her hair, while wrapped in her own mother's arms. They remained like that until Eirini broke the silence with a whimper, wriggling beneath Skyemera's weight against Lyra's chest. They all pulled apart to look down at the infant and burst out laughing.

Lyra unstrapped Eirini and handed her to Skyemera who quickly pulled the babe into a tight embrace. Dynami had already taken a seat on the settee, and Lyra joined her, clasping her hand.

"I was afraid..." Dynami began somberly.

"I wish you trusted in me a little more, mother. I'm no longer an impulsive child."

"No, but..."

"No buts. I will see 100 winters sooner than you know, and yet you think me so weak-minded. I told you that Vasilios has continued to call my name all these years, all these years that I have remained here, and yet you imagined me running back to him now."

Dynami opened her mouth to speak and then closed it again. Lyra knew it was not easy for her mother to admit when she'd been wrong, and she didn't push. Instead, she turned her attention back to her daughters. Mera had relaxed much more and was rocking her sister. She must have felt Lyra's gaze because she looked in her direction.

"Where did you go, mother?"

Lyra's heart contracted at the pain in her daughter's voice. When she left the house earlier that afternoon, her pain had been so great, she could not have foreseen the consequence of her search for breathing space. She simply needed to get some air and gather her thoughts.

"I went to visit your trees."

"The Strimmena?"

"Yes. I went to thank them for providing you a place of solace, and I had hoped to receive the same sense of calm you describe getting from them. It's been a very emotional few days, and when you and your grandmother left this afternoon, the house felt like it was closing in." Lyra left her perch on the settee and knelt before Mera again. "I am sorry I hurt you. I am sorry that I made you worry." She looked over at her mother as she made the last statement. "I was not thinking, and I was too far away when I realized something was wrong."

Mera looked up at Lyra with an eyebrow lifted, and Dynami cleared her throat. It took a moment before Lyra understood their responses, and a flush crept up her neck. Turning to her mother, she said, "Maybe I am still a bit impulsive. I'll work on that." They both smiled.

"Are you ready to reconvene with the others, Mera," Dynami asked.

Mera nodded, passed the babe back to Lyra, and stood.

"Mother," Lyra said before Mera could open the door. "I'm afraid I may have mortified the elders during my entrance. I also owe Helena an apology."

Dynami sighed but said nothing before gesturing for Mera to lead the way out of the room.

Chapter Twelve

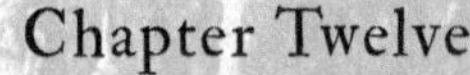

"I am not sure how well The Maenad and her family will take this, but I will need to take her away with me for a while in order to help her learn to control her powers or, at the very least, to channel her anger," Callisto said to Helena once Lyra had entered the receiving room and left them alone.

"Great Mother," Helena said with a bow of her head, "I'm concerned for the entire family here and our community as a whole." She walked to the window, looking out at the street through the twilight. "I'm afraid our decision over a decade ago will cause more harm than we ever considered."

"Decision?" Callisto asked, looking up at the community elder. "What has been done that I do not yet know?"

Helena looked down the hall and listened. The humming and lullaby continued, and she sighed. "Eleven years ago, when Mera had seen but nine winters, we, her grandmother, mother, and I, agreed to have all the memories of Skyemera removed from everyone in The Thicket for the years she and Lyra were with the dragon."

"What?" Callisto said, rising from her seat. "You stole the memories from your community?" She raised her fist, finger wagging in Helena's direction. "Who did this, as I know you all are not strong enough for that work."

Looking at the ground, yet not moving from her spot by the window, Helena responded. "We first appealed to Morpheus to take away Mera's nightmares. They were so bad. When he refused, we begged Lethe to remove Mera's own memories from the time." She looked up directly into Callisto's eyes. "She suggested that it would be hard for Mera to never be reminded of those lost years if we did not also remove those memories from the community collective." Tears began to fall from her eyes. "We didn't want to steal anyone's memories. We just wanted to help the child who was suffering terribly."

"Nightmares, you say?" Callisto asked, and Helena nodded. "And Morpheus refused to intervene?" she continued her questioning, nostrils flaring slightly.

"Yes, Mother. We went to him first. I still can't understand why he wouldn't help."

"The gods always have a reason, and it does not usually bode well for the rest of us regardless of the decisions they make." Callisto walked over to Helena and lay her hands on the elder's shoulders. "I cannot condone the action, but I can understand the reasons and difficulty of the choice. I cannot help but think there is a more nefarious reason for one god's refusal and the other's agreement with conditions."

Helena nodded quickly. "We thought much the same thing but couldn't think of any options besides agreeing. Things were absolutely terrible, and Mera's nightmares had started affecting other members of the community who lived within earshot of her screams."

"I can tell from The Maenad's visceral response to the dragon's portrait that she was somehow traumatized. I can also tell that in order to safely and effectively help her tap into and control her powers, I must remove her from The Thicket." Both nymphs turned when they heard a gasp followed by footsteps entering the room.

"I'm sorry to eavesdrop, Mothers," Kari stated, joining them. She dropped to her knees before Callisto. "May I accompany Mera? I promised to help her find her sister, and though that is no longer necessary, thank the gods, she is my cousin and best friend," she continued, words rattling off her tongue nonstop.

"Hush now, child," Callisto said, placing a hand on Kari's head. "I have no doubt you love and want to assist The Maenad, but neither of you are of an age or sufficiently in control of your powers to be any help to yourselves, or each other, right now."

"But, Ancient One," Kari began before Helena grabbed her hands and pulled her off the floor and over to the seats.

"Do as you were told and hush," Helena said, turning at the sound of more footsteps coming down the hall. She gestured for Kari to be silent with two fingers to her lips. Kari pouted, looking both ready to yell and cry, but she remained quiet.

"Have you gained control of yourself once again, Maenad" Callisto asked when Mera entered the room before her mother and grandmother.

"Yes, I believe so, and I apologize, Ancient One," Mera said, eyes downcast, as she approached the sitting area.

"There is no need to apologize. The outcome was what I had hoped to see, so I could know how to help. You are young and untrained with heightened emotions that are not aiding, other than to generate uncontrolled power," Callisto said with a wave of her hand dismissively. "There is no blame or shame here."

"Thank you, Mother," Dynami said, taking her seat next to Helena opposite Kari whose eyes were both set and rimmed with tears. "This is my daughter, Skyemera's mother, Phialyra." Lyra knelt in front of Callisto, infant still tied to her chest and began to prostrate in front of the ancient nymph.

"Please rise, Mother of The Maenad. We are all family here, and you may not feel so reverent after you hear what I have to say next." Looking at Mera before turning back to Lyra, who had risen to a seated position and clutched Mera's hands to the point her knuckles were white, Callisto said "I must take the Maenad away for a short while." Dynami's eyes went wide and a single tear slipped down Lyra's cheek, but no one spoke. "I both feel and understand your apprehension, but your lack of response says that you also understand why it is necessary."

She looked around at everyone in the room, her eyes resting on Skyemera. "Maenad, you are yet unaware of the extent of your powers, and you are untrained on how to control and wield them. Your emotions are a dangerous driving force." Callisto tilted her head in the direction of the hall. "You have not hurt anything or anyone yet, but the possibility is there. So I will take you to a location that is safe should your powers exceed your capacity to contain them." Her gaze matched Mera's in conviction.

"I don't want to do any harm to my family or my people, but where will we go?"

Kari got up and crossed to the window, turning away from the conversation. Helena glanced in her direction before turning her attention back to Mera's exchange with Callisto. There would be time for sadness later.

"I will not give specifics, as we do not want anyone trying to follow us," Callisto said with a knowing smile, eyes cutting to Kari. The ancient nymph was astute in recognizing Kari's impulsivity. "It would not be safe for someone to come upon us unaware when you are trying to wield your powers. I will also need to protect the identity of the one who will help us."

"You will involve someone else in Mera's training," Dynami asked, grabbing her granddaughter's hand protectively. "So few people know what she truly is, and with the dragon's return, I worry that the more people who know, the more danger she will be in."

"There has not been another true maenad in a millennium at least." Callisto reached one hand toward Dynami and the other toward Phialyra. "As I was still in exile during that time, I have minimal knowledge of their capability. I do, however, know of someone with firsthand experience with the last maenad. I hope to enlist their help."

Lyra held fast to Mera, but Dynami took Callisto's offered hand. "Please understand that I trust your judgment, Mother, as I have even less experience. The recent scare of thinking I had lost my daughter and youngest granddaughter to the dragon has me even more apprehensive. My heart cannot take much more."

Callisto's gaze softened. "Once she has a better handle on what her powers are and how to use them with control, The Maenad will be free to return. I suggest you use this time to put plans in place for protecting the village from the dragon, should your fears of his wanting The Maenad be warranted." She looked pointedly toward Kari who was still looking out the window. "I also believe it would be wise to provide explicit training for the young one there, as I have no doubt she will try to follow the Maenad once she leads the charge to confront the dragon."

Kari turned sharply at that, but her face held no argument. Helena couldn't help but smile at the look on her granddaughter's face. She recognized the loyalty and conviction, as she felt the same for Dynami.

"I will take care of that task personally, Ancient One. Kari will be as ready as she can be when Mera returns," Helena offered, smiling at Kari who silently mouthed her thanks.

"And I will take your suggestion to the council, so we can begin preparing our defenses for whatever may be coming."

"When will you be leaving?" Lyra asked, unsuccessfully hiding the emotion from her voice.

"On the morrow, if The Matriarch will allow me to spend the night," Callisto responded, and Mera gasped.

"Tomorrow?" Mera asked quietly, less of a question than a statement.

"Based on what I saw tonight and your emotional state, we

must get started sooner than later. We also must go to the human town on the other side of The Great River first." Mera moved closer to her mother, brushing through the fur on her own thighs repeatedly. It wasn't until Dynami reached over and placed a hand on Mera's shoulder that she stopped fidgeting.

"Helena, please show the Ancient One to the spare room, and I will help my granddaughter pack for her adventure," Dynami said, ending the conversation. They all rose from their seats as Callisto stood to leave the room.

"This way, Mother," Helena said, gesturing down the hall toward the back rooms. She nodded toward Dynami before leading the ancient nymph to her room.

Dynami turned to Kari then. "Please say your farewells, and then return home to explain the training plan to your mother. She must know that your education will be advanced and arduous. If she has any questions, she can ask Helena when she gets home." She stood and held her hand out for Kari's. When she had both of the young ones in front of her, she placed one hand on each of their heads. "You have not been separated for years, but now you must each follow your own path, so you can come back together as an unbeatable team." She nodded to each of them. "I will give you a moment alone, and then I expect both of you to follow my directions. Mera, we will be in your room." She kissed both of their hair and turned to grab Lyra's hand before leaving the sitting room as promised.

The cousins looked at each other for a moment. "So..." they said simultaneously, followed by a nervous laugh. Kari got her thoughts together first. "So much has changed in such a short time, and I don't know how to handle it. I don't feel any different, and yet everything is different, and now you are leaving, alone, without me," she said while grabbing both of Mera's hands. "We were supposed to grow up together, train together, and I would be with you wherever you might go. It seems wrong to let you go alone."

"I know," Mera stated, "I feel so lost, like I don't know who I am, Kari." She allowed the younger nymph to pull her in for a hug. The hug was more of an awkward grasping, considering their height and size difference, but they leaned into each other's comfort and love. "I do know I will be back, however, and I'll be taking you with me in the adventures to come, regardless of how this so-called training goes." Kari pulled away enough to look up into Mera's eyes, smile, and nod. Then she let go of Mera completely and ran out of the door. Mera watched her go and whispered, "I love you" to her fleeing form before closing the door and heading upstairs to her bedroom.

Mera woke the next morning before her grandmother who had insisted on sharing the room with her. She did not openly confess her fears the way Phialyra had the night before, but Mera could feel them. Her grandmother was worried for her, and she was also anxious about the possibility that Mera's mother and sister could be taken by the dragon's call. If anyone asked, Mera would admit that she, too, was worried about leaving her grandmother to shoulder that concern alone. She knew that Helena would always be nearby and that her grandmother would have much to do with the preparations, but it was still difficult to imagine leaving her family matriarch. She was the one constant in Mera's life, her rock. She lay there listening to her grandmother's light snores and smiled. She knew she had to leave to grow into her own, but leaving was not going to be easy.

She heard a noise in the hall and looked to see Callisto standing at the door. Mera still didn't know what to make of the ancient nymph. The elders trusted in her words, but to Mera, it seemed odd that they knew nothing about her except the ancient lore, which said she had been placed amongst the stars, presumably dead. Yet, here was this unbelievably beautiful nymph who looked no older than Dynami with the wisdom of millennia in her eyes. Mera imagined she'd find out soon whether or not the nymph was genuine as they set out on this adventure to begin her training.

"It is time to go," Callisto said quietly from the doorway, her voice as if a whisper on the wind that made Mera wonder if she'd spoken at all. The gesture for her to come from the room, though, was very clear. Mera looked back at her grandmother who continued to sleep. Should she wake her? Would it be any easier if her grandmother was able to say goodbye? She thought about how hurt she was to think that her mother had left without a word, and she rose from the bed to dress. "I will be out in a minute," she whispered to Callisto who walked away toward the stairs.

Mera pulled on the clothes she'd had made only for entering the human town, as her people were comfortable with nudity within The Grove and The Tribunal Forest. She had a linen gown that was much wider from the waist down to accommodate her haunches and touched the ground to hide her hooves from sight. She then took a cloak from the hook and folded it over her arm. Once dressed, Mera turned back to the bed and her sleeping matriarch. She lay her hand on the elder nymph's hair, brushing it back from her beautiful, though worn, face and bent down to kiss her grandmother's forehead. "Yaya, I have to leave now. I didn't want to go without saying goodbye," Mera whispered in her grandmother's ear. The Matriarch's eyes fluttered open, and she smiled at seeing her granddaughter standing over her.

"I thought it was a dream and you were already gone," Dynami whispered, lifting her hand to brush Mera's hair back behind her ear. "You are absolutely beautiful, Meraki, and you will return more powerful than any of us can imagine. I believe in you," she said, the look of pride pulling a sob from Mera. Dynami lifted her hands and pulled the gilded ring from her index finger. She took her granddaughter's hand and placed the ring on her middle finger.

"I love you, Yaya, and I will return as soon as I can," Mera said with tear-filled eyes.

"I know, and I love you as well. Now go."

Mera hugged her prone grandmother before she stood to her full height, put on her cloak, and grabbed the pack they had prepared before going to sleep the previous night. Mera walked through the door and paused. She considered turning back to wave but wasn't sure she would be able to resist the urge to run back to her grandmother's arms. After a few seconds, she turned toward the stairs and descended into the sitting room.

As she reached the bottom of the stairs, she noticed her mother in the entry to the hall. She was leaning on the frame as if she needed support. They locked eyes, and the swelling beneath those green pools made Mera's own eyes twinge. "Mother," Mera said quietly as she walked to stand in front of Lyra.

Lyra put a hand on each of her daughter's cheeks and smiled through the tears. "You, my beautiful child, are stronger than I have ever been already, and you will return stronger yet. I am sorry for..." Mera cut her off with a tight hug.

"Please stay safe while I am gone. Yaya and Eirini need you. I need to know you're all right. Stay close and fight against his call until I am strong enough to pick up the battle for you."

"Why do you sound like the mother?" Lyra said with a smile-cloaked sob. Mera shrugged before turning toward the main door where Callisto waited.

"Wait, I almost forgot." Lyra ran down the hall toward the inner kitchen. She returned a moment later with a woven basket. "I packed you some food for your trip." She handed the basket to Mera before turning to Callisto. "I know you will take care of my Mera. I thank you for your help and wish you both safe travels." Callisto inclined her head toward Lyra and then opened the door to leave. Mera looked into her mother's eyes for a few seconds more before she left the house without another word.

Chapter Thirteen

❧

Callisto and Mera left the boundaries of The Thicket and were far outside The Grove before either of them spoke. They were following the clearly worn path over the flatlands. Trees grew in sparse copses on either side of the path. "Now that we are out of earshot of your community and nosy nymphs, I would like you to release the emotions you have been harboring since you rose from the bed this morning." Callisto stopped to look into Mera's eyes, and Mera felt the compassion coming from the ancient nymph. She shook her head as a single tear rolled down her cheek.

"If I start, I'm afraid I won't stop. I'm also afraid of what I might do in the process."

"If you are worried about harming me or anything around us, do not. I can counteract anything you do in your untrained state. I also believe that since you are much more aware that your emotions trigger the outburst of power, you will be more likely to notice it happening."

"I don't know what to feel," Mera said, turning away from Callisto and walking toward one of the small groups of trees. She placed her hand on the tree nearest the path to steady herself. "I'm still reeling at my mother's disappearance and then reappearance. I'm afraid for my sister because my mother is still so vulnerable, and I don't yet know what happened to me with this dragon. I feel broken."

As Mera continued talking through her feelings, vines crept around the trunk of the tree she was grasping. The tighter her handhold became, the more the vines continued up the trunk, lacing their way around and through the branches. "I'm afraid to be away from home without my family to center me, without the comfort of the Tribunal Forest. I am afraid I will never again get to commune with the Strimmena along the sea."

"Strimmena," Callisto repeated with a tone that sounded more curious than judgmental, which broke through Mera's emotional display. Mera stood looking at the tree she had released and the vines she didn't remember being there earlier.

"Did I do that?" Mera asked in a breathy whisper tinged with worry.

Callisto reached for Mera's hand. "Place your hand back on the tree, Maenad." She guided the hand to the tree trunk when Mera failed to move. "Tell me about the Strimmena."

"A sea nymph Kari and I met the day after my sister's birth told us that was the name of the majestic gnarled oaks that grow alongside the sea."

"Yes, I know what they are. Tell me about what they mean to you," Callisto urged. Mera went to take her hand off of the tree, so she could walk away, but Callisto held her there. "Keep your hand on the tree and tell me."

Mera's brows knitted in frustration before softening as she thought about the Strimmena. "I feel safe around them, like I'm one with them." She thought about the times she'd sat for hours beneath their twisted branches, pretending the cave-like features they created were her secret lair. "Whenever I feel overwhelmed or isolated in The Thicket, I go to the sea and sit within the cradle of their strong branches. I listen to the sounds of the ocean and pretend that no one can find or harm me so long as I'm there." She laughed at this last part and said, "Except Kari. She always finds me."

As Mera talked this time, the strangling vine pulled itself from the entanglement of the tree's branches. It retreated along the height of the trunk until it was fully retracted into the copse. At Mera's laughter, new leaves sprouted from the trees' branches. One of those leaves tickled her shoulder, and she smiled.

"You have the power of nature within you. That includes the power of destructive and constructive forces," the ancient nymph told her. "Right now, those two forces are being driven by your emotions, but once you learn to control them, they will become part of your consciousness," she said, "rather than your subconscious." She placed her hand on Mera's shoulder. "You will get to decide which force manifests."

"Ancient One, will I ever feel like myself again? Will I ever feel normal?"

Callisto turned to walk back onto the path. "Let us continue our journey." Rolling hills spread ahead of them with only small groves of trees visible along the horizon in the direction they were traveling. "We do not want to arrive too late, else we might miss the person we seek."

"Are they human? Can humans live long enough to have known the last maenad?"

Callisto chuckled. There was a musical quality to her laugh, and Mera was reminded of the chimes her grandmother kept hanging from the canopy over their outside kitchen. She smiled despite the nervousness that grew, as they drew closer to the human town. "No, the person we seek is most definitely not human, but they do have an affinity for many of the goods humans have created, so we can find them there, if we do not dawdle."

"Will you not tell me who this person is?" Mera asked in both curiosity and frustration, causing her to sound more forceful than intended. Callisto's sideways glance and pressed lips reminded

Mera to do a better job of controlling herself. "My apologies, Ancient One. I mean no disrespect. I am simply nervous. I have always hated the human town and the looks I get from humans and other creatures alike. And now we are going there to potentially ask one of those creatures to help me."

Callisto's face relaxed, and she spoke quietly while they continued walking. "I do not speak this person's name outside of their presence. The mention of their name can be carried across the wind and cause trouble for them and us." She turned to watch Mera's profile for a minute and only continued once the maenad had nodded her understanding. "As to your other concern, I cannot say for certain when you will begin to feel like you not only know yourself but are in control of yourself again. Your world had been spun on its axis and is gyrating in multiple directions at one time. It will take time and understanding of how things are now before you begin to find your footing again."

Mera was so caught up in the ancient nymph's gestures demonstrating the world's movement, she nearly tripped over a rogue tree root. Instinctively, she reached down to touch it and unleash the emotions she held on the unsuspecting root. Callisto put a hand to Mera's shoulder and said three words that put things into perspective, "destructive or constructive."

Mera paused for a moment and then grabbed the root. She pushed at it instead of the previous urge she had to yank it from the ground. She pushed it fully into the dirt and felt it become pliable in her hand. She held it underground for a minute and felt new growth sift through her fingers as a sapling sprouted beneath her hand. She smelled the acrid scent of well-fertilized soil waft up from the hole her hand had made. The sapling grew alongside her palm, and the trunk widened until she could no longer close her hand around its girth. Hardened bark scratched the inside of her palm as the tree matured, branches sprouting above their heads. When the branches were covered in new leaves, creating a canopy to protect them from the sun, Mera removed her hand completely.

She looked up at the tree she had pulled forth from the buried root and then to Callisto who smiled.

"I think this is the perfect place to take our midday meal." Callisto grabbed the basket Mera had dropped when she first beheld the root. Placing the basket on the ground between them, she sat and gestured for Mera to do the same. They ate in the peaceful, protective shade of the tree that had not been there minutes earlier.

Hours later, as the sun began to dip beyond the horizon, they could hear the roaring rapids of The Great River. When the human town came into view, Mera began pulling at her clothes, trying to stretch the fabric looser around her wide hind quarters, and she loosened the hem to cover her hooves completely. She even pulled her cloak tight and raised the hood to shield her hair and face, though the temperature was warm. If she had known how to make herself invisible, she would have. Instead, she settled for ensuring she was covered from head to toe and unrecognizable. Mera felt Callisto look at her, but the ancient nymph said nothing. Thankful for the continued silence, Mera maintained her pace as if nothing were wrong.

"We will likely find our quarry catching a performance at the Grecian Urn," Callisto stated as they ascended the bridge that separated the hills outside of The Great Forest from the human enclave. "The humans love to think themselves clever, and our friend finds the irony of their signage funny." Mera caught the hint of a sneer on the otherwise impassive face.

"I have rarely visited the town, and I don't believe I've ever seen anywhere called The Grecian Urn."

"That is not surprising. I do not believe your matriarch would take her people into such a place without reason. Again, our friend patrons the establishment because he finds it ironic. You will see why once we are there and have greeted him." Callisto's air of finality held Mera back from expressing the other questions swirling in her mind.

The times Mera had visited the town with her mother and grandmother, they had walked straight into the heart via the main path from the bridge she had just crossed with Callisto. This time, however, the ancient nymph led Mera to an alleyway on their left that ran parallel to the river. The main path took them between well-preserved inns, shops, and homes as one moved further beyond the town's center. The alley, on the other hand, took them past docks and run-down taverns. Mera's nostrils were overwhelmed by the combined stench of fish and filth. She was glad for the large hood that kept her face hidden, lest she offend someone with her response to the odors.

They had arrived to the town soon after the typical dinner hour, right before dusk kicked in fully. As they walked, shadows elongated across the path, as if reaching for the edge of the river covering everything between. "Stay close," Callisto said quietly, as if there were any possibility Mera would let herself be left alone in that place. Mera could not see much with her hood up, but she could hear gravely voices all around, calling to each other. Bawdy banter passed between scantily dressed human women on iron-fenced balconies and both humans and non-humans alike at ground level. Mera felt herself jostled when she bumped into a hard-bodied human male walking in the opposite direction from them.

"Pardon me," she blurted before thinking better of it.

If she wasn't already on edge, his response would have made her hackles rise, "You should show your face when you make an apology for rudely walking into someone. If that face matches the voice, I may just forgive you."

"Do not make any move to show your face, Maenad," Callisto

said in her ear. "Continue walking at this steady pace to not draw attention to yourself, and do not stop for anyone until you reach The Grecian Urn."

"What do you mean? You're not leaving me, are you?" Mera squeaked. Her heart rate spiked when she imagined being alone here in the darkening alley.

Callisto pushed her forward lightly. "I will be right behind you. Just do as I say."

"Don't just walk away," the man said, moving to follow Mera. The maenad kept walking as she had been instructed, but she struggled to get her breathing under control. She tried to listen for the man's footsteps behind her, but she couldn't hear over the sound of her own heartbeat in her ears. She heard nothing until there was a loud grunt and then a splash as something heavy went into the river. Mera wanted to stop and look, but she saw a sign that read The Grecian Urn. The sign had a picture of an urn decorated with the form of a centaur on it. It took all of her willpower not to run the final yards to the tavern, but she was afraid of drawing additional attention to herself from others skulking around the shadows.

As she reached for the door handle, a hand grabbed her arm, and she let out a squeak. "Shh, it is me. I did not want you to enter the establishment alone." Mera reached out and grabbed the nymph in a tight hug.

"I was so afraid you were the man reaching for me."

"He will not be reaching for anyone ever again." Callisto opened the tavern door without another word.

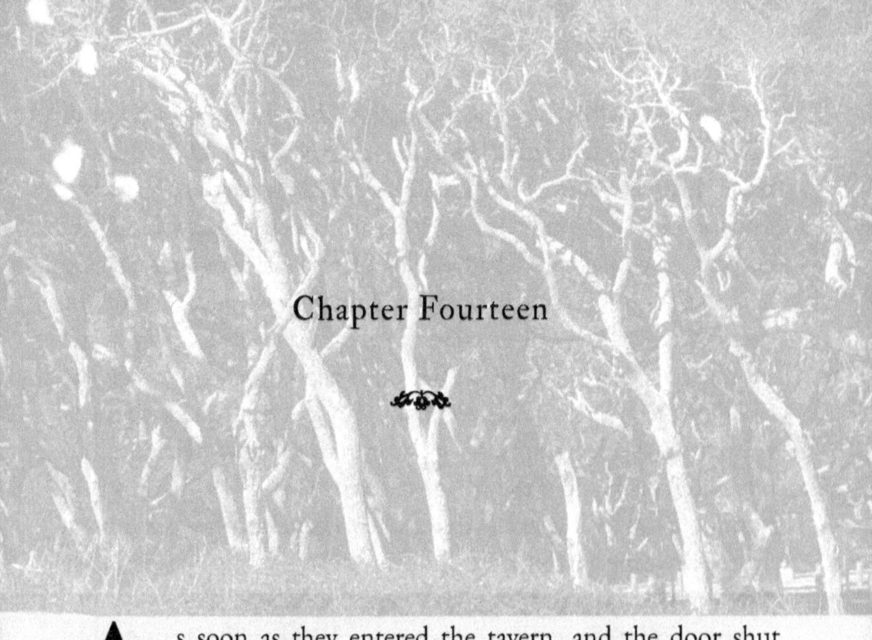

Chapter Fourteen

s soon as they entered the tavern, and the door shut behind them, Mera again had to steel herself against her overwhelmed senses. The stale stench of smoke, liquor, and vomit were just as strong inside as the smells of sewage and fish guts were outside. Mera felt eyes turn on them, but when Callisto made no move to progress further inside the dimly lit tavern, Mera took a moment to look around.

The bar itself took up most of the back wall with its half-dozen stools and display bottles reaching toward the ceiling. Though the rest of the tavern was expectedly dark and eerie, the bar area was well-lit with some type of reflective material Mera didn't recognize hanging above the candles burning in sconces at either end of the counter. There was a performance stage raised two feet off the ground at the rear left corner of the open hall, but all attention was pulled to the bar with its ostentatious glow. What took Mera most by surprise was the silence in the tavern. The stories always told of taverns being raucous environments. Was The Grecian Urn always this quiet?

There was a piano at the left end of the stage, and an aged curtain keeping the performer carefully ensconced until they were ready to show their face. Mera imagined the ash and spilled liquor making the curtain volatile should a stray flicker of the candle reach that way. Though her grandmother rarely partook, there was alcohol in their home for guests and special occasions. Mera guessed they might have had a drink after her sister's presentation had the dragon not arrived. That thought reminded her of the occurrences at home when her powers took over and how afraid Helena had been that she would burn the house down with the candle flames. She shuddered at the thought and quickly looked away from the curtain, turning her eyes to the rows of booths on both sides of the door they'd just entered. Most of the booths held nothing more than a small table and two benches only big enough for four nymphs. Mera doubted four satyrs could sit comfortably in one of those booths.

In each far corner, there was a larger booth with a round table. The semi-circle bench appeared to hold 6 or 8 nymphs by Mera's judgment. Then she noticed that the corner booth on the far right was occupied by a lone figure, and that person...was it a person, she wondered...took up nearly half of the seating themself. Was that a...no, it couldn't be. She went to nudge Callisto to gain her attention when she realized the ancient nymph was looking in the same direction and had begun to move that way. Was that who, what, they came to see? Mera got ahold of herself and followed the ancient nymph who walked to stand right in front of the round table.

The booth's occupant had been looking down, head and face hidden by an overly large hood attached to the black, or was it green, cloak they were wearing. They had massive hands that were clasped, index fingers steepled as if they were waiting for something, or someone. Mera took in the broad shoulders and odd way they sat atop the bench rather than on it. She knew the feeling of sitting on thick, heavy haunches, but the height at which this creature sat told her they were not a satyr, nor were they a faun.

There were very few other creatures with human-like hands and large hind parts, and most of those were said to be extinct.

"Hello, Pholus. It has been a long time," Callisto said, cutting the silence sharply. The half man lifted his head and looked at the ancient nymph from beneath the hem of his hood for what seemed an eternity to Mera. The endless stare cloaked the tavern in an eerie silence again before a wave of recognition passed across his face, leaving a smile in its wake.

"Callisto," he said as a half question, half statement. "I can't believe it's you!" He pushed the table out of the booth so quickly that Callisto and Mera barely had time to jump out of the way. He jumped to his feet, or rather hooves, all four of them. Mera stood in awe as what appeared to be a human man reached out and grabbed Callisto in his strong arms and lifted her off her feet in a tight hug. It wasn't the sudden movement or unexpected affection that held her in place but the view of the rest of his body that caught Mera off guard. He looked like a human man head to waist from the front, but he had the legs, hind quarters and tail of a horse.

"Put me down, you," Callisto said with a forceful tone that belied the huge smile and tinge of laughter in her voice. "You are too big, and we are too old for all that," she chided him still smiling. The centaur put the nymph back on her feet before inviting her to join him for a drink.

"The show starts shortly. I hope you had planned to stay for a while," he said, moving back into the booth to re-situate himself on the bench comfortably before stretching to pull the table back in place. Mera watched him wide-eyed. That was the most unusual way to enter and exit a booth, she thought to herself. Would it not have been easier to just sit at one of the tables where he could easily pull the seat back far enough. Maybe he could have grabbed two chairs or one of the loose benches against the side wall. Surely that would have been less trouble than rearranging the furniture just to take a seat. At least that's what she would have done to draw less attention to herself.

Mera heard Callisto mention her name and was pulled from her thoughts. She apologized, and Callisto repeated her introductions, "Pholus, this is Skyemera from The Thicket, granddaughter of the community matriarch. Mera, this is Pholus, a very old friend of mine." Mera was caught off guard by the beautiful blue eyes, like the azure sky after a storm set in a handsome face of smooth skin the color of life-giving earth after a summer rain.

"You're a centaur," she blurted, surprising herself, as she felt her cheeks flush.

He laughed. "And you are a maenad."

She wasn't ready for that response. No one else had known who, or rather what, she was until Callisto looked at her. Well, her mother, grandmother, and Helena knew, but they had always known. Callisto was the first person to have just met Mera and immediately recognized her identity. The fact that another stranger, one who was not a nymph, so easily recognized her made her instantly self-conscious.

"Relax, young one," he replied in a deep resonant voice that reminded her of thunder accompanying a storm. Its rumble eased her spirit in a way she did not understand but was grateful. "I know who you are because I have been alive long enough to have known the last maenad."

"How?" Mera asked, voice barely a whisper. "We learned that centaurs were extinct."

"Far as most people know, we are, and I like it that way," He said in response. "It simplifies my life." The low rumbly chuckle that accompanied that statement made Mera giggle. "Really, people just believe what they want to believe." He shrugged. "Take my story, for example. People really believe that I was dumb enough to accidentally prick myself with an arrow I knew to be poisonous. I believe I once heard it told that I wanted to check out the arrow," he said gesturing with his hand to emphasize the absurdity of the idea. "I don't want to be around anyone that illogical. I disappeared when the rumors started, which allowed them to flourish. Nearly a millennium of peace and quiet. Well, except for when I come into town for supplies and a little entertainment," he finished with a smile.

"Don't look too surprised, Maenad," Callisto added, "I was supposedly dead as well."

"Yes, how was it that you managed to hide from the gods?" Mera asked, eyes bright with curiosity.

"I did not exactly hide from them. More like I was hidden from them, and by the time I reemerged, Hera had more important things to deal with. It's not like Zeus suddenly became faithful to his wife after he sent me away to the stars." Callisto smirked. "Let's be clear, though," she continued with a point of her finger, "I do not go around flaunting my continued existence, and I generally try to stay away from the gods."

"Exactly," Pholus agreed. "So how did you know I was still around, my friend?" he asked Callisto.

"A little birdie keeps me informed of what happens here. As humans have expanded their populations and the gods' power has waned, my people have somewhat isolated themselves. This is the closest town to several enclaves of alseides, so I try to keep an eye on things without interfering. At least, most of the time..." she grew quiet and let her eyes shift to Mera who suddenly grew uneasy in her seat when Pholus also turned his eyes on her.

Before anyone could say anything more, piano music began, and the centaur turned his attention to the stage at the rear of the room. Mera was grateful to have their gazes directed elsewhere. She took in the changes of the tavern hall since they had joined Pholus in the booth. The room was now full of people. Mera looked over her shoulder down the rows of booths and saw that every one of them held at least one head. The tables in the middle of the room were mostly occupied. There were a number of humans there, and a few satyrs. She even saw two barmaids, both nymphs, who she hadn't notice earlier. The barkeep, presumably the owner, was a satyr, which Mera found surprising, as she always thought of this as a human town where the forest folk traded.

She also realized that the noise level had risen significantly. Numerous conversations were happening. Simultaneously, a glass shattered behind the bar, and the human piano player picked up the pace of their tune. Mera could feel anticipation in the air, and she realized why when the curtain on the stage parted to reveal a siren.

"Of all the creatures," Callisto said under her breath, her brow furrowed in disgust.

Pholus turned his eyes to the nymph for a second. "You have to admit it's smart business. Who else would call the patrons in, so they would spend all their coin?" He returned his attention to the stage without waiting for an answer. Callisto scoffed but also turned to watch the show. Mera was already drawn into the haunting tune. She didn't think the lyrics themselves were what gave the song its haunting quality. The siren was living up to its reputation by promising a beautiful, sensual death with its voice.

When the song was finished, it was as if everyone, or at least all the males in the room, were in a trance. They sat there staring at the siren, unmoving, until the piano player began clapping. Then the room erupted in applause. Conversations resumed, and drinks once again made their way around the room. By the time a barmaid had gotten to their table, Pholus was sharing another of the rumors surrounding his supposed death, and she caught them all mid-laugh.

"Can I get you or your friends anything to drink?" The scantily clad nymph directed her question at Pholus with a big smile.

"Yes, Chari, grab us a round, and a meal for my guests. It is past dinner, and I am sure they are hungry."

"Chari," Mera asked.

"Yes," the nymph responded. "My name is Chariclo, but most of the patrons here just call me Chari."

"Oh, I see. My best friends name is Kari. I'm from The Thicket," Mera continued, though she wasn't sure why she felt compelled to share all of this with the barmaid.

"The Thicket?" She looked Mera up and down, at least the best she could when the maenad was seated in a booth inside a relatively dark and smoky tavern. "You're not a nymph, yet you're also a nymph," she said, brows drawing together.

"I'm both."

The nymph looked at Mera for a short second and then looked at Callisto, but when the ancient nymph said nothing, she walked away to fetch their drinks and meals.

Mera looked up at her companions, noticing the odd looks on their faces. "What?"

"I found your answer, 'I'm both,' both accurate and unexpected," Pholus said in response to her question.

"Why did you not simply say what you are?" Callisto asked, and Mera felt herself getting defensive at the question.

"I'm not fully sure what I am, Ancient One, or even what it means to be one," Mera responded tersely. "How do I claim something I don't understand," she asked before turning silent again.

"You are The Maenad," Callisto said decisively. "It is not just a description but a title. You are the only one of your kind. Your birth was heralded across the skies and through the trees." Once again her hand gestures emphasized her words, but she must have felt her voice raise above the din of the crowded tavern because she lowered it to say, "You belong to and receive power from two pantheons."

"I hear you say that, but I don't feel it. I don't know what I'm supposed to do with that information. Do I just announce it to everyone I meet," Mera asked, her voice becoming more frantic with each subsequent exchange. "My mother's mate showed up because my birth was announced to the world, and then he somehow terrorized us both. Should I be happy about that or announce that part too? What does this knowledge do for me? How will it help me protect my family? My home?"

"By the gods," Pholus interjected. "I feel like an outsider in this conversation. I had guessed it was not just coincidence that brought you to The Grecian Urn this evening, but now I must ask. Why have you sought me out, Callisto?"

Callisto rested her elbows on the table and put her head in her hands, rubbing her temples through her hair. The barmaid, Chari, brought their drinks and food before Callisto could say anything, and she waited to respond until the young nymph was out of earshot. "Outside of the gods themselves, you are the only other being I know old enough to remember the last maenad." She paused, looking at Pholus until he acknowledged the statement's accuracy with a nod and a shrug. "Right," she said, "and I was still in hiding, exile, however you want to put it at that time." She looked around to make sure no one was close to their table or listening intently to their conversation. "The Maenad is just beginning to come into her powers, but they are untrained and dangerous. She already unleashed a small cyclone inside of her home." She made a swirling gesture with her finger. "And a massive tornado outside without even realizing it was happening. I was hoping that between the two of us," she said, pointing back and forth between herself and Pholus with the same finger she had used to gesture the cyclone, "we could teach her the extent of her powers and how to wield them safely and effectively."

"Is that all," Pholus asked with a chuckle, gesturing for Mera to begin her meal.

"There is more, but that will have to wait until we are somewhere alone," Callisto said and began her own meal.

Pholus sat up a bit straighter, as he considered her request and that last statement. "I cannot promise anything about how well I can help train her, as that was such a long time ago, but I'm willing to try, for you." Callisto smiled at him and then turned that smile on Mera before she grabbed her next bite of food.

Chapter Fifteen

M era found herself thinking about her family and how much had changed already though she'd just left them two days prior. What were they doing? How was her mother holding up? What preparations was her grandmother putting in place to protect The Thicket? She wondered about Kari's training and when it would start. What would it entail? Would it be different from what she was going to go through? She had a strong sense of homesickness suddenly, and she'd just left.

"How long will I be away from my home?"

Pholus turned sympathetic eyes toward her. "Homesick already, young maenad?"

"I've never been away from them for any longer than a few hours when I'd go to the shore at the edge of The Grove."

"Never?" Callisto asked. "I had been told you were away at the mountain house for months at a time."

"I don't remember much of that except what has come back in visions and nightmares. I can't really say, but from what I do remember, I've always been near my family and my home in The Thicket."

Callisto glanced at Pholus. Something passed between the two of them, but Mera had no idea what it meant. "I hadn't considered how difficult this separation might be on you Maenad. Though I still feel it absolutely necessary, I apologize for my lack of consideration. I might have left you more time to say your farewells."

"I cannot give you a timeframe for how long your training will take," Pholus said, trying to assuage her fears. "But, as I work through what you already know and can do, I will have a better idea to share with you. I imagine it will be at least a year or more." He turned up the final drops of his ale. "We will spend the night upstairs here in the inn, and then we will leave on the morrow, as I had originally planned."

"Where are we going?"

"It's better we do not speak specifics in this place surrounded by prying ears. Just know that it's a long journey from this town, and we will go on foot, so it may take even longer, as I will be forced to slow down for you."

Mera bristled at this statement. She had always been the fastest nymph in the forest. "You'd be surprised at how fast I can travel. My cousins can never keep up if I don't want them to."

"Ah, yes, you have the power of the faun in your legs. That will be helpful in many ways, even beyond the journey to my training lands."

"You have training lands, as in you train folk regularly?" It was Callisto's turn to be surprised at the conversation.

"Much has changed since we last saw each other, old friend." Looking at each of them in turn, Pholus asked if there would be anything they required from the town before they left tomorrow. At Callisto's response, both of their jaws dropped.

"I will not be traveling with you two, though I will check in with you periodically to get updates on the Maenad's progress."

"You're not..." Mera began and Pholus finished, "traveling with us?"

"No. If danger is, in fact, coming to The Grove and my people, I should be near to help council the elders. I have every faith in your ability to care for the Maenad in my absence."

"We have much to talk about this evening before we leave then. I thought we would have the journey to discuss what is to be done."

"I am sorry for any confusion. I brought her to you because I knew you were her, our, best hope. I also knew that I needed someone I could trust to care for and protect her while I work to make sure her home is fortified and ready for whatever is to come."

"Do you think it will be that bad while I'm gone?"

"I cannot say, Maenad, but I do not want our people left unprotected. You will, once your training is complete, be their best protection, but for now, I will stand in your place."

"Thank you," Mera said with a trepidatious smile. Turning to Pholus, she asked, "Is there a place to relieve oneself in this tavern?"

He smiled, "Of course, though it is not a space large enough for my needs. On the other side of the tavern, beyond the stage, there is a short hall with facilities."

"Indoors?"

Callisto and Pholus both smiled at her. She imagined they wanted to laugh and was grateful they did not.

"You'll find that there are many places in the world that are more advanced and very different from your home in The Tribunal Forest," Pholus answered. "When you return, we will head upstairs, so you can rest while Callisto and I work through logistics for your training."

Mera nodded and squeezed herself out of the booth. She had been sitting a long time on the hard bench, and her haunches were screaming their disapproval. She wondered how Pholus could stand to remain seated the way he was folded into the back of the booth. Once her muscles relaxed enough to walk, she made her way to the other side of the tavern. She was nearly there when she felt eyes on her from all directions. She picked up her pace at the stage area.

"I bet that ass is a sight to see," said an unknown voice from her left.

"Come show us what's under that cloak," another voice chimed in from her right.

"Don't be shy. I bet you're a beauty."

The voices sounded like they were closing in on her, some of them slurred with drink and others were more sinister. Mera tried to fight down her panic and prepared to run. Then, someone grabbed her wrist while another hand pulled down the hood of her cloak.

"Well, hello, gorg..." one of them started before Mera screamed, "NO!" Both hands released her, and everyone standing within ten feet of her was thrown to the ground as if hit by hurricane-force winds. Before anyone on the floor could recover, Mera saw the table of the booth she'd just shared with Callisto and Pholus fly from its nook to the center of the room. They both stalked toward her, power emanating from their forms.

"What the..." one of the men on the floor began, after he recovered from having the wind knocked out of him.

"Move or finish that sentence and it will be your last utterance," Pholus said from his full height above the man who instantly paled. "Come, Mera." Pholus held his hand out to her, and they walked toward the rear hall stairs.

The barkeep stepped into their path from behind the bar. "I have never had any trouble from you, Pholus."

"And you will continue to have no trouble from me so long as your other patrons learn how to respect young women." The barkeep turned from Pholus to look at Callisto before his gaze landed on Mera.

"That is no human woman. No nymph either," he said suspiciously.

"She is from The Grove," Pholus said matter-of-factly. The

barkeep's eyes stayed on Mera for few more uncomfortable seconds before he shifted them back to Pholus.

"Be that as it may, she is no nymph, and that," he said, gesturing at the people still getting up from the floor or walking around dazed, "was no mere nymph magic. Do you still plan to leave on the morrow."

"Yes, after we break our fast, we'll be off." The barkeep nodded and stepped back behind the bar, allowing the three powerful creatures to exit the bar proper.

"A round for everyone, on the centaur," they heard behind them. Pholus' eyes hardened in the hall's dim light as muffled cheers rang out, but he said nothing.

Back in his suite of rooms, Pholus turned on Mera, "What happened back there?"

She shrank and backed away from him. "I don't know. I was going where you directed me, and they started saying things, telling me to remove my cloak and show them my haunches. I tried to walk faster to get away from them, and then someone grabbed me. I froze. Someone else pulled down my hood, and I don't know what happened at that point, just that I told them *No!*"

He shook his head and stomped around a bit.

"She's telling the truth, Pholus. I have seen what happens when her magic spurs. She remembers nothing of what happens nor how it happens. It takes control of her. That is why we need your help."

The following morning, they left the tavern soon after they had eaten. Gathering a few necessary items for Mera, including material for new clothing and cloaks for the journey, Pholus and Mera prepared to head south. Mera was surprised that she managed to hold back her tears when she said goodbye to Callisto. She wasn't sure when or if she would see the ancient nymph again. This goodbye reminded her that she was not sure when or if she would see her family and home again.

"Young one, are you sure that you will be able to make this entire journey on foot?" Pholus asked as soon as they left the edge of town.

"I have no problem walking," Mera responded, not bothering to look up. "My legs are just as strong as yours. I simply have two of them." Pholus chuckled at her response, and Mera felt her sadness wash away in his laughter. "Ancient One," Mera said, turning to look at him this time, "what can you tell me about the last maenad?" He looked down at her, which was a surprising comfort, as normally, she was the one looking down on everyone else.

"First," he said, "we will be together for a long time. Please call me Pholus. I am old, but I do not need to be reminded of it on a daily basis." Mera turned her face away with a half smirk before she nodded. She could feel heat creeping up her neck. "Good. As far as the last maenad is concerned, I was lucky enough to have known her well. She was born in the forest I called home. Thus, we knew who she was from the moment of her birth, and my family had been called on to ensure her safety until she grew into her powers." He continued walking while he spoke, and Mera had to force herself to keep up as the shock of that revelation set in. "Unlike you, she had the benefit of knowing who she was, and what she was to become, from the beginning. In that way, she also held a bit of arrogance in her youth, and that arrogance is what eventually led to her demise."

"So she knew both her parents?"

"Yes, she knew them both, but no, I will not share the details of her parentage. As I said, I grew up in the same forest as the maenad, but growing up, she was little more than another forest creature like we were. We played. We ran. We watched each other grow."

"So you were friends?"

"Yes." There was a distance in his voice.

"I occasionally see some of the forest creatures and might run alongside them, but my only real friend, my best friend really, is my cousin Kari. Her real name is Karielle, but we call her Kari just like everyone calls me Mera though my name is Skyemera. I don't know what I would do if I didn't have Kari as my friend." Mera realized she was rambling, but she continued with a sigh. "Everyone else treats me so differently."

"Well, that is a similar experience to the last maenad," Pholus inserted when Mera grew quiet. "Everyone treated her differently as well, at least everyone in her village. They treated her differently because they knew that she was to become more than they were."

Mera stared into the distance. "I just always felt like I never fit in. I look different. I stand different. I walk different. I am so much taller than everyone else. I stand out, and, most of the time, all I want to do is hide. What was her name?"

Mera saw Pholus turn his head and look off into the distance. She began to wonder whether he was going to answer the question or not as his pause dragged on. "Her name was Truisha." Mera stopped walking for a second and looked up at him, her head tilted slightly to the side. Why did that name sound familiar? He turned back to her saying, "We have a long road ahead. We cannot stop every time you ask a question." When he kept walking, Mera jogged to catch up.

"Sorry, her name just caught me off guard. I know that I have never heard of a maenad until someone told me I was one, but I believe I've heard that name before."

"Her story, much like my story, and that of Callisto, has been relegated to mythology."

"That can't be right. We learned about you two as part of our history."

He laughed again with that resonant voice of his. "Ah yes, young one. You are still measuring life in winters, and yet my life has seen so many that I no longer measure it. The last maenad has been gone for nearly 1000 years, and yet she had seen 300 winters before she was stricken. Your people in The Grove are some of the very few who still maintain the old ways as if they were common. You venerate the old gods. You practice the old rituals. You even continue to mate in the same patterns..." He paused. "...at least most of your people do," he trailed off, looking at her. She caught his gaze.

"Yes, my mother made different decisions, though I'm not sure she was fully aware of most of those decisions. I think she just wanted to get away and be something different."

Mera fell silent. They had long left the human town along the horizon behind them, and in the distance on all sides was little more than grassy plains. She had more questions, though he seemed reluctant to give many answers. At the same time, thinking of her mother provoked a strange melancholy in Mera. She wanted to be mad at her mother, knew she should be mad at her mother, and yet all she knew was that everything had become so complicated. She had been lied to her whole life, and knowing that lie had been to protect her, didn't make it hurt any less. Mera felt the familiar sting behind her eyes and knew that she had to distract herself from those thoughts.

"Great Pholus, what kind of powers did Truisha have?"

"Now we have come to important questions," he responded with a tone that nearly made Mera laugh. "If you're thinking that you will have the same powers that she had, I'm afraid that may not be so. You see, she was not the first maenad, and, in our history, that maenad had different powers as well. It appears to be a matter of the specific combination of parentage that determines the type and strength of the powers you will have. For example, the first maenad I knew of had the power to speak to birds, all kinds of birds. She could use them as her spies, as her messengers, and as weapons in battle. She was also able to tap into them directly and fly."

"Fly?" Mera nearly jumped up and down in front and around him like a baby goat when she heard that. "She was actually able to fly?"

"Well, I didn't get to see it. Contrary to what you may believe, I'm not that old." He winked at her. "She lived far before my time. I'm not quite as old as the gods themselves."

Mera smiled at him, holding in her laughter at his insistence that he wasn't all that old. "What about the one who was your friend? What were her powers?"

"Oh, she was able to control all things made of water. She could make it rain or melt the snow. She could easily divert a river. I once watched her make the ocean recede so she could study the sea life that was near the shore.

Mera beamed at him. "That sounds amazing!"

"Yes, it was amazing to watch, until..." He paused his steps.

"Until what," Mera asked, drawing up next to him.

"Until I watched that sea life gasping for air because it was unable to breathe outside of the water. She and her hubris were so excited to be able to touch and observe those previously unseen creatures without getting wet that she watched and allowed them to die, suffering the whole time. My friend had a hard time understanding the responsibility that came with her power. In all her years, she struggled to learn that simply being able to do something did not mean it should be done." He turned to look directly at Mera, and she started shifting uncomfortably under his gaze before he continued his thought. "As we come to learn your powers, Skyemera, I hope that you will learn that lesson. Now come, there is a small city over this next hill. We will stop there for the night."

Mera spent the next few minutes thinking about what he said. She wondered if Truisha had intentionally peeled back the sea and killed those creatures or whether in her excited state she had acted on instinct not realizing what was happening around her. Mera couldn't help but wonder at the stories her own people were already telling about her in The Thicket because of her power manifestations when she was upset. She wanted to ask Pholus about the possibility that his friend's behavior had been misinterpreted, but the sadness on his face told her now was not the time. So, they walked in silence toward the tall hill.

Chapter Sixteen

They were silent as they crested the hill. When Mera came to stand beside Pholus, she remained silent, for no words would form. Sprawled before them was a village, no, not a village, nor a town. Pholus had called it a city, but this was far beyond anything Mera could have imagined. There were buildings of various heights and sizes as far as she could see. Unlike her own village, or even in the human town, these buildings did not appear to be made of twigs and sticks. Nor did they appear to be made of carved wood. They stood tall and wide and shimmered in the sun.

They had traveled a full day, and yet they had ventured two days worth of distance from the human town, their powerful legs moving them much faster than human or nymph could travel on foot. Mera saw the sun leaning toward the west, reaching to hide behind the cover of mountains in the distance. The grandeur of those mountains would be nothing compared to the view in front of her. She felt Pholus' gaze fall on her, but she could not look away. It was the most amazing sight she had ever seen, amazing and yet confusing.

"How do the houses glimmer like that?"

Pholus chuckled. "Have you never been to the city, young one?"

"Is this a city? I've never heard that term. I've never seen anything like this." She wondered at the sight before her. "The gods know, I have never been any further than the human town outside The Thicket. At least not that I can remember."

Pholus smiled at her and turned his gaze on the city. "This is Krinosera, named for the lilies that grew in this valley when the city was founded. It is called a city because of its size, the number of peoples who live here, and the types of buildings. The glimmer, as you put it, comes from the windows."

Mera pressed her lips together and shook her head. "We have windows in The Thicket. They have windows in the human town." She gestured back the way they had come. "These..." she said, holding her hands out toward the city and spreading her arms wide. "This is magic."

He chuckled again. "Your homes have holes in the walls. Holes that you cover with grass rolls when it rains. In the town, they have holes in the walls, holes they cover with wooden shutters. But here..." He gestured toward the city as she had. "Here, they have windows, windows made of glass. As for magic, I suppose they are probably one of the most magical things created in my lifetime."

"Glass," she whispered, feeling the word in her mouth. It felt as magical to say as it was to see. When her eyes fell on a tall spire reaching above the other buildings to the east, she pointed and asked about it. "I cannot see anything more than that tall point stretching toward the heavens."

Pholus turned to follow the direction of her hand. "That is what the humans call a church. It's where many go to worship their god."

"Like an altar?"

"There is an altar inside, yes, but it's not like you imagine. In The Thicket, your people hold onto the ancient traditions and the old gods. Many here have forgotten, or forgone those traditions in favor of new gods. Truth be told, there are many who believe there is only one god. Yet, in this city, like many others, they build different churches to worship that same god." He pointed toward different areas of the city, and Mera could make out similar yet smaller spires across the landscape. "They also call this god by many different names and argue amongst themselves on how to worship him properly."

"Have you been to many cities like this one and seen many of these churches and their gods?"

"I have no time for worship or gods, be there many or one. I have seen too much in my lifetime." He turned toward the city and began walking toward what appeared to be a steep cliff. "Come. I'll show you glass up close before the sun sets, or you will no longer be able to see its glory. Tomorrow, we'll explore the city, so you can see what all the humans and other creatures of the city have managed to create with glass." Mera marveled at his descent as if dropping into the hill she stood upon. She hurried to catch up before he dipped out of a sight. He was following a steep path toward the valley below.

As they neared the closest building, Mera realized her earlier assessment of the city's scale was grossly underestimated. This city had to be at least the size of the Tribunal Forest, and some of the buildings seemed nearly as tall as the sentinel pines that protect it. The closer they got to the buildings, the more she had to crane her neck until she was almost bent over backwards like she and Kari used to do when they were small children preparing to do flips. Still, she could no longer see the tops of the buildings, just the light glimmer of rainbow colors until they passed into the shadow of an alley between two buildings.

"I have never before felt so small," she mused. He laughed, and his voice echoed in the alley as they walked between building after building. "Do people live there? Way up high? In The Thicket, my grandmother's house is one of the tallest with only two floors. In the town, our room at the inn was also on the second floor, though there were a couple of buildings with a third floor. The gods know this," she pointed at the building to their right," must have at least 100 floors. It has to be like climbing a mountain to get to the top."

"Not quite 100." She could hear the mirth in his voice. "The tallest building in the city is a mere 10 stories high, but I understand why it feels much taller from down here," he said while looking up as she had.

They stopped walking outside of what appeared to be an inn of sorts. It had a sign out front, similar to those she had seen in the human town, but this building was made out of some kind of stone-like material. She wasn't quite sure what it was, but she knew that is was definitely not wood. After counting the windows, as Pholus had called them, she concluded that the inn must have five floors, and she wondered what the view would look like from that height.

"Will we stay at the top?"

"I can request a room up there if you'd like."

"I want to see the view. I want to look through these windows from the inside."

Mera screamed. She felt the beating of wings around her and the heat of his breath. She ran, searching for somewhere to hide. She banged on doors, running between the buildings, rushing down different lanes, trying door handles, hoping one would be open, but they were all sealed shut. A torrent of light shot across the sky, lighting up the lane she was on, as if morning had come. Just as quickly, the shadows returned, reaching for her with claw-like fingers. She ran into something hard and screamed again. She turned down another lane, lungs burning. Where could she go? There were so many buildings and doors and clawed shadows. She needed to find somewhere to stop and think and breathe.

The sound of footsteps grew, and Mera backed herself into the shadows, slowly making her way along the wall hoping she could find another lane to disappear into. Finding a doorway in the wall, she tried the handle. When someone banged on the door from the other side, she put her hands to her mouth to stifle the scream bubbling up from her stomach. The banging grew louder. She turned to run and got caught on the hem of her robe. The momentum carried her forward until she was face down on the ground, wrapped in layers of cloth. She didn't remember a robe in all of the time she'd been running from the dragon. She kicked her feet and reached up to her shoulders thinking she could pull it off and crawl out of the twisted fabric.

Skyemera.

She heard the voice calling from the other side of the pounding door and looked up to find herself inside of a room. Wasn't she just outside?

Skyemera.

The voice called again, and she looked around for somewhere to hide, for some weapon. The robe still had her legs wrapped up tight like a constrictor. The dragon would break the door down before she could even get up. She pulled herself away from the door until she was up against a wooden post. Could she use that as a weapon or to hide? As she moved into a seated position and reached her hands down to release her trapped legs, keys jingled from the other side of the door.

Hurry up! The Maenad needs help!

Maenad? Wait, I'm the Maenad. The thoughts no sooner entered her mind that her heartbeat slowed, and her breathing returned to normal. Looking at her surroundings, she noticed the post she was sitting against was attached to a bed. She looked to the corner and saw her pack sitting on a chair. A little higher, and there were her robes hanging on the wall. As the door opened and

Pholus came barreling in, pushing the innkeeper out of the way, Mera looked at her legs to find them wrapped in the bed covering.

"What is happening in here? I heard you scream." His panicked accusation had come out before he'd even focused on her sitting on the floor. "Get out," he said to the small human who was standing in the doorway trying to see around the centaur's hind quarters. When the door didn't immediately close, Pholus swung himself around and nearly knocked the man through the wall with his tail. The innkeeper held up his hands as he swiftly backed from the room, pulling the door with him. "Are you alright," Pholus asked, turning back to Mera.

Mera looked up at him. "I don't know."

"Ok, let's get you up." He reached down and began unwinding the cloth from her feet and legs. "How did you get this so twisted around you?"

Mera didn't have an answer. She still wasn't sure what had happened. Fear went up her spine like a chill; it had felt so real. She could still feel the cold of the shadows between the buildings and the light on her face as the dragon's flames flew overhead. He was close. She knew it and wrapped her arms around herself as she began shaking.

"By the gods, young one, you are not alright, are you?" He took the blanket he had just unraveled from her finally-free legs and wrapped it around her shoulders before picking her up from the floor and placing her on the bed. She had not had anyone pick her up since she was...actually, she didn't remember anyone ever picking her up, though she was sure her mother must have when she was a babe.

"Thank you. Thank you for coming for me."

"Do you want to talk about it?"

"I'm not sure what there is to say, honestly. I have nightmares. They are always about a dragon. I am always stuck somewhere and can't get away from him. This time, I was here, in this city, running between buildings, trying to find an open door, so I could hide.

Everything was sealed shut. The dragon flew overhead and released a blast of fire. I could feel the heat of the flames and the sky was bright as morning. It was all so real. The shadows grabbed for me, and I ran. My lungs were burning."

"You said, you were in the city this time. Where are you normally in these dreams?"

"I only recently started having them again, though my family says I had them when I was younger. That is why the village had their memories erased, to protect everyone from my nightmares."

"Wait, I feel like there is much Callisto did not tell me when she left you in my care."

"I'm not sure she knows it all. I'm positive I don't know it all. What I do know is that in every nightmare, the dragon is coming for me. I don't know what he wants, but I can feel him searching for me. I still feel like he's coming now, and I'm awake."

"Perhaps it was the newness of the city. You were overwhelmed by it all last night when we arrived. Let's explore it in daylight today and see if we cannot dispel some of the unknown."

"I'm not sure that will work, as my usual nightmares were of a place I didn't even remember existing, but I would love to see this city of yours." If she were being honest, she would've said how she wanted to stay hidden inside forever, possibly burrowed inside of the small wardrobe on the wall. Instead, she turned her mind's eye toward the wonders of the city.

He laughed. "This is not my city, young one, but it is one of the closest large cities to where I reside. I usually come here for supplies or send my wards here for supplies once a month. It would help for you to know this place."

"Where do you live? Where are we going?"

"I don't want anyone overhearing, lest we have unwanted guests, but I will tell you once we've left the city." She nodded. That made sense to her. He said he was a bit of a recluse, so it would make sense that he didn't want others just showing up.

"I think you may have scared the life out of the innkeeper. Will we be staying another night? I'm not sure he'd be too happy with that."

"He, like all innkeepers, are happy with coin. He will be fine, but we will not be staying. I prefer to leave as the sun is setting. Others are less likely to follow us into the night, and those who do are always an enemy."

"I'm sorry for waking you."

"I don't sleep late. Wash and get ready. We'll do some exploring." He got up and opened the door. "Are you alright now?"

"Now that I'm awake, yes." She couldn't shake the feeling of something searching for her, but she wouldn't have him thinking her crazy. She remembered her grandmother's face, and her own heart, when Phialyra admitted to still hearing the dragon's call after all these years. No, she would mind her own internal battles. Pholus bowed to her and left the room, pulling the door quietly behind him.

Mera didn't know why this nightmare kept such a grip on her, but the excitement of exploring the city would be a welcome distraction. She quickly washed in the basin and donned her robes. She stood for a moment remembering the feeling of her legs being wrapped in the nightmare and then looked toward the bed, reminding herself that it was just the bedclothes.

Chapter Seventeen

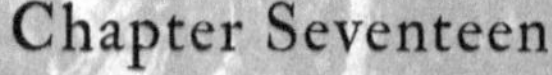

Mera gawked at the church with its colorful and multi-shaped window panes. "Those are beautiful. They make images, but images of what, Great Pholus?"

"I don't know, for I know nothing of these gods and their churches beyond what I told you last night. I imagine they are similar to the images your history lesson have taught about the ancient gods."

"The most we have are images painted on parchment and skins. This is something extraordinary. Do you think I could see inside?"

"I have never been inside, but I don't fit inside everywhere. You may try, but do not tarry. There's still much to see of the city before we depart."

Mera didn't wait for him to finish his admonition before she bounded up the stairs and into the open hall of wooden seats. She didn't know what to expect, but she was struck by how shadowy the interior of the church looked...and felt. There was a coldness to it that she expected of the Greek temples and their marble pillars, entries, and floors the elders described in their lessons. From the outside, particularly with all of the intricately placed windows, she expected far more light, more warmth from the sun, but the sun didn't penetrate here. The doors closed behind her.

Come inside, child, find your place here.

Mera looked around quickly trying to find the source of the voice that appeared more in her head than coming through her ears. She had not ventured too far inside the building, and there was no one standing around or seated on the rear benches when she had arrived. There was nothing but an abundance of candlelight flickering from behind the pillars to her right until he stepped out of the shadow.

He was a man not much taller than Kari with a light hunch in his back. Mera could see that his robe expanded behind him, though it moved far more than she would have expected for a satyr or other forest creature she was familiar with. His ashen face and head were shadowed as if he had removed all of his hair at once and it was forcing its way back through the skin. His eyes were small and dark, the color of burnt wood after a lightning strike. Everything about him reminded Mera of the remnants of a fire.

"Be not frightened. You are welcome here. We accept all visitors, though they be but few."

"I'm sorry I did not see you there and was startled." Mera's calm response belied the bristling of the hairs on her arms and the increase in her heartbeat. Though his welcome remained warm and inviting, there was a distinct difference between the voice coming from his mouth and the one she'd heard in her head, a difference she could not put into words.

"Be not worried, child. I forget that the shadows hide my presence, as I am always here and often shadowed. Have you come to speak to the God of Light?"

"God of light? Is that the patron of this, I believe its called, church?" Mera found herself looking around as the shadows appeared to move more than just with the flicker of candle flames.

"Yes, did you not notice all of our beautiful windows allowing the light to pierce this space and concentrate on the altar? Have you yet approached the altar?"

A shiver went down Mera's back as the man...was he a man... approached her, gesturing toward the front of the church beyond the wooden benches. She, again, thought she saw the shadows move out of the corner of her eyes as she focused on the altar. Someone was kneeling there, and Mera felt relieved to know she wasn't alone with this person from the shadows.

"Come. The altar is a beautiful testament to the God of Fire," the acolyte said as he ushered her away from the door.

"Fire? I thought you said this was the church of the God of Light," Mera asked, pulling herself up straight and stopping mere feet from the person knelt before the altar. From her spot in the aisle, she could see the pinpoints of light from the colorful windows coming together to create a flame in the middle of the altar. The person kneeling stood, and Mera could make out a very feminine shape within a thin, hooded robe that seemed to caress her skin as a waterfall grazes a mountain side. As the hooded figure turned toward them on the aisle, Mera saw the shadows she'd been watching flicker and float toward the person until they spread out around her in the shape of wings.

"Welcome, young one." The woman's voice spread over Mera like cool water on a hot day. She could feel the sun's heat while she and her cousins played along the rivers edge before diving into the cool waters. She smiled before she felt the undertow pulling her down in the daydream as her feet moved forward in the church. "When my shadows said you'd arrived last evening, that they'd felt your presence in the city, I almost didn't believe them. I had not thought to meet you yet and definitely not here."

Mera returned to herself when she was standing within an arms' length of the woman. "Do I know you?"

"No, my pet, you do not, but I've known of you for years now." Again, Mera felt the cold seep into her skin and shivered.

She wanted to run, but her legs were frozen to that spot. The woman's voice was warm, seductive, and yet icicles were forming in her breath.

"Who...no, what are you?"

The woman reached up gloved hands and pushed her hood back to reveal an ashen face similar to the shadow man's. Hers, though, was beautiful where his had been disquieting. She had golden eyes rimmed with red, eyes that seemed familiar as a memory she could not grasp. Unlike the man, her head was crowned in a series of horns from the longest in the middle to shortest near her temples. Each horn looked dipped first in black and then in red, as a volcano mid eruption. Mera imagined a river of magma deep within the woman, flames aching to reach up to the sky and cover her in ash. Behind the crown flowed a thick mane of red and black hair that reached to her waist in cascades of fire.

"I am Yevondra, Mistress of Shadows, and chief priestess to the God of Fire. It is a pleasure to meet you, Maenad."

Mera's heart pounded in her chest. The shadowy wings moving behind the priestess gave the appearance of fireflies as the light from the altar flickered in the spaces between each feather, though they were not feathers. The wings were made of individual shadows, shadows that had been stalking around the church since Mera entered through the door. Remembered Pholus was right outside, she turned toward the entry only to find the shadow man directly behind her, his eyes flickering like the altar flame.

"You already know Mingus. He is an acolyte of Sizzsear and my faithful servant." The acolyte smiled at her, and Mera noticed the jagged edges of his teeth and the darkness around the inside of his lips.

"I have to go." Mera made to move around Mingus without looking back at the priestess.

"So soon? Did you not come to learn about the God of Fire?"

Yevondra's words didn't come across as a question, and Mera, again, looked toward the door willing Pholus to step inside and find her. "Come now, there is plenty of time for you to find your destiny."

Mera turned back toward the priestess. "I wanted to see the pretty windows, just the pretty windows." Her voice squeaked as she blurted out the first thought she had that might break the spell holding her still. Yevondra smiled.

"Of course you did. The thing with windows and doors is that they both invite you in and keep you isolated from others. Much like fire that touches the outside and yet completely alters all that is within. Such is the touch of the God of Fire." Yevondra reached her hand out toward Mera's shoulder at the same time the front door flew open and the deep resonance of Pholus' voice calling her name came through along with the sunlight. Yevondra hissed as the shadow wings behind her broke apart and flitted to the far back corners of the church.

"I really must go," Mera said, first to the priestess and then to Mingus. "I'm coming," she yelled toward the open door. Mera's eyes widened, though she did not stop, when Mingus bowed his head and moved to the side to let her pass.

"I will see you again soon, Maenad."

Mera had to stop herself from running out the door at the priestess' ominous goodbye. As it was, she couldn't help but run down the stairs to reach up and hug the unsuspecting centaur when she finally exited the church.

"Gods, is everything all right, young one?"

Mera let him go and turned back toward the church. Both doors were wide open, and she could clearly see all the way to the altar, with its brightly lit interior. She blinked multiple times and then turned back toward him. "Yes, I'm just glad you called me out. I guess I lost track of time."

"You weren't in there that long, but I felt that you would also like to see other parts of the city in the time we have here." He must've read the question on her face because he followed up with "I just saw you standing there in the middle not doing anything, so

I called you out. You're welcome to return inside if there was something that had caught your eye."

She looked back up at the church and watched humans enter and exit. No one had entered or exited while she was inside. She never heard or saw the door reopen until Pholus called for her. There was no way he could not have seen Mera standing there with the priestess and acolyte when the door opened. She shuddered at the memory. "No, we can go elsewhere now."

They explored the city from one end to the other, walking through the man-made parks where groups of people congregated in open fields. She felt the now familiar sting of homesickness, as she watched various families, both human and forest folk, who had come to live in the city. She'd barely been gone a week and was missing her family terribly, as if it had been months already.

She wished Kari was there to wonder about the beautiful glass and crane her neck to see the tops of these buildings. Mera longed for her grandmother's wisdom and strength. She twisted the ring on her finger in the same way her grandmother did. She'd begun doing that whenever she thought of the matriarch, and it brought her comfort. She hoped her mother was standing strong against the dragon's call and wondered whether Eirini would remember her by the time she returned. She was here for them, to protect them. How sad that she was also here, following the centaur around, to protect them from herself.

Thinking of Pholus brought her back to the present where they had stopped in front of the tallest tower at the heart of the city.

"Do you know what this tower is?" he asked.

"No," she said looking up at its fully-windowed height. She wondered whether the windows were either shadowed or covered in some way because the walls looked like solid sheets of reflective stone. "What is it? Is it somewhere important?"

"What kind of feeling do you get from this building?"

There was a coldness that came from the building itself. "Well, it feels very cold and imposing. It is beautiful in a way, but it almost makes me uncomfortable, like I don't belong here." Of course, she thought to herself, she had been feeling like she didn't belong here the entire day, so she didn't necessarily trust those feelings.

"This building is where the leaders of the region come together and make decisions meant to benefit the people of the this city and other towns in the area. Generally, though, I think the only people that are benefited from these meetings are the people inside the building. You've seen the disparity between the town we came from where we met and the city, as well all villages in between. In my mind, decisions that were meant to support everyone in the area, would have reduced some of those disparities."

"I see what you're saying. So who runs this place? Is it like our council meetings? My grandmother runs those, as she's our Matriarch, but there are other family leaders on the council as well."

"Well, on that small scale, that would be the equivalent of the village elders in the small village that we passed yesterday. In those cases, members of the community are generally on equal footing and come together to try to support each other as best as possible to help support the community. When it comes to towns and larger cities, the size of the council doesn't change, but the number of people they are meant to represent changes significantly. Then you take into account here, where those who come together meet to discuss the needs of the region, you have even more people represented by fewer leaders. Somewhere along the lines, somebody gets left out."

"So how do they determine who the leaders are?"

"That is a great question," he said, and she sensed something in his voice that told her he did not approve. "The majority of the leaders who will come to this place to make decisions, belong to the different religions or different churches that we have walked past. They claim to represent their congregations all over the areas, but they really just tend to make decisions based on what will bring more people, money, and power to their specific church."

Mera thought that sounded very selfish, but before she could say anything, she was reminded of her experience in the church this morning. She still hadn't told Pholus what happened because she was no longer sure it actually happened. Everything in the city seemed so normal, well, as normal as a place this large with this many different creatures could be. Pholus began walking away from the building, and she was not upset about leaving. The place did make her uncomfortable.

"Great Pholus, I have a question about these churches." He turned to look at her with a raised eyebrow. "I know you said that they are different from the way my people still venerate those of the ancient pantheons, where we had gods and goddesses who reigned over many different things that we find in the world. Of course, we forest folk follow Dionysus, but we also venerate Artemis as the goddess of the hunt, right. We don't necessarily just look to one god all the time." He leaned his head a little further to the side, so she continued. "When I started having nightmares again, the elders told me about other gods they sought out to help when my nightmares first started many years ago. That doesn't even include my father and all the gods of his pantheon."

He snorted, turned away and started walking again. Undeterred, Mera followed him, quickening her strides to match his. "You said that the churches here are generally built to worship one god, sometimes the same god that the people here call by different names. I'm not sure I understand that at all."

"You are full of questions this morning, young one..." Before he could say more, they heard a voice calling his name. At first, it sounded like a whisper because it was squeaky, almost as if a mouse were calling for him. The voice grew louder until finally footsteps to accompanied the voice.

"Master Pholus. Master Pholus!"

They both turned to see what appeared to be a young boy running toward them.

"Master Pholus, I didn't expect to see you here."

"Hello, Gery."

As the boy got closer, Mera realized this was not a boy at all. He was quite small like a human boy, but he wore a full beard, had a bold, bulbous nose, and large cheeks that looked like he was always smiling. No one could possibly frown with cheeks that large. "What are you?" Mera asked aloud before she could stop herself.

Pholus looked at her and shook his head before Gery turned to her, finally noticing she was there.

"What am I?" he mimicked with that squeaky voice that matched his size. "What am I? Who asks such a rude question like that? My name is Gericole, and I am a gnome from a long line of gnomes. I serve as the right hand of Master Pholus here."

His indignation almost overpowered Mera's sense of guilt and embarrassment.

"I'm sorry," she said. "I feel like I have no idea what is happening in the world I live in. I have never known any creatures outside of my forest except for having heard of the great Pholus before I met him. Though I do vaguely remember hearing about gnomes in our lessons, I've never seen one before. I do apologize. You're right, that was very rude of me."

"Don't do it again. It is bad enough that we live here in this big city that is run mostly by humans. We are either treated like second-class citizens if we don't live in a big house, or ignored altogether even if we do. So we don't need outsiders looking down on us too!"

"Ok, Gery," Pholus intervened. "She has never been outside of the forest."

"The forest?" he asked. "Which forest?"

"The Tribunal Forest," she responded. "I lived there my whole life, or at least I thought I had. I just recently learned that many things I thought I knew were actually not true. It's been a very long and strange couple of weeks."

"So, do you have a name?" Gery asked.

"My name is Skyemera, but my friends and family call me Mera."

"Then I will call you Skyemera."

She did laugh at him this time. Gery scowled, which made her laugh even harder because of his ever-smiling cheeks. He turned away from her and began updating Pholus on all that had been happening since he left the training grounds. Pholus still hadn't told Mera anything about where they were going, other than it is where he sometimes trains others who need his help.

"Gery," she interjected, "How did you manage to find us here in the city? This place is huge."

It was his turn to laugh now. "I come from this place," he said. "This is where Pholus found me and gave me my job. I used to run the streets all the time, and now I only come here for business. But, as you probably know, there are not many centaurs around anymore, so word gets out pretty easily when Master Pholus is in town.

"Oh, that makes sense."

"Mera," Pholus said, drawing their attention. "Before Gery found us, you were going to ask me something."

"Oh yeah, I was wondering about the different churches here and the religions."

"We have a multitude of churches here," Gery answered, not giving Pholus a chance to speak. "Some of the humans have churches to their one god, and others attend those churches too, but even some of the humans also attend the other churches. It is interesting to watch the different groups go in and out of the different churches on different days."

"Old habits of worshiping multiple gods are hard to break," Pholus jumped in when Gery took a breath. "Some of the most powerful, or rather popular gods here, are the elemental ones."

"Elemental gods," Mera asked.

Gery took a deep breath as if preparing to give a long answer, and Pholus stopped him. "Relax, Gery. Again, she is new to all of this, so you do not have to drown her in information."

The gnome nodded, but Mera could tell that he was slightly disappointed at not being able to share everything about his city.

"The elemental gods," Pholus turned to her, "are said to be older than our ancient pantheons. They are said to hold the power of the four elements, earth, wind, water, and fire. So while our gods reign over many things, including the winds, like Aeolus, these gods are told to be masters over their specific element with no one being strong than the other."

As he was speaking, Mera could see Gery bouncing with excitement. Pholus must have noticed this too because he motioned for Gery to share.

"I can't say that I believe in these elemental gods, but I can tell you that the stories about them are very interesting. If you go from one of the churches to the other, to another, to the last," he repeated with a wave of his hands, "you will hear the same story but with a slightly different perspective. So if you let them tell it in the church of the God of Water, water is the most important element there is. If you then go to the church of the God of Earth, they will tell you that all things grow from the earth, and therefore, their god is the most important and strongest..."

"What do you know about the God of Fire?" Mera asked, stopping his redundant story.

"The God of Fire? Why do you specifically want to know about the God of Fire?" Gery's demeanor had turned serious, though Mera wasn't sure why because surely he was going to mention that god anyway. She just wanted him to get to the point.

Mera looked around to see if anyone else was watching them as they walked or close enough to overhear their conversation. "Something happened this morning," she started, and Pholus stopped in his tracks to look at her. She took a deep breath to ground herself. "Something happened while I was inside that church this morning." Her voice sounded much weaker than she expected it to be.

Pholus continued to stare at her, his brows furrowed. "Go on," he said.

"Please don't be upset with me, Great Pholus. When I came out of the church, everything seemed so normal that I wasn't really sure anything happened at all. I thought I imagined it. Now that Gery is describing these elemental gods, I'm beginning to think that maybe something did happen, though I'm not exactly sure what it was."

"What church did you all go to this morning," Gery asked, his question more to Pholus than her, but she answered anyway.

"Oh, I don't know the name of it, but it had very pretty windows that were colorful and made pictures. I really wanted to see what they looked like from the inside."

"It was in the East Division," Pholus said, "the church with the tallest spire. She had noticed it from the cliff when we first came in last night. So, I thought that it would be good to take her to see it up close."

"The church with the tall spire," Gery asked, his already squeaky voice pitching higher. "That is a human church to their one god. What does that have to do with the God of Fire?"

"I don't know," Mera said, "but that is where I learned about the God of Fire, and by learned, I mean heard of him."

"That's enough," Pholus said forcefully. "Let's find somewhere to sit and talk where we can be very mindful of who is around. This is not a conversation that we want to have out in the open."

"Did I do something wrong," Mera asked.

"If you're saying that you learned about the God of Fire inside a human church..." Gery trembled like a chill went up his back, and he shook his head. "There are no churches to the God of Fire allowed in this city."

Chapter Eighteen

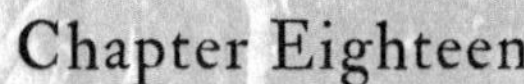

Pholus led them twenty minutes away to a wide open square on the southeast side of the city.

"Great Pholus, I thought you were looking for somewhere more private?" Mera asked.

"Master Pholus said somewhere we could control who overhears what. If we are in an open space, the only ones who could eavesdrop without us knowing are the birds."

Mera nodded, though she still didn't quite understand why the secrecy or why it would be fine to discuss the other gods out in the open but not this one. Similarly, why would a city ban churches to a specific god if they allow open worship to many others?

"I can see by your expression that you have lots of questions, young one. Before we address those questions, let us hear what you imagined happening this morning," Pholus demanded.

"Well, I went into the church and was immediately surprised by how dark it was inside." She was watching Pholus's face and didn't see anything in his expression change, so she continued. "There was no one inside that I could see except for one person kneeling near the altar. A man's voice invited me to come further inside. The thing was, though, that I heard the voice in my head rather than with my ears."

"Interesting," Gery said.

"When I turned toward the shadowed corner, a small man, at least I think he was a man, emerged, telling me not to be afraid. His face was gray, and he had a bald head that had black blotches all around it like his hair had been burnt off. It was difficult to look at him. He appeared to be covering some large hump that moved on his lower back."

This time, she did see Pholus' head come up, and his gaze became more intense. He looked around, prompting Mera to do a sweep of the square as well. When he said nothing, and she saw nothing, she continued. "As the man, I believe his name was Mingus, was talking to me, I thought I saw the shadows dancing in the candlelight. They seemed to follow us when he lead me toward the altar at the rear of the building."

"Mingus," Gery said with a perplexed expression. "I've not heard that name before."

"They said he was an acolyte..."

"An acolyte to the human god?"

"No, to the God of Fire."

Pholus had again been looking around at the alleyways that surrounded the square when his eyes snapped back to her. "He told you that."

"No, the priestess who had been kneeling at the altar did."

"Priestess?" Gery squeaked, and he turned to look at Pholus. "This cannot be good."

"No, Gery, this cannot be good." Pholus turned all of his attention on Mera. "What did this priestess do?"

"When she rose from the altar, it was as if the shadows came to her, collecting at her back like wings. I thought it was just the candlelight playing with my imagination." They both shook their heads at her, and a shiver ran down Mera's back. Should she tell them how beautiful the priestess was or how hard it was to turn away from her gaze?

"She told you the acolyte's name, but did she share hers?" Pholus asked.

"She introduced herself as Yevondra, Mistress of Shadows."

"We have to go," Pholus stated with an urgency that shook Mera to her core.

"Master Pholus, dusk will be upon the city soon."

"Too soon, Gery. Go home and tell Purivia to find us. And..." he continued in a language Mera did not understand. As soon as he finished, Gery disappeared with a pop.

"Wait, where'd he go?"

"We can talk as we move!"

Pholus had already begun making his way down an alley to the right of the square by the time Mera put her pack across her shoulders and followed him. She nearly had to run to catch up.

"What is happening? Why are we running? I don't understand what's going on."

"I don't know what's happening either," Pholus responded, "but I do not want to be here when dusk falls."

"What happens at dusk?"

"Mera, did you not mention shadow demons in your nightmare this morning? Did you not just say that you thought you saw the shadows moving? I don't believe that was your imagination or a coincidence."

"Are you saying those really were shadow demons?"

"If that was truly a priestess of the God of Fire, yes, I do believe those were shadow demons, which means they're here in the city."

Mera was trying very hard not to panic, but her heart raced as images from inside the church replayed in her mind.

"Where did Gery go?" she asked. "I didn't realize gnomes could just disappear like that."

"One of the reasons I chose Gery as my personal assistant is because he has the ability to get from one place to another very quickly to pass messages or collect things that I need. Remember how I told you that sometimes I send others into the city to gather supplies? Well, Gery is the one that I send most often."

"Where did you send him now?"

"I sent him for my weapon and some help." He hadn't turned to look at her, just maintained his quick pace toward the eastern end of the city.

Mera had no response, but if Pholus was worried enough to need a weapon, they might really be in danger. She silently vowed to never enter another church if this would be the outcome.

"Keep up the pace, Mera. We are still quite a while from getting out of the city and away from all these alleys. Keep your eyes open for anything moving that might mean to do us harm. If I say run, you better run."

Mera turned around to look behind her and saw the sun was setting much more quickly to the west than she had noticed when they were in the square talking. She didn't even remember it setting that quickly last night when they first arrived at the city.

"Why does it seem like the sun is setting much faster now?"

"We are talking of the God of Fire, right? Do you not realize that the sun is little more than one large ball of fire?"

"By the gods!" Mera exclaimed.

When they had passed several more intersections, and the sun's light began to dim between the buildings, Pholus turned his head to her. "Mera, tell me about these powers of yours before we have to think about using them?"

"My powers? The only thing I know that I've done is created a tornado that I don't even remember and can't tell you how."

"That's it? I'm going to have a long conversation with Callisto about what she thinks I can and cannot do."

"Callisto did have me grow a tree on the way to the human town. I might be able to do that again, maybe."

"We don't need any more places for shadows to hide right now. What we're going to need is to fight fire with fire."

"Is that even possible?"

Before Pholus could give her an answer, they heard the flapping of wings above them. Pholus looked up and told Mera to run. Just as she was about to lift her hooves, she saw a shadow demon climbing down the building that they were walking next to. Its body was the size of a newborn child, but the way its wings spread from torso to claws made it much larger and reminded her of a bat. The difference between a bat and this thing was that smoky tendrils floated around its edges, as if it wasn't fully formed. When it hissed down at her, showing its mouth full of fanged teeth, Mera froze.

"They're real!" she exclaimed. "I didn't actually think they were real!"

Just then, claws scraped against the building on their other side. Pholus grabbed her hand, pulling her along with him as he picked up the pace to a trot. "Run, Mera! We have to get from between these buildings. On the open plain, there are no places for shadows to hide and regenerate themselves."

Mera screamed and her hand was jerked from Pholus' grasp. One of her own shadows had caught her hoof and was pulling itself up her leg. She tried hitting at it with her fists to no avail. He turned around in the tight alley and ran back to her side. Grabbing the demon by its wings, he pulled the creature apart with his hands before throwing it against the building. He grabbed Mera's hand anew and began to run.

"We have to go faster," he said. "There will soon be too many of them."

The scraping grew louder, and more wings beat above their

heads until the sound was like drumming in Mera's ears. She wanted to hide and curl into a ball on the ground. She wished she was back home and could go hide beneath the gnarled oaks of the sea. Instead, she was stuck there in the open alley of a strange city with the sun going down and Pholus pulling on her hand. She heard him grunt as one of the demons climbed onto his back. He reached around trying to swat it off, but its claws had dug in. Pholus howled at the grooves being cut into his skin.

"Get off me!"

Mera didn't know what to do. She didn't have a weapon. She didn't even know how to fight. She was supposed to start learning during her fifteenth year; instead, it was her twentieth, and she had missed her window of opportunity. She felt the panic rising in her throat like bile. Suddenly, she heard a loud pop and then a screech from the demon on Pholus' back as it went flying and hit the side of the wall. Gery was there with a hammer of sorts in his hand.

"Stupid shadow demon. Stupid, stupid shadow demons are not allowed in my city!"

From behind her, Mera heard what sounded like an arrow's thwump before flares of light bloomed around them.

"Run, Skyemera, and don't stop running," Gery screamed at her.

"Gery, go with her."

"What do I look like, a babysitter?"

"Go!"

"Fine, fine. I'm going."

"And grab her some kind of weapon, a stick or something!"

The last thing Mera heard from Pholus sounded like a call to someone else. "Purivia, let's light this place up and give us safe passage out of the city." Then she heard more arrows. Thwump. Thwump. Thwump.

"Gery, should we really be leaving him alone," she asked when Gery caught up to her with a pop. "What if he needs some help?"

"He has help." Pop. "I brought him help." Pop "Much more

help than we have." Pop. "Here, take this," Gery said as he threw her a short but sturdy tree branch. He continued to pop in and out as he gave her instructions. "If one of those demons gets close enough, start swinging that thing, but keep running!"

Mera was impressed with his ability to keep up with her, even if it meant popping in and out of the alley.

You cannot run from the shadows, Maenad.

"Did you hear that," Mera asked.

"All I hear...is my heartbeat inside my ears...and my breathing picking up...because we are running. I would rather just teleport out of here, but I cannot leave you, so keep running." His breath was labored, but he continued popping around to stay by Mera's side.

The light continued to grow, and before long, there were flaming arrows sticking out of the buildings on both sides of the alley. The arrows were now in front of her instead of just behind her.

You will not escape the shadows, Maenad.

"Run faster!" Pholus' voice came from behind her, breaking through the warning in her head. "The demons are moving ahead of us, ahead of the light. They're going to reach the other side before we can catch up. We will run out of arrows before we get out of this alley."

Mera looked up at the swarming shadows moving along the tops of the buildings far above the light. They were moving so fast, clinging to the buildings' sides too far away for her to have heard their scraping but not far enough for her to miss the shroud of darkness they created above.

There were so many, she internally screamed.

"We're almost through the tallest buildings. There will be fewer shadows once we get out of this maze," Pholus yelled over the sound of the whirling demons above and the flame on each side of them.

The noise of their beating wings began to drown out the

thwump thwump of the arrows, and then Mera saw her. The cloaked figure of Yevondra stood at the end of the alleyway, and Mera stopped running. She still hadn't fully convinced herself that the morning's event was real, and now here the priestess was standing in front of them.

"I told you that you could not outrun the shadows," Yevondra said aloud, so all could hear her.

Next to Mera stood Pholus and Gery, and someone else that Mera did not recognize. They must have been the one helping Pholus because they had a bow in their hands and an arrow already strung up.

"How many arrows do you have left," Pholus asked, his voice quieter than normal.

"This is my last one," the stranger said in response. "I could direct it at her."

Though she was focused on Yevondra, Mera heard Gery's retort. "They said she is a priestess of the God of Fire. What in the gods would make you think about sending that flame to her? What do you think she's going to do, pick her teeth? No! She's going to send it back and burn us all!"

"If she were going to burn us all, she probably would have done it already, silly gnome," the stranger responded.

"Who are you calling silly? Do you see all those shadow demons? They're not going to let you get any closer to her with that arrow."

"They have been running from the fire all this time. They will continue to run from the flames themselves. They are shadow demons, not flame demons."

"Enough," Pholus said, interrupting their argument. "We will use that arrow, but we will use it when I say."

Mera watched as the shadow demons circled around Yevondra and settled into place as the wings on her back. When she lifted off the ground, the group let out a collective gasp, and Mera felt frozen in place much like she had in the church. She wasn't sure what would happen now because she didn't know what might've happened had Pholus not called for her through the open door. The gods knew she wasn't even sure how that door got opened in the first place.

"Sizzsear, The God of Fire, has business with the young maenad. How very nice of you all to bring her to him, or at least to bring her to me, so I can deliver her. Come, Maenad, we have business to attend to, and we have wasted enough time now with this cat and mouse game."

Mera felt herself being pulled forward, though she wanted to stay as far away from the priestess as possible. The last thing she wanted was for those demons to grab her and lift her up into the sky. She turned her head from left to right as if trying to find an exit. Her nightmares were coming true, and she had no way of stopping them.

Pholus put his hand on her shoulder. "We are going to get out of here," he said decisively, though his voice was kept low. The weight of his hand and strength of his conviction bolstered her resolve.

"I'm not going anywhere with you," she yelled.

Yevondra broke into a laugh. It was an evil and yet seductive laugh that again made Mera question the powers this woman had.

"You do not have a choice. We are in the time of shadows, and the shadows answer to me. I answer to the God of Fire, and soon all will answer his call."

"Get ready, Purivia. When I say loose, run as fast as you can, and swing with all your might. We simply have to get out of this alley into the open."

"What am I aiming for, Master Pholus?"

"Aim...Aim for...Aim for one of her wings."

Mera felt his indecision, and she understood his misgivings. "They are not really wings. They are demons. If they hide from the fire, then they will scatter, leaving her in place. I don't know what she can do, but she can't fly without them."

"Are you sure?" the archer, Purivia, asked. "If I only hit one of them and that demon falls, the flame will stay with that demon."

"We will be running as soon as you loose that arrow," Pholus interjected. "Hopefully, we will get there while they're distracted and can knock as many out of place as possible."

"What if I start running first?" Mera asked. "What if I act like I'm going to sacrifice myself and get close enough to distract her?"

"That's a stupid idea," Gery squeaked. "If you get close enough to those demons, they are going to grab you up and take off with you, but do what you want."

"What other options do we have?" Mera countered. "You somehow flashed out of the city and back again with someone else, and yet you haven't offered to pop us all out of here. There must be a reason, so what else are we supposed to do?" She looked pointedly at each of them.

"You're beginning to waste my time now, Maenad. Your fires will only last so long, and then we will have you anyway. Better to save your friends and come along with us. We will leave, and they will be left to go on about their lives." She was still hovering above the ground, but she had not come any closer to the group.

"Do you promise that you won't hurt them?" Mera asked, turning back toward Yevondra.

"You have my word. The God of Fire's business is with you, not with them. But if you continue to waste my time, and we have to come in there after you, then I make no promises about your friends."

"Keep your demons off of me. I don't want them touching me. I will come, but I don't want them touching me."

"Very well." Yevondra said something in a language Mera did not understand, and Mera watched the demons on the building lift higher above the alley, almost creating an archway for Mera to walk through. It could've easily been an archway of flowers that Mera had seen her people use multiple times, as nymphs like her came of age. She nearly broke into tears at the thought of how she had missed her chance for that now. She wasn't walking into the next phase of her life. She felt like she was walking into the end of it.

Holding the stick Gery had given her in both hands, Mera willed her hooves to move forward. Behind her, she heard the arrow being lit. "Please fly true," she whispered under her breath. Mera was halfway under the arch of demons. Although the priestess had promised they would not touch her, Mera kept watching and waiting for one of them to grab for her. Suddenly, she heard the familiar thwump of the arrow's release as the mass of demons writhed above her head.

The demons screeched and beat their wings as they broke formation. The flapping came closer, and she felt claws in her hair. She swung her stick in all directions, knocking away ten of the beasts before one pulled it free from her hands. She cried out in indignation. Her fear and anger coalescing into a thrumming in her chest. Then, as the winged creatures descended to grab her, a sudden gust of wind circled around Mera, emanating from her, and catching the flame from the arrow. The flame burst wide in all directions between Skyemera and the priestess, filling the width of the alley's opening, catching the demons. They screamed and tried to fly away. The more they beat their wings, the more they caught the wind, and the more the fire grabbed them. In a flash, the demons that had been blocking the alley disappeared, and though Mera struggled to get her bearings, she could hear Yevondra screaming at the end of the alley. The Queen of Shadows was screaming for her demons. As the winds continued pushing the flames forward toward her, the demons on her back detached, depositing the woman back on the ground. She turned toward the alley and lifted her hands.

Still in the trance of her powers, Mera was only vaguely aware of her companions. She felt Pholus grab her in his arms and start running. She heard Gery's hammer hitting what must've been demons because the thud was sickening. Then there was a pop.

"Control the wind, Mera. Control the wind and push it out of the alley. Push it out in front of us."

Mera heard Pholus' voice, much like she had heard her grandmother and Kari singing, like she had heard Callisto guiding her to choose the outcome of her powers. She heard his voice, and she felt for the wind just like she had felt for the root with Callisto leading her. She called for it to spin and travel forward as a shield. She willed the gust to pick up the flames and push them outward, so her friends would not be caught in the inferno.

Unlike the uncontrolled fury that took over her powers back in the Thicket, leaving her confused and full of adrenaline, this unpracticed control drained her. She would not be able to hold onto the wind for much longer. As her energy slipped, she was grateful to still be held in Pholus' arms, cradled like a doll. When she felt him rear up on his back legs and then felt his front legs come up underneath of her kicking at whatever was in front of them, dizziness nearly consumed her. Still, by sheer will, she pushed the wind forward, afraid they wouldn't make it to safety. How were they not out of the alley yet? How many more paces did they still need to run?

She wasn't sure how much longer they had fought to escape. She couldn't tell whether her wind had managed to stave off the demons. Her eyes felt like lead, but the silence jolted her from the exhaustion threatening to pull her under. She opened them to look up at a clear sky. In the wide-open prairie, there were no shadows. There was no fire. Her wind had dissipated. Pholus put her on the ground, and she took deep, steadying breaths.

"You did well, young one. You got us out of there."

With her hand on his side for support, Mera moved to look behind him at the city. She could see the outline of wings flapping above the ground where the buildings stood. Flames littered the ground on what must have been shadow demons that had fallen in the inferno. She could see the outline of the priestess floating in the air.

You will not be so lucky nor will my invitation be so nice next time. Mera would never get used to hearing the priestess' voice in her head. She took a deep breath and turned to Pholus.

"Thank you for not leaving me there alone."

And then she collapsed in sobs.

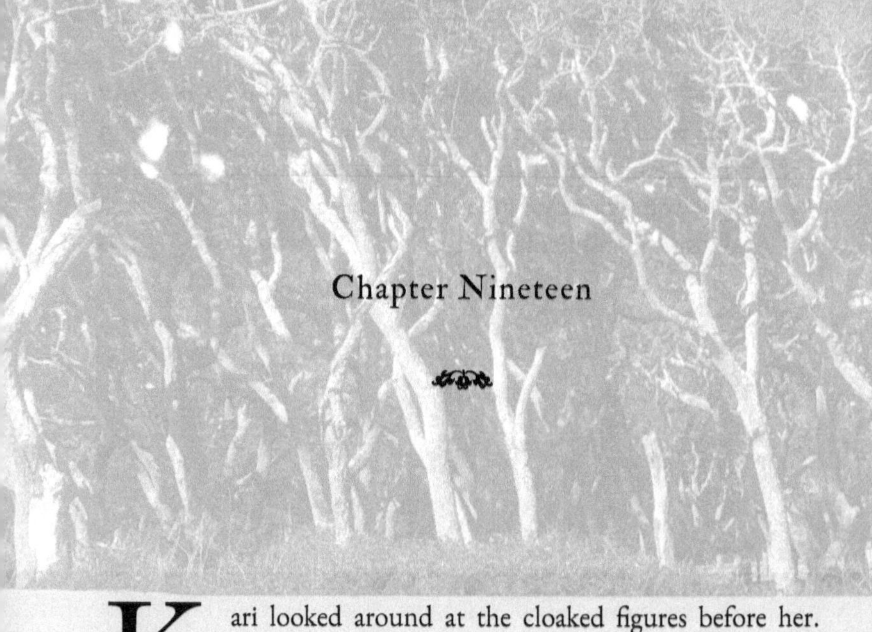

Chapter Nineteen

K ari looked around at the cloaked figures before her. Only two of them had visible weapons, and three of them were taller than her.

"Talk to me about what you're thinking, Kari," Eustis yelled from the edge of the field. Eustis was one of The Thicket's most capable protectors, so it was a surprise when Helena told Kari that she would be combat training with her. Usually Eustis was out patrolling in The Grove or training other guardians to protect The Thicket.

"Seven of them is a lot," Kari called out.

"Yes, but do you think that if there's an invasion, they're going to count the odds in your favor?"

"No, but I did maybe think that as a practice exercise, it might be comparable to what my mind and body was ready to deal with."

"The gods know, Kari, that if talking down your opponents could win a war, you would have won it before it started."

Kari giggled and thought of how often Mera had teased her about talking constantly. She wondered how her cousin's training was going. Had she gotten to the place where she would be training yet? Weeks had passed since Mera left The Thicket, and Kari had been training consistently from day one with Helena. She wouldn't say she'd gotten good or anything, but she at least knew how to hold a staff and to call a swarm of butterflies.

"Focus Kari," Eustis called. "What are you thinking should be your first step?"

"So, what I see right now," Kari said, coming back to the present, "is there are seven of them."

"Yes..." Eustis gestured for Kari to continue.

"Three of them are taller than me, but I don't see any weapons. I don't know what they might do. Two of them are my height and look to be about my size. If I knew how to fight better, I could probably beat them...or at least put up enough of a struggle to try and get away." She laughed at herself and the image of distracting them with butterflies. "Two of them have obvious weapons," she continued after getting herself back under control. "They're about my height, so they could be strong opponents, but at least I know what I'm dealing with. If they're holding those weapons with purpose, at least I know the type of fighting needed to beat them. I can watch those weapons."

"So what are you going to do first? Who are you going to engage?"

Kari looked back at the group of hooded figures. "I'm going to engage the ones with the weapons first. I know what I'm dealing with, and if I can get them out of the way, that reduces the number against me. It also gives me the chance to get additional weapons if I don't have any by my side."

"Good, and then who would you engage next," Eustis asked, moving onto the field and approaching Kari.

"That's a harder one. The three who are my size, are still a higher number than the others. If we were reversed, I would be expecting them to come after those of us who were the same size. I mean, it would make sense to be afraid of those who are bigger. So

I'm going to take out the tall ones." She paused for a moment, reviewing her options. "Yes, I'm going to take my chances with the tall ones over there because there are only two of them." She pointed to the figures in question off to her right. "I don't know what they're fighting with, but I'm hoping it might catch everyone off guard if I engage them first."

"Sound logic. If I told you that the two taller ones were there to provide protective magic over the others, would you change your plan at all?"

"Does this magic protect against other magic, or does it protect against physical harm as well?"

"Now you're thinking. You don't know."

"If I don't know what they do, then I'm going to stay with my original plan." She thought through the scenario again. "If I can somehow tell they are providing protection, like when I bounce off their shields as I'm engaging the others, for example, then I might rethink things a bit. If, however, I have no idea what their purpose is or what they're capable of, I'm sticking to my original strategy, until I learn otherwise."

"Very well." Eustis turned to the cloaked figures. "You may go now, and thank you."

"Do I not even get to see who they are?"

"No. Just know that at some point, they may engage you unexpectedly because what is authentic practice without an element of surprise."

Kari caught the glint in Eustis' eye and began to worry that her tutor was planning something. They both turned at the sound of footsteps. Eckasia, Euonsise's daughter, was running toward them.

"Kari, Helena has need of you near the meeting hall. She said you're to come right away."

"Did something happen?"

"I'm just the messenger. My feet move faster than my mouth," and she took off running again.

Kari turned to Eustis who nodded permission for her to leave.

She ran from the field where they had been training to the meeting house on the opposite side of The Thicket. As she approached the long, wooden building, she saw Helena standing by the door.

"You sent for me," Kari asked between breaths.

Helena turned and smiled at her. "Yes, Karielle. You have been summoned to today's council meeting, and I wanted to…"

Kari's palms began to sweat as Helena's pause lengthened. They were standing outside of the one communal building in The Thicket she had never entered before. Until Mera went there just a few weeks ago, no young nymphs had ever been invited inside.

"Have I done something wrong?" she asked.

"No, child. You have done nothing wrong. In fact, you have done great things."

Kari's brows drew together as she tried to imagine what she'd done good or bad to warrant an invitation.

"Relax your brows and your mind." Helena reached out to rest her hand on Kari's shoulder. "There will be some decisions made today about the preparations we need to begin based on everything that's happened."

Kari knew exactly what Helena meant by preparations. Ever since Mera left The Thicket, they had all been talking about "the preparations." What would they do should the dragon return? What would they do if someone else invaded The Thicket? What could they do to keep their community and their people safe? How would they prepare for the "just in case"?

"The council is considering you for an important role in those preparations. I suggested you hear those considerations directly and be able to share your thoughts."

Kari's eyes went wide. The council made decisions, and the nymphs of The Thicket followed through on those decisions. As if reading her thoughts, Helena continued.

"After much discussion, we have decided that it is no longer fair to make decisions about individuals in the community without their input and full understanding of what they're being asked to do. The return of Mera's nightmares is a perfect example of how this practice was unfair. I want you to know, though…" She gave her granddaughter an admonishing look. "Whatever you hear inside of this building is for your ears only until it has been announced to the community." Kari looked at her for a minute before nodding. "We want you to be honest and thoughtful and truly take into consideration what we will be asking of you. Can you do that?

"I can be honest, yes," Kari said with no hesitation.

"Can you be honest without talking everyone's ear off?"

Kari looked at her with a bit of a quiver in her lip, and Helena smiled. They both laughed.

"Come, let's go inside."

Kari didn't know what to expect when she walked inside the meeting house, but she definitely did not expect to see Phialyra with the baby or other mothers of younger children from the community. Helena must have understated the changes the council had been making. The room was so full that Kari had to sit on the bare ground right beside the entrance door.

"Welcome, Karielle," Dynami said with a smile. "We are sorry to have called you from your combat training, but we thought it important for you to be here for this part of our conversation. You will notice that we have additional visitors today as well." The Matriarch gestured around the room to everyone seated against the walls. "We thought it important for you all to be here because what we are about to discuss today will affect you and your young children."

Helena spoke up then. "We ask that everyone in attendance not share anything that is discussed here with anyone outside of this hall until an announcement has been made to the full community. We have some decisions to make, but then we must also have some explicit plans for how to implement those decisions before we start sharing. Can you all agree to that?"

Each of the nymphs in the room raised her open left palm to the sky like the trees of the forest to gesture their agreement.

Dynami nodded in acceptance of their gesture. "I know many of you have questions, but please hold them until you have heard what we have to say. Mother," The Matriarch said, with an open palm addressing the eldest of the community leaders.

Canea stood at her seat, as there was not much room for walking around the hall. "It has aways been our way," she began, "to begin training our youngest nymphs once they had seen fifteen winters when their magic begins to spark on its own. Events of the recent past have drawn attention to the folly of some of our practices, including this one. It is not that our young nymphs lack magic until their fifteenth winter. It is simply that their magic is easier for them to control in a short period of time at that age."

The elder nymph began to move her hands rhythmically in front of her and above her head. Swirls of smoke formed ringlets and lines, painting pictures in the air. "We are born with magic. We are born from the earth. We are born in the forest and from the forest. Our magic is not something that is simply bestowed upon us by the changing of the seasons."

Kari watched as everyone around the room, including the parents, began to nod in agreement, almost as if they were bewitched by the spectacle.

"Mothers," Kari interjected. "I'm sorry. I'm not sure I understand. Are you saying that I've had magic all along? I have actually had the ability to do magic and nobody told me this?"

She saw Helena cover her face with her hand and shake her head.

Euonsise, the community's premiere grower, spoke up. "Yes. In short, the answer is yes, you have had magic. You'll aways have magic, and that magic just continues to get stronger and more focused as you hone it. We don't always have the same level of ability in each area of our magic, but we all have magic."

Nerin, another of the matriarchs, continued where Euonsise stopped. "Some of us just have a little too much impulsivity to be allowed to run around wildly practicing this magic."

Kari began to glare at the nymph she considered the crankiest of the elders when Helena added, "but this doesn't mean that impulsivity should be the reason young nymphs are taught they don't have magic until they reach a certain age. In fact, it is that same impulsivity that led us to determine how important it is we begin to train our young nymphs at a much younger age than we have been. This way, when their magic comes in, it will not be a danger to them or anyone else in the community. They will already have an idea of what to do when the full strength develops."

Kari's shoulders relaxed, and she sat back with a nod. "I guess that makes sense."

One of the parents from the other side of the room asked, "What does this mean for our children? Why are we here? If our matriarchs have already decided that our children should learn about their magic at a younger age, why do we need to be here for this discussion?" There were murmurs of agreement from the other younger mothers.

Sapharnia, one of the younger and most beautiful of the matriarchs, stood. "Young mothers, we have brought you all here today because of the situation that happened with young Skyemera. We still don't know quite why, but we know that her magic was triggered by strong emotional responses. One thing we do know about our young nymphs is that even before they reach fifteen winters, they are already prone to strong emotional responses for any number of reasons. Of course, due to her nature, and her parentage, Skyemera's magic is understandably stronger than most of ours..."

One of the other mothers sitting just a couple spots away from

Kari cut into her explanation. "What do you mean 'her nature'? What are we saying here? We all know she's different, but what exactly does that mean?"

Kari's eyes immediately turned to her aunt. The way the hair on the back of her own neck bristled at the questions must have been ten times stronger for Lyra. How dare they ask a question like that with Mera's mother in the room?

Lyra, poised as ever, took a deep breath. "Yes, as everyone knows, my Mera is different," she said with a tone that did not allow for interruption. "We didn't know how different other than her physical appearance until recent events. Skyemera's father is the god Bacchus who comes from a pantheon different from our own. Because of her mixed heritage, she has inherited a form and strength beyond anything that has been seen in over a millennium. Skyemera is a maenad, the only maenad."

Collective gasps around the outside of the room brought Kari back from her wandering memories. She remembered the last time she saw Mera and how worried her cousin was about what was happening to her. Kari wouldn't have wished that on anyone.

Dynami spoke then. "Let us continue. Again, Skyemera's powers came in unexpectedly and much later than we initially thought, as she is not a nymph of fourteen winters but a maenad of twenty. The tornado that happened nearly a month ago was just one manifestation of her powers. We are sure that she has more power she is not ready to control."

"Is that why she's been hiding? Are we safe here in The Thicket? That tornado could have torn the whole village apart," came voices from around the room. "Should she even be here?"

"That is enough!" Canea had once again stood from her seat and held her cane in the air to gain everyone's attention. "We are not here to discuss Skyemera's place in this community. She is one of us. She comes from one of our oldest families. But, she is not here. She has been sent to learn her powers, which are far beyond anything we could teach. So there is nothing to concern any of you about her for the moment. The concern now is protecting our young nymphs from themselves and from what might be coming with the dragon's return."

Whispers floated around the room. *Return. What do they mean by return? It was the first time we saw the dragon.*

"We know you have a lot of questions regarding the why behind this conversation," Dynami said, taking back control of the gathering. "There are many announcements to be made to the entire community, rather than small conclaves like the group joined here today. So, let us return to the point of this meeting. What we are proposing is that we begin to introduce our young nymphs to their magic much earlier. We would like input from all of you on what would be a good age. We are thinking ten winters, but we have also had discussions about bringing it back to those who have five winters, of course on a much simpler level."

"Right now, young Karielle has been having individual training and has been doing a wonderful job at honing her magic, though she has not yet met fifteen winters," Helena said. "The gods know, she is stronger at fourteen winters than I was at seventeen." Kari snapped her eyes to Helena who shook her head for quiet. "So many of us begin our training at fifteen, and we don't begin to produce spells for safety until we are well into our eighteenth winter. She can already produce spells that protect her from bodily harm due to physical weapons."

"And I can produce swarms of butterflies too," Kari said under her breath. While Helena's words made her proud, she really didn't think she'd done anything out of the ordinary. Heads turned to look at her and then at each other. She wondered if they also struggled to understand the purpose of her attending the meeting when she was already being trained. She sat on her hands and tried to hold the swell of questions at bay, but the murmurs around the room were more than she could take.

"Yes, I haven't quite seen fifteen winters yet, but I'm already receiving this training. Why was I invited here," Kari blurted to the chagrin of the matriarchs. They all looked like she had caused a storm to blow in during the summer solstice.

After a few moments, Danalise, the other younger council member, stood, smiling warmly at Kari. "You've been invited, young one, because we feel like you would be one of the best supports to help train the younger nymphs. As you are still learning yourself, and still have much left to learn, we don't think you're ready to support those your age or older because their powers are much stronger. We do, however, believe that you have the wherewithal and demeanor to help train our youngest."

Kari couldn't believe what she was hearing. She wasn't a teacher. She didn't even know anything and was still in training herself. How was she supposed to help train others? None of that was making sense. As she thought about it, she began picking at her fingernails. Ever since she was little, she had the nervous habit of picking the skin around her fingernails, sometimes until they bled. Someone sat on the mat next to her that had been vacated the last time the council visitors jumped to their feet.

"This is a good thing. Be proud of yourself. Mera would be so excited for you." Lyra reached over and grabbed Kari's hand.

Kari missed her best friend. Looking into her aunt's eyes, she saw the same emotions mirrored there. Tears stung the back of her own eyes. She nodded and leaned into Lyra who still had the babe tied to her chest.

"All of you in this room have learned and heard much today," Dynami began anew, addressing the now quiet room. "Of course, there are more questions, but what we need are ideas and thoughts. We need your input as mothers and community members. We cannot, and we should not be making these decisions on our own." Kari felt Dynami's eyes drift in their direction, and she looked up. "Recent events have shown us that secrets held amongst a few can be dangerous to the many."

For the next hour, Kari listened, sometimes intently, sometimes barely, to the decisions being made that would affect her drastically. She was going to be a teacher. A teacher, her! None of that even made any sense. She was Kari. The impulsive one. The talkative one. The playful one. And now, she would have to be the responsible one. Mera was always the responsible one. Gosh, she wished Mera would come back home.

Chapter Twenty

Mera lay on the makeshift bed that had been quickly prepared for her arrival at what would now be her new home. It was after dinner on the night they arrived, and she didn't get to see anyone else besides Gery who had shown her to her room. The room was little more than a cleaned out cave with a small window for light carved through the mountain rock. She wasn't sure how that was possible, but she was glad since the sun had long passed over the mountain on the western side. There were candles, of course, but the candles would not stave away the cold and isolating feel of the rock-enclosed space.

Her cave was one of many cut into the sides of a canyon surrounded by mountains and cliffs. The canyon was virtually invisible to anyone traveling the mountain pass on either side of the range. To arrive, she and Pholus had to do quite a bit of climbing and descending before they entered the canyon, and some parts of the trail perched precariously on crags and ridges. Mera didn't think she could find her way back alone if she were to leave. Somehow that thought was made more disquieting by the fact that it might be more than two years before she'd be able to return home. She'd been away from her family for little more than a few weeks, and it already felt like months.

Everything had happened so fast: her sister born, the dragon flying over their heads, meeting the ancient ones, learning that so many of the creatures from the histories and myths of her people actually existed, and then the shadow demons. They still haunted her dreams, though nothing like the nightmares that started all of this. Those nightmares were unfathomable because they were things she couldn't remember, that she had no reference for, except for feeling that they were very, very real. The demons, however, were real. They had run from them and fought them.

Oddly enough, she was less afraid of the priestess who led them than the demons themselves or the dragon she'd only seen from a distance. In fact, the priestess never came to her nightmares. Her voice didn't come to those dreams either, but Mera could remember how seductively that voice rang through her mind. She could also remember the acolyte with his charred appearance and hunched back. She had no idea what tomorrow would bring, but she felt like the memories of recent weeks would continue to haunt her forever. She covered herself in the rough blankets and tried to get some sleep.

Morning came far too early, even here in the mountains. She wondered if that was because they were further east than The Thicket. It seemed she had just closed her eyes when Gery came calling her name.

"It's time for breakfast. Hurry up, there's no time for dawdling! There's a lot to do today. I have to get you measured for clothing because it appears you don't have anything acceptable to fight in." Mera rolled over and covered her head with the blanket that quickly pulled up her legs. "And Master Pholus is expecting you and the others in the heart of the canyon in less than an hour."

Less than an hour. What was he thinking? Who got up to actually do things this early in the morning? "What time is it?" she asked aloud before clamping her hand over her mouth when she almost blurted out a question that sounded more like Kari would ask.

"Time doesn't matter. The sun is up, so it's time to get started."

His nagging changed her mind, and she decided to channel her cousin after all. "It would seem that time is important if, as you were telling me, I have less than an hour to get up, get ready, get measured, eat breakfast, and be in the center of the canyon for my initial training session." He clicked his teeth and gave her a scathing look before she heard the pop of his disappearance. Addressing the rock walls, she said with a smirk, "Isn't that odd that he did not pop into the room but decided to leave that way." Oh well, she thought. It was probably time she got up and ate the breakfast Gery had left for her on the table by the cave wall anyway.

Putting on her coarse robes, she wondered what he had meant about needing appropriate clothing for training. Though Callisto had taken her to purchase material in the human town, she had no clue what she might need. Her people didn't really wear clothing, and she had never found any to fit in the shops they occasionally visited in the human town. The only things she owned were her simple robes that had been made by doubling her mother's robes to fit over her extra large haunches. It wouldn't do her any good to dwell on those things. If Gery wanted to measure her and try to find clothing that fit, so be it. The gods knew he might have better luck than she ever had.

As she took the last bites of her breakfast, she thought about who the other trainees might be. Would they always eat their meals alone? Is that how things were done in other places? She couldn't help but feel the loneliness from the previous night creeping into her skin, and she hugged herself, rubbing her hands along her arms. She had never eaten a meal alone before. Either her mother, her grandmother, or Kari was always there. Somehow that simple thought brought a sob to her chest, so she tried to think of something else, hoping she wouldn't spend the next two years alone.

What would the next two years be like? The centaur consistently mentioned training. Callisto had said Mera needed to learn her powers, which she honestly did, but what would that entail? What would it look like? She had so many questions. Looking around the cave, she realized that none of those questions would be answered in there. She took a deep breath and walked out of the cave to look down on the canyon floor below.

S he found Gery waiting near the main entrance into the canyon proper. He was leaning against the rock wall looking nonchalant, but his foot was tapping the rhythm of his impatience. His crankiness by far overwhelmed his diminutive frame. When he turned to look at her, irritation marking his brows, she nearly laughed.

"It's about time. Let's go into Master Pholus' study to get these measurements, and then we will head down to the training field." He ran through the words so fast that Mera had to take a moment to process it all before she could respond. Then he didn't even wait for her response, just walked toward the large cave near the entrance and ducked inside. She hurried to follow him.

"Go ahead and remove your cloak," he said, climbing on top of the boulder that served as Pholus' seating area. "I will need to measure your neck, chest, waist, hips, and then the lengths of your arms and legs." Mera shuddered. She had no concern with her own nakedness, generally, but the fact he would need to touch her in various places, including those parts that made her uncomfortable, was unnerving.

"Is this truly necessary? I could just make do with the spliced garments I already have."

"No, no, that is unacceptable. You need adequate clothing for training. You can't move comfortably in those clothes, and there are often trainees who are uncomfortable with nakedness, though I've heard that is not an issue for your people."

Mera paled. "I..." She looked at the stone floor of Pholus' office, finding the cave entrance from the corner of her eye. "I'm not..."

"Hey," Gery said, face softening. "You don't need to be afraid of me, yeah. I have measured every trainee we've had here, male and female, without incident. I will not hurt you or try to take advantage. I have no interest..."

Mera didn't give him a chance to finish his sentence, as guilt set in, pushing her to speak. "That isn't what I meant. I am not afraid of you, Gery. Though you're obviously, not happy that I'm here, you're not my concern."

"Then what is making us spend this time talking that you could be training already?"

Mera's brows knitted together at his matter-of-fact question. Why did he hate her so? "If you must know, I stay covered because people are disgusted by the shape of my body. I am a gnarled, hairy mess on the bottom."

Gery nodded, as if he'd made some kind of silent decision, and Mera's spine went rigid. If he reached out a hand toward her with that leering look, she would run out of the cave and leave the canyon completely. "Turn around, Skyemera. If your concern is what you think my visual response to seeing you might be, I will measure you from behind, so you cannot see me my face, yeah. That should take care of it."

Mera blinked rapidly. Was he serious? There was no way something as simple as turning around would make this situation easier. He was so misguided she wasn't sure whether to laugh or cry.

"Come on. Time is ticking, and we have other things to do. Turn around, yeah."

"Gery, I don't think..."

"Don't think, just do. Turn around." His tone bore no possibility of argument, and Mera followed his direction, steeling herself for the panicked discomfort that would come as soon as he measured her haunches.

"Now lift your arms straight out, and don't move."

The process of measuring her from head to hoof took less time than their entire conversation beforehand. Mera stood perfectly still and barely flinched when he got to her hips. Everything went so smoothly and quickly that she didn't have time to register him touching the uncomfortable parts of her body with the thin rope he used.

"All done. Now, it's time for you to meet Master Pholus in the training field."

"That was it?"

"Yes, of course. Did you think you'd have to stand on your head or something?"

"Well, no, but..."

"No buts. It's done, yeah, and it's time to go outside."

Gery jumped down from the boulder, his soft shoes lightly thumping on the stone floor.

She could already see the great centaur in the middle of the canyon's heart, and there were other figures standing around him, but she couldn't make out who they might be. After taking another deep, steadying breath, she began her descent.

"There you are," Pholus announced, as she entered the canyon bed. "I thought I would have to send Gery after you."

"I'm here. This morning was a little disorienting, but I'm ready for what's to come."

"Good to hear. Let me introduce you to the others who share the space with us." He turned toward the small gathering. "You have already seen, though not officially met, Purivia, our paladin. Though she is human, she has a keen eye and a steady hand needed for archery. She also has an affinity for healing magic."

"I'm also pretty good with a sword," the archer said nonchalantly with a wink. She had piercing blue eyes and hair the color of pitch. Now that Mera saw her in daylight, she realized her skin was tawny beige, rather than the dark ochre she had appeared in the shadows mingled with firelight of the alley days past.

"I didn't get to see that the other day," Mera said with a giggle.

"Of course, you and Gery are already friends." Gery scoffed and Mera smiled, barely holding back a guffaw. "Well," Pholus added, "you're getting there." Mera saw his shoulder bounce with a silent chuckle before he said, "Next is Tarkegan Plessis, who has been with me for a number of years. His training ended many winters ago, but he just seems to enjoy this mountain solitude." The broad-shouldered cyclops with pale pink skin and equally pale hair winked at her. His single eye nearly as far above her head as her own eyes were above Kari's. All Mera could do was stare.

"And this is our newest trainee," Pholus said gesturing to what appeared to be a young human male. "He comes to us from a far away land. Much like you, he was sent here to hone powers his community wasn't quite expecting." Mera saw the young human smile at the same time she heard Gery snort. She was learning that the gnome made noises when he didn't agree with something said, but she didn't get a chance to dwell on that thought when the human reached out a hand to her.

"My name is Gaeleath." He was much younger than the others she'd been introduced to, probably close to her own age. He had a beautifully chiseled face that was still youthful and soft. He would be stunning as he aged. His hair was brown with hints of honey blonde and it fell in loose curls about his shoulders. Mera smiled at him before Pholus interrupted their greeting.

"Sometimes, we have a bigger group here, but for now, this is everyone, and everyone, this is Skyemera, The Maenad. She is the first of her kind in over a millennium." Mera felt herself blushing from such a formal introduction. "I will not bore you with stories of the previous maenad nor regale you with her great works today. As we all know, coming into our own is often a very solitary thing, and it is deeply personal." Pholus looked at each of them solemnly. "No one who has come to me for aid has ever come because their process was easy or fit into the normal mold of their people."

Mera looked around at the group as Pholus made his point. Each of the others were nodding in agreement. Would they really accept her? It was obvious there were many differences between them all, but could it be true that they had similarities too? Mera once again found herself silently asking lots of questions and nearly missed when Pholus addressed her directly.

"Mera, you will do more watching today than anything else, so find yourself a rock over there that looks comfortable and have a seat. What I would like everyone else to do is share a little of what you have learned while you've been here. You do not have to share anything overly personal, but I would like you to give a little demonstration of your skills."

"It's nice to meet you all," she said before turning to do as Pholus commanded.

"Gery, as I know you have other responsibilities to get to, including going back to the city for our belongings, I would like for you to start."

"Really? I really have to do a demonstration?"

"Yes. Your skills and abilities are different from everyone else's. Show us what you can do."

If Mera didn't know any better, she would think Gery was little more than a teenage boy with all his pouting, scowling, and huffing about. Of course, she did not have much experience with teenage human males, but she had plenty of experience with Kari and her whining and incessant talking. Gery made her laugh just like Kari did, and that endeared Mera to his temperament.

"Fine. As all of you have already seen, I have powers of teleportation. I snap my fingers and I go from here to over there." As he said the words, he disappeared from the center of the canyon floor and reappeared at the far end, second level, where Mera had left her cave this morning. In a blink, he was back. "I'm also pretty good with a hammer, the bigger the hammer, the better. I know I am little and you all think I'm not strong, but give me a hammer, and I'll show you how strong I am."

"No one thinks you're not strong, Gery," Pholus interrupted, which produced a sharp look from the corner of Gery's eyes.

"I'm also very good with money, collecting it, stealing it, spending it, hoarding it, and counting it. So I maintain most of the finances that come in for this little thing we have going on around here," he said gesturing widely around the canyon. "If you find that you need anything, you come to me. Can I go now?" he asked, turning to Pholus.

"Gery, that is not all you can do."

"Why can't I keep some things to myself? I'm old, and they don't need to know everything that I've known how to do for all this time. I've learned a lot in my 500 years."

Mera choked before blurting, "500? That is more than my grandmother has!"

"See, that is why I don't like to talk about myself!"

"I'm sorry...truly. I would love to know what you've learned in these 500 winters."

His stare bore into her before he looked around as if remembering there were others in the canyon. Mera's thoughts began to wander around different possible powers the gnome might have. She was suddenly brought back to the present by what sounded like explosions. She looked around. They were explosions.

One after the other, the sides of the cliff exploded outward in shards of rock all the way around the cavern.

"I'm also really good at making things blow up," he said matter-of-factly.

Gaeleath, who was obviously as impressed as Mera, asked, "Can you blow up anything, or just rock?"

"Anything."

"So you can blow up people?"

"Can I? Yes. Do I like to do that? Absolutely not! It's messy and it makes me feel bad. And do not ask me how I know it makes me feel bad or how messy it can be. I don't want to talk about it. Can I go now?" Gery had turned back toward Pholus again with a pleading look Mera recognized. She'd used it many times to escape to the gnarled oaks at the shore.

"Yes, Gery. Thank you," Pholus said with a nod of respect.

Before Gery had the chance to blink away, everyone else in the canyon, including Mera, were on their feet clapping. His already round and rosy cheeks reddened even more before that familiar pop happened.

Chapter Twenty-One

❧

"Are you telling me that after all you made me do, you didn't make Gaeleath show all of his powers? You actually let him keep something secret? I had to show everything that I can do, but other people got to show what they wanted to?" Gery was pacing back and forth through the cave while Pholus rubbed his temples. "Master Pholus, I believe you to be fair, which is why I work for you. That's why I trust you. But," he said with a sigh, "I don't believe this was fair."

"Gery, there is a very good reason why I specifically told him, as I told you while we were in the city, that he could not share everything. Knowing your powers might make her feel more comfortable and safe here; knowing his might do the opposite."

Gery huffed and continued pacing, waiting for Pholus to share this 'oh so important' reason. He was so frustrated by the unfairness of it all, he was caught off guard by Pholus' next question.

"Do you know what her greatest fear is?"

Her greatest fear? What did he care about her greatest fear? At least that's what he wanted to say. When Pholus raised an eyebrow of impatience at him, though, he gave the only answer he knew to be true. "Yeah, those shadow demons we fought the other day."

"No, it's..."

Gery cut him off with a finger to his lips and a hand pointing toward the mouth of the cave. Someone was out there listening. He'd heard footsteps, but when they stopped outside and didn't continue walking, Gery knew the person was intentionally stalling outside of the cave. He hated nosy people. *Pop*.

Pop. "What are you doing out here?" he said to the startled face of their newest trainee. He didn't trust her one bit. How did she even know to find them here? "Why are you listening in on our conversation? Do you know how rude that is?" He folded his arms as he looked up at her. Sometimes he wished he were taller, so he could appear more intimidating.

"I'm sorry. I came out here to ask a question, but I didn't want to interrupt your conversation."

Gery wasn't sure he believed her, so he continued waiting for her to elaborate. She looked down at his tapping foot and scrunched her nose. He couldn't believe it. She actually scrunched up her nose at him like he was the one caught doing something wrong.

"Look, I didn't actually come intending to hear what you were taking about, but I heard enough to know that you were talking about me. Is it not rude to talk about someone when they're not present?"

He glared at her. "As if you've never talked about somebody who wasn't there before. I'm sure that you've had plenty of conversations about people who were not in the room at the time. That doesn't mean that those conversations were for those people to hear."

"Gery, bring her inside," came Pholus' voice echoing from the cave's entrance. Gery stared at her for another moment before he stepped out of the way and gestured for her to enter Pholus' cave. She actually had the audacity to start talking as she entered the space, not even greeting their patron first. He followed her inside and hoped she could feel his disappointment.

"Great Pholus, I promise I was not here to listen in on your conversation. I honestly didn't know Gery was here until I heard you two talking. I came to ask you something." When she paused, Gery rolled his eyes. "You know what, it doesn't even matter what I came to ask you. I would like to know, though, what you think my greatest fear is and how you came to that conclusion because I'm not even sure I know."

Gery took a step forward, ready to put her in her place. How dare she address Master Pholus like that? He stopped, though, when Pholus held up a hand.

"We will address that in your training. Part of what we do here is get you to explore and recognize things that are affecting you. Fear can be both a help and a hindrance to using your powers, but that is not an office conversation. Just know that all decisions I make are based on conclusions I have drawn and nothing is done out of malice, as that helps no one."

Gery would never understand how the centaur had so much patience with everyone here. Truly, Gery wasn't sure how Pholus had so much patience with him either. He was moody, argued with him regularly, didn't always follow directions, and was sometimes extra stubborn. He knew he brought value to The Palaestra and the work they did here with the untrained magical beings who came for help. He was sure the centaur would not have kept him around for these past 400 years otherwise, but Gery knew he wasn't easy to live with. This nymph, no, maenad, he thought with irritation, was going to get on his last nerve. She spoke then, breaking him from his thoughts.

"By the way, what I'd come here to ask was if there was any way for me to communicate with my family. I miss them, and though I know I cannot go back home right now, it's very hard to be here and to really know no one."

Gery wasn't sure how Pholus would answer that question. He

didn't know that anyone had ever asked before, and the asking made Gery look at her again more closely. He read no guile in her posture like she was wanting to share their location with the outside world. Maybe she was telling the truth. He remembered that feeling of loss and loneliness when Pholus had first plucked him from the streets of Krinosera and invited him to the castle on the cliffside. No, he would not feel bad for this ill-mannered goat-nymph.

Pholus walked around his tall table and took her hands. "I will find a way to send them a message. You can give the message to Gery, and I will make sure it gets to them. I will also make sure that you receive any responses." Gery thought she was going to jump up and down like a rabbit on those legs of hers, but Pholus kept her hands in his. "I know that you left in haste and that separation is difficult, but know that this will not be a regular thing."

"Thank you. Thank you," the maenad responded, visibly shaking with excitement.

Pholus dropped her hands. "Now, go have dinner with the others. The rest of the trainees should be in the dining hall, which is in the cave on the far end of the cavern. I know that you've been keeping to yourself, so go and try to make friends, or at least get to know them a little."

Gery stood there perplexed by the whole exchange. Somehow, she had not gotten reprimanded for eavesdropping, and she had gotten Pholus to promise that her messages would be sent. And who, he mused, would be asked to deliver and return those messages? Nope, he didn't like her one bit. He was so deep in his thoughts that he didn't realize she had turned to leave the cave until she nearly ran him over. She stopped mid-stride when she realized he was still standing there in the entrance. It took a moment before he recovered enough to step to the side and let her leave.

"Master Pholus, do you think that's wise? Has anyone else had the opportunity to correspond with their family once they got here? Why does she get such special treatment?"

Pholus turned to face him directly, and Gery barely held himself still under that gaze. He already knew the answer before he heard it.

"Gery, I respect your input, and I trust you as my assistant and friend, but I don't answer to you."

It wasn't until Pholus walked back to the other side of his table that Gery realized he had been holding his breath waiting for a tongue-lashing and exhaled. Even after all these years with Master Pholus, he still couldn't forget the number of times his temper got him in trouble. He didn't move, however, knowing there was still more to be said. He stood completely still watching Pholus situate himself on the bench Gery had specially made for him. It was built for him to lean against if he was tired enough or sit on comfortably if he chose to, though Pholus did not sit often.

"She is not, as you say, getting special treatment. She is getting necessary treatment for what she has recently been through, and what, I'm afraid, will be coming soon for her, both here and at home."

"Wait, do you think something is going to be coming here? Do you think something is going to happen here? What are we supposed to do?"

Pholus leaned on his elbows and folded his hands until Gery stopped asking questions. "There is something we need to do to get ready, but as I said, I don't answer to you. When I'm ready to share the plan, you will be the first to know it, as you always are. Now, before you get started again, I do have a task for you."

Gery was shuffling from one foot to the other. They hadn't had any significant issues at this location in the 200 years since he had blasted out this canyon and each of the caves. No one knew their exact location, and someone would have to randomly scale the right peaks to see them from above. There must be something else Master Pholus is considering a threat, maybe her uncontrollable powers. No way some invader is going to find them.

"Gery, are you listening?"

Gery shook his head to clear it and then nodded.

"I will be sending you to deliver her correspondence and return with any messages for her. But, there is a greater purpose for your travels to her forest home. Once you have her message, come see me, and I will share that purpose with you."

Gery caught himself before his face fell at the thought of playing messenger, especially to the forest. Thankfully, Pholus didn't seem to notice his hesitancy.

"Now go have dinner. I will not be joining you all tonight."

"Would you like me to have something sent up for you?"

"Yes, please."

"Speaking of blowing stuff up...welcome back, Gery," Tarkegan yelled across the cave. Mera, who had been enjoying the friendly banter of the others, hastily shoved a piece of food in her mouth and looked down at her plate. She'd had enough of Gery's attention for one day.

"Watch out now, cyclops. Your head's already almost too big for this cave," Gery retorted to raucous laughter from everyone around the table. Everyone except Mera. She nearly choked on the bite of fowl she hadn't quite finished chewing. She snorted in an effort to control her breathing until she, at last, managed to swallow her food. Gery was funny when he tried to be, and he still reminded her of Kari. She needed to send a message to Kari. The cousins had been inseparable for as long as Mera could remember.

"So what have you lot been working on the past two days? Tell me some stories," Gery said.

"I was finally able to set my sword aflame," said the paladin, Purivia, who had helped them escape from the shadow demons in Krinosera. "I don't think I can replicate it very easily yet, but I was able to do it."

"Really? I know that is something you have been working on, pulling in the power of your god," Gery responded, thumping her on the back.

"Which god do you gather power from?" Mera asked.

"I cannot say that I draw power from just one god," she responded. "That would be to say that my power is limited by the reach of that god wherever others reign. Rather, I believe that I am here to support and protect the people, which to me would be the goal of all the gods. So, I try to remain respectful to whichever god the person I'm helping believes in. It has served me thus far, but I'm relatively new." She took a bite of her meal and chewed it before the other new trainee, Gaeleath, shared his story.

"I knew quite a bit when I got here, but I've learned a lot since. For example, I've learned that conjuring fireballs in my hands is not as easy as one would think. I can conjure them sure enough, but they go out in a puff of smoke. I know there's an easier way, and I will continue to find time to practice it that way, but in the meantime, it is rather frustrating to have your fire just fizzle out. Kind of depressing really. But, my ice is getting stronger, so it is no longer immediately melting into a puddle of water."

Gery chuckled at that. Mera wasn't sure what was so funny, but apparently there was something of a joke in the retelling.

"Do you want to know what I have learned since I got here?" she asked.

Gery cut his eyes at her, but simply said, "Sure, tell me what you learned." She knew the tone of insincerity and almost thought to just get up and leave, but the great Pholus had told her to come and make friends, or at least get to know everyone. That meant she couldn't just run away every time Gery decided to sneer at her.

"Well, I learned that caves are chilly, the beds are hard, and I have absolutely no idea what I'm doing." Everyone stopped laughing and looked at her, but she continued unperturbed. "I have magic. I know I have magic because I have used it in times of great need or in times of great emotion, but that's it. Nothing happens when I'm not scared or angry," She sighed. "My people learn to start controlling their magic at fifteen winters. By latest calculation, I have seen twenty. I'm supposed to be this great, powerful being, and the most I can do is conjure a little wind when I'm really upset. My cousin Kari talks so much that she conjures wind as soon as she wakes." She looked at Gery, not sure what she was expecting, but his slack jaw expression wasn't it. "I don't know what the point of all this is..."

"What do you mean by last calculation of your age," Gaeleath asked.

Mera took a deep breath, and then that single breath spilled out the shortest version of the long story that explained how her family had erased the memories of everyone in the village to save her from nightmares that were ruining everyone's lives, including her own, resulting in the loss of six years of her life.

"Goodness, that is a lot to take in," Purivia chimed in.

"You're telling me."

"It seems like you come from a family who really cares about you," the paladin responded with a smile.

"They do. I know they do. I'm just a little frustrated with all the lies and pretending and having to learn so much in so little time. I can't help but think they would've never told me had the dragon not flown overhead."

"Dragon?" Gaeleath looked at her intently.

"Yeah. On the day of my sister's birth, a dragon flew over our community, blasting fire and scaring everyone. That night, my nightmares came back. Then my powers kicked in, and everyone was afraid for me, and of me, in little more than a day. And it all had to do with that dragon."

The room was silent for a minute before Gery took control of the conversation. "Let's talk about something less stressful for a minute. We know that everyone is here to do a job or to learn something, but what is something you like to do for fun?"

"Oh, that's easy," Mera answered. "Ever since I was really young, I have loved to go to the sea and burrow beneath the gnarled oaks that grow along the shore. They're super strong and powerful, but my people are afraid of them because they look different. I always feel safe around them, so I sit there and listen to the waves. It gives me a sense of peace." She smiled to herself as she thought of them. "I recently learned that they're called Strimmena by our sea nymph cousins and that they're known as the Watchers of the Sea. It doesn't matter what they call them, I love them because they are gnarled like me. They're misshapen, but they still stand strong." Mera looked up then to find all eyes staring at her, and her cheeks turned pink. Usually, she was the silent one because Kari couldn't keep quiet. Were those looks meant to say she'd been talking too much? "What," she scowled.

"You have a loving family that you miss, and yet you just said that your favorite thing to do is to hide underneath of some trees by yourself," Gery responded before anyone else could say something.

"Yes."

"Interesting."

Mera was about to ask him why they would think that was odd when someone else decided to share their favorite activities. There was lots of talk of games they used to play when they were younger back in their homes, and Mera was surprised to hear that Gaeleath, who seemed to be the youngest of them all, loved to read. Reading wasn't a big thing in her community. A few of the nymphs had scrolls, like Helena, for her healing spells, but very few of them did any real reading. Now she was wishing that she could read and write well since she wanted to send a message home.

"If you will all excuse me, I need to do some thinking about what the great Pholus told me earlier. Gery, I will have what you're waiting on in a couple of hours."

As she walked to the cave that was serving as her room in the canyon, Mera wondered what she could possibly tell her family. She would tell them that she was safe, of course, and that she missed them, but would that make anybody feel better? She wished she could tell them something magical was happening, and that she expected to be home soon, fully charged up and ready to protect everyone. She nearly laughed at the absurdity of that statement. Her laughter was stifled, though, when she walked into her cave and saw a large parcel on her makeshift bed.

She had never gotten a gift before, at least not a wrapped up like this, though she'd heard about them on the rare occasion they'd visited the human town. She couldn't imagine any reason why she should be getting a gift, not here, at least. She walked over to the brown-paper-wrapped package and recognized her name scrawled across the top in block letters. Still skeptical, she ran her hands around the package, noticing it wasn't soft like she'd expected. She carefully pulled the tip of the twine bow and let it unravel. When the paper flopped open, Mera gasped. Sitting before her was a stack of clothing. There were different fabrics and different colors.

She stood frozen for many moments, almost afraid to touch them. What would she do if they didn't fit? How would everyone react if she pulled the items on and ripped them. She turned away and walked back toward the opening of the cave. "I'll just tell Pholus that I'm good and don't need them," she said aloud to the empty room, but as she made to leave the small space, she put her hands on the cool cave wall and looked back. There sat one of the things she had most wanted in the world, clothes made to fit her for when she traveled outside of her community rather than the coarse robes from her mother's closet that had been spliced together. Curiosity got the better of her, and she walked back to the bed.

Opening each of the items carefully, she found a beautiful tunic of cerulean blue, leather breeches, soft simple shirts, and a warm woolen cloak in the deepest green of the forest. She lifted the cloak and stared. The color was magical, almost iridescent. If she thought that was an amazing piece, what was underneath it literally stole her breath. Moving the cloak to the side, she found a gown of shimmering white that transitioned to the palest green along the bottom edges. The sleeves followed the same pattern. She had seen humans walking around in beautiful dresses and long gowns before, but she never imagined she'd have one herself. Where would she possibly wear something so beautiful?

She wasn't sure how much time had passed while she stared at the clothes, but when she heard the familiar pop outside of her doorway, she knew it had been long enough.

"Skyemera?"

"Come in," she said with a hitch in her voice. As Gery entered the cave, she was wiping tears from her eyes.

"Is everything good?"

"Yes, everything is fine."

"Do the clothes not meet your needs or your approval?"

"With my approval," she said in a giggly whisper. "I don't even know what to say. Gery, I have never seen anything so beautiful before in my life. I have never owned anything so beautiful in my life." She looked down at the garments carefully placed around the bed. "I'm afraid to try them on."

"What do you mean?"

"I've never been able to buy clothes that fit the way my body is made. My people look at me like I'm some kind of misshapen monster sometimes, and they don't know how to fit me. The same has been true in the human town. Clothes there don't fit either. No one is this big on the bottom and this small on top," she punctuated her statement by gesturing at her body and wrinkling her nose. Without looking up at him, she said, "I remember trying on my mother's clothes when I was younger, and I tore them. It was terrible. I felt terrible. She didn't get upset, but I was miserable." She looked at him then. She could feel the sting at the backs of her eyes, but she held the tears in. He was not someone she wanted to cry in front of. Instead, she gave him a half smile, half laugh as she pointed to the brown cloak hung on the wall and at the one robe she was wearing. "That's how I got the clothes I'm wearing. My mom took the one that I ripped and sewed it together with another one of her old, simple dresses."

He stared at her for a moment, and she almost thought his eyes were glistening, but then he blinked. "Skyemera, look. Before I left, I took all your measurements, yeah. All your big parts and all your little parts. Do you remember that?"

She sniffled and laughed. "Yes."

"Good. If these clothes don't fit, I am going to go blow up the tailor who doesn't know how to make clothes according to measurements."

This time her laughter was genuine. "Thank you."

"So try something on right now, yeah. What better time than right now?"

"You know, Gery, you remind me a lot of my cousin Kari."

"Is she old and cranky?"

"No, just the opposite," she said shaking her head as she ran her hands over the different fabrics on her bed. He looked at her with one eyebrow lifted and lips twisted, which made her bust out in a fit of laughter. "She could always make me laugh too."

"I'm going to step outside for two minutes, and I want you to try something on. I need to know whether this tailor gets paid or blown up."

"Fine," she acquiesced, throwing up her hands in surrender,

and he left the cave. She wasn't quite ready to put on the beautiful gown in case it didn't fit, so she opted for a pair of breeches and a shirt. At least if those didn't fit, she could possibly have the others. When she pulled them on, though, bottom up and top down, they were absolutely perfect. She ran her hands down her legs. She had never felt her legs fully covered before, and feeling the leather instead of her fur made her fingertips tingle. The tunic fit perfectly as well. It didn't bunch anywhere. It wasn't tight, and it didn't look like it had been spliced together from two other pieces of clothing.

"Can I come back in now?"

"Yes, Gery." She turned to face him, so he could look her up and down, well, mostly up. His natural smile grew.

"They fit very well, yeah."

"Yes, yes they do. Thank you, Gery!" She almost went to hug him, but his next words stopped her.

"Did you get to the bottom of the package yet?"

"There's more?"

"Yeah," he said with a sheepish grin that once again made him look like a young boy rather than the hard gnome of 500 winters she'd grown accustomed to. She turned around, lifted the dress gently, and set it to the side. Underneath, she found another wrapped package. She looked back at Gery over her shoulder.

"What is this package?"

"Open it," he responded enthusiastically. She did and found a pair of beautiful boots.

"Gery?" He didn't say anything just raised his eyebrows when she turned back to look at him holding the tops of each boot by the tips of her fingers. "Gery..." she said again, "I don't have feet."

"No, you don't. I can see that."

"So why did you give me boots? What am I supposed to do with these?"

"Pull them on and tell me how they feel."

"Is this your way of getting back at me for all the times I've irritated you?" He crossed his arms and stayed silent. Her lip quivered involuntary as she tried the first boot on. When her hoof hit the bottom of the boot, it was snugly held in place. When she flexed her ankle, the toe kicked up and down. She pulled the other on silently and felt the same enveloping from her hoof to her calf before she stood up from the bed. She wasn't sure what to expect when she took a step, but the perfectly weighted toe felt like an extension of her hoof, allowing her to walk in a circle around Gery. This time, she did hug him.

"By the gods, Gery...how? How did you do this?"

"Magic," he said with a wink and turned back toward the cave entrance. Before he took his exit, he looked back over his shoulder. "Not my magic, of course, but my cousin is amazing." And with that, he popped out of sight.

Chapter Twenty-Two

S he followed Pholus up to the rim of the canyon on the opposite side from where they had arrived months ago. The afternoon sun was high overhead, illuminating a clear blue sky. As they descended the mountain ridges, Mera noticed an increase in foliage. Their ascension on the other side was dry and bare. The mountain and its ridges were covered in various shades of copper clay bespeckled with gray rock. This side, however, wore a cloak of green hues that Mera hadn't seen since leaving the Tribunal Forest. She breathed in the scent of pine and noticed the rhododendron leaves peeking out from beneath the trees growing in more sparse groups. The weather slowly began to warm, as winter passed into early spring. The flowering buds should be opening soon, and then the mountainside would be awash in a rainbow of colored flowers.

"What are you thinking right now, young one? I feel your excitement."

"Spring is coming, Great Pholus, and I noticed the bushes growing between the trees on some of the ridges along this side of the mountains. I can't wait to see them in full bloom. It will be a spectacular sight."

Pholus smiled at her, stopping their descent near one of the bushes. "When Callisto first left you in my care, she told me of how you had grown a tree in seconds." Mera's shoulders slumped at the memory of strangling the previous tree she'd touched that day. "Callisto was encouraged by your ability to command the earth to sprout forth life."

"I did not do it on my own. The only thing I did on my own was kill a tree with a strangling vine. If Callisto had not stopped me the second time, I might have killed an entire copse of trees."

He turned his entire body around to look at her fully. "Do you remember what I told you about the last maenad and the way she had peeled back the ocean to see the sea life?" Mera nodded. She had spent weeks trying to reconcile her own magical manifestations with the story he told. "When Truisha pulled back the sea, she did so intentionally. She watched the urchins and fish dying with complete understanding of what was happening. Even after I begged her to release her hold on the sea, she refused. She told me that they were too beautiful to be covered from her sight."

Tears filled his eyes, and Mera had to look away to wipe at her own. "You do not have to relive that moment again, Master Pholus," she said, trying to control the catch in her voice.

"I would relive the memory aloud one hundred times if it helped you realize that what you have done with your magic unintentionally does not make you a bad person. It does not make you a danger. The fact that you are bothered by what happened means that you will try to control it the best you can."

She shook her head. She was not ready to accept his platitudes when she still wasn't able to bring forth her magic intentionally. What if it came when she was least able to control it, when her emotions dominated her control?

"Do not misread me, young one. You have capabilities that absolutely can cause damage if left unchecked. We both understand that fact. That is why we're here today. The more you practice manifesting and controlling your magic, even when it seems impossible, the more you will learn to recognize when it does and doesn't emerge from within you."

Mera looked around the mountainside again, trying to gauge what he might want her to do here. She turned a questioning gaze up at him. "What do I do?"

He gestured toward the bushes at the base of the nearest pine. "When we first arrived, you noticed the lack of flowers on these plants. I want you to make them bloom. There are plenty to practice with here, and there is still plenty of time before spring produces the rainbow you were envisioning. I fully expect you to win this race against Persephone's return.

"Ancient one, I don't know how…"

"Then I suggest you get to trying various means. Nymphs have earth magic. You are a nymph as much as you're not a nymph. Call on your magic. Feed it your happiness. Feed it your positive memories. Believe in yourself and allow your magic to flow through that belief. I will send someone for you when it is time for the evening meal. Hopefully, you will have made multiple attempts and had some successes." He turned to make the climb back to the canyon's rim.

"But what if I fail," she called after him.

"Oh, you will fail. You will fail numerous times."

Mera's mouth fell open at his words, and her chest tightened as she considered the challenge before her. How was she to make all the bushes bloom without killing them? How was she supposed to make anything happen when she didn't know how to call forth her magic? The centaur quickly disappeared over the ridge, his sure footing and familiarity with the terrain driving him swiftly up the mountain. Mera's heart bottomed out as soon as he slipped out of sight, and she slid to the ground, leaning against one of the strong pines.

She had no idea how long she sat there, but her legs were stiff when she finally rose and began exploring the ridge and the flora present. There were far more flowering plants than rhododendrons peppering the landscape. She walked up to one of the large bushes with its thick, pointed leaves and touched a small sprig with tentative fingers. There were no buds along its length yet, just hearty leaves. "What do you need to bloom?" Mera asked the plant. She had seen Euonsise talk to the gardens often when she'd wander out to the village farmlands. According to the master grower, plants were sentient and responded positively to direct communication.

No response came from this plant, and Mera retracted her hand, moving along to another one. This bush was closer to the ridge's edge, and its leaves were dark green from the extended sunlight rather than the bright green of those hidden amongst the trees. "Will you help me?" she asked this one, stroking its smooth leaves. The sprigs shuddered as if a gust of wind had blown through their tangle, but nothing else changed. This was going to be useless. She couldn't just talk them into growing. She looked out over the ridge's edge on the mountain below, and defeat built in her chest.

Mera threw her hands in the air and screamed her frustration. She needed access to her magic, and just sending her here to touch plants didn't help her gain that access. No sooner had the thought passed through her mind, the ridge seemed to shift under her feet. She turned back to the plants she'd walked away from, and they all shifted backward away from her. She blinked multiple times thinking she must've imagined it. When they all leaned toward the wall of the next ridge up, she rubbed her eyes. What was happening? "Hello."

She felt ridiculous out there talking to the plants, but she didn't know what else to do. In succession, they each shuddered with a slight twisting motion, their leaves waving. "Are you afraid?" Her brows knitted even as she asked the question. Though she trusted Euonsise's ability to grow enough food to feed the village and provide for trade, Mera did not subscribe to the notion that the plants were listening to her. Well, that wasn't true completely. She had always felt that the Strimmena listened to her and wrapped her in their calming branches. Was it possible? She watched the waving of leaves happen again, this time vertically up and down the length of each bush. "Are you afraid of me?" she asked. The rattling leaves answered with their vertical undulations.

"How goes it?"

Mera jumped and whirled around. She recognized the cyclops gruff voice, but it startled her nonetheless. "Tarkegan, what are you doing here?"

"Pholus sent me for you. It's nearly time for the evening meal."

Her shoulders fell, and a groan left her throat before she could stop it. She had gotten no further toward meeting the challenge than she'd been when Pholus left her alone hours before.

"Are you not tired? Hungry? Do you not need a break to regroup?"

She huffed. "I'm no closer to making these flowers grow than I am learning to fly."

He chuckled. "You're not a patient one, are you? I remember being young and idealistic. It's difficult to learn the hard lessons when we're so sure we should already know the answers."

Mera turned and began her ascent up the ridge.

"Did I say something offensive, Young Mera?"

She didn't respond, but she did slow down and allow him to catch up. The cyclops was much taller than she, nearly matching the difference in height she had on her own people. It took him but a few seconds to join her on the next ridge. "No, you didn't offend me, but I'm frustrated." Though 'frustrated' didn't feel like a strong enough word, Mera couldn't think of another that fit. His words had hit home. She wanted to already know what to do. She wanted to already know how to use her magic. She wanted to be ready to return home, and she wasn't any closer to meeting that goal than she had been the week she left The Thicket.

"That's understandable. You're young. Others have made you promises of great things you will do, but none of them have told you how to do those things. That doesn't mean you skip the process of learning. We all must fail to win." With those words, he lengthened the stride of his long legs, and crested the remaining ridges in moments. Though she could have caught up with him easily, Mera slowed her steps to mull over his words. Her people didn't have time for her to fail. The dragon could already be there.

Oof. A ball of ice hit Mera in the back of the head. She spun and threw the blunted dagger in the direction of the ice ball. Gaeleath was too quick, and another ball of ice hit her hand, knocking away the second dagger.

"That's not fair," she yelled. "I can barely hold onto these things as it is."

"Don't be ridiculous, Mera," Gaeleath chided. "You hold a knife every evening at dinner. Holding a dagger is no different."

"Of course it is," She responded, marking her words with outstretched hands. "I am not planning to use it to fight someone else or to potentially stab them."

She turned to pick up the dagger he knocked away. He shook his head and walked to where the other she had thrown lay on the ground.

"Mera," he said when he returned and handed her the dagger hilt first. At the look on her face, he took a deep breath. "You spend so much time concerned with what you think should be natural that you're unable to see what might be possible. You're holding yourself back."

She gave a frustrated screech, threw the daggers on the ground, and stomped off toward the sleeping quarters. Gaeleath's shoulders slumped as he watched her retreat with sad eyes.

"You're right, fireball. She is holding herself back. Don't feel bad for stating the truth."

Gaeleath shrugged, picked up the daggers, and handed them to the cyclops before exiting the inner circle to practice his fire. He knew how frustration felt.

Mera held the sword the cyclops had handed her. It felt unbalanced in her hand. She lifted it anyway, slashing back-and-forth like he'd shown her. It wasn't that the sword was heavy, but it felt uncomfortable. If she imagined using it against someone, she couldn't picture ever managing the strike. In fact, that had been the trouble with all of the weapons she had tried since her arrival at The Palaestra. None of them felt right.

"Come on, Mera. You have to at least try." Tarkegan was very patient with her, but she knew he was exasperated.

"I am trying," she said.

"No, you're not," he retorted with a chuckle. "I could walk up to you right now and pluck that sword from your hand just as easily as plucking an astera from the puffed weeds there on the ground." His patience did not tamper his sarcasm, and Mera felt her frustration rising. Did he not see that she was trying? "Since I have felt your kick and your punch, I know you are strong enough to wield a sword, but you're spending so much time in your head about it, you're frozen."

At those words, Mera deflated. He was right. She had done the same thing with daggers, scimitars, and Gery's axe. Even when Tarkegan placed short sticks in her hands, she could not picture herself using them.

"No one is a master of a weapon until they get a feel for it. I don't mean 'feel' like you were looking for it now. I mean through comfortable practice. They don't become accustomed to the weight and movement until the weapon becomes an extension of themselves." He went into a fluid demonstration with his own sword, spinning and slashing, kneeling and squatting, his body harmonious with the weapon. "I didn't pick up a sword on my first day and become the weapon's master. In fact, I cut myself more times than I cut anything else. But I kept working at it." He picked up her sword from where she had dropped it in frustration and handed it back to her. "And once I mastered one weapon, I picked up another."

He walked over to the weapons table he pulled out every session Mera was meant to try and find her weapon of choice. He picked up each, in turn, and flipped it around in his hand as if it were another appendage. "Now, I am comfortable with nearly anything you put in my hands, though I have an obvious preference for my spear." He picked up the weapon he regularly sparred with and carried each time he left The Palaestra. Mera watched in awe at the confidence and competence he demonstrated with the long weapon. "The spear, like me," he said as he continued his demonstration, "has one point of view. It is steady, straightforward, and true."

He finished with a flourish that left the pointed end inches from her chest. She gasped in surprise at his stealth and quickness. He could have easily pierced her. She had been too distracted by her own failures and insecurities to follow his movements. Both he and Master Pholus had been warning her to stay out of her head while in the training ring and in a real fight. Even in this, she failed. She looked up at Tarkegan, expecting another look of exasperation, but when he turned his one eye on her, she read compassion in his gaze.

"You will, at some point, find your preferred weapon, Mera. Until that day, you will want to practice with many weapons because your enemy will not wait until you have perfected your fight before attacking."

"I have my wind," she countered, not knowing what else to say.

He laughed. "I've been around enough to see magic fail, including your magic. My hands, though, they never fail me."

Mera sighed. She wondered if Kari was having just as much trouble as she was in her training. She wished it was just the weapons that were the struggle, but he was right, her magic was just as elusive. It only came when she was angry or sad, when her emotions were high. Here on the training grounds, she was more frustrated than anything. Whenever it was time to train or spar with Tarkegan, he threw everything he could at her to try and trigger her magic, but she always knew he would not hurt her. He was one of the kindest people she'd ever met. Though she'd heard his stories of great battles, she couldn't imagine him hurting anyone. So, nothing he did brought forth a magical response from her. Each day, they both left the inner circle tired and discouraged.

Chapter Twenty-Three

Kari looked up from where she'd been writing in the dirt with the young children she was teaching. She still wasn't quite sure what she was doing with them, but the weeks she'd spent introducing them to symbols and what it means to have magic, so they would be prepared when they began to feel their own flutters, felt right. What she felt now, though, felt very wrong. She turned to Eckasia, "Take care of the children. Something is happening, and I need to check it out."

Kari didn't wait for a response but took off at a run. She didn't know what she was feeling exactly, but there was something in the forest that was not normally there. The elders didn't know, but she'd been placing security spells throughout the forest to warn of any unknown or unfamiliar creatures. Eustis' wards protected the actual community, but Kari didn't want them to be caught unawares if something entered the forest, and right now, something was definitely in the forest.

As she ran from the fields through The Thicket to the forest, she passed Phialyra walking with the babe, Eirini.

"Kari? Where are you off to so quickly? Is everything alright?"

"I'm not sure, Lyra, but I feel something. There's something or someone in the forest that doesn't belong. I need to check it out, if only to know I'm not losing my mind." She had turned to address her aunt but looked back the way she was running as if to bolt off again.

"You shouldn't be going alone."

"I promise I won't get too close, but I need to see if my spells are working."

"Spells? Oh, what have you been up to?" The thing Kari loved about Lyra was that she did not judge anyone. Her tone was one of mild curiosity with a sprinkling of concern.

"I'll explain later. I have to go."

"Wait," Lyra said, putting a hand on Kari's arm. "Do you even know where you're going or how far away it might be?"

"No, that's why I have to go. It might take me a while to find it." Kari was growing impatient but trying not to shout in the face of Lyra's concern.

"Here, let me help."

Kari looked at her with wide eyes and shook her head immediately. "You can't leave the baby."

"No, but I can help in another way."

Lyra held up her hand, closed her eyes, and before Kari realized what was happening, a large stag came walking through the opening in the hedgerow that led to the forest proper.

"Gods! You'll have to explain to me how you did that later."

"He will take you where you need to go much faster than you can on foot, and he will protect you. The gods know we don't need to lose anyone else."

Kari saluted her with an open palm raised to the sky. Then, she patted the buck's head and jumped on its back. She hadn't ridden a deer in years. When they were younger, she and Mera would often play in the forest. The fawns always wanted to play with them, probably because Mera appeared as kin to them. Kari had forgotten how fast they could run and was grateful to Lyra for calling the stag to carry her. She patted its neck and leaned down to whisper in its ear, "Do you feel the stranger too?" The stag snorted. "Let's go find it."

After seeing and hearing nothing for what seemed like forever, Kari was about to give up. Maybe she had imagined the sensation of a stranger in the forest. When they approached the dunes at the forest's eastern edge, however, raised voices echoed from the other side. Though she could not make out their words, or who they belonged to, Kari knew the argument she was hearing had something to do with the sensations she felt. "Stay here," she told the stag, as she climbed off its back. "We may need to get out of here very quickly." She slowly crept toward the dunes and climbed to the top on her knees, keeping low, so she would hopefully remain unseen by whoever or whatever was arguing on the other side.

"I mean no harm," came a squeaky voice. "I heard of these trees, and I wanted to come see them. Is that a crime?"

"Coming to see the Strimmena is not a crime. Coming to take from them is. Now, what do you want here?"

As Kari topped the dune, she saw Nelaira in battle stance before what appeared to be a gnome. Kari had never seen a gnome before, but this one sure matched the descriptions. What was a gnome doing here? Other than the dunes, there were no hills in the forest to make their homes, and she'd never before seen one.

"I didn't come here to disrespect the trees or you or anything else."

"Lies. I saw you with your little knife heading toward the Strimmena. What did you hope to take?"

"I," he stammered a bit before finishing. "I thought maybe I could get one of their branches."

"What? You would pluck a branch from this sacred place?"

He put his hands up protectively, and Kari almost felt sorry for him. Nelaira looked ready to tear him apart. "Look, I didn't realized it was sacred, yeah. The crazy nymph-goat girl said that this was her favorite place, and I was trying to get something for her."

Kari jumped up from her hidden spot. "Nymph-goat girl? Who are you?" Nelaira turned suddenly, prepared to attack until she locked eyes with Kari. "Sorry to interrupt," Kari said sheepishly, "but what did you mean by goat girl?"

"Yes, I think he needs to start talking," Nelaira said, turning back toward him.

"And I told Master Pholus that this was not a good idea for me to come out here. You forest folk are out of your minds."

Kari wasn't sure if he was talking to them or himself, but Nelaira was not having any of it.

"And the gods know you are about to be without a head if you don't start telling us who you are and why you're here."

Kari watched the small man as his eyes flitted about. There was something important Kari needed to remember about her lessons on gnomes. She stared at him trying to remember what the elders had taught them.

"Look, I came here for a reason. I could tell you my reason, but she probably wouldn't believe me," he said directly to Kari while pointing at Nelaira, "and then you still wouldn't let me go and do what it is that I need to do, so really, there's no point. I think I'll just go now."

"You're not going anywhere," Nelaira growled at him.

The slyness of his smile reminded Kari what she was forgetting. They can teleport! That would explain how he ended up in a random part of the forest, and she couldn't figure out where he had entered it. Quickly, she wove a web of magic around them, a protection spell of sorts that would neither let anything in nor let anything out. She wasn't yet strong enough to cast this type of protection spell over the whole forest, or even the entire thicket, but she could cast it over the three of them.

"I will leave when I'm ready, and I'm ready," his squeaky voice declared in triumph. He closed his eyes in a blink and then opened them again...and again. He repeated the process once more before his eyes went wide. Suddenly, he started looking from side to side.

"Are you trying to figure out why you're still here," Kari asked. "No one is going anywhere until we get answers. Now I want to know what you meant by nymph-goat girl."

"See, try to do something nice for somebody. I knew I shouldn't have done anything. She irritates me, and yet I try to do something nice for her. Now I'm stuck." He rambled on as if he hadn't heard Kari address him.

"Alright," Kari said, pushing her hands toward the ground in a calming gesture. "Let's try this again and start over completely. My name is Karielle, and I'm from The Thicket. This is Nelaira. She protects this part of the beach. She is a protectress of the great Strimmena here, and you are..."

"Still can't believe this. What in the world was I thinking? I should've just delivered my message, and I could've been gone. No, now I have to figure out how to get out of here."

"That's enough," Nelaira said sitting down in the sand. "You're acting like a child. You have a beard, so I assume you aren't a child."

Kari watched as his entire demeanor changed, and his glare grew strong at Nelaira. "No, I'm not a child."

"Then stop acting like one and sit down. Let's have a conversation because right now I'm thinking taking your head off is a good idea."

Kari was having a hard time hiding a chuckle at both his incredulous face and Nelaira's serious one. "Again, what is your name, and where are you from?"

He stared at Nelaira for another moment, still scowling with the rosiest cheeks Kari had ever seen. It made his scowl less menacing and more comical. Finally he took a breath and looked at Kari.

"My name is Gericole, and I'm a gnome from the city of Krinosera. I am the assistant to Master Pholus, yeah."

"Pholus the Centaur?" Kari's incredulity must've come across a little too much because he turned that cheery scowl on her, and it was all she could do to not break out in a fit of laughter. "I'm sorry. As far as I know, Pholus died hundreds of years ago."

"And as far as you know, so did the nymph Callisto, but I'm here to see her and deliver a message, yeah. So what do you really know?"

Kari did laugh at the look on his face that time when his scowl deepened and his brows drew together in anger. She held up her hands. "Yes, that's fair, we did think that Callisto was dead, at least most of us did until we recently found out otherwise. So let me get this straight, you are in the forest to deliver a message from Pholus the Centaur to Callisto the Nymph, both of which are supposed to be long gone. That still doesn't explain the situation happening right here along the shore."

"This was a misunderstanding."

"So help us understand," Nelaira said matter of fact, with just a hint of menace that nearly sent Kari into shrieks of laughter again.

"Alright. I can only teleport to places I have previously visited. I have been to this forest, so I came to the forest. I couldn't control where in the forest I was going because I didn't know where your thicket was, yeah. When I arrived, I didn't know which way to go, so I started in one direction. After walking a bit, I heard the waves of the ocean and..." he gestured widely to the surf. "I hadn't seen the ocean in centuries, so I decided to come have a look."

"Walking in this direction wasn't the only mistake. You came to take something from the Strimmena," Nelaira snarled.

"That was not my initial intention," he said in response to her accusation. He climbed back to his feet and walked toward the trees. Kari had to put her hand out to keep Nelaira from jumping after him. "When I came over to see the water, I saw the trees.

When I saw the trees, I remembered how important they were to Master Pholus' new pupil."

Kari and Nelaira looked at each other. "Are you saying that Pholus is training The Maenad," Nelaira asked.

Gery turned around, mouth agape. "Wait, do you know her?"

"She's my cousin," Kari said.

"And I am her protector as well, when she is here at the sea," Nelaira shared.

"Oh my goodness! Oh my goodness!" He rubbed his hands on his face ruffling his beard. "Is your name Kari?"

"I already told you it was." Kari put her hands on her hips.

"No need to get testy. No need to get testy. I missed that, yeah. I have a message for you from her, but I have to see Callisto first." His eyes sparkled in what could only be excitement.

"You still haven't answered to your intentions with the Strimmena," Nelaira said, drawing both of their attention.

"I can't say anything until I talk to Callisto. Then I can explain it all, and you can either believe me or not, yeah. But I can't say anything until I speak to Callisto."

"Very well. Nelaira, I will take him back with me to The Thicket."

Nelaira grabbed her hand and pulled her a few steps away from the gnome. "Are you sure that is safe? Might it not be a better idea to bring Callisto to him," she whispered.

"I'm sure that my aunt and grandmother would also like to hear how Mera is doing. If he's lying, it will be just as easy to kill him there," Kari whispered back, looking over her shoulder at their strange visitor.

"I'm not lying! I'm not lying. There's not need to kill me, yeah. I really do like my life."

They both turned toward him. Nelaira's eyes had widened and then narrowed. "Has anyone ever said that you talk too much?"

He smiled, and Kari sputtered with laughter. "I'm sure he's

heard it as many times as I have. Come, Gericole, and tell us of my cousin."

"Have you ever ridden a deer before?"

"Have I ever ridden a deer?" Gery's voice trailed off as the majestic stag stood in front of them. "No, no, and I would prefer not to right now."

Kari laughed. "Well, since you don't know where you're going, and I'm not going to walk the full day's path to get there, we're going to ride." She jumped on the stag's back and got comfortable. "Do you need me to help you up?" she turned and asked behind her. She watched Gery close his eyes and gulp before she watched him disappear, and then just as suddenly reappear behind her. "What was that?"

"What do you mean?"

"How do you do that? How do you move from down there to up here?"

"Do you not have people who can teleport?"

"No. But how convenient would that be! I could get into so much trouble with that power." Gery looked at her. "You are interesting," he said.

"If you ask my family, that is an understatement. Now, hold on, and if you try anything, I will kill you myself." Of course, she wasn't sure how she would do that when he could just vanish, nor did she know if he had any weapons. Suddenly she was considering Nelaira's words about whether it was wise to bring him into The Thicket or not. She quickly reestablished the spell she had placed over them on the beach to contain his moving around and tried to think of her options.

"Is it really that far?" he asked, breaking her from her thoughts.

"Far enough. It takes my cousin no time to get out here with those strong legs of hers, but the rest of us have to trek it the hard way."

"Doesn't look like you're trekking it the hard way to me," he said, looking down with a shudder.

"Are you alright?"

"I'm just not the biggest fan of heights, and while it might not seem too high to you, this buck is double my height. We might as well be standing on a cliff, or rather sitting on one."

She stifled a giggle at his comparison, considering this cliff was moving at a very swift pace, but then she said quietly, "just close your eyes. That way, you won't be looking down." She was actually hoping he would close his eyes, so he wouldn't see the direction they were traveling in. Then she willed the deer to vary his route.

When they stopped, Kari turned and watched the gnome open his eyes and look around confusedly. "This doesn't look like a village," he said.

"It's not, but it's as close as I'm taking you."

"You don't trust me," he said as more of a statement than a question.

"I don't know you, and the last time a strange man showed up to The Thicket, bad things happened. I would rather not be the one to repeat those things. So you will stay here with the stag, and I'll return with the others. Know that there is a spell wrapped around you to dampen your ability to just go teleporting about." She waved her hands in his direction hoping her gesticulations would seem more ominous than the words of a nymph of barely fifteen winters.

He immediately tried to teleport, and she could see on his face his resignation at being unable to do so. "There aren't things out here that will eat gnomes, right? I would hate to have gone through all this to bring a message and get eaten by a forest creature before you get back."

"You'll be fine. Stay there, and stay on the stag. If something happens, he can try and give you an escape. I'll return shortly."

He likely didn't intend for her to hear, but she caught his "Please hurry. I don't like to be in the forest alone," and she almost changed her mind about leaving him there.

Chapter Twenty-Four

G ery wasn't sure how long he had been waiting there on top of that deer, but shadows were starting to fall, as the sun moved further away from the forest. It reminded him of their race against time in the city, and his nerves made him irritable. "What's taking her so long?" he asked of no one. "Just leave people out in the middle of the forest by themselves." The buck snorted, but Gery ignored him and continued his descent into self-pity. "Why did Pholus have to send me on this fool's errand anyway, and for that annoying goat-girl? I have got to learn to say no." He would've continued the tirade had he not heard voices drawing near.

At first he couldn't hear what they were saying at all, and he wasn't quite sure it was the nymph who left him. Then he heard her voice.

"I was afraid to bring him into The Thicket. I know that we can protect ourselves when we know something is coming, but this gnome has the ability to teleport himself in and out of places. I didn't want to give him our location to come back later."

If they hadn't been talking about him, he would've smiled at that. It was one of the reasons he'd created their training arena and living space the way he did. He didn't want anyone who just happened to be traipsing around the mountains to stumble upon them. He thought it a very good plan, even if hearing her words reminded him that he wasn't trusted, or really welcome, here.

"Hurry up," came an older and more powerful voice. Gery could only imagine that it must be one of the village elders, as even her voice delivered a sense of authority.

"How much farther until we find this gnome of yours? He said he had information about my Mera, right?" came yet another voice, this one more lilting and excited than the others.

He wondered how many nymphs she was bringing back with her.

"If he has truly been sent by my friend, he will have information about your daughter. I left her in his care, and he does have a gnome who works for him. From my understanding, he is more family than employee."

That statement made Jerry smile, and he had to work real hard to relax his face before they appeared from between the trees. He wanted to yell at the young nymph for taking so long, at the same time that he wanted to know how they just appeared through the trees without him being able to see them approach the clearing. He suddenly felt intimidated by the group standing before him and said nothing.

They were all beautiful, though he could tell that three of them were much older than the other two. He'd been on this planet long enough to realize that elders carried themselves differently. "Good afternoon," he finally said in greeting, knowing it would be considered rude to stand there gawking at them when he had intruded on their land.

"Good afternoon to you," said one of the elder nymphs. "I heard that you were sent to look for me, and I am hoping that is the truth."

"It is definitely the truth. If you're Callisto, I was sent here to look for you and deliver a message, yeah."

"I am she, and your name is?"

"My name is Gericole, and I work for Master Pholus the Centaur."

"Very well, Gericole, what is the message that your master has sent to me."

Gery looked around at the group of nymphs. "He said that I was supposed to give you this message in private." The faces of the other nymphs darkened in impatience, though it did not look like Callisto was perturbed in any way.

"I understand. He was always very secretive. My friends here are concerned about a young maenad in his care. Can you tell us about her first? Then we will be free to speak privately."

Gery knew that he had to choose his words carefully. He could not be overly honest about how he felt about their family member, and he wondered how much he could tell them about what happened when they left the city. Master Pholus hadn't given him explicit instructions about that. "Can I get off this deer now?" he asked to give himself some thinking time.

Kari laughed. "You could've gotten off the deer a long time ago. I'm sure the stag will be happy to relax his back."

He scowled. "What are you trying to say?"

"Simply that he's been standing there for hours now with you on his back."

"You told me I couldn't go anywhere."

"No, I told you that you couldn't teleport anywhere. I didn't say you couldn't get off the deer, just that you would be safer on him if something were to come after you while I was gone."

"You tricked me." She laughed even harder then but did not respond.

"Let us sit on the ground," offered Callisto, refocusing the group, and all of the nymphs found soft places to sit while Gery hopped down from the stag's back. "Feel free to stay on your feet, Gericole. We know you have been sitting for a long time. So long as you intend us no harm, no harm will come to you."

"I thought nymphs were very hospitable to those passing through their territory. You all seem very worried. I feel like there are things that Master Pholus did not warn me about when he sent me here."

"Forgive our lack of hospitality, Gericole," said one of the other elder nymphs. "We have had some concerning situations in recent times that make us a little more wary of unexpected visitors. My name is Dynami, and I am the matriarch of The Thicket. I believe that your master has one of our own in his care. "This is her mother," the elder said, pointing to the younger nymph.

"Please tell me that my Mera is well," the maenad's mother pled.

"She's fine. When I left this morning, she was trying to grow a tree in the middle of the field. I thought I overheard her say you'd shown her how to do that," Gery said to Callisto. He watched as the others turned surprised gazes on her.

"Young Mera has very strong emotions. If she cannot learn to control those emotions, she must learn how to channel them through her magic." The other nymphs nodded in agreement, and Gery was sure there was a story behind those nods. "As we were walking to meet up with Pholus," Callisto continued, "she had a very emotional moment and grabbed a tree nearly killing it." Kari gasped, and the other nymphs looked down in their laps, but Callisto did not pause her tale. "I helped her figure out how to channel and control those emotions to create new life, and we talked about how her magic could be either destructive or constructive." He noticed tears in Skyemera's mother's eyes. "With just a little bit of prompting, she grabbed that same tree's root and grew another entire tree before my eyes. She was quite powerful already, and we have no idea in what ways or how far that power goes."

"Yes, Master Pholus feels the same way, and when I saw her using her magic, oh my goodness it was amazing! She knocked those demons right out of the way..." He froze. He should not have told them that. He stood silent for a moment waiting for their response, hoping maybe they'd overlook the details, but he'd never been that lucky.

The elder nymph who hadn't spoken yet gasped before they all responded in unison, "What do you mean demons?"

Skyemera's mother jumped to her feet, "You told me my Mera is fine. What do you mean by demons?"

He held his hands up in front of him. "She is fine, yeah. She's fine. I left her this morning, and she was fine. She was with all the other trainees, and she was fine."

Callisto lay a hand on the mother's arm, and he watched as the nymph visibly relaxed, before she began pacing back and forth.

"She does that too, you know?" He smiled at the visibly shaken nymph, though he knew a smile would not be enough to reduce her worries. "That back and forth. When she's thinking or when she's worried or when somethings not going her way, she has to walk. She does it a lot." The young mother turned a sad smile in his direction. "I'm sorry if I made you worried and spoke out of turn." He addressed the whole group. "Can I know your names? It seems very weird to be having this long conversation with you all, and I don't know your names. When I go back, I'm sure Skyemera's going to ask who I spoke with."

"That is understandable, Gericole," Callisto answered before any of the others spoke. "I am sure that she will indeed want to know who you saw here, providing Pholus lets her know that you came."

"I would tell her anyway," he said, and he meant it. "I would tell her, yeah." He saw the young one smile again. He turned to her first. "I know you told me your name, but I'm sorry, I was too busy talking, and I don't remember what it was."

She giggled before saying, "My name is Kari."

"Oh yeah, you're the one she talks about all the time. She said we're very similar, you and me, though I can't imagine why." Kari laughed so hard she began coughing, drawing a stern glare from the village matriarch.

"That's enough Karielle," admonished the elder nymph.

"Your name is Dynami," he said, drawing attention away from Kari. You just told me that. I remember that. And you are Skyemera's mother," he said to Lyra once she stopped pacing.

"My name is Phialyra."

"Phialyra, yeah. Good, I got that." He then turned to the last of the elders, "and you are?"

"My name is Helena."

"Oh, Helena. Good, I got it now. I will know who to tell her I talked to. I think she'll be glad to hear those things."

The nymph, Helena, spoke up again, "now tell us about these demons, Gericole." By the gods, they were not going to overlook his slip.

"The demons? Right, right." He closed his eyes and inhaled deeply. "So there was a situation in Krinosera where we got chased by some shadow demons and had to run, and there was fire, and there were arrows, and there was a priestess, and the priestess tried to get Skyemera to go with her, and she didn't because the maenad set a strong wind on her and blew all the fire her way and burned the shadow demons, and we all escaped."

"I'm sorry, what!" Kari exclaimed.

He looked around at them, and all of their mouths were gaping. He rang his hands, as the matriarch's surprise turned to anger. Her eyes then shifted to concern before she got control of her emotions and was able to speak.

"I'm sorry, Gericole, did you just say that my granddaughter was nearly captured by a priestess with some shadow demons?"

"Your granddaughter? Never mind, not important, and not exactly. She and Master Pholus had passed through my city, and she was fascinated by all of the churches that we have there."

"Churches? What are churches," Kari asked.

"They are places where people go to worship their different gods."

"Oh, like our temples of old."

Callisto turned to her, answering before Gery could respond. "Not exactly, young one. In larger cities, such as the one I believe Gery is telling us about, the people believe in many different gods, not necessarily the ancient ones that we remember and venerate here. In The Thicket, you all still follow the ancient ways and worship the ancient gods, but in other parts of the world, there are many gods worshipped and called upon."

"Right," said Gery, "Many different gods. So Skyemera wanted to go into a church, and she went in by herself because Master Pholus takes up a lot of room and often feels uncomfortable inside many buildings. It should've been fine. It should've been safe. They've always been safe. But we found out later, after I met up with him, that she had come to meet up with a priestess of the God of Fire."

"God of Fire," the elder nymph Helena asked. "Who is this God of Fire?"

Callisto stood and Gery felt the silent command to remain quiet. "There are four elemental gods that many on the planet worship. These gods are said to have existed before even Zeus. Many believe they were the embodiment of The Titans we've learned about through our histories. There is the Goddess of the Earth, the God of water, the God of wind and the God of Fire. While they may sound familiar, they are very different from the ones you all know to exist in The Thicket. Together, these gods control all of the natural world, and those who worship them believe that their god is most important for preserving and protecting everyone in the world and all of its creatures."

Gery watched the faces of the other nymphs, which ranged from concern to confusion. Kari's face, however, was set in excited curiosity. She appeared to be taking it all in like a child listening to a bedtime story. He understood why Skyemera seemed to miss her most of all. She was unfettered in her response to everything. When she turned to look at him, he realized he was staring and turned his focus back on Callisto's lesson.

"They are said to have worked together, but this God of Fire, Sizzsear, has not always played nice with the others. Not only do his people, his followers, if you will, believe that he is the most important because he can bring destruction to everything and everyone, he also believes that he is the strongest of them all."

"Yeah," Gery interjected, "so in my city, they do not allow followers of Sizzsear to build churches. That priestess should've never been there, but somehow she was, and she met Skyemera in the church. It wasn't until the coming dusk that the maenad shared what had happened with us. Dusk means shadows, and the priestess' shadow demons chased us out of the city. Master Pholus and one of the other trainees used flaming arrows to keep the demons away from us...until they ran out of arrows. It was Skyemera's wind that saved us and allowed us to escape. She made the wind push the fire and burn everything in its wake."

"Wait," interrupted Kari, "this is supposedly the priestess of the God of Fire, and yet she and her demons were stopped with fire? That doesn't seem to make much sense."

"As Master Pholus explained it, they are shadow demons, not fire demons. Too much light kills the shadow, and that is exactly what happened. The priestess was not hurt by the fire, but her demons were, at least enough for us to escape." At the horrified looks around the group, Gery added, "There have been no issues since, yeah. She is safe and she is working hard."

"My poor Mera. We sent her away to make sure she was safe, to make sure we were all safe, and she walked into...I don't even know what to call it." The nymph looked like she was about to cry.

"Please don't cry. I don't do well when people cry, and, like I said, she's fine, yeah. She gives me a hard time all the time, but she also cries. I think she misses you all, but she is working hard to master what she needs to, so she can come back home."

"I wish I could see her," Kari said.

"I don't know if that would be a good idea. Right now she is working hard, so she can return."

"That is not a good idea," Helena said. "You still have much to do and learn, Kari, as does Mera. These are things you both must do on your own, so that you can be stronger when you are back together."

"I know, but I miss my best friend." She turned away for a moment before twirling back to the group. "Oh, so when I found Gery, he was at the shore, trying to pull a branch from The Strimmena."

"The Strimmena?" Dynami asked.

"Yes, the trees that Mera likes to hide beneath when she goes to the beach."

Callisto turned to him. "What were you doing?"

"Master Pholus thinks that it might help if Skyemera had some kind of relic or item that would help her feel connected to and channel her magic. I know that for some people they might have an amulet or a ring or something else, but other than the ring she said she got from her grandmother," he paused looking at Dynami, "from you, she doesn't appear to wear anything like that." Dynami nodded at him in a way that said he wasn't wrong in his conclusion, so he continued. "She's also had difficulty determining what kind of weapons she'd like to use for fighting. When we were attacked by the shadow demons, I had given her a broken tree branch to use as a staff, and she did pretty well knocking the demons away with that. So I thought maybe a rod of some sort would be good for her."

He recounted how Mera had spoken so fondly about the white oaks along the shore that when he was wandering through the forest and came to the shore, he was drawn to the trees. He thought that her connection to them would help her somehow. "I didn't realize they were sacred, though. I just thought they were regular trees that she like to sit by, at least until that sea nymph tried to kill me."

"That's where I found him and Nelaira arguing," Kari said. "He wouldn't explain to her what he was doing, and she was protecting The Strimmena." Kari turned a sly smile on him, "I guess it's a good thing I came along, huh?" He was in the middle of thinking up a sarcastic retort when Callisto addressed him.

"Gericole, is there anything else that you need to share with The Maenad's family?"

"No, I don't think so."

"Thank you, Gericole, you have provided us some comfort," said the matriarch. "Ancient one, we will leave you alone to get your message in private. Do you need us to stay close?"

"No, Mother. I will be fine."

Gery didn't know what to say in response to their words of departure. Should he say thank you, you're welcome, nice to meet you, thanks for not killing me? So he settled for "Hey, will I be able to leave here when I'm done?" Without turning around from where they were leaving the clearing, Kari lifted up her hands and snapped her fingers. Gery felt a weight lift off his shoulders. "Oh, thank goodness! I thought that young nymph was going to keep me here forever, and I don't like the forest too much."

Callisto smiled at him. "Now share what it is your master needed me to know."

Chapter Twenty-Five

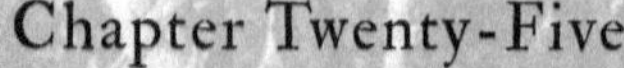

Once he had finished recounting Pholus's message, Gery was prepared to leave. "I will now return to The Palaestra. Is there a message you would like me to send back?"

"Yes, but you will have to wait until the morning."

Gery looked around nervously. Was she going to leave him alone in the forest? Did she expect him to just stay here? Kari had given him the ability to leave again, but Callisto sounded like she expected him to stay. "You want me to stay here in the forest?"

"No." She laughed a beautiful, twinkling sound, much like he imagined the stars sound when they blink on and off, like little bells. He understood why Pholus admired her so much. She was beautiful, even at her advanced age. He would have never guessed that she was nearly as old as the centaur himself. More than that, she was kind and wise. He had met many wise people in his life, but very few were kind to him.

"I am inviting you to join us for dinner."

He looked at her for a moment not sure he understood what she meant by us. "You want me to accompany you to The Thicket? I'm not sure the others will be very comfortable with that."

"The others will be fine, but to satisfy their concern I have a question about your teleportation powers. I need an honest answer, or you will not only lose the trust of everyone here in the forest, but I will also tell Pholus of your treachery."

He nodded. He had lied to many people over the centuries, but he had no desire to ever lose favor with his friend and mentor. Pholus had saved him and given him something to belong to, and something to believe in. He would protect that relationship with everything he had. He nodded at her again. "I will answer you true, yeah." She looked at him steadily, and his palms began to sweat. Were nymphs able to read people's minds? He hadn't even considered that. Though, he imagined if that were possible, he would not have spent so much time sitting on the sand earlier.

"I understand that you are only able to teleport to exact locations where you have been. If you are taken somewhere without knowledge of how to get there, would you be able to give directions to others, or would you only be able to teleport there directly?"

He had to think for a moment. That was not a question he had ever been asked before, and he wasn't sure whether it was a situation he had experienced. "Honestly, I don't know. That's not a situation I've been in before, at least not that I can remember. I am half a millennium old, so if it was something that happened when I was a child, I don't remember."

"Let's try something." That nervous twitch went up his back again. "If I asked you to teleport back to the Strimmena, could you?"

"Yes. I've been there. In fact, I spent the whole morning there."

"Good. Would you then be able to find this location again?"

"Sure. I'm standing here with you now, so I can come back here."

"Can you show me the way to the Strimmena? I've not seen them."

He looked at her, and then he turned. He turned again in a

different direction. When he had turned all the way in a circle back around to her, his head tilted to the side, and he frowned. "I don't know which direction we came from."

"Did you not just come here this morning?"

"Yes, but I had my eyes closed most of the way. I was really nervous sitting on that buck's back. It made me so uncomfortable, and Kari told me to close my eyes, so I closed my eyes."

"Did you fall asleep," she asked with a bit of a smile that he knew could become a laugh in no time.

"No, I was awake the whole time. I think that deer was walking in circles or zigzagging."

"Alright, let's give this a try. I heard that you could take people with you, so let's go to the sea where I can see the Strimmena."

"Are you sure that's a good idea? That sea nymph did not seem like she would be too happy if I returned."

"I will make sure that you are safe."

His shoulders were tight, and his whiskers itchy. "I'm trusting you," he said, looking into her eyes. "Put your hand on my shoulder." Callisto had no sooner followed his instructions, that they left the clearing and arrived to the sounds of the ocean, their feet in the sand.

"That was impressive," she said after stabilizing herself and releasing his shoulder. "I haven't been teleported in years, nay, centuries, and I don't remember it ever being that smooth of a transition. You have a gift, Gericole."

"Please call me Gery. You are a friend of Master Pholus, and now you have traveled with me."

"Very well, Gery. We should not be here long, so let us commune with these Strimmena."

Gery stood back a bit. "I think I will stay right here and not get too close. That way if the nymph comes, she will see that I'm nowhere near those trees."

Callisto laughed with her melodious sounding voice and said

"yes, but if you are too far away, I may not be able to protect you when she arrives." He looked around quickly, and then hurried to stand closer to Callisto, who was looking at the trees with soft eyes. "They are rather beautiful, aren't they," she mused.

"I'm not sure that I would have said beautiful, but they are definitely different...curious, maybe."

"Yes, they are different, and they have survived millennia beside the sea without any protection from the winds and the storms. Their strength amidst everything thrown at them is what makes them beautiful."

"Skyemera said that this was her favorite place to be, with these trees, because they make her feel safe, because they are so similar to how she is. She doesn't think she is beautiful. But she sees these trees that remind her of her own differently shaped body as beautiful."

"You appear to have developed a fondness for her, Gery," Callisto said, turning to look at it him.

"Ha! I don't know about any fondness. We argue all the time. But when she talks about how different she feels, and how alone, even amongst her people, she feels, I recognize that feeling." He paused for a moment wondering how much he should share with her. Then he remembered how kind she had been and deemed her safe. "It's why I stay with Master Pholus. I never feel that way with him or the others at The Palaestra." She moved closer, stopping him before he could share more specifics.

"I understand," she said before she reached out a hand. Gery's body tensed when she touched his shoulder. He wasn't sure the purpose of the gesture, so he wasn't sure how he should respond. Then she reached out and touched one of the trees.

"What are you doing," he asked and cringed at the fear in his voice.

"I am allowing the Strimmena to feel the empathy you have for Skyemera. They have always protected her, watched over, and been a solace for her. I want them to know that you are also, in your own way, watching over her now. I want them to know that you can be trusted."

He looked at her until he could no longer see her clearly. He didn't know what to say, or if he could even get the words out. He turned his face away, so she wouldn't see the tear running down his cheek, and that's when he saw her.

"What are you doing back here?" Nelaira screamed as she ran across the sand, spear lifted. "You are not welcome here!"

Callisto turned. "Lower your spear, Nelaira. We will have no violence here today."

The wind rattled through the Strimmena behind Callisto, and Nelaira stopped in her tracks, dropping to one knee, mouth slacked open, eyes wide. Gery looked back and forth between the sea nymph and Callisto not knowing what was happening between them. He also couldn't tell why the wind had picked up so heavily, until he heard a crack from the tree copse. His attention drawn to them, his own mouth dropped open.

He knew that Nelaira hadn't been lying, and that Skyemera had been honest when she said it felt like the trees themselves were alive and somehow protecting her. He just never expected to see anything from them, at least nothing like this. From within their depths, a branch came forward. It left the copse of trees floating horizontally. He could see what appeared to be the shape of a hand at the top like five fingers open, stretched forward, space between them and a palm in the middle. When it cleared the trees, the branch turned vertical and stood its full 6 foot tall height. It was pure white from the top to the bottom, and the hand, as he knew it now to be a hand, reached toward the sky.

He turned his head slightly to ensure that he wasn't the only one who was seeing this happen, and he found both Nelaira and Callisto with their left hands lifted toward the sky in the same way as the branch. He watched that very same branch float toward

Callisto until she grasped it. Once she had her fingers around the staff, she lowered that hand and touched the staff to the ground, the other hand still lifted in salute.

"Thank you," she said to the trees, and then she turned to look at him. "The Strimmena offer this staff for Skyemera. We will trust you to deliver it to her along with the message of the trees."

This time it was he who dropped to one knee. The love and acceptance the trees had for Skyemera humbled him. "I will deliver it and the message." He lifted his hand to receive the staff and sniffled, simultaneously wiping his eyes. "I have seen a lot of things in my five hundred years, but I have never seen anything like this."

"Come Nelaira, I would also invite you to dine with us tonight. We are all in this together, for what comes affects us all."

Nelaira stood and nodded. When she looked at Gery, he could not help but notice that she no longer held him in contempt. Was that awe in her eyes? He wasn't sure, but he was glad to see that she no longer looked like she wanted to tear him apart.

"Gery, are you able to take two people with you," Callisto asked.

"Of your size, yes. Unfortunately, in the fight with the shadow demons, I could not take Master Pholus and Skyemera together. We had to find another way to get them out."

"And she did escape, and we thank you. Come, Nelaira, touch his shoulder."

"Forgive me, Ancient One, but what is about to happen?"

Gery didn't wait for an answer. As soon as both nymphs touched his shoulders, they returned to the clearing where the buck still stood.

"What was that?" Nelaira asked.

"That was teleportation," answered Callisto. "This gnome has a wonderful ability."

Gery watched Nelaira open her mouth and close it multiple times before she said, "I'm not sure how I feel after that. It is strange to be in one place and then another within the same blink of the eye."

"Yes," Callisto said, "it is strange at first, but very convenient." Gery smiled at her. It was definitely convenient and had gotten him out of many difficult situations before.

Chapter Twenty-Six

The weeks passed while Mera worked on making the flowers bloom. Spring was quickly coming around, and Persephone's light would soon shine on the mountain. The buds would sprout and the flowers would bloom in spite of Mera's attempts not because of them. Though the plants no longer shied away, Mera's magic continued to elude her.

They no longer see me as a threat, she thought to herself. There was no need to fear her when she could do nothing to them besides talk. So, she talked. She begged and coerced. Still, nothing happened.

"Still no luck, young Mera?" The cyclops' voice up here on the ridge no longer startled her. He was always the one Pholus sent to find her at mealtimes.

She shook her head. "I have tried everything I can think of." She leaned against the nearest pine and slid to a seated position. He did the same against another tree facing her.

"There was a reason Master Pholus believed this a strong challenge for you. What was it?"

She stared at him for a moment. The question was not one she had been expecting, and she wasn't sure how to answer. "He told me Callisto had shared how I had grown a tree simply by touching the root." Tarkegan's eyes lit up, and she shook her head sadly. "Don't get excited. She didn't tell him that before then, I had nearly killed a tree by strangling it with a vine." Her throat constricted thinking about the potential for destruction her power held. As much as she wanted to bring it forth, the fear was overwhelming. "I just never know what will happen."

The cyclops eyes shone with compassion. "The first time I fought outside of my own kind, I did not realize my own strength." His gaze slipped away, as if he were looking through time. "It was many moons ago, long before Master Pholus found me. I was wandering and came across a kingdom preparing for a grand celebration that included competitions of strength and dexterity. They even had men demonstrating their abilities on horseback." He laughed at the memory. "Our Purivia could've beaten them all with her archery and horsemanship."

Mera agreed with his assessment. Purivia had been fearless when she came to help them escape the shadow demons and Yevondra. Mera shivered at the memory and turned her full attention back to Tarkegan to keep from reliving that moment.

"I did not yet have mastery over any weapons except my spear, and the only men there fighting with spear-like weapons were on horseback. Can you imagine me riding a horse?"

Mera laughed aloud at the image. "Your long legs would be running along the ground on either side," she said between chortling breaths.

He, too, was laughing. "If the horse could even run under my weight." Mera's mirth died, as she considered her own size difference, but he continued his story with the same energy. "So, I signed up for the hand-to-hand combat competition. I figured that would be one I was bound to win. I was young, in my prime, and naive." His laughter faded. "I won my first three trials. The humans were much smaller and weaker than I, even those they considered their champions."

The long pause left Mera with a sense of foreboding. His stories were always leading to some kind of lesson, but she couldn't imagine what this one might be. Did he lose the last match? He had said he didn't know his own strength, so maybe he broke someone's weapons.

"In the final trial, I went against this brawny human. He was, indeed, much larger than the others, and he put up a great fight. We landed on the ground, grappling." His face contorted in a grimace. "This was never meant to be a fight to the death. We were to immobilize the other person, but he was much more aggressive than I expected after the first three fights." Mera held her breath waiting for the revelation she knew was coming. "I managed to get my legs around his barreled chest, and I was trying to wrap my arms around his neck to incapacitate him. He would not stop fighting. I squeezed, hoping he'd drift off to sleep. Time stood still, and when it began to pass again, his head was in my hands."

Mera gasped, hand coming up to her mouth. She knew Tarkegan was strong, but she could not imagine him doing this. He was always so controlled.

It took a few moments, but the cyclops refocused his attention on Mera. "So much changed for me in that moment. I had been the favorite to win the competition, and suddenly, I was a demon in the eyes of everyone there. I could barely catch my breath to process what I'd done, and I had to run away to not lose my own head. The guilt haunted me for years, still does sometimes."

Mera gaped at him. "But you didn't mean to kill him, right?" She could not reconcile her compassionate weapons trainer with an intentional killer.

"No, young Mera, I did not intend to kill the man, but I did kill him. I must live with that. I have since killed many men in battle, intentional and not, and I must live with those deaths as well. I simply hope that the work I've put in to hone my control, skills, and impulsivity is enough to ensure any further deaths by my hand are intentional. I also hope that the lives I touch with my training keep more people alive. I hope for balance, not absolution."

His gaze was intense. Mera considered his idea of balance. Could she find balance between the destructive potential of her magic and her desire to use it positively? She had managed to grow a tree from the root, hadn't she?

"Whenever I begin to feel overwhelmed by the damage I've done in my life, I think about the friends I've made and the trainees I've helped," Tarkegan told her. "You need to find something positive to hold onto for when your fear tries to overpower you. Now, we are missing the meal, and I do not like to go to bed hungry."

They both stood, and the cyclops began to climb the ridge. Mera, still processing everything he'd told her, looked around at the bushes that still refused to bloom for her. She thought about the tree she'd nearly killed and the tickle of the new leaves on her shoulder when it had regrown. She may have been unsuccessful today, but she would try again, and she would make the intentional choice to use her magic in a positive way. She turned to follow Tarkegan up the ridge, a smile on her lips. A light breeze swirled around her and through the ridge, touching the pines and rustling the leaves of the bushes in her wake. A small bud formed on one of the rhododendron stems.

"I guess they can teach an old bird new flight patterns if you're giving up your hammers."

The cyclops had been her sparring partner this morning, and she was so surprised by his outburst, that she nearly fell face first in the dirt when he sidestepped to address whoever was coming up behind her.

"Still can't see the forest for the trees, I see," came a voice she recognized. Mera spun around and smiled.

"You're back!"

Gery looked around as if surprised. "Who? Has someone been gone?"

She smiled at his teasing. They had gotten off to a rocky start, but she had grown fond of the gnome and was excited to hear of his trip to her home.

"So what's with the stick?" Gaeleath asked from one of the other training circles where he had been sparring with a new trainee.

"Staff. It is a staff, intentionally made, not a stick."

"Staff. Stick. Looks like it fell out of a tree to me."

"You have no idea," Gery responded before he turned to Mera. "I will tell of your family later, but first, a gift."

"What? From home?"

"From the Strimmena," he said.

"The trees sent me a gift?" She didn't mean to sound as incredulous as she must have because his smile turned serious.

"Yes, and if I hadn't been there myself, I would not have believed the story. As it is, I still have a hard time believing it."

His words and demeanor gave her pause. What in the world could have happened to make him so unnerved? In his hands, he held a beautiful branch of white oak. It stood nearly twice his height, and at the end were gnarled shoots that formed what almost looked like a hand. He had been carrying it horizontally, which made sense considering the difference in his height and the length of the staff. When he stood it up, the gnarled fingers at the top, Mera felt herself audibly gasp. She reached her hand slowly to the sky, palm up and fingers open. It was the salute. She couldn't believe what she was seeing. He was holding a symbol of her people.

She looked at him, but there were so many questions going on around her head that nothing came out. Instead of teasing her, he simply nodded and held the staff in her direction. No one in the canyon bed spoke. The sparring had stopped when Gery joined them on the field, but they were now all watching Mera in silence. She doubted they understood the significance of the staff's form or its origin, but she wondered if they could feel the sense of peace that enfolded her as she reached out and lightly stroked the wood with the backs of her knuckles.

A smile took over her face, and she opened her hand to grasp the staff fully. Wind whistled through the canyon, wrapping around her in the same way her hand wrapped around the staff. Hair whipping about her face, she lifted the staff from the ground a few inches, enough to feel its strength. She felt the power of the Strimmena channel through the branch and into her hand. The power caressed her mind with warm memories of her time spent amongst them on the shore. She knew then that Gery had not made up the story of the staff's origin. The trees had plucked one of their own branches and fashioned the staff just for her.

"The gift comes with a message," Gery said, intruding on her communion with the trees. She turned on him more sharply than she might have otherwise, and he took a step back. "The trees gave me a message to share, yeah," he quickly continued. The wind receded and Mera sat the staff back on the ground before he visibly relaxed.

"Please share the message, Gery," Mera said, letting the others on the field fade from her thoughts.

"They said…" he started timidly, and Mera almost sighed her impatience. "The staff is for Skyemera. It will help her hone and focus her magic. It will remind her that she is loved and protected as a part of this world. This staff will remind her that she is worthy and that she is strong. It is as unbreakable as the Strimmena who made it."

By the time Gery had gone silent, Mera's eyes were overflowing her emotions. How had they known how much she needed this message and how alone she'd been feeling all these months?

"Thank you, Gery," she said without immediately looking up at him. When she raised her face, she saw everyone looking at her and wanted to run back to her cave. Their eyes held so many questions she did not think she could answer.

"Skyemera, please come see me," came Pholus' voice from outside the opening that held his living quarters. Relief and nerves ran through her simultaneously, and it took several moments before she could will her legs to move. "Gaeleath, I will see you next. Please join us in thirty minutes." Mera didn't wait to see the other trainee's response before she made her way toward Pholus and out of the sparring field.

Chapter Twenty-Seven

"How are you feeling?" Pholus asked when Mera entered the cave that served as his office. He had already settled himself down on his bench and was looking at parchments strewn across the table.

"I'm not sure how to answer that, Great Pholus. I have too many emotions right now, but I am grateful to you for pulling me from the field before I had to answer any questions."

He simply nodded to her. She had learned that his nod was a general acknowledgment of her words whether or not he agreed with them. She had also learned that when he did this, he was preparing to counter with some other reason or task she might not be as grateful for. She held back a sigh and sat on one of the boulders that served as chairs in front of his desk to wait for him to say why he called her.

"I can tell by your countenance that you know I didn't just call you in here to gauge your temperament." She nodded when he paused, and he continued. "You've been improving with your training and your practice, but I feel that the routine and formality of our methods here may not be serving your needs."

Her stomach quivered. "Are you sending me away?" she

blurted. She knew she hadn't made as much progress as he had hoped. She could see it in his eyes whenever he was training her himself. "I can do better. Now that I have the staff, I will do better!"

Pholus held up a hand. "Who said anything about sending you away?"

Trying to keep the panic from her voice, she countered, "You said this might not be the best place for me." How could she help her family if she couldn't train? Where else could she possibly be safe enough to train? She couldn't be sent away. She felt her heartbeat pounding in her chest.

"Skyemera, I need you to breathe. I need you to breathe and to listen before your wind picks up and blows everything off my desk."

The calmness in his voice brought her attention to the edges of the parchments lifting slightly from the wooden slab they lay upon. She closed her eyes and tried to bring her breathing under control. She didn't open them again until she felt her heartbeat relax. It wasn't until she looked at him that he spoke again.

"I didn't say you would need to leave. I was saying we need to try something different to help you feel the urgency to tap more deeply into your magic. If we had any inkling of your capabilities or their developmental properties, I could probably make this training more systematic, like I have been able to do with the others. Instead, I only have my memories of the last maenad to guide us, and she began developing her powers much younger than you are with the support of her family."

She looked down at the floor. She didn't like to think about how much time and practice she had missed out on because of her family's decision to erase everyone's memories, including her own. Time had not erased the feeling of betrayal. She shook her head to clear those thoughts and felt the urge to run. Instead, she stood slowly and began pacing a circle inside the cave.

"I have an idea, something to make the fight a little more

urgent and authentic, so you feel the need to use your magic. I believe that you hold back with us because you're afraid of it, or rather, afraid of the unknown of your powers."

She stopped and looked at him. "I'm trying my best." Did he think she wasn't trying? Did he not realize how much she wanted to go home?

"I know you are. I don't think your restraint is intentional, but it is delaying your progress."

"So what's your plan?" she countered, her back stiffening.

"I will share that plan when Gaeleath joins us, rather than repeating myself twice. His training will continue with yours, as I think this experiment will be good for both of you."

She slumped back onto the boulder when Pholus went silent. Apparently, there would be no more discussion of her lack of progress or plan. He hadn't even mentioned her staff and how it might give her the boost she needed. She definitely felt more connected and powerful when she held it out on the field. She itched to grab it from the wall where she'd left it leaning upon entering the room.

"Can you believe he's sending us on a mission already? Do you feel ready for a mission?" Mera walked back outside to the vastness of the cavern and began pacing along the edge. Gaeleath watched her. "Aren't you going to say something?" she asked, turning to face him.

He opened his mouth a couple of times before any words came out. "I'm not really sure what to say, honestly. I don't think he's wrong...you are holding back."

"What? He's not wrong? I'm holding back? What about you?"

"Well, maybe he's not wrong about me either. There has to be some reason why I'm struggling to maintain my fire. It shouldn't be this hard."

"So you think sending us out on a mission when we're unprepared and not fully trained is going to make it easier?"

"I don't know," he said quietly.

His somberness caught Mera off guard, and she turned to him, looking at him fully for what might have been the first time since she got here. He looked young, maybe closer to Kari's age than her own. Why wasn't he training with this family? On her first day at the Palaestra, Pholus had mentioned Gaeleath had powers his family didn't know how to handle, but she had only seen him fighting to maintain his fire conjurations and throwing snowballs and ice at the others. That didn't seem like anything too complicated. What could be holding him back, and why did he seem so sad all of a sudden?

"I'm sorry, Gaeleath. I shouldn't be railing at you. None of my frustrations are about you."

"No, but it's a lot safer than railing at him." He looked back toward the cave and pointed with his thumb.

She laughed. "You're right about that."

She grabbed his arm, hooked her arm through it, and began the descent into the cavern bed, so they could join the others for lunch. When they were almost to the other side, Gaeleath spoke again.

"Who do you think is going on this mission with us?"

"Oh. I hadn't even thought of that." Mera tried to think about her other companions and which one of them would be sent to lead the mission. "I don't know," she finally responded. "Would you care to speculate?"

He shook his head rapidly. "I'm not sure. I know who I would want to go with us, though."

Mera stopped before they neared the other edge of the cavern. "Oh really?" Her response must've had a sharper tone than she intended because his head jerked up and then dropped just as quickly. "Hey, tell me. You know everyone here better than I do."

"I got here just a couple of moons before you did."

"Still, you seem to have formed a much closer connection to them all than I feel."

"That may be true, but you have spent a lot of time by yourself since you got here. It's hard to get to know people when you don't spend time with them."

Though his face was neutral, his words were a slap. He might as well have thrown one of his ice balls at her. It would have stung less. Had she been isolating herself?

"I'm sorry, Skyemera. I shouldn't have said that."

"No, I'm fine."

"Are you sure? I didn't mean to hurt your feelings. I just thought you should know that everyone would like to know you better. Maybe you would feel more comfortable and better able to focus on your fighting and your magic if you weren't trying so hard to stay away from everyone." He paused and looked at the staff she carried. "And you don't need to protect us. We're not afraid of you."

"Ha! I don't know that I should thank you for your honesty because I'm not sure I appreciate it, at least not now."

He laughed then. "That's alright. I really didn't mean to hurt your feelings."

She felt him staring at her, obviously waiting for a response. "Thank you," she said quickly, and then hooked her arm back in his, leaning in conspiratorially. "Now back to your thoughts on the mission." They both laughed and continued walking slowly toward the cave where lunch was served.

"Well," he began thoughtfully, "since it's a situation in the forest, I don't know that Tarkegan is a good idea. He's big and runs headfirst into a fight without thinking. If the forest is already in danger, and we don't know why, I'm not sure he would be our safest bet."

She couldn't disagree with him. The cyclops did lead with his strength and try to overpower rather than think through and strategize when fighting.

"I also don't think Gery would be good for this mission."

"Really?" She was more than a little curious about his reasoning for eliminating Gery from the options.

"Well, yeah, he's not comfortable in the forest. I would use him for any mission into the city but not the forest. He gets nervous and skittish and might not be able to focus on the mission."

She hadn't realized that about him. He just spent all that time in her forest. Had he been scared the whole time? She couldn't even imagine there being anything scary in her forest.

"Do you know why he's afraid of the forest?"

"No, but I heard him mumbling when he was asked to go to your home. He didn't seem too keen on spending time in the forest trying to find the location of your village. He seemed really nervous. So, I'm not sure he would be too excited about another mission to another forest."

She nodded in agreement. She was even more grateful to Gery for having gone, knowing that he was so uncomfortable with going. "Well, we are running out of leaders," she said to get them back on track as they neared their destination.

"Of course, the obvious answer is Master Pholus himself," Gaeleath answered without breaking stride. "He's from the forest, and he's our leader, right. But I don't think he's going to choose to go on this mission with us."

"Why not? Like you said, he is our leader and our trainer. Why wouldn't he accompany us on this mission if it's part of our training plan?"

"I think he would've told us if he'd planned to go himself. I also think he doesn't necessarily want us to rely on him, so he's going to put us in a position where we can't rely on him."

Mera turned her eyes on him for a second, thoughts running.

"So that leaves Purivia. What do you think about her as our leader?"

He stopped walking and turned to fully face her. "Though she is not much older than us, I think she's probably the best choice for this mission." Mera raised an eyebrow. "Seriously. She is meticulous and calculating. She is very comfortable in a forest environment and resourceful. She has great fighting skills, is able to hunt, and can speak multiple languages in case we run into people who can't understand us."

Mera's eyes widened. "Really? That wasn't one of the things that was shared when everyone introduced themselves."

"I don't think she thinks about it as one of her major skills or powers. Remember how she talked about not following just one god and that she wanted to be able to help people regardless of who or what they believed in?" Mera thought for a second before nodding, and he turned for them to continue their stroll. "I think the languages just go along with that. It's part of the process for her."

"I guess that makes sense. When do you think Pholus will let us know who is going?"

"His plan was to let you all know during lunch, if you would ever enter the cave."

Mera flinched at the booming voice behind her. From the looks of him, Gaeleath had nearly jumped out of his skin.

"Master Pholus, we didn't realize you were coming up behind us," Gaeleath sputtered as they pulled apart.

"Obviously not," was his only response before walking between them and heading into the cavern entrance. Mera and Gaeleath looked at each other and hurried to follow him.

Chapter Twenty-Eight

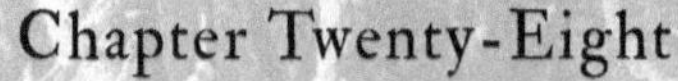

era sat on her bed at the end of the day. She was sore from the afternoon's training session. It seemed Master Pholus was determined to push them even harder before they left on their mission. She finally felt good about her progress this afternoon, though. While sparring with her staff in hand, the movements had begun to feel more natural, as if it were part of her. Tarkegan had been right. She knew she shouldn't take that for granted. It's not like she might not one day be caught without her staff. But for today, she chose to feel proud.

A familiar pop came from right outside of her cave's entrance. "Come in, Gery."

"No one else ever notices my arrival, and yet you do."

"I hear you popping about."

She looked up to see Gery standing there with his head tilted. She raised her brow.

"I don't make any noise when I teleport."

"Gery, your popping is loud." When he stood there silently shaking his head, it was her turn to look confused. "No one else can hear you?"

"No. I grew up around others who could teleport, and I never heard them either."

She shook her head. That didn't make any sense. "Not even Master Pholus."

"No," he said more securely. "He is always complaining about me showing up unannounced."

Mera felt her shoulders slump.

"Don't look dejected. I'm the one who should be upset."

Mera saw the light in his eyes and smirked. She really did like the gnome when he wasn't being so grumpy. "How is my family?"

"Your grandmother is intimidating and amazing." He paused when she smiled, but he must have known she was waiting to hear more when she remained silent. "They miss you. They're nervous about the dragon possibly returning and not being ready. From what I saw, though, they are more than ready."

"What do you mean?"

"They have started teaching the little ones about their magic, so they are at least aware that they are supposed to have magic and what that means in case they need it."

Mera's jaw slacked. "What? How? We don't develop magic until we've seen fifteen winters."

"Apparently, that is just a story the elders told because they were scared of a bunch of uncontrollable children running around shooting their magic off unexpectedly here and there."

Her face hardened. "Of course they'd keep that from us!"

"Now, don't get angry. We both know what happens when your temper shoots off. This cave is too small for all that wind."

He winked at her, and all the anger dissipated. "Are they really teaching the young ones about magic?"

"If by 'they' you mean Kari, then yes."

"Kari?" Her eyes shot open.

"She's an amazing young nymph. When I first met her, she saved me from that sea nymph Nelaira. That one was scary, yeah.

Anyway, I should've been mad at Kari, but I was too much in awe of her ability."

"Angry at Kari, why? Other than our grandmother having to silence her regularly, no one is ever angry at Kari."

"She cast a spell that kept me from teleporting. She basically imprisoned me in that forest!"

Mera's brows knitted, "Kari, cast a spell on you? She didn't even have magic when I left."

"Oh, she has it, and she is amazing. She's so good that they have her teaching the youngest nymphs glyphs and theoretical magic, so they'll know what to do when they feel their magic quicken. She told me they also acknowledge her as a youth leader in the council."

Mera had started pacing and quickly sat on the bed. So much had changed since she left. The more he told her, the more disconnected she felt. It's as if Kari had passed her by in magical ability, and yet she was supposed to be the big deal sorceress. "What am I doing here, Gery? I feel like such a failure."

He walked over, jumped up on the bed, and grabbed her hand. "You are not a failure, Skyemera. You have had to overcome so much and have learned more about yourself than anyone even thought possible."

"But you said Kari has already mastered her magic, and I've barely been able to blow things around. Is that all I'll ever be able to do?"

"I didn't say mastered. She's good, but she's still learning as well. The big difference is that she's always known who she was and the type of magic she could expect to do. Now, it doesn't appear anyone expected her to be as good as she is already, but she's not doing anything surprising to your people. She has the benefit of comfort and tradition to support her, two things you've not had."

Mera looked up at him with tear-filled eyes and sniffled. She read no guile in his eyes and gave him a weak smile. After a few moments, she squeezed his hands where they still held hers and let go. "Thank you, Gery. I miss her terribly and am so glad she is coming into her own, really I am."

"She misses you too, and asked at least three times if she could come visit you since I'd be able to immediately return her to The Thicket. Of course, she couldn't, but she asked repeatedly, and gave very strong arguments." He laughed, and Mera smiled.

"Oh, I'm sure her arguments were strong. She always had a way with words...all the words." This time, she laughed along with him, a genuine laugh.

"And my mother?" He hadn't mentioned her, and Mera was almost afraid to ask why. Was her mother not in The Thicket?

"She is worried about you, and she looks tired. I don't know that it's a physical tired, or even one that comes from caring for a babe."

"His call must be getting stronger or more consistent," she said more to herself than to him.

"What do you mean? His who?"

"Oh, they didn't tell you about my mother and her... situation?"

"Is she ok? She seemed very nice."

"She is one of the nicest people you'll ever meet. As much as I hate all the lies she's told and things she's kept from me, I can't stay mad at her." He nodded in understanding, and Mera wondered what type of relationship he might have had with his own mother since Pholus had found him on the streets of Krinosera. She decided not to follow her train of thought and ask him. "My mother is mated to the dragon, and all of the secrets of my village are due to something that happened while we lived with him in the mountains." The words flew from her mouth like bees from a disturbed hive. Gery's eyes were nearly as wide as his mouth, and he almost fell from the bed when he shifted to look at her.

"What?" he sputtered, his eyes never leaving her face. Mera knew he was looking to see if she was joking.

"Imagine my surprise when I found out less than two weeks before I came here to the Paleastra."

"You're serious? I knew you had some fear or situation related to a dragon, but I just thought it was something recent or else nightmares that might have been a seeing."

She shook her head at that last part. "My mother met the dragon in his human form, and he won her over. It wasn't until they were mated, and we were living with him that he showed his true self in form and personality. I'm still not entirely sure what happened, but I developed nightmares, and when we came back to The Thicket permanently, my family implored the gods to help rid me of those nightmares. The gods' answer was to remove my, and the entire village's, memory of those years spent with the dragon. I essentially restarted my childhood with Kari as best friends of the same age, though I'm much older than she."

She watched his face as he tried to make sense of what she'd just dumped on him. She waited for the barrage of questions, and realized how tense she was when her jaw began quivering, teeth scraping against each other. He stood and began walking toward the cave entrance. Was he going to leave her?

"I'll be right back," he said not even turning toward her before he popped out of the room.

Mera wasn't sure what had just happened. Even early on when she and Gery had shared mutual animosity, he'd never walked out on her. He looked angry. Was his anger at her? Why did she have to tell her mother's secret? He didn't need to know that if no one in The Thicket thought to tell him. Still, it didn't seem to be anything that would make him angry. She was lost in her thoughts when he popped back into the room directly rather than outside the entrance, catching her off guard.

"Please come with me."

"Did I do something wrong?"

"No, we did, and I would like to fix it."

She raised an eyebrow at him, still not comfortable with his behavior or response, but she followed him out of her cave and down the trail toward the training grounds. In the inner circle usually saved for demonstrations stood Pholus and Gaeleath, each holding torches that bathed their faces in light. She slowed her descent at the sight of them standing there watching her with a look of... What was that look? Anticipation? Nervousness? She must have slowed more than she thought because Gery came back for her.

"Don't be afraid."

"Why should I be afraid of Pholus and Gaeleath?"

"You shouldn't, but you look like you want to bolt, yeah."

She looked down at him, trying to read his face in the dimly lit corner of the canyon without responding to his observation. "Is this about the mission?"

"Yes and no, but you need to know what they have to tell you before the mission happens."

"Gery, I don't know if you realize this or not, but statements like that do not breed calm."

He smiled before he turned away and began walking back down the trail. She followed a few seconds later with a last look toward the two figures waiting below.

"Good evening, Maenad," Pholus said when she walked into the circle.

"Great Pholus," she responded with a nod. "Gaeleath," she said, turning to address her fellow trainee. Up close, she could tell that his expression was definitely one of uncertainty and discomfort. "Is everything alright?"

The centaur snorted, shaking his long mane behind his back.

"It was brought to our attention that a decision made months ago to keep some information from you is no longer appropriate and..."

"Just tell her, Master Pholus. It doesn't matter the decision or the why. She needs and deserves to know. I need her to know."

She looked back and forth between Pholus and Gaeleath willing one of them to speak again. "What decision? What do I need to know? What is happening?"

Gery laid a hand on her arm as her heart rate escalated. "Breathe, Skyemera. You are safe. Your family is safe. We're all safe here." When she looked at him, he raised his brows, and she smiled. Before she could say anything else, he turned toward the others. "If you can't or won't tell her, I will, but since I never agreed with the decision in the first place, I don't think I should have to be the one to do it."

Pholus' scowl nearly sent her over the edge. Why should he be angry with Gery if they had been keeping something from her? Shouldn't she be angry? Then he turned his head and locked eyes with her. She read regret, and her anger dissipated. "Please, just tell me." After a few more seconds of reading her face, he must have recognized the calm resignation, and he acquiesced.

"That first night in the tavern, after you went to sleep, Callisto told me about your first outburst of magic, and how it was triggered by your thoughts of a dragon while looking at a painting in your grandmother's meeting room. At that point, we didn't know if your magic was being controlled by anger or fear, but it seemed to be tied to the dragon. As such, we decided it best not to mention dragons."

"But we've talked about the dragon since then, in your office."

"Yes, we have, on occasion, mentioned the dragon. Your nightmares have been few, and it's been many months since he showed above The Thicket."

"So, why is he a concern now? Has something else happened? Has he been seen?"

"No. We're not speaking of the dragon from The Thicket," Pholus said, his eyes briefly gazing upon Gaeleath with that look of regret she had seen earlier. She turned away from Pholus and faced Gaeleath directly.

"Why are you here for this conversation? What do you know of the dragon?"

"I know nothing of your dragon, Mera." He paused for just a second. "But I do know dragons, intimately." She looked at him. What did that mean? Dragons were rare. Her people didn't think they still existed until the day of her sister's birth, well, except for her mother and grandmothers. None of them had mentioned more dragons.

"Dragons, as in plural? How? We thought them extinct until he came during my sister's presentation."

"We are far from extinct, Mera," he said, reaching out to take her hand.

"We?" She stepped away from him, pulling her hand behind her back. "We?" She repeated, her voice a little sharper. She knew the answer, though she hoped she was wrong. But he couldn't be a dragon. He was a human, like Purivia. Right?

"I want to show you, but I'm scared," Gaeleath said, looking straight into her eyes. "I'm not scared for my safety. I am scared for you and how you might respond. I can promise you have no reason to fear me, that I'm your friend, but I know you're afraid. I can smell it on you."

Pholus stepped forward toward them. "Soon, you two are going off on a mission with Purivia. If something threatens your safety, I want both of you to be able to throw everything you have at it. He cannot protect the group with everything he has if he's afraid you will panic on the mission. Do you understand that?"

Logically, yes, she understood. There was, however, no logic in this conversation at all. The existence of multiple dragons. The fact that this person she'd known for months now supposedly was one. The lies and omissions it took to keep this secret. All of it. None of it made much sense. "This is a lot," she admitted looking around at the faces standing near her. Each face held a different level of tension. Gery's perpetual smile was pulled taut with worry. Pholus was watching her like she might fly away on a tornado. Gaeleath's countenance held the most concern, genuine concern for her and not just of what she might do if her fear was triggered. It was his look that relieved some of her tension. She reached out and took his hand before addressing the small group.

"I won't lie. I'm angry...no, not angry...hurt. My family's decision to keep secrets is a big part of why I'm here now instead of with them. I can't take any more secrets." She turned to look directly at Gaeleath. "Please, no more secrets." He nodded at her, and the rest of her tension melted away. "I trust you not to hurt me."

Gaeleath squeezed her hand before he stepped back into the center of the circle away from them. Gery tugged on her hand, pulling her to edge of the inner circle, and she saw Pholus back up to the edge as well.

"How big are dragons anyway?" She asked aloud.

Gery giggled and Pholus snorted. Neither answered, as Gaeleath asked if she was ready. She gave him a nod before she could change her mind. He winked and snapped his fingers. The hairs on her legs stood on end as electricity pulsed through the air. Within an instant, Gaeleath faded from view and the form of a dragon faded in until it was corporeal and... "Huge!" She didn't realize the word had left her lips until Pholus's laugh bellowed through the canyon, its echo reverberating.

She smiled and took a step forward toward the dragon. "How'd you do that?"

Step back for a second. She heard the words in her mind and quickly jumped back between Gery and Pholus.

"Watch this," Gery said. She didn't have time to look at him before a rush of light and heat hit her as the dragon opened its mouth toward the sky. Flames burst at least fifteen feet into the air above its head. It rocked its shoulders back and forth, the flames following the pattern.

"Doesn't he need to breathe," Mera shouted over the sound of the flame, as the spectacle continued on for what seemed an unnatural amount of time. She looked at Gery and Pholus, but they were both watching the dragon, awe on their faces. Clapping and cheering came from the direction of their sleeping caves. The others had come outside to watch the show. None of them showed any fear, and Mera was once again drawn to look at Gaeleath's dragon form.

The flames had begun to recede, and she watched him, his golden eyes glistening in the dimming firelight. His scales were gold with flecks of scarlet that shimmered like droplets of blood running to his feet. Mera was struck by his beauty. He was by all counts a handsome young man, but this form was stunning. She watched as his fire died, and the cavern again filled with shadows. The air had grown cold without the flame, and a chill ran up her back when she noticed the dragon looking directly at her.

How are you? Are you alright?

Can you hear my thoughts, she asked silently in response.

Yes. In this form, I can. It is not as easy in my human form.

Mera was reminded of her mother's situation with her mate constantly calling her telepathically. She'd never mentioned whether the dragon could hear her thoughts as well. Did she answer him?

Mera, I can hear all of your thoughts right now, whether you want me to or not.

"Oh," she said aloud, drawing the attention of everyone else standing there. Tarkegan and the other new trainees had joined them in the circle now. She tried to ignore their questioning glances and pretended that her shocked outburst had been for the view and not the voice in her head. She heard Gaeleath laughing and looked back up at his large, reptilian eyes.

You are surprisingly easy to read, Mera, like you're also

telepathic. She shook her head. The first time she'd ever heard anyone's voice in her head had been the priestess, and that was a terrible experience she did not want to repeat. *I'm going to shift back now before you think something you don't want me to know.* She silently thanked him and turned back to the others.

"Wow!" exclaimed one of the newest trainees. "A dragon up close." Mera turned in his direction and then nearly laughed at the change that came over his face when Gaeleath shifted back. It was a hilarious combination of awe and confusion. She felt the change as soon as it began and knew when it was over without having to watch. The electricity that touched her skin and traveled through her hair told the story. No one else seemed affected by the change physically. They all just stood watching in his direction. She walked away to a group of rocks and sat down. It was all so much.

Chapter Twenty-Nine

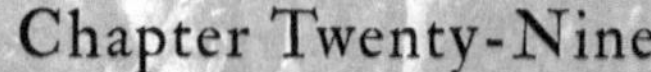

"Hey," Gaeleath called from the training grounds. "Do you want to spar?"

"I have something else I need to work on," Mera called out. She continued toward the trail that led to the canyon's southwestern ridge. She clasped her staff tightly, using it as a walking stick on the upward climb. The sun shone brightly overhead, and there was a hint of rain in the air, though no clouds were near enough to threaten her work. Determination encircled her like a cloak. She would make something grow today.

She crested the ridge and wound her way down to the same third level where Pholus had originally issued that challenge weeks ago. Nothing had changed from that day, except the days lengthening and the weather warming. She looked at her staff and smiled, feeling a level of confidence she hadn't achieved in over a year. If she could master weapon fighting, she could master her magic, or at least begin to.

She looked over the plants closest to the trail. They were beautifully lush and green. Willing to try every strategy she could think of, she started talking to them. "How are you doing, friends?

Ready to bloom yet?" She stood still waiting for the familiar rustling that she'd come to recognize as their collective response. Instead, one bush began to quiver its leaves. She walked over and addressed it. "And what is happening over here," she asked reaching out a hand to touch its leaves. The leaves parted, showing a small bud. "Oh!" Her surprise was punctuated with a rustling of leaves all around the ridge.

How had that happened, she wondered. It was obvious by the lack of blossoms everywhere that Persephone had not yet arrived, so something must have happened to cause the bud's appearance. "Can I help you blossom?" she asked the bush. "I'm not sure how exactly, but I would love to try if you'd let me." The leaves quickly closed around the bud, hiding it from her sight. Rather than the normal frustration she felt each time they shut down from her, Mera smiled in her new-found confidence. "I understand your fear. I, too, have been afraid of myself and what I might do. Then I received my staff." She held it up in the air, and a light breeze blew across the ridge.

More rustling came from the bushes at its sides, those leaves shaking in excitement. Mera moved first to one bush and then the other, her smile growing widely. "Look at those beautiful little buds you've grown. They are going to make this mountain a gorgeous rainbow of colors." She smiled at the rustling bushes. A warm breeze caressed her cheek reminding her that she was not alone. She had the love and support of the Strimmena with her. As the breeze floated across the ridge, her attention was drawn to more elated rustling along the edges. Buds had begun sprouting everywhere.

Mera turned back to the small bush with its tightly closed leaves. "You were the first to bud, little friend. Will you be the first to bloom?" She reached out a hand and ran a finger along the length of each leaf. Slowly they began to peel away from each other until she saw the bush filled with tiny buds along its stems. She blew out a long breath, admiring the changes. It was not yet the scene she had envisioned, nor did it meet Pholus' challenge, but it was improvement, a step forward.

Something happened when her breath touched the buds. They twisted left and then right. Mera sucked in, holding her breath, afraid they might pop right off their stems. Then, they opened in a sudden burst of color. She fell over, landing on her backside, and giggled as giddiness overtook her. A sound on the upper ridge caught her attention, and she jerked around, staff raised, ready to protect the fragile flowers, but nothing was there.

Turning back to the fully bloomed bush, she thanked it for sharing its beauty with her. Maybe Euonsise was right about the power of talking to the plants. Whether it was true that they responded or not, Mera was grateful to see the blooms and proud to know she'd had some part in it.

"Do the rest of you want to bloom too?" she asked of the others on the ridge. The excited rustling of bushes made her laugh. Even the pine had gotten in on the excitement, twisting themselves to and fro in a dance. "Ok, let's see if this gives your little buds a push." She stepped back a few paces, so she could see the entire ridge and blew out a deep breath, turning her head slowly from left to right. Simultaneously, she lifted the hand holding her staff and swept it behind her breath, imagining the wind pushing out through the trees onto the bushes.

Tiny pops of color began to emerge from the greenery. There were pinks and purples, reds and oranges, and even blues and whites. The ridge was suddenly awash in colors. Tears formed in Mera's eyes when she took in the sight. Applause, complete with cheers, came from the upper ridge, and Mera swiped at her cheeks before turning around. She knew someone would eventually come looking for her, so she wasn't surprised to find she had an audience. She was, however, surprised at how many of the others were looking down upon her work with mouths agape.

Pholus made his way down the trail toward her, clapping all

the way. "I knew you could do it," his voice boomed. She gave him a shy smile.

"I didn't get the whole mountain to bloom though, so I haven't met the challenge."

"Have you tried?"

She shook her head, brows creasing. "No, not yet."

He gave a gesture that said 'go ahead and try it.'

She swallowed, suddenly nervous amidst the stares of the others still watching from above. Turning, she walked toward the edge of the ridge she'd stood upon most of the afternoon. As she passed the already bloomed bushes, they shook excitedly, and she felt that they were cheering her on. It was enough to calm some of the nerves.

Grasping her staff, she held it aloft over the edge, and she brought to mind the Strimmena. "Please be with me," she whispered. Once again, the warm breeze caressed her skin and ruffled her hair. She smiled and swept her hand with the staff over the mountainside below. Slowly turning in a circle, she continue to push the wind up the mountain toward her audience. When she'd returned to her starting position, a cacophony of rustling noises began from the base of the mountain to the top, rising in a crescendo until the entire mountainside exploded in a rainbow of blooms.

The crowd once again erupted in cheers, and the Great Pholus reared up on his hind legs in celebration. Mera sat on the hard ground, her breaths quick and shallow. Her eyes welled at the beautiful sight, and her heart swelled, even in her exhaustion. She sat there long after the others had returned to the canyon floor. This was the happiest she'd felt in well over a year, and she was determined to hold onto the feeling. When dusk fell, she made her way down for the evening meal. Tomorrow, she, Purivia, and Gaeleath would begin their mission.

Mera dressed in her travel gear of soft brown pants and loose top Gery had specially made for her. She put on her leather boots she only wore when they left the confines of the canyon, and grabbed her pack and staff. The pack held some medicinal supplies and snacks in case food was difficult to come by in the forest. She quickly glanced around the cave, taking stock of the last year and a half of her life and how this mission was a culmination of that time. If successful, she'd return soon. If something went wrong, she might never see this space again. Her chest tight, she turned and exited to the labyrinth that would take her outside into the canyon proper.

Mera could hear the noise of breakfast as she neared the hall's entrance. Hooves in the dirt stopped her progress, and she turned to see Pholus trotting up behind her.

"Good morning, Great Pholus."

"Do you have everything you need, Maenad?"

"I believe so. We don't know exactly what we'll find, so it's hard to say, but I've packed everything we discussed last night, and a couple of extra poultices Gery brought back from his last visit to The Thicket."

"Good. Remember what I said. I don't want you to hold back if you all are in danger. Use your logic and magic to help the forest folk as you can, but protect yourself and the team as a priority. I do not want to have to send word to The Thicket that something happened on a recognizance mission. I have given the same command to the others."

"I understand. We'll be careful, and we will come back. I must make it home to help protect my people."

He dipped his head at her response, and she knew he

understood her meaning. "Let's get some breakfast before you leave."

They entered the cave just as Tarkegan clapped his overlarge hand on the back of one of the new trainees. The young paladin's face was beet red when a chunk of meat flew from his mouth to hit the floor on the other side of the table. The boy took two deep breaths before gasping out, "I was fine, ya big brute!" Everyone at the table laughed. Pholus cleared his throat, and the laughter died, all eyes turning on the centaur who took up over half of the entryway. Mera stood off to the side, out of everyone's direct sight, barely stifling her laughter.

"What is happening in here this morning?"

"The whelp couldn't handle his meat," Tarkegan said, lip quivering as he tried to hold back a smile.

The paladin, whose name Mera couldn't remember, glared at the cyclops. "You're too big to be so childish!" He looked back toward the doorway. "Master Pholus, I was not paying very good attention to my eating and got choked laughing at Gery's story. Mr. Big and Brutish here..." He gestured toward Tarkegan "thought it necessary to break my back with his big hands."

Pholus shook his head and made his way to join the table. As he took his place, the conversation relaxed back to its normal volume and flow. Mera watched the room, still amused by the easy banter and yet regretful that she was unable to integrate into the group as easily as the new trainees had in their short time at The Palaestra. She still had trouble considering herself part of this unlikely family. Her family was waiting for her return. The familiar burn stung the backs of her eyes as it did whenever she thought of the family she hadn't seen in nearly two years. Before she could give herself over to the melancholy, she caught Gaeleath staring at her.

Even in the dimness of the cave, She could tell the color of his eyes from where she stood. She had spent hours the other night looking into them after the excitement of his shift had subsided, and everyone else had gone to bed. Gaeleath had explained why he went along with the plan not to tell her about his dragon form and how hard it had been to keep that secret. She understood, knowing that Pholus was attempting to protect her from the nightmares Callisto told him about. She understood it, but she was still angry about the additional secrets.

Still, she had enjoyed his company and learning about what it meant to be a dragon. His life and stories were nothing like she'd imagined based on her nightmares and her mother's recounting of the years spent with her mate. He spoke of his family and growing up in a colony. She never realized, and she was willing to bet that no one else in The Thicket knew, that enough dragons still existed for there to be colonies.

She had been taken with how beautiful his dragon form was up close with its shimmering colors and how well the colors of his eyes matched that form. It seemed more natural than this human form staring back at her. She couldn't say that she was no longer afraid of dragons. Fear still gripped her when she thought of her nightmares and those lost memories, but this friendship helped reduce it. Her thoughts returned to the cave when she realized he was no longer seated at the table. She hadn't seen him get up, but within seconds, he was standing by her side and whispering.

"Are you alright? You seemed very far away right now."

She smiled, more out of habit than genuine emotion. "I'm a little nervous about this mission, lots of 'what ifs' on my mind. I'm also a bit anxious to get going. It's a weird mixture of feelings."

He laughed, and she smiled, this time genuinely. "I wonder if somehow we couldn't just sneak out. If no one noticed, we wouldn't have to go through the process of goodbyes to everyone," he said.

"Not gonna happen," came a voice to Mera's right, stopping her question about the 'process.' She didn't have to look to know that Gery would be standing there watching her, his foot tapping.

"Good morning to you too, Gery," she said without turning.

"We have a process for sending people off on their first mission, and you don't get to skip out on that process."

Her chest tightened at the second mention of 'the process,' but she managed to hide it behind a quick "Fine, but do we have to wait all day for it to happen?" She didn't have to wait for an answer, as Pholus stood up and addressed the room.

"For as long as I've been training fighters, the moment comes for them to each embark on their first mission. Today we send off two. Skyemera and Gaeleath, please come stand by me."

A shiver ran down Mera's spine. She hated being the center of attention. She looked to Gaeleath, but he just shrugged and walked to stand on the other side of Pholus where she could no longer see him behind the centaur's torso. Great, she thought, way to leave me on my own.

"Stop sulking," came Gery's squeaky voice at her side. She nearly jumped, forgetting that he had been standing there before the announcement started. She turned to deny his assessment, but he pushed her forward toward Pholus' side.

"Each of these trainees has made strides to mastering their powers and abilities, but there is more they must learn about themselves. They must step out of the safety of The Palaestra and into the wilds. There have been rumors of entire villages disappearing in The Palacial Forest." There was a collective gasp around the table as every eye, even those that had previously been distracted, trained on Pholus. "The goal of this mission is to gather accurate information, and, if possible, find people from the villages. The goal is not to engage with whatever is happening in there."

"Master Pholus, is it safe to send trainees into an uncertain situation like that alone," the young paladin whose name Mera still could not remember asked. She really did need to do a better job of getting to know the others here.

"No, it's not," Pholus responded, looking around the table. "Don't worry, young ones, your first missions will never be completed without a leader who has already had success. Purivia will accompany Skyemera and Gaeleath." He nodded down at each of them. "I have no doubt the three of them will return successful."

Mera beamed, and though she couldn't see him, she knew Gaeleath was smiling at Pholus' remarks. She may not feel that her training had been successful thus far, but hearing the Great Pholus' confidence loosened some of the tightness around her chest.

"And now it is time for the sending-off process," Gery said, climbing onto the table to get everyone's attention. Mera's jaw clenched. "Everyone meet outside and form a straight line across the canyon to the trail that leads up to the northeastern ridge." He jumped down and made his way to the cavern's entrance, gesturing for the other trainees to follow him.

"Wait here, you two," Pholus said, placing a hand on each of their shoulders. Mera watched everyone stream out of the cavern, her anxiety building. She looked up at Pholus, wanting to ask him what to expect when they went outside. She doubted he would give an answer, so she kept her mouth shut. Instead, the centaur gave her a knowing look and winked before turning to leave the cavern himself.

"I do not want to walk out there," Mera whispered to Gaeleath, lest Pholus hear her.

"Unfortunately, caverns do not have back doors," he said with a wry laugh. He held his hand out to her, and she grasped it like a lifeline. They were in this together, this ritual and this mission. Their job was to protect each other, and making it out of the cavern was the first step.

Outside, the misfit collection of Palaestra inhabitants stood in a line that stretched from Pholus, who was standing right outside the cavern's entrance to Gery at the foot of the trail 100 yards away. There was significant space between each person, and Mera could only imagine that she and Gaeleath would have to pass by each one. For what reason, she had no idea.

They stopped in front of Pholus, who once again put a hand on their shoulders. "I do not promise that this mission will be easy, just that you have the collective intelligence, strength, and perseverance to see it through. Trust in each other and stay together." He squeezed each shoulder and gestured for them to move forward to the next person.

In similar fashion, the trainees standing between Pholus and Tarkegan wished them well and squeezed their shoulders or shook their hands/arms, as was each of their custom. The cyclops stood at his full height waiting for them with hands on hips, his countenance serious and imposing.

"You have both come so far. You still have much to learn, including trusting yourselves to have the ability to meet whatever challenges you may face. Don't give up on yourselves or each other."

Tears welled in Mera's eyes at his words. He had never once failed to believe in her, even when she vehemently doubted herself. She quickly reached out and threw her arms around his waist, sliding her arms between where his remained bent in that formidable stance. She felt him relax, and he hugged her back. Tarkegan released her when he put his hand on Gaeleath's shoulder to give it the same reassuring squeeze everyone else had done before directing them both further down the row.

By the time they reached Gery, Mera's eyes were burning with unshed tears, and her heart was overflowing with emotion. Though he stood on a boulder to better meet their gaze, the gnome still had to look up at her. With a sheepish smile, he said, "I told you that you didn't want to miss this." No words formed in her throat, so she reached out and hugged the gnome. His voice cracked a bit, but he hugged her back before waving them forward up the trail to where Purivia waited. "You will do great things, both of you."

Mera took Gaeleath's hand and headed up the trail until it became too steep and narrow for them to walk side by side. When they reached Purivia at the top of the first ridge, all three of them turned and waved to the crowd below. There was no guarantee they would return, nor was there a promise of their success, but Mera felt buoyed by the unwavering support and well-wishes of their friends.

Chapter Thirty

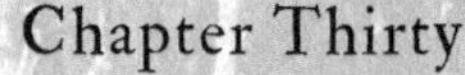

The trio had been traveling two full days when their destination came into view on the horizon. From that far away, the forest looked much like her own, and she felt the same pang of longing to see her family. Thankfully, the steady and comfortable conversation between Gaeleath and Purivia allowed her to stay in the moment rather than continue those sad musings. She would have thought missing her family might have become easier to handle after all this time, but the pull to go home seemed to get stronger as the months passed.

"How does it not bother you two being away from your family for so long?"

Purivia stopped walking. "That's pretty presumptuous," she said with a raised brow.

It took a moment before Mera realized the accusation her words had held. "That's not what I meant," she said. "I meant that you make it look so easy. You've been away from your people for longer than I have, and yet, everyday, I feel this urge, this pull, to run back home. Some days, it's so strong I want to cry."

The paladin's eyes softened, and she opened her mouth as if to say something before closing it again. Instead, Gaeleath spoke.

"It's not that I don't miss them, but it's gotten easier for me over time. I left because I wanted to. I knew I was different from the other dragons in the colony simply because I could breathe ice when all of them could only breath fire. I knew that I would not continue to grow in both of my abilities if I stayed home. They would have tried to limit my skills with ice because it was so different from them."

He paused for a long moment, lost in some memory. When he finally continued, his tone was more introspective than directed toward Mera and Purivia. "It's not like we don't have lore of ice breathers. We do, and part of me still hopes to find one. In the meantime, I have found a family that fully accepts me and encourages me to be my complete self. That keeps me here and looking forward rather than backward."

Mera was torn between wanting to hug him for that feeling of aloneness she had always felt amongst her people and her own jealousy of that connection he found amongst the others in The Palaestra. She wished she could have that too. Before she could do anything, though, Purivia responded.

"I wasn't quite sure how to put it myself, but I think you just made the point I wanted to. I think it's the purpose and reason for coming to The Palaestra that makes it a bit easier for us."

Mera watched and waited, thinking the paladin would continue. Instead, the woman turned and started walking again without another word. Mera looked at Gaeleath, and he shrugged before turning to follow their leader.

"So what is your story?" Mera heard him ask Purivia when she caught up with them. "What brought you here away from your people?"

The paladin turned to look at him for a second and Mera caught that gaze flicker back in her own direction. She didn't answer right away, and Mera figured she wasn't going to. Gaeleath, however, didn't let it go.

"Seriously. I know you came here to hone your magic and

continue your training with the sword and bow, and all of that, but I have a hard time believing that the humans just knew to send you to Pholus for that training."

Purivia responded with a snort, which was the first sound she'd made since turning away from the conversation earlier. "No," she said with a shake of her head. "My people are afraid of magic. We have been so disconnected from it for so many centuries, basically since the old gods went silent, that we turn away from anything magical and try to explain it away with logic. Sometimes the only logic is magic." She turned back toward the distant forest before adding, "I could not tell my parents that, though. I also could not tell them what I had seen the day before I chose to leave either."

That statement, and the raw emotions behind those words, caught Mera's attention. The event had been life changing. "Did you see the dragon of your nightmares," Mera asked without accusation or sarcasm.

The trio went quiet until the paladin stopped. "Let's have lunch here. This isn't a story I want to tell in the shadows of the forest, but it's a story I'm willing to tell."

They set their packs down and sat upon them as they began to pick at the rations they'd brought from the cavern.

"I hope we're able to find some better food in the forest. I'm tired of eating the same thing," Gaeleath said.

Purivia's lip quirked up, and her eyes sparkled. Mera could tell she was trying to hold in a laugh.

"Alright, so tell us about what you saw that day," Mera prodded once they were fully settled.

The paladin took a bite of her food, chewed it slowly, and swallowed. "So, you have to remember that my people do not speak of magic. They do not speak of anything supernatural. They really do not speak of the gods, any of them, other than to say they were in control, and we were just to follow the teachings of whichever one was in power at the time." She swung the hand holding her lunch around as she said the last part with a sneer.

"My specific community worships what they call the One God. I think they believe it's easier to choose one god than to try and keep the multitude straight with ample time and equitable worship. It was expensive and time-consuming to pray to the God of Grain for a healthy harvest and pray to the Sun God or the God of Wind for good weather. Then there were all the others for everything else that would happen in our daily lives. I really think consolidating them into one god and one belief just felt easier. But in doing that, they had to let go of all the mystical that had surrounded those earlier gods our people worshipped. So they relegated them to myths, stories for children. Finally, they shunned taking about them altogether."

Mera thought about all she'd learned these past couple years about the gods, old and new, and how much her worldview had expanded due to her experiences. Her people had always only worshipped the old gods, Zeus and his kin. They were isolated enough from the rest of the world to maintain those beliefs, although their practices were far less emphatic than previous generations. She could see how, with more time, her people might disconnect completely and look to other deities, or a supreme one, for a simpler life.

"It was hard for me," Purivia said, breaking into Mera's drifting thoughts. "When I realized I had abilities that better matched those myths than the mundanity of my people, there was no one I could tell or ask for help. At best, my people would have shunned me. At worst...well, 10-year-old me didn't want to think about that possibility." She shuddered. "Let's just say that I'd heard enough stories of people in the village disappearing. Imagine my surprise, then, when something straight out of those fairytales flew down the middle of my street."

She paused for another few bites of food, and Mera took a moment to look at Gaeleath. The dragon was fully engrossed in the story and waiting for Purivia to continue. His eyes were bright and so fully fixed on the paladin that his lunch sat virtually untouched on his lap. The paladin began speaking without looking up from her half-eaten meal.

"I was standing on the stoop of my house when I heard the screech. It wasn't loud or piercing, more like an achy moan. I looked up to see a bird of prey circling overhead. At first, I thought it was an eagle, but they don't usually circle like hawks. Curiosity drew me into the yard, as the bird descended slowly. I could see its motions were much shakier than I'd originally thought. The thing was massive, though. It had a tremendous wingspan, and its torso was nearly this big around." She gestured with her arms outstretched like she was preparing to hug someone with a chest the size of Pholus.

"From the corner of my eye, I saw the neighbor's dogs. I tried to shoo them away, but they, too, were fascinated by the bird's descent." She admitted to hating those dogs, so Mera found it interesting that she was going out of her way to protect them. "And then voices came, louder as the bird got closer. 'Get off me,' came the first voice, rough and obviously angry. 'We must deliver the message," another voice said. I looked around trying to figure out where the voices were coming from..." Her face got that far away look, as if she was reliving the memory.

Then she described the creature that landed. It was nearly the height of a grown human man when it stood fully, and it had an unnaturally round abdomen. Mera gasped when Purivia described how the creature pulled a second creature from its side like a mother ape might remove her child.

"I watched the monstrosity unravel itself where it had landed when the creature threw it to the side. It was much shorter than the bird that had flown in, or maybe it just appeared that way because it was hunched and mangled, like it had been stripped of its feathers...and its skin. Places where skin should have been were blackened, and the smell of ash wafted from them."

Mera and Gaeleath sat in silence, rapt in the tale she was

weaving. Occasionally, they would look at each other, wide-eyed and slack-jawed.

"So you're saying these creatures, these birds of sort, were burnt?"

Mera nearly laughed at the dragon's half question half statement. The story was so unbelievable.

"Yes. It was as if they had been touched by fire and one of them was far more traumatized than the other. I could see his bones and the singed flesh around them. I could tell where his feathers had been burnt off. The flesh underneath looked like a chicken that had just been plucked. I still see it in my mind. The skin was raw and red like it has been scalded, but more than scalded. There were obvious signs that it had been directly touched by fire, unlike the other that only had singed feathers. That one was fully covered and still able to fly with its wings intact. It wasn't their appearance that told me I not only had to keep the story to myself but that I also had to leave."

She stopped talking, and Mera could see her eyes glazed over, as if she was once again stuck in the memory. Mera, desperate to hear the rest of the story, interrupted that daydream. "What happened?" The paladin blinked and shook her head. It was a while before she spoke again, and then the story took on an even darker tone.

Purivia explained that the first creature flew away, while the other stood begging it not to leave. Its pleas were intertwined with reminders of a message that must be shared, though it never articulated the message. Once it grew quiet, realizing its ride would not return, it noticed the dogs and hobbled its way behind a bush in the yard. As the dogs approached around the bush, its pleas turned to whimpering. When she couldn't take it anymore, Purivia had walked around the bush. One dog stood there snarling while the other had the creature's leg locked in its jaw.

She reached down to grab the small dog, thinking to save the creature from its jaws. Her fingers sunk into oozing flesh, and she realized the whimpers were coming from the dog, not the creature. The monster, as she had called it, had newly formed, though still blackened, flesh covering its previously visible skeleton, and its feathers, though burnt at the ends, had begun to fill in anew. She'd dropped the dog and watched in horror as it wasted away while the creature became stronger. The newly formed bird pulled the dog's jaw off its leg with its talons and stood to its full height. Squawking again about delivering a message, it took flight.

"Gods," Gaeleath said. "I've never heard anything like that, and I have lived in the supernatural my entire life with people who breathe fire. Are you for real?"

The paladin cut her eyes at him, ready to reprimand his rudeness when Mera stopped her with a simple "I believe you." Purivia and Gaeleath turned to stare at her. She could read the shocked surprise that shifted through various emotions in the late afternoon sun before finally landing on incredulity.

"I've seen people who looked similarly singed, like they had been touched by fire and forever changed but not killed."

"How? Where?" Purivia's questions were direct and held an unexpected air of hopefulness.

"In the city where we first met. I'm surprised you haven't heard the story. Did you not see the priestess?"

"The one with the shadow demons we were fighting?" the paladin asked.

"Yes. The priestess who stood at the end of the alley had been touched by fire, much like you described." Neither of Mera's companions said anything at that revelation, so she continued. "I had seen her earlier that morning inside a church, but she was not alone. The person who was with her was far more ravaged by the flames. He had scars and scabs, and missing patches of skin, like he had been freshly burned while she had been reborn from the ashes."

Gaeleath watched her and began to bite his nails. "That is really strange," he said.

"What part?" Mera asked.

"The part where the two of you see similarly burnt creatures, for lack of a better word, in different places at different times, and yet find yourselves here together."

Mera wondered aloud if the Fates were somehow responsible, but he just shrugged.

"I don't believe in fate," he said. "My people come from fire, have been here much longer than any of yours, and the vast majority worship the God of Fire."

This time, it was their turn to look at him incredulously. Mera's heartbeat quickened, but he once again shrugged when she asked him what he could tell her of this god she'd only learned existed in the past two years.

"I know you don't want to mess with him. I know that he and his siblings have been around forever, since the world began. I know he is powerful and seeks to have everyone follow him. I also know that his siblings have been fighting against that ego for at least as long as my people have been around."

With genuine surprise, Purivia asked, "Your people are taught that?"

He laughed and shook his head. "No. There is, however, a threat given to every dragon child that if you blaspheme against the God of Fire, you'll lose your ability to breathe fire. We're told we will blow nothing but smoke and be shunned as a liar. It's a consistent threat by our parents that I don't believe, nor will I worship a god who would threaten children."

Mera agreed with him there, and it reminded her of how the gods wouldn't help her family with the nightmares. They just left her to suffer. What kind of deities would do that?

"Anyway," he said, "I have the ability to both blow fire and ice, ice that should be in the realm of the Goddess of Water, so my beliefs matter not."

Mera could only stare at him. The way Gery talked of the god and his followers, they were pretty scary, so she was not really surprised they would threaten their children with exile. It was different, though, to hear them described by someone from that belief system. It would make sense that a god who believed himself the strongest and worthy of being the supreme god above others would teach his followers that loyalty to him was the only way. Still, she was saddened to think of Gaeleath being exiled from his family. She couldn't imagine being threatened with excommunication just for asking questions. Not for the first time that day, she wanted to hug him, but his next words made her smile.

"There is no other way with him, follow or perish in the flames. It's all about him and his flames," he said with a sneer. "Well, I have my own flames, so I don't need his. Just one more reason why I needed to leave my colony. They would consider me pretty radical, especially now."

Purivia laughed and stood, lifting her pack and wiping the dirt from it before situating it on her back. "We will camp right outside of the forest for tonight, and in the morning, I will hunt us some fresh breakfast before we try to find out what is actually happening in there."

Mera followed her lead and began grabbing her belongings. "How do we even know where to start looking?"

The paladin pulled out a map and showed them where it was marked with the names of different peoples. She pointed to one prominent spot in the middle of the forest. "Hopefully, we'll be able to find them, unharmed, and get some answers. Either way, it would be safer to camp outside the forest when we don't know what we're walking into."

They all agreed and made their way toward the trees in the distance.

Chapter Thirty-One

They walked through the forest for hours, seeking the inhabitants according to Pholus' marks on the map. All they found was scorched earth and singed trees. Each marker triggered the unending refrain "What happened here?" They found no clue, no movement, no life. Yet, they also found no bodies, no death.

The sun was directly overhead before they found anything that might give them a clue of what was happening. The trees opened on a large clearing that had not been marked as inhabited, yet there was something about it that caught their attention. The center of the clearing was clean, almost too clean: not a branch to be found, the dirt and grass appeared untouched, and random leaves were strewn as if the wind had carried and lain them gently on the ground. The idyllic scene was out of place within the ravaged forest.

The hair at the base of her neck bristled, and Mera gripped her staff tighter. "Does anyone else feel like we're missing something here? I don't know what it is, but I don't like this feeling."

"Yes," Purivia said behind her. "This is not a natural clearing.

There should be footprints and forest debris, or animal droppings at least. There should be some sign of life."

"I don't think we're alone," Gaeleath said between clenched teeth. "I feel a presence, but I can't place it."

Mera turned her focus back to their surroundings, scanning the trees and coming back to the empty clearing. She also felt a presence she couldn't identify and wondered if they shouldn't head back under cover among the trees. Purivia gave the command before Mera could voice her mounting concern.

"Stick together, but let's get back to the tree line. We're too exposed here."

She didn't have to say another word before they all began moving in unison, turning as they walked to watch for any movement. There was none, even once they were fully ensconced beneath the canopy. The clearing remained silent, and yet, Mera's fur was bristling now too, tingles from her ankles to her head. Something was very wrong here. Movement between the trees to their right caught her attention, and she pointed in that direction. They'd taken one step when Purivia jumped to the left, pointing at something in the trees there.

They were all looking back and forth when leaves began falling around them. First it was just one or two individual leaves floating to the forest floor. Then pine needles began to drizzle upon them. The rustling of leaves and creaking of branches caused them to look upwards into a sea of dark waves undulating beneath the canopy, obscuring the sun completely.

"The shadows," Mera whispered, heart beating in her throat.

"Shit!" Purivia brandished her sword. "I don't have any flaming arrows."

"What are those things," Gaeleath asked, pulling out his kukri. Though he was just as skilled with the two short swords in his hands as the icicles he'd throw at his sparring partners in the Palaestra, Mera knew he'd rather use his magic, or even better, unleash his dragon. The forest, however, wasn't the safest place to blast with flames, and she was glad he had the presence of mind to realize it.

"They are shadow demons with terrible claws and teeth," Mera said.

"They were unstoppable in the city. Why haven't they attacked yet?" Purivia's voice was both strained and determined. "They clearly have the advantage of number."

The rustling in the trees grew louder until the sounds seemed to come from all sides. There had to be hundreds of them pushing into each other, closing off all bits of sunlight until the forest mimicked the caves along the cavern they lived and fought in. The only light came from the clearing, now more than twenty yards away.

"If we can get to the clearing again, we'll be safe." Though she'd said the words aloud, Mera wasn't sure they were true. The number of demons and the way they were patiently waiting made her skin crawl in anticipation. What were they waiting for?

"It is good to see you again, Maenad."

Mera jerked around away from the clearing and gaped at the ashen face of Mingus. He was not wearing the acolyte robe he'd had on in the church, but she would recognize his gray face with its singed edges anywhere. Her breaths quickened and her heartbeat raced as she tried to look around him. He turned to follow her gaze and she gasped at the sight of his full body. Had his bottom half been fur-covered, he might have been mistaken for a satyr, though he had no horns. Instead, his entire body was gray and black with thickened skin, as if he'd been overbaked, and his tail was long, hanging toward the ground like some strange lizard creature. She now understood why his robe seemed to move behind him in the church, though he'd stood still.

"Be not afraid. You're amongst friends here." He gestured toward the trees with his arms wide.

"Where is your priestess," Mera choked, sounding far less secure than intended.

He had the audacity to smile. "Our Mistress of Shadows regrets her absence and looks forward to seeing you soon. I was sent to find you and extend an invitation for a private meeting."

"Wait, how long have you been looking for me?"

"Oh months, Maenad. I dare not return without your acceptance. My mistress is a patient woman, but she does not accept failure. But I did not waste the time. No. I preached the strength of our Lord, The God of Fire, to the forest's inhabitants while we searched for you."

"Months!" Purivia stepped forward to stand at Mera's right side. "You've been terrorizing the peoples of the forest for months?"

He wrinkled his nose in disgust, and his tail began to swing side to side behind him. "You dare question our faith and ways?" The shadows in the trees worked themselves into a frenzy as his agitation grew.

"We need to get to that clearing and quickly," Gaeleath whispered in the space between Purivia and Mera's ears.

Mera didn't take her eyes off of Mingus, though he no longer spoke. His nostrils were flared and his hands clenched and unclenched. He was preparing for something, and she feared it would not bode well for them. When the shadows gathered behind him in the shape of wings, she began walking backward away from him.

"Be not afraid, Maenad. I won't harm you. I must bring you to the Mistress." His eyes drifted between Purivia and Gaeleath, and his brows raised. "Your friends are not invited."

The fluttering of wings and squawking above them was deafening, and she felt the moment he released his hold on the demons. The rush of energy took her breath. "Run," she squeaked and lifted her staff. Wind began to push forward in front of her, knocking demons from her path, as she ran toward the light of the clearing. The sun was calling her name, and her strides lengthened. The air around her began to warm the nearer she got to the light, and the sounds of the demons receded. "Hurry, we're almos..." She looked first left and then right for her companions.

She dug into the ground so hard to stop, the soles of her boots shredded. She turned and looked back into the forest. She couldn't see anything beyond the expanse of black undulations, but she could hear the grunts and thuds of a fight. Oh no! She'd left them. She hadn't meant to leave them. They were running beside her when she heard her name called. "Shit!" She repeated Purivia's favorite epithet and ran back toward the sea of shadows, staff lifted above her shoulder, ready to swing on whatever demons were in the way. She heard Purivia's grunts of exertion and demon shrieks.

She let the staff do the heavy lifting, first left then right, trying to clear her way back to the team. Why had she not heard Gaeleath? Where was he? She swung again, knocking a demon twenty paces into a tree trunk. They seemed oblivious of her, focused on swarming her friends. "Hold on!" She swung the staff around her head and pushed forward with her magic to make her way through the wall of shadows.

It took several seconds before she could fully take in the scene before her. Purivia was in the center of the circling shadow demons swinging her sword and kicking at four of them while they yanked her hair and flew at her feet. The wall they created was frenzied with excited shrieks. Why did she not use her magic? "Call to your god!" Mera screamed over the din of the creatures encircling them. "Use your magic!"

Purivia screamed as one of the demons scraped its claws across her shoulder. She pivoted and slashed it in two. A scream caught in Mera's throat as she watched the demon lift from the ground and knit itself together with smoky shadows. Her chest tightened as she watched Purivia continue the deadly dance. Mera could tell they were toying with the paladin. She jumped into the center of the circle, her back to Purivia. "How do we win this?"

"We can't, not with weapons," she said with a grunt as she parried and swung, lopping a wing off of one of the creatures. "I've not found anything that actually kills them. They regenerate everything."

"Where is Gaeleath?" Mera asked, knocking another demon toward the wall until it melded in with the others.

"They separated us with that damnable wall of shadows."

"We have to find him! Can you bring forth your light?"

"There are no people here. No god to call upon in their time of need. None will answer me."

They both turned their attention back to the flock of demons that seemed to have doubled to eight currently in the fray. Rage welled in Mera's chest. They had no idea where Gaeleath was, and the game the demons were playing grated on her. Why weren't they attacking in earnest? What was this gladiator-style arena they'd created? What was their end game besides taking her to the priestess? She needed time to think, and these shadows were in her way.

"Which direction was Gaeleath when you last saw him?"

Purivia pointed to Mera's right, as she kicked at the nearest demon. Mera channeled her anger into the staff and swirled the top above her head. The dust began to kick up and around them, separating them from the demons. Each time one tried to get closer, it was caught in the wind and toppled head over tail, flipping through the air, wings flailing within the cyclone Mera created. Soon, the cyclone was as dark as the wall of shadows had been, and just as noisy with shrieks of surprise and confusion rather than rabid excitement.

"When I let this go, run toward the clearing. I'm going to find Gaeleath!"

"I'm not leaving you in this forest alone. We are a team. It is still too dark here in the forest, and they will just come back with more energy."

Mera watched the cyclone, taking in Purivia's words. They would just come back again when she let them go. How could she give them some reprieve? She tried to look beyond the swirling wall of topsy turvy creatures and caught a peek of sunlight at the clearing's edge. Could she funnel them there, to the light? Was that possible?

"Stay close to me. I don't know if this is going to work."

Purivia opened her mouth to say something when Mera stopped her stirring of the staff and pushed it forward with all her will. The cyclone broke, and the wind burst forth toward the clearing like a river flooding through the trail between the trees. Demons bounced off branches and trunks, pushing forward toward the light. The howls of the creatures bounced back in waves as each shadow burst into tiny bits of ash in the sunlight. Mera breathed a sigh of relief and her knees weakened when Purivia cheered at her side.

"That was brilliant!" she cried. Mera swayed and reached out a hand to Purivia's shoulder to steady herself. "Are you alright?"

Mera nodded and took in two deep breaths trying to slow the pounding of her heart and keep the dizziness at bay. "We have to find Gaeleath."

They looked around to reorient themselves after the cyclone had obscured their view.

"He should be this way," Purivia said, grabbing Mera's arm, and pulling her forward. They took off jogging. When they caught wind of what sounded like a voice amongst the trees, adrenaline pushed Mera to pick up the pace.

The demons here were less frenzied and more watchful. Mera could see glimpses of the scene from between them, as their heads and wings swayed back and forth along the wall of shadow. Finally, she heard Mingus' voice. "You're not what you seem. You're hiding something from us. I feel a heat within you, a kinship. Let us see you as you are." Muffled yelling was the only response Mera heard, and her heart caught. The shadows were so focused on the scene before them that they didn't immediately notice Mera and Purivia behind their wall trying to peek through the occasional openings caused by their movement. Purivia held up a finger to her lips and pointed to their left. Mera followed as quietly as she could through the underbrush.

Rather than a circle of shadows this wall was finite and ended just beyond the trail. They stepped off the trail and behind some dense bushes beneath the thick trees. "Do you see him?" Mera whispered as Purivia peered around the furthest tree trunk beyond the creature collective. The paladin said nothing, but the widening of her eyes spurred Mera to step behind her for a better view.

Mingus stood with the shadowy wall at his back. He was facing what appeared to be a large black blob. In response to his words, the blob flailed about, and a lock of curly hair escaped between the shadows. Gaeleath was inside of that dark mass. Purivia must have realized it at the same time because she gasped and quickly covered her mouth. Mera put a hand on her shoulder, as the paladin reached to unsheathe her sword from its scabbard on her back.

"Come now," Mingus said, "we're all friends here. We are both fire touched, you and I. There should be no animosity between us. The God of Fire calls for us to be brothers."

Gaeleath encased by the demons lurched forward trying to get to Mingus. Mingus, waved his hand at the demons. "Let him speak. We shall converse like brethren."

"We are not brothers! You are an abomination! A creature no different from these incorporeal shadows."

"Incorporeal? Could they hold you if they had no shape? Could they have torn at your friend until she had no fight left in her if they were nothing but smoke? Could they have carried the maenad to our priestess if they were nothing but the absence of light?"

"No!" Gaeleath screamed in frustration and tried to break free from the creatures' hold. His human form was significantly weaker than their collective strength when they knitted their wings together. His screams turned to whimpers and then silent sobs. Mera's heart broke, as she tried to figure out how to free Gaeleath and rid the world of that ashen-faced menace taunting him.

Purivia's sword would not help against the shadows, and Mera wasn't yet fully recovered from the last round with the demons. She leaned heavily on her staff and held her hand on the nearest tree for added balance. She looked up into the canopy, wishing it were winter without the full coverage of the leaf-laden branches. When the wind blew up through the trees, creating a small opening between the branches, light penetrated the canopy to touch Mera's face. There were no demons above them.

"I have an idea," Mera whispered and pointed at the tree tops. The paladin smiled as the plan unfolded. Sword in hand, she took a wide stance, ready to run with the blade at her shoulder. Mera looked to the hand at the end of her staff and reached deep within to feel her magic flow through the branch. At the same time, she pushed her magic into the tree she still touched. Wood creaked and leaves rustled as the wind picked up just under the canopy. Sunlight began to poke through in narrow streaks. The first one to touch the wall of demons earned a piercing screech and then a hiss as the demons slinked away from the ray, huddling tighter together.

The branches began to separate themselves more, allowing the penetrating rays to grow in dimension and strength, illuminating the dim forest floor. Mera focused her energy, pushing for the canopy to fully open above their friend. If Purivia was surprised by Mera's powers, she didn't show it. She relaxed her knees and shifted to the balls of her feet in preparation to run. As soon as the sun blasted through the wide opening above, the demons holding Gaeleath disintegrated, and the dragon lunged forward at the same time Purivia ran toward them.

Mingus, caught off guard, looked back and forth between Gaeleath and Purivia before stepping back into the shadows of the trees where the canopy remained intact. The demons swarmed around him, lifting him into the air, as if to carry him away. Mera locked eyes with him just as an icicle pierced his side. He nearly lost control of the demons and began to slip toward the ground before they grabbed him again and disappeared into the dark.

"Let's go after him," Gaeleath shouted, but Purivia held him around the waist.

"We need to get out of the forest before they rally and come back," Purivia said in the sternest voice Mera had ever heard her use.

"Let's get back out to the clearing and make a plan," Mera said, limping over to them from behind the trees.

"Are you hurt?" Gaeleath asked, eyes intently searching her face. Purivia released her hold on him when Mera shook her head. She tried desperately to hold back the exhaustion threatening to pull her to the ground. Gaeleath grabbed Mera's arm and put it around his shoulder. Purivia came up, behind them and lent her shoulder on Mera's other side. Together, they walked toward the clearing. Each breathed a sigh of relief when they made it out into the open.

Though the sun would be setting far too soon, the trio rested in the center, as far as they could get from any tree. Mera was too tired to think, so she lay on the grass watching a pair of large black birds circle above the clearing. They would disappear beyond the trees and then return again, making their circles in the sky. Their steady pattern lulled her to sleep while Purivia and Gaeleath argued over the best way to get them back to The Palaestra safely.

Chapter Thirty-Two

✣

Muffled voices penetrated the fog in her brain. She couldn't make out the words, but the tones were obvious: anger, disbelief, and concern. Purivia and Gaeleath couldn't still be arguing about the best way to get home, could they? They'd need to leave soon if they were going to make the long trek back through the forest. It was important that they traveled by daylight. Why was that important again? She shook her head, trying to clear her thoughts and block out the voices. There was an important reason they couldn't rest for too long in the light of the clearing, and she just needed a quiet moment in the sunlight to remember. She shivered and threw her head side to side. Where was the sun? The demons were blocking out the sun! By the gods, the demons had found them in the clearing and blocked out the sun completely!

She tried to scream. She tried to get up. Nothing worked. She was trapped in the cold darkness. The voices got closer and she froze with a soft whimper.

"She's still asleep," came a squeaky voice. "I told you she needed rest." It was followed by a booming one.

"This rest is unnatural, and she needs to wake up. It's been three days."

The voices sounded like Gery and Pholus, but they weren't in the forest. She must be dreaming, wishing they had been there to help against the demons, against Mingus. They had to save Gaeleath. He was encapsulated by demons, their shadowy wings blocking his face and mouth. She didn't know how to help him. The demons were unstoppable. They would kill him if she didn't do something! She raised her staff and shouted his name, "Gaeleath!"

Hands grabbed her shoulders, holding her in place. She fought them, kicking and screaming. They were too strong and held her. Where was her staff? She needed her staff. "Let me go, demons! I will not go to your priestess. Let me and my friends go! Gaeleath! Purivia!"

An out-of-breath voice called her name. "Mera! Mera, wake up." The voice came from far away, and she opened her eyes to look for him. She stared straight into the eyes of...

"Gery?"

"Oh, thank goodness. You're back, yeah. You're not gonna kick me anymore, yeah."

Gery still had his arms around her ankles, and he was eyeing her with suspicion and hope. She had forgotten that she was also being held down at her shoulders until she felt the weight of that hold lift slightly. She shifted her gaze from Gery and found Pholus looking down at her. Concern clouded his large crystal blue eyes. Neither of them fully released her, though. It was as if they were waiting for something. She looked around the cave, her cave, and her heartbeat spiked. The hands on her tightened again, and she had to fight her panic to breathe normally. She needed to get them to release her.

"How did I get here? Did you say three days? Where are Purivia and Gaeleath? Can I please sit up?" She looked at both of them in turn, trying to convey a sense of calm she didn't feel. They both looked back at her intently neither releasing their stare or their hold until her heart rate had reduced again. When she took a deep shuddering breath, they simultaneously released their breaths and her body.

"How do you feel, young one?" Pholus's deep baritone was heavy with worry. The contrast between it and Gery's squeak of "You're probably hungry, yeah," coupled with the aftermath of her panic nearly sent her into a fit of hysterical laughter, but they hadn't answered her questions.

"Where are Purivia and Gaeleath?"

"I'm here," came the one voice able to fully calm her. She had to sit up in the bed and strain her neck to see him standing near the cave entrance behind Pholus' imposing mass.

"Oh!" She clasped her hands to her mouth, tears stinging her eyes. He walked over and knelt by her bed between Gery and Pholus who still stood within arms distance. Gaeleath reached up and pulled her hands from her face, holding them in his own.

"I'm here."

"You were covered in demons. They were all over you, covering your face. If it wasn't for your hair," she reached up and twirled one of his curls around her finger, "I wouldn't have recognized you at all."

"You saved me, saved us."

"Purivia is here too."

He smiled at her. "She is down in the dinner hall regaling everyone with repeated retellings of the encounter and how amazing you were."

Mera laughed and shook her head. "I nearly left you two behind. You were left to fight those demons and Mingus, alone."

"You came for us. I only wish I could have seen you in action. Stupid demons covering my eyes the whole time."

She laughed again, but then remembered her other questions. "How..."

Pholus interrupted her. "We will discuss the how's and what's next after you get something to eat."

She took a deep breath and agreed, asking them to give her a moment alone to collect her thoughts before she joined the group. They all left the cave, and she shifted to sit on the edge of the bed. Her head was pounding with questions, or maybe it was just hunger, as they all suggested. Had she really been asleep for three days? She looked around and saw her staff standing against the cave wall. The gods knew she was grateful to still have it and that it hadn't been lost in the forest. She walked over and lifted a hand in matching salute. It had helped her and her friends escape the shadows.

She turned to leave the cave in search of dinner and quickly returned for her staff. "I think I'll just keep you with me," she said aloud to the familiar piece of wood, much like she always spoke openly on her days hidden among the Strimmena.

Conversation in the dinner hall was already loud and raucous, and Mera looked forward to soaking in the normalcy of it all. She smiled when she saw Purivia and Gaeleath seated next to one another at the long table. Relief washed over her. It's not that she hadn't believed they were both here and all right, but the images of Purivia scratched and exhausted from fighting the shadow demons and Gaeleath smothered by their shadowy forms kept replaying in her mind.

"Mera!" Purivia stood and rushed around the table to grab her in a tight hug, nearly knocking Mera over. The shocked looks around the room verified what Mera was thinking. The paladin never showed outward affection. Mera leaned into the hug and wrapped her arms around her friend.

"How are you?"

"How am I? You're the one who'd been unresponsive for days! I even tried healing energy from the various gods represented here, and you didn't wake up."

"Thank you for trying. I'm sure it helped." Mera pulled away to look in the woman's eyes and smiled warmly. Purivia squeezed her shoulders one last time and walked back to her seat.

"Join us, Mera," Pholus said from the head of the table. "There is a seat next to your teammates."

She made her way around the table, greeting all of the others on her way, and took her seat. The food had already been presented, and everyone else had nearly finished their meal. She dug into her plate, hunger pangs kicking in as the aroma reached her nostrils. When had she ever been this hungry? Her plate was nearly empty when she looked up to see everyone staring at her.

"What?"

"That's three days of not eating on display, yeah," said Gery from across the table near Pholus.

Heat rushed into her cheeks, and she sat up straight, pushing her dish away.

"Eat your fill, Maenad. You earned it."

"Her appetite is not the only thing that grew over three days. That's an impressive crown."

She jerked her head toward the voice and saw Tarkegan smiling at her. His awkward smile brightened, and his single eye traveled up and down from her face to the top of her head. She looked toward Gaeleath at her side, and he smiled too. She tentatively reached up and brushed her hair back from her forehead. She gasped when her hands caught on her horns, but they weren't her horns. Those were short, furry knobs. Using both her hands, she traced the hard antler-like points up from her scalp across the short, pointy protrusion about three inches off her head before the rest continued to their points another three inches into the air. A lump formed in her chest, and her breath caught. She couldn't hide these like she'd hidden her small ones for all these years. Would she never fit in?

"What has happened to me?"

"Skyemera," Pholus called, breaking into her thoughts. "Let's discuss the mission and that will hopefully answer your questions."

"I thought Purivia had already told everyone." She looked at Gaeleath who shrugged sheepishly and then to Purivia who shook her head.

"I wanted you to be well before we told the full story."

"I know some of what happened, but it is our practice to share with everyone, so that we all might learn something from each mission. So, start from the beginning."

They did just that. Taking turns, they told of the journey to the forest, leaving out Purivia's private tale. They explained about it taking them hours within the forest to find the clearing. They spoke of the weird emptiness of that field and how they had mistakenly thought themselves safer beneath the tree cover. Then Skyemera shared all she knew about Mingus and the priestess' invitation. She told of feeling the break in energy when he released the demons to attack, and how she had used her wind for them to run toward the clearing. Tears filled her eyes as she recounted the moment she realized her friends weren't with her at the forest's edge.

Purivia shared how the demons had closed ranks around her and Gaeleath and then built a wall separating them. She spoke of the inability to kill them with her sword and how Mera had come back to fight alongside her, using the cyclone to gather the demons around them before sending them into the sunlight on a current of wind. Mera blushed at Purivia's descriptions and the awe in her voice. The combination of gratefulness and admiration triggered fresh tears, though for a much different reason.

Gaeleath's story was a similar combination of surprised confusion at the events, and pride at how Mera took control of the situation, using the trees as a weapon against the demons. He'd had no idea how they'd so thoroughly overpowered him in the span of seconds. It was as if they'd known his true form and were prepared to keep him from changing. He also shared that he was afraid of further harming the forest and its inhabitants if he would have changed and blasted fire there on the forest floor. He showed no outward emotion in the retelling of his capture, but he never met Pholus' gaze.

"But how did we get back here," Mera blurted, unable to hold back the question any longer.

"I brought you back," Gery answered simply. "Don't look so surprised. I am the king of quick travel," he concluded with a flourishing wave of his hands, which earned him a laugh from the younger trainees.

"He brought you and Purivia back together," Gaeleath stated, as if that had been the plan all along. "I used my telepathy to bring him to us, and then I flew myself back, as it was safer than waiting in that clearing alone. I needed to release some of my own energy anyway."

"You really don't remember anything after we made it back to the clearing," Purivia asked, genuine surprise in her voice.

"I remember you and Gaeleath arguing about the best way to get out of the forest." Her head tilted, and she added, "and I remember large birds circling over the clearing. They would circle, then fly off over the trees before returning to circle again."

Purivia and Gaeleath both looked at her.

"What birds," Purivia asked. "What did they look like?" Her voice had risen to a pitch that caused the hair on Mera's arms to bristle.

"They were black with wide wingspans. I couldn't see many details, but I remember thinking how large they must have been to be so clearly visible from the ground."

Purivia looked from Mera to Gaeleath and then to Pholus.

"Did you see any birds on your flight, Gaeleath?" Pholus' voice boomed through the large cave. Though his face remained impassive, Mera felt a change in his energy, as he stared at Gaeleath's uncertain look.

"I may have seen some birds, but I never pay them any attention when I fly. I didn't thi..." He turned back to Purivia. "Do you think these are the birds from your hometown?" When she didn't answer, he let fly a slew of words Mera had never heard used in The Thicket. "Master Pholus, I would never intentionally..." Pholus silenced him with a wave of his hand.

"We must be prepared for nothing and everything at the same time."

The newest trainees looked around at each other and then at the others. The uncertainty and fear was palpable. The conversation turned to one of general practicalities related to preparation. Gery must have noticed their fear because he began making jokes about not preparing enough dinner for all the hungry mouths around the table. The overall tension in the room slowly began to recede, as laughter took over.

Something moved where the cave wall met the ceiling. Perhaps it was one of the small, reptilian creatures that also called the mountains home. They would often skitter across the walls of the cave, and they made Mera scream more than once when she first came to the Palaestra.

"What's so funny?" Gaeleath asked with a smile.

"I was thinking about the little creatures that run around the caverns and how often they have made me jump and scream." They both laughed. "Ironically, I don't remember screaming once in the forest."

"No," he said. "You were in your element."

"I was, wasn't I?" She still wasn't sure she felt any different or any more secure in her abilities than she had before the mission, but their belief in her and their pride in how far she had come gave her confidence.

"What was that?" One of the younger trainees yelled. "Ow!"

Another screamed, jumping on his bench. "Something just scratched my foot." Mera jumped to her feet, staff in hand. Everyone else looked around in silence.

"There!" Mera pointed to the far end of the room where the light from the candelabras didn't reach.

"Grab whatever weapons you can and get out of the cave," Pholus' deep voice bellowed, echoing around the chamber.

Chapter Thirty-Three

❦

S hadow demons flooded through the cave entrance as if a dam had broken. They made their way around the chamber in a torrent, staying as far away from the candlelight as possible.

"Gaeleath, your fire," Pholus called over the din of flapping wings and squeaks of excitement. Gaeleath opened his palm, conjuring twin flames. "As soon as you're outside, set as many fires as you can. Make sure all the torches are lit. These demons shy away from the light." All of his directions were given within a matter of seconds as he began moving toward the opening.

"Shoot your flames at the high corners of the cave," Mera whispered to Gaeleath.

She had never heard the shadows speak or seen them respond to spoken word, but she didn't want to take a chance. With a wink, Gaeleath turned mid-stride and shot flames up toward the darker corners of the cave. The demons hissed. A few were hit directly and burst into ashes while others fell from the wall or flew across the cave to find cover.

"Remember they are shadows," Mera yelled amongst the throng pushing toward the exit. "They cannot exist in the light."

The young paladin, whose sense of justice and faith were stronger than anyone Mera had ever met quickly pulled his sword. It sparked into a bright white flame. "Let me clear the opening, Master Pholus," and he slipped around the centaur to lead the escape.

Mera watched everyone empty out of the cave. She didn't know what was outside, but she knew what was in here. "Gaeleath, we either have to destroy these things, or we have to find a way to contain them in here. There are too many places to hide in the shadows out there, even with torches."

"If you can gather them, I'll burn them."

Mera pulled forth her magic, channeling the support of the Strimmena, and sent her cyclones out around the inner perimeter of the large cave, making sure to reach to the ceiling for all those that might be hiding in the crevices and under the table. They could rebuild the table later, she thought, as it splintered. The shadows screamed and hissed while being sucked into the swirling wind.

"I think I have them all."

Gaeleath shot his flames at the cyclone, and they listened to the screams and screeches of the creatures. He stopped when all that was left in the wind were ashes and soot.

"That was awesome," he said with glee. "I didn't really get to see your power in the forest, but this was spectacular."

She opened her mouth to thank him when they heard voices yelling from outside in the canyon. They both took off running out of the short tunnel without a word. At the mouth of the cavern, Mera stopped in her tracks. Gaeleath ran into her back and had to grab her arms to keep them both from toppling over. The melee before them was tremendous. There were shadow demons everywhere, and every inhabitant of the Palaestra was caught in the middle of a group of demons. Pholus had no fewer than eight clawing at his back while he fought others in front of him.

"Light the fires," Pholus screamed as another set of claws

found purchase in his flank. Gaeleath sidestepped Mera and ran toward the first set of torches.

Mera couldn't move. She saw the priestess standing on an overhang halfway up the cliffside. Next to her was a beautiful, middle-aged man with a face that had been seared into Mera's memories. It was the face her mother had painted and hung on her grandmother's wall. "Vasilios," she whispered. Her mother's mate was here in the Palaestra with Yevondra. She froze staring at him, watching the two of them look over the scene on the ground.

Oh, there you are, Maenad. I was very disappointed that you did not accept my invitation. I was hoping we could meet under much quieter terms. The priestess' voice echoed through Mera's mind making her skin crawl. *If you come with us now, all of this will end.* Yevondra gestured widely at the canyon floor.

Mera tore her eyes from the canyon ridge and took in the scene. The demons continued to torment her friends and mentor. They seemed to be everywhere at once in overwhelming numbers. The only person not besieged by shadows was Gaeleath who ran from torch to torch, lighting them with his conjured fire. It was slow going, as there were people in the way from him being able to shoot the flames across a distance.

The torches wouldn't be enough, though, if the others couldn't grab them to fend off the creatures. Even the young paladin with his sword of light was struggling against their numbers. As soon as he'd destroy one and turn to help someone else, others would attack him from behind. The best any of them could do was knock the creatures away and breathe for a moment, but each of them were covered in scratches and bite marks on the exposed parts of their bodies. Even the cyclops had a long gash from the left of his eye around to the back of his head to the nape of his neck where a demon must have latched onto him.

You can stop this, Maenad. All you must do is come with us.

Mera's breath quickened in anger at the two fiends perched on the ledge above the fray. Magic tingled within her veins like tendrils straining for release. She watched Gaeleath running around between demons and his friends trying to get the torches lit, and she waved her hand. The breath of her wind caught his flame and lit every torch, one after the other, until they were all blazing, bathing the cavern bed in light. The demons screeched, and those that did not burst into ashes, slunk against the edge of the cavern in the shadows, creeping into cave openings, anything to get away from the flickering light.

As soon as the demons had gone into hiding, everyone on the cavern floor stopped. Time stood still for a moment, giving them reprieve to wipe sweat from their brows and blood from their skin.

I warned you, Maenad. Now your friends will have to contend with more than just my demons.

Mera and Yevondra stared at each other when energy sizzled through the air. Mera gasped, as Vasilios jumped from the edge of the cliff.

"Dragon," she screamed.

Gaeleath must have also felt the shift of energy because he stopped and turned, leaping into the air and transforming in the span of a heartbeat. His dragon form careened toward Vasilios who was much larger than himself. The two clashed in a flurry of wings and claws before Vasilios overpowered the younger dragon. He swung Gaeleath around through the air and flung him against the side of the canyon.

Mera screamed, lifted her staff, and blew the winds with all her might. She caught Vasilios off guard when his wings were lifted by the current. He twisted in the air flipping head over tail until he, too, hit the canyon wall, falling to land on his feet. He looked at her, ignoring everyone else in the canyon.

I know you. She heard his voice in her head as clearly as she had heard the priestess and Gaeleath. *You have grown since I last saw you, Skyemera. You were but a young babe of barely nine winters.* The images from her nightmares flooded her thoughts, and her knees nearly buckled. Somehow, though, she managed to stay on her feet and maintain his gaze. *You do not belong here. You are far beyond this simple stock.* He swung his head from side to side, his blue and red scales glistening in the torchlight as he gestured to Mera's friends. *You belong amongst the elementals, the gods of ultimate power. The God of Fire would have you as his own, sitting by his side. You would have a throne of obsidian, not a simple cave for a room.*

"I want none of that and nothing to do with you," she yelled, forgetting that he could hear her thoughts. The others turned to look at her in surprise of her seemingly random outburst.

We will see once all of this is over. He took a deep breath.

"Take cover," she screamed. She prepared her wind to try and block some of the fire's force as it shot from his mouth. She felt his power pushing against her own, a mixture of element and magic that threatened to overpower her. She hoped that her friends were out of the way in case she couldn't hold it, but she dared not look away to see.

You are not yet strong enough against me.

She is not alone! Another voice broke into their conversation. Gaeleath had recovered from his crash and fall. He opened his mouth, but instead of flames, he blew ice and snow. It weakened the fire, and its cooling power washed over Mera. The cold pushed against the receding flames.

What is this? Vasilios bellowed through the telepathic connection they shared. His flames had stopped, and he turned his attention on Gaeleath who had stopped breathing his ice crystals. *You're an ice dragon.* Though his thought was more a statement than question, his tone was incredulous. He turned his head sideways to take in the younger dragon. *I'm surprised your people didn't kill you as a child. They must have hidden your existence from the God of Fire. I shall remedy that situation now.*

Gaeleath roared at him and shot fire in his direction. *I have my own fire.* He leapt into the sky above the canyon with Vasilios in pursuit. They attacked each other, claws seeking purchase. Their flights might have been considered majestic if the battle hadn't been so deadly. Flames and ice, and even more flames, burst forth from them in rapid succession, lighting the sky.

Now that your dragon is occupied... The priestess' voice rang in her head. *Let us talk up close and personal.*

Mera had barely turned around when the priestess landed on the ground twenty yards away in the shadows. She was just as eerily beautiful as Mera remembered from the church with her long black and red hair and crown of horns above her ashen forehead. She did not wear the same gown, but she was still dressed all in black. Tight pants were tucked into knee-high boots, and the low-cut tunic hugged her curves.

Mera's silent appreciation was cut short when Yevondra with a sly smiled said so everyone could hear, "And to ensure we are not disturbed, Mingus has brought some friends to the party."

The sudden rumble of flapping wings was deafening, and excited shrieks came from the caves and dark crevices around the canyon. Mingus' gray form appeared against the night sky atop the canyon ridge in a flurry of winged shadows. His features were barely illuminated by the blasts of flames from the dragon fight that continued overhead. A rush of winged creatures passed over him and swooped into the canyon.

"Incoming." Pholus' voice bounced off the canyon walls. Everyone turned to look up, and Mera gasped as she saw the huge birds flying into the canyon. She clenched her staff and lifted her arms to protect her friends, forgetting Yevondra. A wave of heat hit her chest like a lightening blast, and her knees nearly buckled. She staggered back before gaining her footing and pushed the power she'd been gathering toward the priestess. Yevondra toppled to the ground, her red and black tresses floating about her in a waterfall.

There wasn't much vegetation on the canyon floor, but Mera tapped her staff into one of the spots of green nearest her foot and nudged her energy to grow. Sounds of battle continued around her, but she pushed the fear and concern aside, focusing on the woman before her. Yevondra slowly rose to her feet, shaking her head, angry eyes fixed on Mera. She didn't have to say a word for Mera to clearly read the danger in that look, and she reached further with her magic to find the roots beneath Yevondra's feet. Slowly, green tendrils sprouted forth from the cracked earth and wove their way around the priestess' feet and up her ankles.

Yevondra attempted a forward step, and Mera watched as the look of menace converted into one of horror and then fear. She fell face forward into the dirt and swiftly flipped herself to pull at the vines. "What? How?" Mera smiled at her surprise, but that smile swiftly faded as Yevondra conjured matching scimitars from smoke. With one swipe of the barely corporeal blade, the vines fell from her legs, and she sprang to her feet. She rounded on Mera but not before taking in the scene around them. "That was a nice trick, Maenad. Earth and Wind. The God of Fire will be happy to know you are progressing so swiftly. Unfortunately, the same cannot be said for your friends."

The battle sounds flooded into Mera's consciousness, and her heart pounded at the cries of her friends as they fought off the demon birds. She heard Purivia's cry of warning. "Don't let them hold onto you." The image the paladin had painted of the dogs from her hometown flooded Mera's mind, and she allowed herself a moment to look for her friends.

Purivia was working back to back with one of the younger trainees, swiping her blade back and forth to keep the birds away. Gery leapt onto the back of one of the creatures from a boulder and smashed his hammer into its beak from the side, cracking its skull. The bird fell into a heap, and Gery took off running toward another of the creatures. Pholus was stomping on another that had stood still too long, and yet another took the opportunity to claw at the centaur's back before being knocked to the ground by Gery who appeared unexpectedly.

At the other side of the canyon, near the caves where they all lived, Tarkegan grappled with Mingus over the cyclops' long spear.

What the demonic acolyte lacked in height, he made up for with brute strength and cunning. His long, prehensile tail reached around while they held each other's hands aloft and grabbed at the cyclops ankle, trying to topple him. Tarkegan released one of his hands and reached down to yank the cord-like protrusion. Mingus screamed, reaching for Tarkegan's eye. The cyclops ducked and landed two strong punches to Mingus' side. He doubled over, and Tarkegan brought his knee up into Mingus' face. The sounds of cracking bones permeated the air. He fell, and the cyclops skewered him with the spear.

Yevondra screamed. Her piercing shriek of anger drew everyone's attention, including the dragons still fighting in the sky. She turned toward the cyclops who stood over Mingus' broken body. Cuts and dirt mixed together turning his skin a shade of dusty rose. She flailed her hands around, and with a gust, threw him against the canyon wall. Spear still clutched in his hands, he fell to one knee, the wind knocked from his lungs. Mera watched in horror as the hordes of greedy shadow demons left the caves and attacked him in unison, scratching and clawing. There were so many, Mera could hardly see the cyclops, even with his huge body. He roared. Whether it was in pain or anger, Mera couldn't tell.

Pholus yelled from where he was still battling the birds, his war scythes slashing flesh from their bones, and still, they kept coming. Mera's breath caught as one of the young trainees fell, clutched in the massive claws of one of the birds. Purivia ran over and removed the birds head with one swipe of her sword, but it was too late. Mera turned back to the cyclops who was an undulating black mass. Only his spear was visible amongst the shadows.

"Let's end this," Mera said, running toward Yevondra without waiting for a response. She felt the energy shift as the priestess braced for the collision. Mera held her staff in both hands, twirling it until it fanned out before her as a shield. She kept running, even when the priestess threw her shadow blade that bounced off the staff. Mid-stride, Mera jumped and kicked at the priestess with her strong legs, knocking Yevondra to the ground. She screamed in consternation and jumped to her feet, another set of twin blades slashing in front of her as she attacked Mera. Mera parried with her staff, but the priestess was fast. Had she been holding back?

The thought had no sooner popped into Mera's head that she misjudged Yevondra's move and felt her own arm being sliced open. Mera screamed. It burned more than the heat of the dragon's flames she'd barely pushed away before Gaeleath had stepped into the battle with his ice. She backed away from the priestess again. The blades came forward in a fury, flying through the air, forcing Mera to continue retreating. The force with which they hit her staff reverberated through her already aching arm. Mera gritted her teeth, wanting to call forth her magic but knowing it would be countered by the priestess.

Gaeleath roared above her, and Pholus continued yelling commands at those still fighting the birds. From behind Yevondra, Mera caught the grunts and cries of Tarkegan who was now fully encapsulated in the smokey sarcophagus of the shadow demons. She could not spare a moment to look anywhere but Yevondra and her scimitars. *Back up* came Gaeleath's voice in her head. She jumped to the side away from the priestess who was immediately engulfed in flames. *Now,* he said, before she heard his cry of agony. Vasilios swooped in and dug his claws into Gaeleath's back, swinging him out of the air.

"No," she screamed.

Yevondra snuffed out the flames, but not before her ashen skin laced red and black from the heat. Flesh was missing from her arms, and her clothing was burnt and tattered. The long hair that fell from behind her crown was missing in blistered patches on her head. She brushed the unruly strands from her face and winced. When she looked at Mera, her anger was palpable. "I will kill everyone in this canyon, including that dragon, but you will die first. I will offer myself as the God of Fire's right hand in your place."

She conjured her swords anew and took a step toward Mera. Mera braced herself, staff in both hands as the priestess approached. Yevondra raised the blades to begin the fight again when Purivia streaked behind her and slashed across her back. She screamed and dropped her scimitars, which faded before they reached the ground. At the same time, the cyclops rose up and threw his spear in a final act of defiance, piercing the priestess through her side before he fell to the ground. Mera walked toward Yevondra who was on one knee, breathing heavily and whimpering in pain. Her eyes flashed anger and madness as she she tried to push herself up on her feet. Mera once again grasped her staff in both hands, ready to swing at the priestess when two birds swooped in grabbing Yevondra by her arms with their large talons and pulling her from the canyon bed.

"Let me go," she yelled. "Put me down, you idiots! This is not over. Let go of me! If you try to feed from my body, I will kill you." Those last words faded as Yevondra was flown over the canyon's ridge. In her wake, the rest of the birds followed, thus ending the battle.

The shadow demons, having destroyed the mighty cyclops, slid toward Mingus and lifted his body to carry him off as well. Above the canyon, a dragon screeched. Vasilios, in his blue and red glory was flying in circles. Gaeleath was nowhere to be seen. "No," Mera said, leaning heavily on her staff. Vasilios' voice reached out to her.

You have fought well, Skyemera. I'm sure we'll meet again. Your dragon is on the other side of the ridge. He too fought well but will need to be better next time. And with those final words swirling through her mind, he flew off behind the others.

Mera looked around for Gery. "Gery," she yelled, trying to find the gnome.

"I'm here," he cried from the other side of the canyon where he stood next to Pholus who was still on the ground.

"No," she cried and ran, falling to her knees next to the centaur. "Will you be alright, Great Pholus?"

"Those damn birds started pulling at his essence. We were able to kill them, but Master Pholus fell where he was standing," Gery said, watching the two paladins who attempted their healing magic. "This is not a normal healing," he said. "I don't know if they're strong enough." The latter whispered so low only Mera could hear him.

"Gery, Gaeleath…"

"I know, I saw him fall."

"The dragon said he's on the other side of the ridge."

Gery looked at her with sad eyes. "Poor kid."

"No, he said he needed to be stronger for next time. I think he's still alive. Can you find him?"

Without a word, Gery popped and was gone. Mera watched in silence as the paladins worked on Pholus until her heartbreak was such that she couldn't watch anymore. She stood and looked around the canyon, taking an account of who was still standing and who lay unmoving on the ground. Those who could still walk were slowly making their way toward Pholus. Mera saw one of the young trainees on the ground and said a silent prayer to the gods that he would be taken care of in the afterlife. She didn't know which god he followed, but she hoped they would hear her prayer. She walked to where Tarkegan lay.

If she hadn't known him so well, she would not have recognized him. His face was a mess of scratches and bruises. Flesh was missing in places where the shadow demons had bitten into him. His skull was misshapen, squeezed under the pressure of their tightening undulations. Mera knelt next to him and touched his arm. She'd not been blessed with healing magic, but even if she had, he was beyond her help now. "Thank you. We couldn't have ended this without you." No tears burned the backs of her eyes, as numbness crept in.

Before she could return to Pholus, Gery popped in behind her.

"I found him," he blurted. Mera smiled. "I found him, but he's unresponsive. He's also still in dragon form. I can't bring him back here like that." Any other time, Mera would have laughed at Gery's response to the idea of transporting a dragon. She couldn't laugh, though, not with the broken and battered bodies strewn about the canyon. She couldn't feel anything.

"Can you take me to him?" she asked.

"Do you think it's a good idea to be out there by yourself? What if the other dragon comes back? What if the birds come back or the priestess?"

"Gery, we can't just leave him out there alone. He helped us in this battle, swooping in to protect us...to protect me. He left himself open to Vasilios, and I can't leave him out there alone."

"Fine," Gery said, his jaw set. She touched his shoulder, and they were gone.

Chapter Thirty-Four

✦

Kari felt his presence before he fully materialized. She'd grown used to his comings and goings when he came to bring them updates on her cousin, or to strategize with Callisto. Though he rarely arrived this early in the morning, she walked toward the edge of the forest, which was his designated arrival point. She started running when she saw his frantic waving outside of her protection spells.

"Gery, what's wrong? Is Mera alright?" Her voice carried faster than her legs could go. She released the ward, and he came running to meet her.

"Skyemera is fine. Pholus has fallen. We need Callisto. We need healers. By the gods, we need help!"

"Breathe, friend." She touched his shoulder when they were close enough and helped reduce his heartbeat. When he smiled up at her, more in control of himself, she invited him to teleport them to the meeting house where Callisto was there with the council.

"Please wait here," she said when they stood outside the long building. Raised voices made their way through the open windows. Kari gave him a reassuring smile and a conspiratorial nod of her head toward the windows. She watched him go to stand beneath one of them. She took a deep breath and walked through the doors.

Nerin stood in the middle of the council yelling about something or another she didn't want to do.

"My apologies Mothers, but Gericole has just arrived from the Palaestra, and he is in need of Callisto. Ancient One, I will take you to him."

"He can wait!" Nerin wailed. "Why should the business of the council be interrupted by outsiders?"

"He was sent by Skyemera," Kari said, with all the outward patience she could muster. She still didn't know what he needed, but if Mera needed them, she would be there, by the gods.

"I am tired of so many decisions relating back to that..."

"Nerin," Dynami said with an edge to her powerful voice. "Take care your words. That is my granddaughter you are referring to." She turned her attention on Kari and addressed her with a softened voice. "Please invite Gery to come in."

Gery popped into view as soon as her words had come out. Kari almost laughed at the gasps and shocked expressions around the room. These women needed to be shaken up. They were too set in their ways and too out of touch. Kari didn't know much of the outside world, but the council barely understood those who lived here in The Thicket.

"I'm sorry to interrupt, but there is no time, yeah, no time. Callisto," he said, finding her amongst the sea of nymphs huddled in the chamber. "Pholus has fallen." Callisto's face went white and she flopped to her seat from where she had stood at his arrival. "No, no, he's not dead. At least...he wasn't when I left. He is hurt, yeah. We were attacked, and he is hurt. He's not the only one, but it is a magic our paladins cannot heal. We need help. We need a healer. Please!"

"And what of my granddaughter?" Dynami asked. "What of our Skyemera?"

"Skyemera is fine. She sent me here. She said you have healers.

She is tending to one of our trainees who was badly injured. Please help." His voice cracked at that last part, and Kari kneeled to put her arms around her friend. She turned to look expectantly at her grandmother with a silent plea.

"Matriarch, I must go," Callisto said. "If Pholus has fallen, his trainees, including your granddaughter will need leadership." Her breath also hitched, but she held her voice steady. "I am not the strongest healer, but I will lend my support."

"We understand," Dynami said, her eyes locked on Kari's. "Not long ago, I would have offered for Helena to travel with you as our strongest healer, but I have need of her here."

Callisto inclined her head, and the tears were visible. There was no way the matriarch would send her without any help. She couldn't, not if Mera had sent for help. Kari's breath caught, as she fought the urge to shout at the injustice.

"You will still have our help. Please take Karielle with you. She has far surpassed our other healers and she has developed many other skills that might be needed." Dynami left the council circle and walked to Kari, never breaking eye contact. She opened her arms, and enveloped her in the tightest hug she'd ever received from her grandmother. "Keep yourself safe, and bring your cousin home," Dynami whispered in her ear. Kari's chest tightened with pride and excitement.

"Thank you, Matriarch. I will send both of your granddaughters home safely once we have stabilized the situation." Dynami inclined her head to them and returned to her seat. Without another word, Callisto and Kari each touched Gery's shoulders and were whisked away.

G ery flashed them into what appeared to be the middle of a canyon. The sun's morning rays had not yet reached this place. The only light came from torches set in circular patterns, which allowed views of caves at various heights along the canyon walls.

"There," Gery said, pointing in the direction of a crowd seated around a large figure on the ground. "They still haven't moved him."

Callisto ran across the canyon and fell to her knees next to Pholus. She spread her hands over him searching for his energy. Kari followed her and began the same process. Callisto raised panicked eyes to Kari who continued searching. She needed to find just a tiny spark, and she could begin the healing process. Callisto stopped her search and ran her hands lightly over his face.

"What did this to him?" Kari asked the crowd.

One of the paladins who had stepped aside when the nymphs arrived said, "If it pleases you, my name is Purivia. We were attacked by many demons of the God of Fire, including shadow demons, a dragon, a priestess, and some accursed birds that not only attack with talons and beaks but also suck the life from you to rejuvenate themselves."

"One of those birds grabbed him and wouldn't let go. I crushed his head with my hammer, yeah, but Master Pholus still fell." Gery's raw emotion broke Kari's facade, and she averted her eyes as a tear slid down her cheek.

"The Rheizaldaru were here?" Callisto looked up at them. "They're not aggressive, at least the stories I've heard do not mark them as aggressors.

"You've heard of these birds before?" the paladin asked. "I saw them once years ago in my town. One was emaciated and burnt. He was left by another, and in trying to hide from one of our neighbor's dogs, it killed the poor animal."

"According to the stories, the God of Fire keeps them as

messengers, harbingers if you will, of his desires. He holds them above the fire pits, so their feathers are always singed, and when one of them gets close to the death, the others feed off his essence until he's nothing more than bones."

"By the gods, they are life suckers," Kari exclaimed. Callisto inclined her head and turned her sad eyes to Pholus' face. "Thank goodness Gery rid the great centaur of the creature as quickly as he did. There is still much life left in him, though it is weak." Kari's words triggered murmurs of gratitude throughout the small group.

"This will be easier with positive energy in the air. I need something to pull from. If you could all imagine Pholus at his strongest." Kari reached out her magic and pulled on those positive threads of energy swirling through the group, those coming from Gery the strongest. She weaved them together into thread that she wove through the metaphysical wounds stitching them closed. "I have done all I can do. He should wake soon."

A collective sigh rose from the group. Callisto was the only one who did not look up at Kari. She was staring into the face she still held in her hands, the look so intimate that Kari turned away.

"Thank you for your help," Purivia said, standing to clasp Kari on the shoulder. "We healed his body," she said, gesturing to a younger human male who had been at her side when Kari arrived. "We could not have helped his spirit." Kari gave her a gracious smile and turned to Gery.

"Where is Mera?"

"She's with our dr…"

Gery cut off the paladin. "She's with Gaeleath. He was hurt on the other side of the ridge. I can take you to her." Kari was uncertain about the look exchanged between the two, but she was too anxious to see Mera to analyze it. She reached out and grabbed Gery's hand.

Before she could take a breath, they were standing on the

canyon's ridge, and the winds whipped her hair about her face. "Gery, you said Mera was out here. Where is she?"

"I need to tell you something first before we go to her exact location."

"I don't like the sound of this."

"You're not going to like what I have to say either, but I would rather you get upset with me than to panic in front of everyone who just watched you heal our leader."

"Tell me where my cousin is, Gery, or the one who will be panicking is you."

He looked directly into her eyes and took a deep breath. "She is around these trees and beyond those bushes on the next ridge with Gaeleath. I did not lie, yeah. But Gaeleath is..."

"Is what? Dead? One of those creatures you all just described?"

He shook his head. " No, he is not a life sucker. He is a dragon."

"A dragon! You left my cousin with a dragon!" She took off running before he popped in front of her to slow her down.

"It's dark out here, and you could fall into a ravine, yeah. Gaeleath is a dragon, and he is one of our family here in the Palaestra."

"Kari?" Mera's voice came from below. "Is that you?"

"Mera, where are you? Are you hurt? Does the dragon have you trapped?" She started down the ridge again, sliding around Gery. She did walk slower this time, and he followed her rather than trying to impede her progress.

Mera's laughter traveled up to her. "Trapped? Absolutely not."

Kari looked back at Gery who shrugged. They curved around the small copse of trees, giving them an unobscured view of the lower ridge. Kari stopped in her tracks, mouth slacked open with a startled gasp frozen in her throat. "Breathe," Gery said, grasping her hand. "I know he's a sight, yeah."

"Kari? Please don't be afraid. He's hurt, and I can't leave him."

"By the gods, he's a whole rotting dragon!"

"He is, and he's my friend. He was hurt protecting me." Kari's eyes went wide, taking in the dragon and looking back to Mera. She looked unhurt, and he was obviously not.

"Take me to them, Gery," she said, squeezing his hand that still held hers.

They no sooner popped onto the lower ridge that Mera enveloped her in a hug. Tears sprang to her eyes and her breath hitched. She pulled away and looked her cousin up and down. "You're really alright?"

Mera nodded with a smile. "A little bruised and tired, but otherwise whole. What are you doing here?"

"You told me to go to The Thicket and bring healers, yeah, so I brought Kari."

Mera inspected Kari with the same scrutiny Kari had looked her over. "Yaya let you come? And you're a healer now? I've missed so much."

"She knew she couldn't have stopped me from coming when Gery said you sent for help. I've missed you." She reached out and pulled Mera in for another tight hug. "Let's look at your dragon. What happened to him?"

"Vasilios, yes, that Vasilios, caught him off guard and dug his claws into Gaeleath's back. Then he flung him down here on the ridge, and he's not woken up since." Her eyes filled with tears as she talked about the dragon.

Gery grabbed Mera's hand. "She healed Pholus' soul. I'm sure she can stitch Gaeleath back together good as new."

"By the gods, Pholus is alright?"

"He still hadn't woken when we left him, but I felt him growing stronger by the second. Callisto and the paladins are there to help continue his healing."

Mera squeezed Gery's' hand, gratitude exuding from them both. Kari hadn't yet shared her ability to read emotions with anyone, but she smiled nonetheless. If they noticed or wondered why, they didn't ask. She turned toward the dragon, taking a deep, steadying breath and looked over his massive form laying on its side. This was likely the same position he'd fallen into when he was thrown. That meant the tears in his back were around on the other side against the trees that had stopped him sliding down to the next ridge, and she wasn't sure if that was the only thing ailing him. The sun had begun to rise on the other side of the canyon, so he had been here for hours without moving.

She reached out with her magic, hoping she'd be able to penetrate his scales to detect his primary injuries. A gasp escaped her before she could hold it back. Mera came to stand next to her.

"What is it? What's wrong?"

She wasn't sure how to answer the question. It did not look good. He was too big for them to move. "He's impaled on a broken tree. It is stuck in his thigh. It missed the artery, so it is likely pain keeping him unconscious."

"Oh no! What can we do?" Mera's voice was a plea.

"If we could pull out the tree, or pull him off of it, I could heal his wound. I think I can even heal the gashes in his back, though it looks like they've already started healing themselves."

Mera and Gery exchanged a look, and Gery shook his head. "I can't teleport him in this form. He's too big for me." Mera's tears spilled, and her chin quivered.

"I'm sorry, Mera. My magic doesn't work on plants."

"Did you say plants? What do you mean?"

Kari shared her thoughts about possibly getting the tree to dislodge itself somehow. It was probably impossible, but she'd learned that much of what she'd thought impossible two years ago were simply things yet unseen. Mera said nothing, but she reached out a hand to touch the dragon's muzzle. Kari felt the energy shift, but couldn't tell what it meant. She watched Mera walk around the dragon's head and disappear behind the massive creature.

"Mera?" The hair on Kari's arms stood as the dragon winced. Gery grabbed her and flashed them to the upper ridge just as the beast shrieked in pain and flames poured from its mouth to the spot they'd been standing moments before. It roared and rolled from its side to its belly, but it didn't spit flames again.

Mera walked from around the dragon and patted his nose, as he nuzzled her hand.

"Gery, what just happened?"

"I'm not sure. I'm guessing Mera removed the tree from his leg."

"What? She can do that?"

He giggled. "You both can do a lot more than you could the last time you were together." Kari watched Mera stroke the dragon's cheek affectionately and smiled at the warmth she felt from her cousin. Gery was right, a lot had changed in these two years. "Come," Gery said. "Gaeleath said it's safe for us to come back down there."

"He said?"

"Yes. He is telepathic in his dragon form."

"He can talk to me too then?"

An unknown voice entered her mind. *Yes.* She screeched just as Gery popped them back to Mera's side.

"By the gods, Gery, you could have done a much better job preparing me for what I was walking into coming here." They all laughed, and smoke wafted from the dragon's nostrils as he held in a chuckle.

"Listen here, you giant torch. I do not want to be a roasted nymph today, but I need to see those gashes and that hole in your leg. Can I climb on your back?" *It would probably be easier for Gery to put you up there.* The unfamiliar voice infiltrated her mind again. "I don't know if I will ever get used to someone being in my head. I already have too many thoughts of my own." The dragon snorted.

Mera stayed on the ground stroking Gaeleath's cheek. Gery and Kari flashed to his back, and she began knitting his wounds closed one at a time. The first time he shrieked and set fire to a small tree across the ridge, Kari made Gery check on Mera. After that, he was able to control his responses to rumbled growls that made Kari's teeth chatter from the quaking.

"How does that feel?" Kari asked when she and Gery returned to solid ground.

"It feels like my body's been torn open."

Kari tapped her foot and looked at him sternly. Mera stifled a giggle and Gery laughed outright.

The dragon pushed himself up to his feet, wincing as he placed pressure on his rear right leg, and looked at her sheepishly, as sheepish as a dragon could look anyway. *I'll live*, he said in her mind. *Thank you*. He lowered his muzzle to her, and she patted it.

"You're welcome," she said aloud.

I need to fly, he sent to all of them.

"Are you sure you're strong enough for that already," Mera asked, concern coloring her voice. Gery looked at him with the same emotion.

I will see you all in the canyon. Gery get them back inside, please. And with that, he took off, massive wings spreading to catch the air.

"Not going to lie, that was amazing to watch," Kari said.

Chapter Thirty-Five

❧

Mera looked around the inside of her cave once more. Little had changed within this space, but she was nothing like that young maenad who'd walked through that entrance two years ago. At Gery's suggestion, she'd worn the gown he'd gotten for her and the green cloak. Her travel/fighting clothes had been destroyed between the fight in the forest and the battle outside in the canyon. She hoped he'd tell her where he had ordered her clothes, so that she could visit the tailor for more.

"Mera, everyone's waiting." Kari's breath caught when Mera turned toward her. "Gods, you look..." Mera's eyes dropped, taking in the gown, and second-guessing the choice. "Powerful," Kari finished. "I have never seen you look so in control and confident." Mera smiled and sent a silent *Thank you*. "I will never get used to you being in my head!" They both laughed and exited the cave arm in arm. Mera wasn't sure how she and Kari were able to silently communicate. Though Gaeleath had previously mentioned how attuned she was to telepathic messages, she never imagined that she had the ability to speak to others with her mind if they hadn't first tapped into hers. Somehow, though, Kari's empathic abilities made it easier for Mera to test those abilities, particularly when emotions were involved, like now.

In the canyon bed below, everyone at the Palaestra stood waiting to say their goodbyes. Pholus wasstanding in the center with Callisto by his side. Gery stood at his other flank. Mera pushed a rogue strand of hair from her forehead and reached to cover her horns with her locks, forgetting that they were now standing off her head as a signal of her maturity. They made her both proud and self-conscious. Kari squeezed her hand, and Mera smiled down at her cousin, absorbing the peace she was sending.

"I am no good at goodbyes," she called out to the odd collection of people before her. She sniffed.

Pholus slowly walked up to her, still weak from his ordeal but otherwise whole. "This is not goodbye, Skyemera. You are a part of our family, and we will see each other again." He opened his arms, and she walked into them for a tight hug. He picked her up off the ground, and she laughed.

"I will miss you until then, Great Pholus." She leaned up and kissed his cheek.

Callisto joined them. "You have become so much more than I imagined when I first met you, Maenad, and you still have more inside of you. I feel it."

"Thank you, Ancient One."

"Please tell the council that I will return once I know that Pholus will be fine."

"I'm already fine, Callisto. I don't need a nursemaid," he said and then swayed. She raised an eyebrow as she grabbed his arm to steady him. They both turned to Kari.

"Thank you for your service. I have never seen a more powerful healer," Callisto said.

"Thank you for my life," Pholus said and hugged Kari tight.

Mera made her way around to the others, giving hugs and saying farewells. This exit was no less emotional than when she left The Thicket, but it was very different. There was no fear this time.

She was going home to her family, and she had made another family here. She knew she would see them again and was proud to know them. She walked over to where Gery and Kari stood together.

"Where are Purivia and Gaeleath? I wanted to say goodbye before you take us home."

"I'm not taking you home. Master Pholus needs me here."

"What do you mean?" Mera asked. She and Kari both looked at him, brows drawn together. He looked from one to the other and laughed, pointing at the space between their eyes.

"You two are definitely related," he said between laughs.

"Gery, what do you mean you're not taking us home? And where are the others?" Mera stood with her hands on her hips.

He stopped laughing, and pointed up toward the canyon ridge. "They're up there waiting for you."

Pholus came up behind them and put one hand on each of their shoulders. "You needed an escort. Our powerful healer deserves to see something of the world, and your friends asked to leave with you."

Mera turned to face him. "Why would they want to leave here? This is their home."

"You'll have to ask them, as they each made the request to accompany you."

A lump formed in Mera's throat. No one besides Kari had ever wanted to follow her anywhere. She didn't know what to think.

"You've earned their friendship and trust, Skyemera. Don't overthink it," Pholus said, as he guided them toward the trail that lead upward to the ridge.

Kari grabbed Mera's hand. "Come on, cousin, let's go home."

They caught up with Purivia and Gaeleath as they descended the second ridge. The latter was back in his human form, and they both carried packs that matched those Kari and Mera wore. Mera wanted to ask them why they were coming right away, but Pholus' admonishment to not overthink their friendship stayed her tongue. Instead she hugged both of them in kind, the hug lingering a little longer with Gaeleath. His whispered appreciation of her clothing choice leaving her breathless. She looked over her shoulder and saw Kari smirking at her. She shrugged and lengthened her strides, laughing when her cousin complained about the pace.

When they arrived at Krinosera a few days later, Mera and Purivia approached the city with trepidation. They explained the events of the last visit to their companions and everyone promised to keep their eyes open for danger in the shadows. An hour later, Kari's eyes were wide, taking in the tall buildings, sheets of glass reflecting the sun, and the spires jutting from the tops of the many churches along their route.

"I've never seen anything so beautiful," she said aloud to everyone and no one. "We have nothing like this in the entire Tribunal Forest. I've not seen anything close to it in the human town either."

"It is something to behold," Mera said. "Pholus called it glass, and there are different types and colors. Some can be seen through from both sides, and some are so reflective in the sun that you can barely see through them."

"We had glass in my small town, but in much smaller pieces. Our windows were nowhere near this size. I'm in awe every time I come to Krinosera or visit one of the other large cities," Purivia shared.

"There are other cities like this?" Kari asked.

"Many," Gaeleath answered. "I have probably traveled the farthest distances of anyone, perk of having wings," he winked at Kari, "and there are many cities this size, some even larger with paved paths between the buildings that they call roads or streets.

"What else have we missed in the forest?" Kari asked. Mera shrugged, and they kept walking.

The journey home was far less eventful but ever more enjoyable than the trek to the Palaestra, and Mera was grateful. She needed time to take in the sights and smells of her homeland. She delighted in the textural difference under her hooves, as they exited the flatlands and entered the forest. The closer they got, though, the more she worried about her friends feeling out of place in The Thicket. Time seemed to have stood still in The Tribunal Forest, and the world remained so small. Now that she'd seen more of it, she wondered if she'd feel at home anymore.

Kari broke Mera from her thoughts, asking "How do you think the council will receive Purivia and Gaeleath, especially Gaeleath?" amongst heavy breaths. Mera turned to see that she had left her friends yards behind and slowed her steps.

"Sorry," she responded with a half smile.

"I missed having to run everywhere just to keep up with you," she said with a laugh. "You didn't answer my question."

"I don't know. He saved my life, so they will have to accept that he is my guest, but I'm hoping they don't make him uncomfortable. I'm not sure they'll be able to keep from comparing him to Vasilios." Kari nodded. "I'm fairly sure they will respond openly to Purivia. She is not much different from our warriors. She is an amazing fighter, and her healing skills are strong. She will be an asset..."

"But?"

"But...will they accept me?"

Kari shook her head and took Mera's hand swinging their arms hard like they did as children. "You are one of us. You are my cousin. Our grandmother is the village matriarch. You belong, end of story." Mera smiled, but she couldn't shake the fear that had crept into her spine. She was even less nymph now than she had been when she left. If her horns didn't give away her changes, her staff and dress would.

At the hedgerow surrounding The Thicket, Mera stopped, looking side to side. "What is that energy?"

"You feel it?" Kari asked with a proud smile that caught Mera's attention.

"Is that you?"

"Those are my security wards. I have placed wards of protection around The Thicket that will only allow us in, and I have detection spells throughout the forest in case anyone should show up uninvited. That's how I found Gery." Her smug satisfaction made Mera laugh and then wrinkle her nose.

"So we can pass through the ward, right? What about our friends?"

"If we're holding their hands, they can enter as well. Their presence will, however, trigger a warning for Eustis."

Mera reached back and grabbed Gaeleath's hand. He had been walking directly behind her since they entered the forest. Purivia had stayed at his side, and Kari reached for her hand. They entered The Thicket two by two with Kari and Purivia in the lead. Mera held back for a second, watching the others slip in easily. Again, the uncertainty that she wouldn't make it past the wards crept in. Gaeleath squeezed her hand, and she looked up into his smiling face.

"I may not have my telepathy in this form, but you are still easy to read," he said.

"What if it doesn't let me through?"

He chuckled. "Then I guess we'll be stuck out here together."

"Come on, Mera," Kari said from the other side of the ward, still holding Purivia's hand.

Gaeleath squeezed her hand once more, and they both took a step forward. Nothing stopped them. Mera didn't know whether to laugh or cry in relief, but she held onto Gaeleath's hand and followed her cousin further into the village.

They'd gotten no further than the second set of homes when a group of battle-ready nymphs approached them. "Karielle? We did not expect you to return from the outer trail, nor did we expect strangers," the leader said, the formation blocking their path.

"Hello, Eustis. I didn't expect to take this path home either, but it was the grandest adventure ever! Welcome my cousin home and say hello to her friends."

"Your cousin?" All of the nymphs turned their attention to the rest of the group and their eyes caught on the horned woman behind Kari. "Skyemera, is that you?" When Mera stepped forward, Eustis smiled. "Oh, welcome home! Your family will be so happy to see you." The tension in both groups eased, as Mera saluted, palm raised and Eustis did the same. "Who are your friends?"

"This is Purivia and Gaeleath. They have both fought by my side and saved my life. They have been our escort home and will remain as our guests."

"You know that will have to be decided by the council, right?"

"I know," Mera responded, trying to hide her discomfort at the idea of presenting them to the council.

"Hurry home now. The council can be addressed after you let everyone know you are both home safely."

"Thank you," Kari and Mera both called as they pulled their friends forward before someone else stopped them.

As they passed through the village, numerous nymphs stepped outside to welcome them home. Kari received many hugs, and Mera waves and well wishes. A few skeptical glances were thrown toward their companions but nothing derogatory was said. Mera began to relax as their grandmother's house, her home, came into view. She wanted to run through the door, but something held her back. Would they recognize her? Again the anxiety crept in.

Suddenly the door flew open and Phialyra flew from the house heading straight for her. She stood and opened her arms, as her mother fell into them, clinging to her.

"My Mera, you're home." She repeated the refrain numerous times, as she alternated hugging her tight and touching her face, her hair, her horns, and her hands. Finally, Lyra pulled back and looked at her fully from head to toe. "How is it possible you've grown more beautiful?" She didn't wait for a response, simply grabbed Mera's hand and pulled her forward. "Your grandmother needs to see you. Come along, Karielle. She needs to see you too. And bring your friends." She called over her shoulder without looking back or loosening her grip on Mera's hand.

Mera wasn't sure about the change in her mother's tone or behavior, but she was glad for the warm welcome. Though she had left home with a mixture of anger and confusion, she had missed her mother and was glad to see her. Before they entered the door, Lyra turned to look at the group. "We will talk about your dragon later," she said with a conspiratorial wink at Gaeleath, but first, you need to see how your sister has grown." She then swept into the house without a backwards glance. They all looked at each other before quickly following her.

THE END

Epilogue

Mera and Kari exited The Thicket, making their way into the fullness of The Tribunal Forest. The forest was still sleeping, so their footsteps echoed through the trees.

"It's a good thing you are one of the most powerful beings alive," Kari said with a giggle. "You'd never be able to sneak up on your enemy."

Mera laughed. It was hard to believe that just two years ago, a comment like that might have sent her running away in tears. She looked down at the hooves peeking out from under her gown and smiled as she watched them crunch leaves along the forest floor. Those hooves had taken her far beyond anywhere her people had traveled and brought her back. They had helped her successfully defend against shadow demons and an enchantress with lightning swift reflexes. They had slid into a perfectly cobbled pair of soft leather boots made just for her, and they gave her a regal stance now.

"They would hear you coming a mile away as well, but it wouldn't matter because you'd just talk them to death once they caught you anyway."

Kari glared at her cousin for a whole two seconds before doubling over in laughter. Mera smiled and kept walking, forcing the nymph into a jog to keep up.

"That's not fair, Mera."

"Don't play with the hooves if you can't keep up with the hooves," Mera retorted but slowed to a more comfortable pace. "Your training has done you well, cousin."

"What do you mean?"

"You've never been able to keep pace, at least not without losing your breath."

Kari smiled, and Mera mused on how much they had both grown in their time apart. Kari had always been enigmatic and energetic, but now she was confident and poised. She had a subtle air of calmness she'd never had before. She put all her energy into teaching the little ones about their magic and honing her own amazing skills that she no longer bounced around The Thicket like a young deer. Her healing magic had far surpassed the elders, including Helena, and the wards she placed around The Tribunal Forest and The Thicket within were nothing short of extraordinary. Those wards were what drug them out of bed and into the forest before dawn.

"Do you perceive when someone leaves the forest," Mera asked as they closed in on their destination within the next copse of trees.

"What do you mean?" Kari turned her head slightly before continuing forward, much like a deer that hears unexpected footsteps mere yards away.

"Well, you feel when someone new, someone who doesn't belong to the forest, penetrates the wards upon entering, but what about someone who was here before the wards were placed? Do you feel them leaving?"

"If you're asking if I feel you sneak out of The Thicket to see your friends, the answer is no, but I do know when you come back."

"How do you know it's me?"

"You're my cousin, my best friend. I would recognize your presence anywhere." When Mera stopped to look at her, she continued. "Gery's been coming and going so often recently that I have grown accustomed to his arrivals. Not to mention the fact that I know no one else with the ability to just arrive in the middle of the forest and not enter from its edges."

Mera nodded in agreement but did not continue their journey. Something was worrying her. "What about unfamiliar creatures?"

"My wards around The Thicket are much more precise, stronger, if you will. I know when deer and birds enter through, though most feel the ward and turn around. The forest is too large with too many creatures for me to consider that level of precision." Mera felt Kari's scrutiny and looked up into her cousin's face. "Mera, what is bothering you?"

"Those birds. I can't remember what Callisto called them, but they were scary. They could fly in and land in the middle of the Forest. A dragon could as well."

Kari stared into her eyes, but Mera couldn't read her thoughts. She was far too quiet, too thoughtful. It had been easier to know what Kari was thinking when she was younger and impulsive. The thoughts left her mouth as soon as they entered her mind. How funny to say "when she was younger." They had both been younger and more impulsive two years ago. Now, they were forever changed. Older, yes, but also wiser, more confident, stronger in ability and conviction. And they were steadfast friends. Mera could trust Kari, and she knew her cousin would take her concerns seriously.

"If those birds had been in the forest before, I would have known; we would have known. The things you described would have left some trace. But your question of other creatures has me thinking. We are not the only forest dwellers. Let me think on it some more."

Mera gave her cousin an appreciative smile, grabbed her hand, and nearly drug her down the trail toward the clearing. They heard

Gery's voice before they had cleared the thick underbrush protecting the camp. Mera had coaxed the trees to create a thick canopy obscuring any view of the camp from the air, and she had grown an unnaturally dense perimeter of thorny bushes with only one entrance from the direction of The Thicket. Kari had added additional protective wards that would warn the clearing's inhabitants of unexpected visitors. Even Gery had to walk through the opening between the bushes and couldn't just pop in.

"Tell us how things are in the Palaestra, Gery." The voice was both sleepy and agitated. Gery must have surprised them with his arrival.

"Once Mera and Kari get here, yeah. You know I don't like to repeat myself."

"That could be hours from now."

As if on cue, the blue bells Mera had grown began jingling, the morning dew reverberating through their petals. Gery laughed. "It never takes Kari that long to find me. Sometimes, she knows I'm here before I do." Mera and Kari both burst out laughing as they entered the inner sanctum of the camp they'd built for Purivia and Gaeleath.

Once greetings were had, Purivia went to preparing a breakfast for the group, and Gery shared news from the Palaestra. Pholus was improving rapidly, and Callisto predicted she would return the next time Gery came this way to see his friends. In turn, the others shared what happened at the council meeting and how the encampment was the council's response to Mera's request Gaeleath and Purivia be allowed to stay. Really, it was their response to having a dragon in their midst. They were more than welcoming to the paladin. She, however, refused to leave him to stay alone out in the forest. Gery expressed his understanding on both sides.

"It's unfair, though, Gery," Mera countered. "Gaeleath and Purivia together saved my life against Yevondra. Him being a dragon doesn't change that fact." Gaeleath's eyes caught hers, and he smiled, warmth emanating in her direction. He understood and appreciated her feelings about the situation, but he also recognized the concerns of the council.

Gaeleath needn't say a word, though, because Gery spoke his thoughts plainly. "No, it doesn't change what you know to be true, but it is hard to reconcile the idea of inviting a dragon into the village when they have spent the past two years building protections against a dragon." He lay his hand on hers. She nodded in understanding, but she still found their exile to sleep in the forest unfair.

"What else has been happening at the Palaestra, Gery?" Purivia asked. "Any new trainees?"

"Ready to come back and get to work already," he responded.

If she wasn't always so serious, Mera could have imagined Purivia blushing in that moment. She knew the paladin had come to The Thicket out of a sense of friendship and loyalty to Mera but that she was struggling with the mundanity of the village. It was much quieter than even the Palaestra, and there were no missions to the city to be had. The alseides were still struggling to accept that cities like they'd described upon arrival existed. They certainly weren't ready to send anyone out there. So she knew her friend was bored.

She wasn't, however, prepared for Kari's response to the question. Her cousin's eyes had widened and then narrowed at Gery as soon as the words left his mouth. Then she sat on her hands and held her breath waiting for Purivia's response. The only time Mera had ever seen her cousin like this was when Callisto told the family Mera had to leave The Thicket and Kari couldn't go with her. That same despondency filled her eyes now. Mera touched Kari's knee, and the nymph let out a long breath.

Purivia looked around at the small group before she answered. Mera couldn't tell if she was searching for approval, but when her friend finally answered, Mera's chest swelled.

"I made the decision to come here willingly to support my

friend. I have not changed my mind and do not regret that choice. I will be here until I'm no longer needed or asked to leave." The collective release of tension from the friends was palpable, and Mera barely stifled a giggle. "I will admit that I'm itching to spar or fight or run, something to release the energy. I'm not used to sitting around waiting without something physical to fill the time."

Kari chimed in. "I know that some of our warriors would love the opportunity to learn new skills. What if we, meaning Mera, cleared another area in the forest for training? That would give us all a chance to learn from each other, practice, and it would help our people get to know Gaeleath."

"When did you become so wise?" Mera teased. "That's a fabulous idea, Kari. I could easily clear an area, but we would have to request permission to allow the others to come train with our friends."

"Since everyone now knows that Vasilios is working for the God of Fire and that he wants you specifically, I bet the council would be willing to allow access to other fighters who have already faced the dragon and the other dark creatures. At least, I hope. I'm going to go ask Yaya right now." Kari stood and made her way toward the opening of their encampment.

"Do you think it would be helpful if I came with you to explain what might happen with the creatures and our techniques?" Purivia asked before Kari could make her exit. "I can accompany you."

Mera watched as Kari turned around, a flush crawling up her neck. "I think that would be smart," Mera said, watching Purivia move to Kari's side. There was something between those two, she thought as they disappeared through the hedges.

"I was wondering," Gaeleath said, interrupting Mera's musing. "Gery, if my telepathy reached you from The Palacial Forest, might it also reach you from here?"

Gery looked pensive for a moment, but then he smiled. "I

think it should. Yes, the distance is further, so I might not hear you as clearly, but I still should be able to recognize the attempt."

"Oh good," Gaeleath responded. "I was just thinking that if something were to happen, we would need a way to let you know rather than you simply finding out whenever you made the journey again. I believe that Master Pholus would want to know sooner rather than later."

"Yes, I am sure you are right."

"Gery," Mera interjected, looking between him and a large wrapped package next to the stump he sat upon. "What's in the package?"

"Yeah, Gery, you forgot your promise to tell us once Mera and Kari arrived."

Gery laughed. "I didn't forget. I simply waited. I do not forget things, young dragon." He climbed off the stump and picked up the package. With a sly grin, he placed it on Mera's lap. "I didn't forget that your clothes had been ruined in the battles. By now, your dress is in need of care, so I brought you replacements." Mera smiled at the gnome and placed the package next to her, so she could hug him.

"Let me go, Skyemera. All this hugging makes me itch," he said with a laugh. "I do believe it is time for me to return to the Palaestra. Master Pholus will have need of my services." He said his goodbyes and then closed his eyes. He opened them again, looking first at Mera and then at Gaeleath. Closing them again, he pulled his face tight in concentration. When he reopened his eyes, a sparkle of amusement tinged with frustration colored his expression. "She's blocked me, yeah. She's good at that!" His admiration made Mera laugh.

"Looks like you'll have to leave the camp like the rest of us. No popping in and out," Mera said, laughter still in her voice. Gaeleath said nothing, but shook his head, a huge grin on his face.

"Fine. Fine." Gery walked toward the opening when he pulled up short as Purivia came barreling into the encampment.

"Mera, your mother...missing...babe gone," she managed with labored breaths before Mera was already out of the camp and galloping toward the village and her home. She didn't wait to see if her friends followed, nor did she ask any questions. She needed to see for herself what had happened. Part of her mind hoped the outcome would be the same as the last time she ran home at her mother's disappearance, but something told her this time was different.

Acknowledgments

Much like Skyemera, when I started writing this novel, I felt completely alone in this authoring world. By the time I finished it, though, I had two groups I was writing with regularly. At the time of publishing, more than a year later, those groups are still going strong, overlap at times, and serve as a constant source of encouragement and motivation. So a huge thank you to my writing friends!

As soon a I knew I wanted to write Skyemera's story as a YA Fantasy, I had my sisters in mind. When I say I could not have done this, or had it come out as good as it is without them, I am not kidding. Dale was there since Day 1, reading the manuscript as I was writing it, catching plot holes and inconsistencies. Then Bev came in and told me where more details were needed. She sketched the characters and created the amazing cover from the words I wrote. The number of message threads and encouragement in all directions was more than I could have asked for. I wrote this story, but it would not be what it is without them!

I also want to acknowledge everyone who has waited patiently for this book to come out. It's been over a year and a half since I started talking about it. You've been extremely patient, and I am grateful for your support!

Finally, a huge hug to the one who encourages me daily. The one who believes I can be more than I'm giving myself credit for. The one who reminds me near daily to get back in my office and get these books out. I appreciate you more than you know!

About the Author

Bobbie Isabel lives in North Carolina surrounded by the people and cats she loves. As a lifelong lover of words, Bobbie is not held to a certain genre. She writes and publishes poetry, fantasy, and children's books that are a combination of the two. She also writes adult romance novels under a separate pen name. When she's not writing, she enjoys spending time with her three-year-old granddaughter, or you can find her in the audience reveling in the language-rich environment of musical theater.

Currently Available Books:

When Can We Be Soft?: Poems of Female Resilience
Lilli and the Nervous Narwhal
Untethered Love

Follow Bobbie all over social media:
https://linktr.ee/bisabelwrites
See the website for the latest updates on her writing endeavors and

a poetry blog. All of her books are available signed in the shop on the website:
https://bisabelwrites.com/shop
<u>Coming Soon:</u>

Sometime 2025: Mother of the Maenad—Age of the Forgotten Ones Prequel Novella

www.ingramcontent.com/pod-product-compliance
Lightning Source LLC
Chambersburg PA
CBHW020236010826
48973CB00006B/1537